Unrecognizable words or ethereal loveliness held Adam spellbound. Beneath dawn's glowing hues and in the center of a triangle formed by three mighty oaks a dainty figure moved, lavender mists billowing around her feet. Delicate face and slender arms lifted to the sky, Llys seemed an elusive fantasy come to light, one whose bewitching spell Adam fought.

"What is this strange dominion you wield over the beasts of the forest?" It wasn't what he'd meant to ask. He hadn't meant to speak at all.

Uncomfortable in the role of spy, he stepped boldly from the shadows, scattering startled animals. He had journeyed from Oaklea on a quest to seek the truth and instead had fallen into the role of secret observer, witnessing a beguiling sorceress's haunting rites.

Suddenly she was swept full against a muscular frame. Adam's nearness was overwhelming and Llys went disgustingly weak. Driven by instinct, and seeking a steady anchor in this shifting sea, she wrapped her arms about his broad shoulders, twined her fingers into the cool gold strands of his hair.

And yet to Adam she appeared in this new role as neither a wanton siren nor a shy and quiet maiden. With this fresh demonstration of her ability to switch between vastly different poses, Adam grew more positive that he never dare trust the devious beauty. . . .

Books by Marylyle Rogers

Chanting the Dawn
Chanting the Morning Star
Dark Whispers
The Dragon's Fire
The Eagle's Song
Hidden Hearts
The Keepsake
Proud Hearts
Wary Hearts

Published by POCKET BOOKS

MARYLYLE ROGERS

CHANTING THE MORNING STAR

POCKET BOOKS

New York   London   Toronto   Sydney   Tokyo   Singapore

This book is a work of fiction. Names, characters, places and
incidents are either products of the author's imagination or are
used fictitiously. Any resemblance to actual events or locales or
persons, living or dead, is entirely coincidental.

An *Original* Publication of POCKET BOOKS

 POCKET BOOKS, a division of Simon & Schuster Inc.
1230 Avenue of the Americas, New York, NY 10020

Copyright © 1993 by Marylyle Rogers

All rights reserved, including the right to reproduce
this book or portions thereof in any form whatsoever.
For information address Pocket Books, 1230 Avenue
of the Americas, New York, NY 10020

ISBN: 0-671-74563-8

First Pocket Books printing December 1993

10 9 8 7 6 5 4 3 2 1

POCKET and colophon are registered trademarks of
Simon & Schuster Inc.

Stepback art by Greg Gulbronson

Printed in the U.S.A.

To
Denise Little, Char Daniels,
Jennifer Halterman, Louise Linder
and Jackie Taylor.
Thank You.

Author's Note

When the Romans invaded Britain in A.D. 43, they found a fierce Celtic race who bowed to the absolute supremacy of Druid priests who claimed to possess the secrets of past, present, and future. The Druid religion was not confined to Britain but rather spread across Europe. However, it is believed that Britain was to international Druids what Rome was to early Christians and present-day Catholics: the center of knowledge and power.

Because the Druids were forbidden to put their beliefs into writing, we have little concrete knowledge of their ways, only the distant echoes of rituals distorted but still observed—dancing with hands clasped about the Maypole, setting bonfires on the night of October 31 (Samhain, eve of the Celtic New Year), and crowning monarchs above the Stone of Destiny, which has resided beneath the British Coronation Chair since 1297 when Edward I took it from the Scots, who had crowned kings over it from time out of mind. We do know that becoming a Druid priest was the highest pinnacle to which a Celtic man could aspire and necessitated memorizing endless poetic chants in the form of riddles whose answers explained natural phenomena—such as eclipses, phases of the moon, movement of stars—and all things unknown to men untaught. These priests held positions of dominant power to which even kings bowed. We know also that they possessed amazing scientific knowledge, some of which modern science has only recently rediscovered, which gave them the ability to awe their contemporaries with, among other things, accurate predictions of astral events. Some wonder what primal knowledge they may have possessed that is now forever lost.

In the Romans' wake came Christianity. Its advance drove the Druids into their natural havens, the wilds of forest and mountain. They were deemed extinct by Roman historians late in the first century A.D., although pockets of them survived for many generations. Indeed, as earlier mentioned, many of the rituals and traditions observed today in Britain and elsewhere have their roots in Druidism.

In A.D. 410 Rome was overrun by pagan hordes and, in a last attempt to save itself, called all its legions home. Britain was left with empty stone palaces and crumbling roads its natives knew neither how to use nor how to maintain. The Romans departed, but Christianity remained and spread.

Another invasion, foolishly invited by one of Celtic Britain's own, began when Angles, Jutes, and Saxons —all of them pagans—crossed the English Channel and the North Sea. They steadily drove the native Celts into Cornwall, Devon, Wales, Scotland, and Ireland. Not until the close of this sixth century did Saint Augustine bring Christianity to these invaders, and then it came unevenly with periods of backsliding into old ways.

It is interesting to note that the Celtic Druids' belief

in the power residing in nature was far different from the pagan Anglo-Saxon's panorama of warrior gods. Also, the Celts' acceptance of Christianity began with the lowliest and worked its way up. The Anglo-Saxons' conversion was accomplished by starting at the top with the king, whose example led entire kingdoms en masse into the new religion. It is important to remember that even after Christianity was accepted by both Celts and Anglo-Saxons the old superstitions remained century after century. Often the Christian church found it easier to cloak the old ways with Christian meaning than to exterminate them.

During these centuries in the Saxon kingdom of Northumbria there were three major figures in the history of the Christian church—Saint Cuthbert, the Venerable Bede, and Bishop Wilfrid. Cuthbert was an ascetic greatly revered by his contemporaries; Bede was a teacher and writer whose books are an important source of the history of this period; Wilfrid was an aggressive, difficult, and worldly bishop who built splendid stone churches in the Roman manner. He was expelled from his see in 678 and spent the last thirty years of his life fighting for his rights.

Thanks first to Roman historians, then to the writings of Gildas, Nennius, and Bede, and last to *The Anglo-Saxon Chronicles, The Welsh Annals,* and *The Chronicles of the Princes of Wales,* we have a picture —often perceived through the eyes and ears of those who were there—of the times and the rulers of Britain's fluctuating kingdoms during the millennium between the Roman invasion in A.D. 43 and William of Normandy's conquest in 1066. The shadowy and near uncharted path through these centuries is rough and patchy at the start but grows smoother toward the end.

Definition of Terms

FROM WALES

Cymry—When the Romans invaded Britain in A.D. 43 they found a Celtic race they called Britons. When the Anglo-Saxons invaded centuries later they drove the Celtic Britons back into the island's extremities—Scotland, Cornwall, Devon, and Wales. The Britons in Wales were cut off from their kinsmen in other areas by the mid-600s and began to call themselves the Cymry (fellow countrymen) while the Saxons referred to them as the Welsh, which in Anglo-Saxon meant "foreigner" (roughly equivalent to modern-day Americans calling Native Americans "foreigners").

Prince—The highest title a man could hold among the Welsh (Cymry). While outsiders referred to Welsh leaders as kings, the Cymry themselves called them princes.

FROM SAXON ENGLAND

Atheling—Anglo-Saxon word meaning "prince of the (royal) blood."

Bretwalda—Excluding the Celtic "outlands" the island of Britain was split into several Anglo-Saxon kingdoms (the number varies, but in the later and more stable centuries it was seven). Each was ruled by its own king. However, at different times one king would gain ascendancy over the others and would be hailed as the overking, or bretwalda.

Ceorl—Yeoman farmer, a free and independent landholder and one of the components of the Saxon kingdoms.

Ealdorman—A member of the ruling nobility of Saxon England, the king's viceroy responsible for a shire's administration and justice system and for calling out the reservist army, or fyrd. "Ealdorman" was not replaced by "earl" until approximately 1010, and was then likely influenced by the Danish word, *jarl*.

Thegn—A member of a select body, usually made up of young warriors, who attended the king and usually accompanied him everywhere, acting as bodyguard and lesser official. On rare occasions, for good service, a thegn could be elevated to ealdorman. Older thegns were among the king's advisers.

Thrall—Bondsman, or slave.

A.D. 678   There appeared the star called a comet, in August, and it shone for three months each morning like a beam of the sun. Bishop Wilfrid was driven from his bishopric by King Ecgferth. . . .

The Anglo-Saxon Chronicles

Prologue

Late Spring, A.D. 678

Leaping tongues of flame lent an eerie orange glow to the sky behind two fleeing women. It provided a false brightness to the horizon ahead, robbed of dawn's natural hues by a heavy shroud of smoke.

"Where have we to go?" the younger woman asked, hastening to keep pace with the older as they sought escape from the scorching heat of fires purposefully ignited to drive them from their woodland home. "What haven can be found for two such as we?"

Gytha heard the stunned distress beneath her companion's undeniable fury over this first defeat at the hands of ignorant and frightened fools. 'Struth, there was pain in this destruction of all that was familiar. But, having suffered much the same many times in her youth, Gytha answered with the shrug of a shoulder cloaked in her long black hair through whose flow wide bands of silver ran like lightning streaking through a midnight sky.

"I've a mind to learn if the *great* Glyndor, of whom we've heard so many praises sung, does indeed possess the powers of a master sorcerer." The sneer in these words made it clear she much doubted it possible.

Elesa was startled to an abrupt halt. The whole of Saxon Britain and the Cymry princedoms, too, had repeatedly heard tales of Glyndor's unearthly powers and of how the magic wrought by his three apprentices had put a massive army to flight without a single blow struck. The prospect of seeing these wielders of mystical powers was appealing but roused in her a curious dread as well. Gytha was her aunt, not her mother, and though Elesa had never known the latter she'd early learned the cost of balking at this powerful woman's commands.

Gytha's wicked laughter rose into a wild crescendo that echoed through the trees, frightening forest animals . . . and any human ones brave enough to linger near their path. Her follower's thoughts were pitifully easy to read. Not deeming it her duty to explain, she spoke only for the pleasure to be had in boasting of her ability to commune with voiceless powers.

"In the deepest hours of night—afore our weak-minded foes summoned sufficient courage to launch their assault—I consulted with the darkness of the new moon. Our future lies to the north, where dwell Glyndor and those who are his. Thus it is certain that the crossing of our paths is destined to be."

A heavy scowl furrowed Gytha's dark brows. She sensed and was impatient with her protégée's lingering regret for what was lost. Repeatedly she had warned Elesa against love, be it for thing or person. 'Twas a useless emotion and a dangerous folly.

"Waste no moment more fretting over things that are gone. Rather, exult in the satisfaction of knowing that those who forced us from our home will ever be forbidden the use of our land, land that I've ensured shall henceforth be known as the vale of doom."

Elesa glared down at blossoms scattered amid the thick grass beneath her feet, striving with little success to find gratification in the prospect of the valley, her childhood haven, as a place of sorrow and gloom. She instead reinforced her inner strength with a determination to see that in future those who thought to keep her from possessing a thing wanted would suffer for both their wrong and this sabotage.

Gytha whirled to face the sapphire-eyed beauty at her back. "How can you fail to recognize this for the goad it is toward the challenging destiny we are meant to pursue instead of wasting our talents in a strength-weakening idleness? Would you dare question the powers that guide our path?"

"Never, Gytha, never." Elesa tossed back a tangled mass of curly black hair and met her mentor's gaze directly. Angry as she was with feeble-witted humankind's dastardly deeds, she must and would insulate herself from their dangers by relying solely upon the powers they two wielded with great skill.

Sapphire eyes went hard and dark as onyx while Elesa reaffirmed her dedication to a role she'd been raised to fulfill. "Without hesitation I will follow your lead to the destiny foretold."

3

Chapter
1

Summer, A.D. 678

Cra-a-ck!

A harshly shoved door smashed against the stone wall. It was the rude announcement of an unexpected visitor's arrival in a small abbey cell. The echoing sound startled the young beauty on her knees before a robed figure into settling back on her heels. She turned jewel-bright eyes toward its source—a tall, black-cloaked figure filling the open doorway and silhouetted against the brilliant rays of a setting sun that glowed on his bright hair.

The intruder's mouth tilted into a cynical half-smile, and disgust darkened the amber gaze skimming over the woman's alluring curves. She was the loveliest creature Adam had ever beheld. But a woman condemned by the fact that as she knelt at the feet of a man of holy calling—worse still, a bishop—only a cloud of ebony hair provided covering, of dubious usefulness, for slender shoulders and lush breasts.

"Who are you?" Bishop Wilfrid thrust his portly form between newcomer and bold woman eyeing the

5

powerfully made man with blatant appreciation. The bishop found in the stranger's wicked good looks naught but a lamentable instrument for paving the path into sins of the flesh.

"And by what right do you enter my lodging uninvited?"

"I knocked—loudly—but no response was forthcoming. Fearing some ill had befallen you, merely did I open your *unlocked* door."

Face flushed with irritation, the bishop shifted his meaningful glare from the stranger to the door, split top to bottom. If such force was an example of the man's restraint, then woe betide any who crossed him. . . .

The still kneeling female softly purred her admiration for strength proven by the abused door. The sound earned a quick accusing glance from the bishop, who then turned back to reproach the intruder.

"Solitude and privacy bring man closer to the divine and are the gifts we here at the abbey seek, gifts we guard for ourselves and one another." The strain underlying his gentle tone made it clear that tight control was required to maintain it. "Thus, never have I had reason to fear trespassers or to bar my door against them."

"Since you have no reason to bar your door, my sudden appearance can hold no great alarm for you."

"You have shattered my privacy as none of the brothers here would've done . . . and at a most inopportune moment. The monks of Winbury Abbey have put aside worldly pleasures and would see this scene for what it is while you, a man of the world, are obviously blind to the truth."

"Truth?" Against his will, Adam's gaze fell to the woman leaning around the stout bishop's robes to continue a leisurely study of him. She tossed her head, rearranging the shiny mass of black curls to permit a tantalizing glimpse of tempting flesh.

By the woman's enticing actions Adam knew she was no penitent sinner come to be saved, and he wasted little effort to dull his contempt as he asked, "What worthy purpose can there be to excuse a bishop alone in his bedchamber with a half-clad female?"

Hearing the stranger's scorn, Wilfrid followed the line of a golden gaze to the seductress wantonly returning the visitor's attention. His teeth gritted against swelling aggravation as he leaned to one side, snatched a dark cloak from a peg in the wall, and swirled it around the woman before pulling her up to stand before him. With hands cupped over her shoulders, the bishop pushed the maid a step toward the intruder.

"This is Llys, daughter of a Druid sorcerer and trained in their black ways. As our God commanded his disciples, I was attempting to drive the demons out from her."

Amber gaze narrowing, Adam studied the sultry woman and, in seeing her subtly shift into an even more alluring pose, missed the mockery flashing through her eyes at the bishop's introduction. Adam had found meager reason in past to esteem the frail gender, and this female's display only deepened his disgust with their number.

The bishop growled his displeasure over the woman's exhibition. "She excels in wielding feminine wiles able to tempt any man into sinful debauchery, but I have not succumbed. And indeed I'd have succeeded in my mission had your untimely arrival not undone what progress had been made."

Cynicism glowed in Adam's eyes. Progress had

indeed been made, but toward what goal? The explanation given did nothing to sway his opinion. The Druidess looked no more a willing candidate for exorcism than she'd seemed a penitent sinner. Her stunning dark sapphire eyes had yet to shift from him, and the invitation in their smoky depths never wavered.

Adam had no trust in the self-important bishop's excuse for this intimate scene, but the scene did offer possible answers to questions he'd come to ask. Disillusionment had rung clear as a church bell in his younger brother's missive. In it Aelfric had suggested the bishop was not what he seemed. It was an opinion surely justified by this apparent sundering of holy vows by a religious leader the boy had previously admired. Too, the man's actions suggested a possible reason for Aelfric's wildly stated intention to flee from this newly formed abbey.

"I am Adam, Ealdorman of Oaklea. Concerned by statements my brother Aelfric wrote me, I have come to visit with him."

Following a momentary widening of the bishop's eyes, Adam saw shutters close the man's expression into a mask of regret.

"I fear, my son, I've unhappy news of your brother."

Thick lashes half shielded the fire of topaz eyes while a frowning Adam waited in smoldering impatience for an explanation.

"Aelfric is dead." Even as Wilfrid spoke he fell a step back, wondering in that moment if it was not this Saxon lord who possessed otherworldly powers. His strange golden eyes flashed with a fire surely hot enough to incinerate the living. Having known only the slight and devout Aelfric, Wilfrid had thought exaggerated the many heroic tales of Adam's physical strength and success as a warrior—but no longer.

"Did some virulent sickness abruptly strike him down?" Like twin barbed maces guilt and regret smote Adam. For the sake of his people at Oaklea, rather than immediately setting off in answer to Aelfric's plea, he had lingered the hours required to properly delegate his shire's management. Now it seemed that delay had prevented Adam from seeing his beloved brother again . . . perhaps even kept him from saving Aelfric's life. The bishop's next words landed another invisible blow.

"I fear it was no ailment of the flesh but rather a weakness of the mind."

Dark gold brows furrowed more deeply still. Adam knew Aelfric better than did any other living soul. Had the bishop claimed his death due to one of the inevitable waves of illness that washed over the land with distressing regularity Adam would not have questioned the words . . . but a weakness of the mind? Never!

"I myself," Wilfrid hastily continued in an attempt to lessen the fierce warrior's obvious disbelief, "saw Aelfric drive the dagger into his own heart."

"No!" Adam felt as if that dagger had instead struck him dead to point, but the shock served to rouse him from the haze of guilt. He was certain the bishop spoke nothing of the truth, an opinion confirmed by the unpleasantly bright smile on the woman's berry-sweet but surely poisonous lips.

"Show me Aelfric's grave."

Adam's demand was answered by a mournful shake of the bishop's thinning iron-gray hair. "I cannot, for I do not know where it lies."

"Is he not in the churchyard?" Repressed fury

curled Adam's hands into fists, but knowing the answer he'd be given, he exercised stern control to hold them immobile at his sides.

Filled with self-righteousness, the bishop felt empowered to meet golden eyes directly. "No man guilty of taking his own life can be laid to rest in hallowed ground."

"Then have the men who buried him lead me to the spot they chose."

"I cannot." The bishop's flat refusal was accompanied by a woman's laughter, humorless and full of cruel glee.

Adam stood as motionless as if struck to solid granite, but the fierce emotion clear in the clenching of his jaw and in the dangerous glitter in topaz eyes forced the bishop into a hasty explanation.

"That night two monks on a pilgrimage to Saint Ynis's grave tarried in our abbey and consented to do the sorrowful deed in exchange for our hospitality. They've been almost a sennight gone." Wilfrid realized he was near to babbling, but despite the acrid taste of disgust for his own weakness, he could not stop. "I know only the direction they traveled and am unable to do more than suggest it unlikely they carried him farther than the forest at the southern edge of abbey lands. The precise spot where he lies I do not know."

"In atonement for that wretched inability, return to me the rosary my brother ever wore. The one given him by the father whose name he bore."

With arms crossed over a broad chest, Adam silently waited, an immovable bar to any attempt at refusal. He would not leave without the demanded crucifix. Blessed by the pope, the rosary had been cherished by Adam's father, who had entered the monastery in middle life, after begetting two sons. By piety and good works the elder Aelfric had earned the reward of being appointed historian. With that honor had come the obligation to write into the chronicles a record of each year's events, a duty he'd discharged with honor until his death near five years past. As the firstborn son, Adam had proudly shouldered the responsibility for Oaklea while Aelfric had followed their father's path to a life in the church. Now the last of his line, Adam *would* have the talisman so prized by the other two.

The bishop's gaze narrowed as for a long moment he pondered what response to make. In no way could this mighty warrior be certain whether or not young Aelfric had been buried with the precious relic about his throat. At length the unwavering intensity of topaz eyes convinced Wilfrid of the wisdom in placating this man insofar as was possible.

Turning, the bishop strode toward a small trunk resting atop one much larger. From a place of importance, obvious by its location near the top, he carefully lifted a heavy gold string of beads embedded with pearls and adorned with a crucifix studded with rubies.

Adam smiled grimly as the precious strand was slowly lowered to become a gleaming pool in the hollow of his cupped hand.

Neither wishing nor having been invited to tarry the night within Winbury Abbey, Adam had rejoined the two supporters awaiting his return beyond the monastery's high palisade. They'd made camp a short distance into the woodland. On the morrow in fervent hope of finding Aelfric's grave he meant to scour the forest edge for sign of recent man-caused disturbances. Adam then would make certain the boy's final resting place was protected against animal marauders by an adequate mound of stones and, no matter the bishop's claim, marked with a cross.

Guilt for having failed his brother and thoughts of an unmourned grave kept Adam awake until the darkest hours had nearly passed. Only then did the soft breeze whispering through treetops and the faint sounds of small animals moving among thick foliage lull Adam into dreams . . . for a brief time.

With the instincts of a warrior trained in defense, Adam abruptly opened his eyes to a flash of descending silver. Issuing a bloodcurdling battle cry, he rolled away, deflecting the descending dagger from its deadly path to his heart. Instead the sharp blade struck just below the ribs on his right side.

In the next instant three mighty warriors stood firmly braced with swords drawn and waiting. The sight sent a small party of craven assailants scurrying into the shadows beyond the dying fire's ring of light. Two of the defenders would have given chase had the third's weapon not fallen from his grip while he slowly sank back against a broad tree trunk, dark liquid flowing freely over hands clasped to his side.

"Pip," Adam's short, husky companion spoke to the other. "I'll remain here. You pursue the wretches and mark where their flight ends. Then later when the time is right we'll wreak our vengeance upon them all."

"Waste no moment on the sorry cowards." Adam's order left his men little choice but to accept the command. "They're neither trained for war nor brave enough to face us awake and prepared. Let them slink into shadows where they belong. They lack the courage to tempt our might again."

"Forest outlaws?" The younger guardsman, russet-haired and called Pip in jest for his large size, was incurably curious and unable to restrain the useless question, though he hastened to atone for his foolishness with an observation. "Wouldn't have thought even their sort likely to prey on travelers this near a holy site."

Adam's smile was cynical. "Forest robbers? Mayhap—but I much doubt it."

His supporters, uninformed of the scene in the abbey, were surprised. Knit brows and silently questioning eyes asked who else the attackers could have been? What purpose save robbery could lie behind so cowardly an act?

Though recognizing their confusion, Adam chose not to voice his suspicion that their assailants had issued from that "holy site"—and not for thievery but rather for murder of the man they'd expected to find alone.

"Help me bind this wound and then let us be off to Throckenholt with all possible haste." Through his discomfort Adam smiled at the others' disappointment. "If Wulfayne's pride in his wife's curative powers is justified, Lady Brynna, will see my paltry injury soon mended."

Although frowning with mingled skepticism at the claim and concern over a deep wound threatening to prove serious, the two still standing bent immediately to do as their leader bade.

Chapter 2

Past the door opened and held wide by a young thrall, two men entered the Ealdorman of Throckenholt's impressive wood frame house. The amber eyes of a third, supported between the pair, struggled to focus on the tall figure striding forward to meet them.

"Wulf . . ." Even lacking the rough bandage heavily stained with blood about Adam's middle, the faintness of his husky voice would have been cause for anxiety. "Need your . . . help. . . ."

Wulfayne's dark gold brows furrowed in concern. Just as the one called reached out to help his friend, Adam sank into oblivion.

After carefully laying their limp burden on the mat hastily laid near the large hall's central hearth, Cedric and Pip stepped back to watch the dark-haired woman who must surely be Lady Brynna approach their fallen leader. She carried a neat stack of cloths, small vial of pale brown liquid, and jar of creamy unguent. To their surprise a second younger but equally beautiful woman sank to her knees across the wounded man from the first.

"Who assaulted you?" Abruptly interrupting the absorption of the wounded man's companions, Wulf demanded explanation. But he added another question before the first could be answered. "Did this harm befall Adam upon *my* lands?"

Cedric, the elder of the two newcomers, responded. "Nay, we were resting for the night only a short distance into the forest beyond Winbury Abbey when the cowards struck. Once we showed ourselves well able to return their attack, they scurried into the shadows like the vermin they are. Only our lord's injury prevented us from pursuing and dispatching them to the fiery end assuredly awaiting."

The tight disgust in these words spoke volumes, although the answers did little to solve the puzzle of who was responsible. Wulf chose not to demand additional information from men likely unable to tell more. This assault merely added another strand, one, of deadly intent, to an already tangled skein of unexplained questions and peculiar events.

Meeting the unwavering gaze of the stocky man near his own age, Wulf tempered his impatience for solutions and smoothed his voice to ask a question surely more easily answered. "What drew you so far from Oaklea?" As Oaklea was situated in the northeastern part of Northumbria, very near the site of King Ecgferth's own hall, it meant a planned journey involving far more than the diversion of a good day's hunt.

Cedric shook his shaggy brown hair. "I know only that our lord received a message from his brother. Doubtless you are aware that Aelfric had been moved from a monastery near our home to the new abbey at Winbury?" Without pausing for a response, Cedric continued. "Ill news it must have been, as afore the

sun rose on the second day, we set off for the abbey.
Adam told us merely that he must speak with the
bishop and see to Aelfric's health . . . but nothing
more."

Wulf frowned. It was plain from the faint echo of
hurt and confusion in Cedric's last words that his
leader's lack of fuller explanation was unusual, a fact
that deepened Wulf's concern. As the holder of lands
neighboring Winbury, he knew Bishop Wilfrid had
arranged for construction at that site of a monastery
crowned by a fine stone church in the Roman manner.
But he had not known and was surprised to learn the
pompous prelate was personally administering the
abbey. With a goodly number under his jurisdiction,
why would such an ambitious man give direct care to
a small religious community so far from his base of
power in York?

"Did Adam visit with Aelfric and the bishop?"

Cedric gave a helpless grimace. "He entered the
abbey alone and, returning in a black temper, said
nothing of what had transpired. Mayhap foolishly, we
chose not to force a discussion he clearly wished to
avoid."

Though nodding a head of golden hair burnished
with strands of silver, Wulf's grim smile was not
reflected in his solemn green eyes.

While the lord of Throckenholt continued quietly
speaking with both the short, stern Cedric and good-
humored Pip, the women worked in silence to rid the
wounded man of soiled bandage and tunic. Once the
pair had washed away dried blood and bathed torn
flesh with an astringent herbal solution, Brynna's deft
hands worked to apply a soothing unguent and cover
the wound with a pad. This left the younger woman

with nothing to divert her attention from their uncommonly handsome patient.

The maid had recently descended from near solitude in the Welsh kingdom of Talacharn, and other than Wulfayne, who stood as foster father to her, she had never seen such a man. However, despite a natural reticence, she found herself unable to look away from the masculine beauty of a face framed by thick hair as bright as sun-ripened wheat and the wide expanse of a powerful chest laid bare. Experience severely limited by years spent in a hill-cave home's seclusion, she had never—save for occasional glimpses of her adolescent brother or the aged Glyndor—seen a male even partially unclothed. Nor had she ever expected to wish to do so. Now, driven by an odd compulsion she was helpless to resist, she let her gaze trace the magnificent planes and ridges of a chest half shielded by a wedge of bronze curls. An unfamiliar, disturbing tension halted the breath in her throat and lent a strange rhythm to her heartbeat.

Brynna glanced up and recognized the startled awareness in the tender maiden's wide blue eyes. While quickly dropping attention to the chore at hand, a warm smile curled her mouth. Here was an echo of her own past. She saw again the scene wherein she'd first found Wulfayne and tended a similar wound. That initial pang of desire was unmistakable and, fond of the girl, she was gently amused.

"If you will finish fastening the pad and then wipe his face with cool water, I'll see to the needs of our other guests." With the request, Brynna gave the maid a reassuring nod and rose to match action to words.

Since Brynna had finished wrapping a bandage around the man just above his waist, the girl had no difficulty in neatly tying its ends to secure a thrice-folded cloth rectangle in place. It was an easy task unexpectedly complicated by the need for a strong measure of restraint to prevent her fingers from straying out to test the tempting texture of rough satin skin.

While valiantly struggling to free herself of useless fascination, she next rose and poured cold water into a basin from a ewer only recently filled at the spring in back of the house. She sank again to her knees beside this patient, this source of dangerous emotional turmoil, causing the faltering of a serenity that must be held most precious to one of her destiny. Already she'd spent years striving to establish mastery over her temper. Now here was a new threat, one she'd no notion how to defeat. She took deep, steadying breaths and forced calm to trembling hands. The erratic beat of her heart she'd no hope of returning to peace and wasted no moment trying.

Wringing out a small linen square, she hesitantly brushed back a swath of the man's blond hair before gently wiping his brow, down strong cheeks to a formidable chin, then around and back up before dipping the cloth once more into the bowl. The water was chilly enough to numb her fingers . . . and cold enough to wake the once unconscious man.

From beneath thick lashes, Adam peered at the source of this frigid caress.

"No-o-o . . ." Shocked, he gritted out his disgust over this apparent return to the abbey. Adam tried to sit up and half succeeded before a wave of dizziness overcame his intent. Dropping against the pillow hastily formed of his own bundled cloak, he clenched his eyes shut in hopes of clearing away this surely false image of the bold female who'd earned his contempt.

He looked again only to find a seemingly sincere frown of concern on the sorceress's lovely face even as Wulf moved to stand at her back.

"Adam, 'tis never a fine idea to attempt too rapid a recovery." Wulf grinned down at the scowling man, apparently irritated by an unaccustomed physical weakness, doubtless a trial to this man whose calm strength in the midst of battle had earned the admiration and respect of both ally and foe. "You've already won a well-deserved reputation as a mighty warrior. No need to continue the fight where no enemy threatens."

No enemy? Adam would've laughed, but the memory of a sorceress's unholy glee strangled the sound. His tawny gaze never shifted from the worry-knitted brow of the woman whom, had he not known better, he'd have thought to be the image of sweet innocence.

From a damp cloth tightly clenched, liquid dripped between slender fingers while the object of his penetrating gaze nibbled her soft lower lip to cherry brightness. The wounded man's fiery glare seemed to brand her with guilt . . . but for what? So far as she knew, she'd never seen him before. What blame could he place at her door?

"Adam." Wulf spoke firmly to break the strange bond. "Meet here my foster daughter, of sorts. Llys and her twin brother, Evain, have long resided with Glyndor in the mountains of Talacharn and descend rarely to visit us here."

Llys? To Adam the fondly spoken name was proof that she was in truth the woman he'd met in Winbury Abbey. A certainty backed by news that she lived with the famous—hah! the infamous—Druid sorcerer, Glyndor.

"Even when they gift us with their presence,

Glyndor and his protégé, Evain, seldom linger. Having accomplished their goal in escorting Llys down to learn more of the healing arts from Brynna, already they've departed to conduct business of their own as they return to Wales." A thread of affection ran through Wulf's mock regret.

Attention shifting to his host, Adam's eyes went to dark amber. Already departed? Were the Druid sorcerer and his apprentice responsible for the harm visited upon him?

Seeing Adam's expression harden, Wulf realized his talk of absent friends had been misinterpreted, and he sobered to quietly request that Llys allow him a private discussion with his friend.

The young beauty could do naught but grant her foster father that boon. Stifling a near overwhelming desire to demand from the glaring patient an explanation for his instantaneous dislike of someone he could know nothing about, Llys rose with exceptional grace. She twitched her simple homespun skirt into place as if 'twere a regal gown before proudly retreating to take over the serving of a tasty morning meal to their other visitors. Thus she freed Brynna to care for her small daughter, who only the past day had been found lying in the forest mysteriously ill.

To Llys's own disgust, she discovered that not even anxiety for little Anya, barely more than a toddler, could halt her intense awareness of their devastating patient—her unexpected antagonist.

Shaken by her newly discovered inability to control either her feelings or her responses, Llys cast many sidelong glances toward the puzzling stranger, too much a dangerous temptation. Bruised and confused by the unwarranted disapproval of this man she found all too attractive, Llys made a silent vow. The reason

for his wrongful condemnation of her she must find.
And more, she must prove it utterly unjustified! Llys
defended her vehement resolution by telling herself it
was not solely for the sake of an anger able only to
impede her path but in the hope of regaining mastery
over wildly fluctuating emotions whose tranquillity
must ever be her goal. It was an excuse of limited
value.

Chapter
3

"Llys?" Brynna called from the corner of the hall whose shadows preserved the potency of her medicinal herbs and potions.

Llys turned, holding a bouquet of dried rosemary. She'd just unfastened the cluster of tiny pale blue blossoms from amid others hanging head down from twine strung along a heavy beam spanning the length of one wall. Though it was midafternoon of a summer day, the two small windows on the wall opposite the door were unequal to lighting the entire hall alone. Thus, to answer her foster mother's summons, Llys crossed a curiously illuminated room. Its outer edges were lit by sunbeams while the center lay bathed in the hearth's golden glow. Even in summer a fire was necessary for cooking and other household chores.

A fortnight had passed since the wounded warrior's arrival. It should have been long enough for Llys's fascination with him to lessen, or leastwise to make it easier for her to keep her eyes averted. It hadn't! Unspeakably worse, his presence left her with an unaccustomed awkwardness that she despised in herself for the betrayal it was of a shameful attraction.

Llys had intended to grind the sweet-scented rosemary into a fine dust easily dissolved in wine and useful when mixed into a variety of tisanes. Instead she carefully laid the dried bouquet atop the long table burdened with an array of vials, measuring bowls, and pottery jars while Brynna continued.

"Cub is asleep, gifting me with sufficient time to administer this fresh elixir to Anya. Toward that end, I ask . . ." Brynna paused. The gray eyes already clouded with deep anxiety over her beloved daughter's unabated illness went even darker with regret for this need to beg of the lovely maid a likely uncomfortable boon.

"Gladly will I do any service to smooth your way," Llys saw Brynna's distress and, suspecting its source, a bright smile of reassurance bloomed on soft rose lips.

"I ask that you repeat our new friend's treatment."

Llys instantly nodded compliance to the other's reluctant appeal. From the day Brynna had gently welcomed the forlorn waifs she and Evain had been into the hill home's haven, Llys had happily given and done all possible on Brynna's behalf. Considering how clumsy and self-conscious proximity with the man left her, it would be a daunting task, yet Llys refused to quail before the handsome stranger. The loving debt she owed Brynna had been increased by the fact that since the day after Adam's arrival the older woman had attempted to shield Llys from his inexplicable contempt. Even had Brynna, between caring for infant son and ailing daughter, found time to apply a healing ointment to Adam's wound.

That reality needled Llys with humiliation for having created excuses to be busy anywhere other than in the same room while the treatment was performed. She'd told herself the action was born of the wisdom in avoiding a situation likely to ignite her temper and put the all-important tranquillity of spirit at risk. But her excuse was more lie than truth, and she knew it. In honesty, Adam was a danger to her serenity but not as a goad to anger. Rather he was a temptation threatening to cloud senses that ought to remain clear.

Though Llys's slender back was turned to the occupant of one of the pair of chairs placed within the hearth's ring of light, she could feel the weight of the heavy scowl Brynna's request had put upon his visage. Adam's rapidly returning vigor had left him impatient with his forced inactivity, and now it was plain that the prospect of her attention irritated him the more. But no matter. Despite the man's relentless disapproval, Llys had agreed and was determined to do what she'd promised.

Brynna disappeared into the small room where her daughter lay on a pallet filled with straw and fresh grasses, leaving Llys to draw a deep breath and gather up a jar of ointment and clean strips of cloth. Clutching these materials against her breast and without regard to the man-made walls forming a barrier between herself and the forces of nature, she silently chanted a triad pleading for calm to smooth her ragged nerves. Then, before her courage could further weaken, she bit trembling lips and turned toward her unwilling patient.

"What ails the child?" Adam asked, amber eyes narrowing on the approaching female, whom he deeply distrusted. In the abbey this undeniable beauty had boldly flaunted seductive charms, but now she came forward with the timid hesitation of a doe sensing danger. It annoyed him that the same woman who once had so wantonly enticed him now would have it seem she was too shy to meet his gaze directly . . . although from beneath demurely lowered lashes she watched him near constantly. Only the knowledge that his host and hostess were fond of Llys prevented him from openly challenging her motives for every action from the offense of laughing over his brother's death to the simple deed of breathing.

Raised by a man later monk, Adam found that his conscience would not permit him to delude himself. His disgust was not all for Llys, could not be when he had repeatedly discovered himself unable to block the mysterious creature from stealing into his night dreams and therein spinning a gossamer web of enchantments. Could he, Adam would refuse that it be so. But his dreams were beyond his ability to halt or control. In his eyes gold sparks burned with the fire of those fantasy images. In them her alabaster skin glowed against a silky black cloud of curls. And, too, the eyes able to rapidly change from tender pansy-blue to glittering sapphire in his dreams turned misty with passion as she drew him down to drink the heady ambrosia of a kiss promising unbelievable pleasures.

Adam abruptly straightened. Finding himself falling victim to the siren's call in the light of day, he curled his hands into mighty fists of resistance. He would *not* permit her seduction of his thoughts as well as his dreams!

Distaste emanated from the golden man in waves, but Llys refused to fail faintheartedly to do her pledged duty. As she had no answer to give Adam as to the nature of Anya's illness, Llys welcomed the prolonged pause that followed his question . . . only to have him repeat the query.

"Have you truly no notion of what ails Wulf's daughter?" The irritation suffered over his lapse in the futile attempt to thwart the enchantress's invasion of his mind put bite into Adam's words.

Llys merely shook her head, stirring the dusky curls cloaking her slender frame. Concentrating on stilling the tremor threatening to overtake nervous fingers, she bent her attention to the task of carefully arranging medicinal supplies atop the circular hearth's stone ledge.

"Ah, then you admit something exists that a sorceress fails to know?" Bitterness underlay his words as, with his own description of her, his memories of the abbey's ghastly spectacle were revived.

Llys felt his scorn like a physical blow and faltered, knocking her hand against the small pottery container and almost sending it into low-burning flames. Adam's hand flew out, saving the near lost cream. Too aware that the lithe speed with which he moved emphasized her clumsiness, and, caught between anger and humiliation, Llys nibbled at a full lower lip.

For the first time in days, Llys's bright blue eyes directly met a topaz gaze—one glittering with contempt.

Llys desperately wanted to lash back at the cynical unbeliever . . . but could not! Immediately lowering thick lashes to shield her from his too perceptive gaze, she stiffened against a fiery temper threatening to sever the tightly wound cords of restraint formed by years of training. Small white teeth released the abused lip to bite her tongue and stifle words struggling for freedom on its tip. Fierce words in defense of Brynna and her own beliefs, words rebuking him with the fact that not even the most powerful Druid claimed mastery over death. Nor did the highly skilled Brynna pretend to possess the formula for elixirs and chants able to heal every ailment.

Furious with herself for the mere desire to speak, Llys's hands curled into fists so tight they'd leave soft palms with the half-moon imprints of her nails. Sharing such secrets with those outside hereditary rings of knowledge was forbidden. To forget that fundamental rule would be to risk sundering her bond with the power in all natural forms—the death of a Druid's soul.

Beneath the burning sun of that truth her anger dissipated like morning mist. Stepping stiffly back from the man made dangerous by his ability to wordlessly steal her all-important emotional control, she stumbled and nearly fell.

Exercising the quick reflexes of a skilled warrior, in one smooth movement Adam rose to wrap strong hands about slender shoulders and steady the off-balance maid. Then, fingers buried in ebony hair as lush and silky-soft as his fantasies had foretold, from his vastly superior height he gazed down at the lissome girl. Her delicate face was filled with the startled desperation of a small wild creature caught in a cruel hunter's snare.

An unwelcome and surely unwarranted pang of guilt struck Adam. Though he had spent but a few days in the retiring Llys's occasional company, he'd seen enough to know her a creature of unusual grace. Therefore, he thought it must be he who was responsible for the skittish maid's awkwardness.

Beneath Adam's scrutiny, Llys stood mute while exquisite heat waves of pleasure were kindled by the warmth and strength of his hold. Unfamiliar sensations swept over her and created an alarming temptation to move closer still, to seek an end unknown. The turmoil deepened by this feeling of self-command slipping from her grasp darkened blue eyes near to jet.

Adam recognized panic in the maid's trembling. Despite irritation with himself for noticing and, worse yet, for caring, he sought to calm her distress. Once the seemingly timid maid's balance was restored, he freed her. Hearing a faint mewling sound recognized from his past and knowing it presaged a coming storm, Adam welcomed the diversion and moved toward the cradle on the hearth's far side, from which he lifted a wiggling babe.

Llys blinked rapidly against the unexpected sight of the famous fierce warrior holding Cub in a gentle embrace. Moreover, as she watched, Adam lightly rocked the babe until his tentative cries quieted. When Cub's dark eyes opened, they trustingly met a warm amber gaze. It seemed certain sure that such a deft and tender hand with children must have been taught by experience. A sudden possibility, nearer to a likelihood, struck hard and deep. Why had it never occurred to her that this famous, devastatingly handsome man was wed? And he was, it appeared clear, a father.

A cynical half-smile flashed as Adam rightly read Llys's stunned expression. "Though 'twas years past, I had a deal of practice in soothing a small boy. More than a decade older than my brother, often was I called upon to care for him."

An adolescent brother—and one well born—expected to care for a babe? The notion roused Llys's curiosity, and unthinkingly she asked, "But surely your mother and her ladies seldom burdened you with such duties?"

Over Adam's face dropped a cold and impassive

mask, closing off the warmth of moments past as abruptly as if a shutter had been drawn to block the sun.

Llys, uncertain whether the fault lay with her careless prying or with the mention of his brother, twisted her hands together while wondering what she might do to atone for the unintended offense.

Cursing himself for opening so personal and painful a subject in the first instance, Adam was intent on leaving no opening for Llys to approach it again. Instead he returned to their initial topic, and so sternly she dared not demur.

"Is Wulf's daughter alone in suffering this sickness?" Rare was the ailment that failed to sprout in clusters like weeds, albeit those that flourished alone were like to be the most deadly.

"Save for a few minor complaints and simple injuries, all others within Throckenholt's borders are well." Llys recognized the tall, intimidating man's motives but could only acquiesce to his lead, although it roused a subject that was painful for her.

"Moreover," she resolutely continued. "Anya was laughing and in good health when she set off to fetch flowers Brynna and I had plucked but left to cure in a glade a few paces into the forest beyond the palisade wall at the back of this abode."

Llys deliberately shifted her attention from the sight of Adam's narrowed glance clearly mocking the folly of leaving gathered blooms behind. She had to struggle to contain the frustrated indignation he so easily piqued. But nowise could she explain—nor was he likely to understand—that a night exposed to the full moon's light added potency to the flowers' curative powers.

The flash of anger in the normal calm of her night-sky eyes surprised Adam. Despite his utterly contrary experience of the sorceress in the abbey, during all the days since his time at Throckenholt had begun, this was his first glimpse of the fire his night dreams suggested dwelt within Llys. Nonetheless he held to the topic he'd raised.

"How soon after the child returned from her chore did she sicken?"

"She didn't return." Llys again bit at a full lower lip to hold back an explanation that she dared not share with this skeptical stranger. "And when her mother went looking, Anya was nowhere to be found until . . ." Never could she reveal how Evain had chanted a mighty plea and followed a trail provided by the forces he'd entreated to where the girl-child who worshiped him lay senseless at the foot of a huge oak. Since falling into that unnatural slumber, Anya had responded to neither Brynna's potions nor her desperate supplications to the powers of nature, which had never failed her afore. And the family's wordless fear was growing apace.

Now worried by thoughts of Anya—barely six summers old, blessed with her father's golden hair and leaf-green eyes—Llys wondered if she was wrong not to have urged her foster parents to send a plea for Glyndor and Evain's return. Their presence would make possible a bond of three. Such triads of power were rarely employed, being most often reserved for matters of grave import, but surely Anya's waning life was that.

Llys fervently wished the two sorcerers hadn't departed the very afternoon Anya was found. Never would they have done so had they suspected either the seriousness of the child's illness or the inability of

Brynna's amazing curative talents to restore Anya to health.

Feeling a traitor for her own lack of trust in her foster mother, Llys subdued a concern likely unneedful. She couldn't suggest the call for aid, which implied Brynna's healing powers unequal to the challenge. Such a deed would surely add a further layer of pain to someone Llys loved and respected.

Giving her head a slight shake, Llys sought to scatter bleak ponderings and force her wandering attention back to the very real responsibility much nearer to hand. She glanced toward the devastating man and the again sweetly sleeping babe. Adam was curiously watching her! Llys realized of a sudden that she'd been standing like a dazed witling for far too long. His penetrating amber gaze flustered her, but not nearly so thoroughly as the physical impact of his slow and potent smile. A single sane thought would be difficult. Serenity impossible! Nonetheless she must try!

"I should like to have done with this treatment afore Brynna returns." Restraining the quaver in her voice was a formidable task but no more so than holding her hand steady enough to safely lift the small jar while he returned the infant to his cradle. She heartened herself with the promise that once the deed was accomplished, she could escape from the man's dangerous presence.

The click of a falling latch broke through the haze of her tangled responses. She glanced toward the outer door and caught a glimpse of the two thralls leaving their lord's hall. They, once busy preparing for the day's last meal, had likely stepped out to fetch fresh bread from the bakehouse a short distance away. 'Twas even possible they'd some reason for retreating to the small hovel they shared—a gift rarely given by masters. Whatever the cause, their departure left Llys alone with Adam, a less than appreciated circumstance. Yet that privacy was a boon for which she soon was thankful—if only to prevent weeds of gossip from taking hold and growing in the ever fertile fields of servants' imaginations.

Adam didn't bother to glance toward the door. Rather his attention was held by the dainty figure with the elegance of a doe and the gentleness of its fawn. Hah! A voice in his mind mocked. And the viciousness of an adder! He *must* stop thinking of her as some innocent woodland creature!

Glaring at blameless floor rushes, Llys resolutely took a step forward. But when she looked up, it was to meet an obstruction hitherto unrecognized as such. Adam again sat unmoving . . . and wearing a fresh tunic. Its rust brown fabric blocked her access to the wound over which she must smooth the cream.

"After a fortnight of inactivity, I am quite capable of applying the ointment myself." Adam's self-disgust had increased and reverberated in low words. Before leaving childhood behind, one painful event had wrapped about his emotions an armor against feminine wiles. Which wasn't to say that by his age of a score and ten, as a powerful, attractive man he failed to possess wide experience of the frailer sex. Nay, hardly that. 'Twas only that no matter their bountiful charms and practiced enticements, his partners had failed to reach a well-guarded heart.

Thick black lashes fell to shield Llys from yet another of Adam's abrupt changes in manner. It seemed he was as skilled at unsettling foes with mercurial mood shifts as Glyndor.

"Unless you insist on using your 'treatment' as excuse to again caress my body?" As Adam purposefully recalled images of the abbey's wanton sorceress, cynicism hardened his eyes to dark amber.

The still glowing coals of Llys's anger burst into renewed life. How dare this wretched toad suggest such a thing? *How?* An inner voice scorned the query. Doubtless her helpless fascination with the devastating man that first night had been all too plain. And yet even that shameful fact surely gave him no reason to assume she'd welcome such a wicked suggestion.

"'Struth?" Through a tight smile, she spoke with a careful, cloyingly sweet concern. Caught between fury for him and self-disgust for her too real attraction to the man, she thought it was a miracle the pottery jar in her hold was not crushed betwixt fingers gone white 'neath the strength of their grip. That strength was necessary to restrain a near overwhelming urge to throw the jar and its contents full in his sneering face! "But the price for your deed may well be the wound's reopening and a return to the first step of healing. And that would, of necessity, mean a repeat of the slow process of treatments—greatly impeding your complete recovery."

"She speaks true. Your injury will be best mended by yielding to the maid's ministrations."

Both Adam and Llys looked toward the open door where stood a curious Wulf. Adam nearly blurted out his reason for distrusting the beauty while Llys's cheeks went scarlet, a discomfort intensified by the sight of the two kitchen thralls returned to gawk on either side of their lord's broad shoulders.

The only dim consolation Llys found in this ridiculous scene lay in the armloads of fresh bread rounds, which offered proof that the two servants had actually been in the bakehouse rather than close enough to hear Adam accuse her of a desire to touch him.

Rather than providing relief, however, the thought intensified her shameful suspicion that his claim held too much of the truth. This was not an admission able to bolster her confidence while Adam blithely stripped off his tunic, wincing slightly with the action. Indeed, his assertion was further confirmed by the fact that even had her life depended upon it Llys couldn't have looked away from the strength demonstrated by rippling muscles. In a desperate attempt to weaken the dangerous man's lure for her, nearly had Llys convinced herself that she merely imagined a masculine beauty of form to match his undeniably handsome face. Plainly that had been a fool's attempt at self-delusion.

Wulf saw his foster daughter's cheeks take on the blush of a rosebud under the other man's unwavering gaze. Thinking her embarrassed by the intimacy, he moved forward to again intervene, this time with a single-word question of paramount import to him.

"Anya?"

"Brynna is administering a fresh potion." Llys was thankful for the diversion and earnestly wished she could provide more encouraging news. Wulf simply nodded, but it was clear in the strong man's clenched hands that growing worries were taking their toll. Forcing a brighter tone, she added, "But Cub sleeps like the wee wolfkin he is."

The mention of his beloved son returned an honest smile to Wulf's lips. He glanced toward the far side of the hearth and the cradle holding a slumbering Osric who at three months threatened already to outgrow his bed. Though as the son of a Wulf he'd been called

Cub from the first, the babe had been formally named Osric in honor of the Northumbrian king who had saved his father's life. It had been a gift repaid in kind. Despite present trying circumstances, Wulf's smile deepened with warm memories of the man who'd restrained a justified vengeance and instead had raised the son of a dishonorable foe with his own heir, Ecgferth—Wulf's present king and friend.

"With my men joining your search, have you had sight of the intruders?" Though honestly interested in the answer, it was in hopes of curbing a resented but continuing awareness of Llys that Adam wielded the weapon of conversation.

"Nay." Shaking a bright head, Wulf turned his attention to the man doubtless growing restless under the inactivity enforced by a wound. "But your Cedric and Pip have improved the likelihood of my quest's success."

Wulf appreciated the two men now returned to the small building they shared with Maelvyn, the smithy, between the hamlet's outer edge and the palisade wall. Fortunately, the pair were unaccustomed to idleness, and as Maelvyn could give men untrained to the anvil and bellows but limited duties, they had welcomed the quest as an honorable pursuit to busy them while their lord recuperated. The pair's aid was the more useful for the fact that Wulf chose not to rouse unnecessary fears by summoning the men of Throckenholt to join him in the search.

As ealdorman, he was leader of the fyrd whose members throughout the shire were men well able to be fierce warriors in battle but in times of peace were farmers, metalsmiths, and millers. And until was found proof of the wickedness he suspected, Wulf would not draw them away from their normal routines, chores that kept vital materials in fine repair and fertile fields producing the foodstuffs required to see them all through another winter.

"Same as each day since you arrived, we located no more than the leavings of the knaves intruding on my lands and making free with beasts and forest fruits that are mine."

"So you've found further proof of their skill at hiding like the weasels they plainly are." Adam's smile was grim while he attempted to temper the warmth sent flowing through his veins by the unknowing invasion of an apparently hesitant maid gracefully sinking to kneel at his side. "And their ability to live by thievery off another's land."

When Wulf moved forward, Adam paused long enough for the weary man to sit in the neighboring chair before asking a question that needed to be asked though already he felt sure of its answer.

"Are you certain they're not simply a breed of common forest bandits?"

Wulf responded with a rueful grimace. "They leave too many traces behind. Common poachers have the wits to conceal their misdeeds by burying the remains of slaughtered animals and scattering the ashes of their fires."

Absently Wulf watched his foster daughter dispense with the old bandage before dipping her fingers into cream she next rubbed over the tender flesh of the mending wound stretching from front to back between lower rib and hip.

Self-disgust hardened Adam's handsome face into a mask of chill cynicism while he pretended a similar detachment to the dark beauty's deed, one he wished he felt. To disguise his unease and restore his peace of mind, he spoke with believable fervor. "The inability to go out and see these leavings for myself is a vexing trial to me."

While maintaining his end of the discussion and feigning a coolness he decidedly did not feel, Adam discovered that remaining immobile beneath the enchantress's gentle attentions was infinitely more difficult than expected. Did the hand smoothing cool unguent over flesh that burned 'neath the touch linger a moment longer than necessary? Or was that notion merely the product of his fevered imagination?

Llys steadily watched fingers whose path she must prevent from widening. Should she fail and surrender to a temptation to boldly caress uninjured areas of firm skin and hard muscle, she would lend credence to his despicable accusation . . . and shame herself with the wordless admission. It was necessary to lean nearer, and she bit her lip to dislodge with pain the wrongful urge to stroke over more flesh than the task required. This close, she couldn't fail to note that the wide planes of his powerful chest rose and fell with greater rapidity as his breathing grew labored. Had the intensity of control required to restrain wrongful desires given her touch an inexcusable roughness? Was she causing him additional discomfort? In atonement for that probability, she took care to be gentle in stroking the last of the ointment from his back around to his side and down to where the bunched cloth of his discarded tunic lay across his lap.

Adam was thankful he'd absently draped the tunic there, elsewise his response to the maid's touch would have been all too evident. Moreover, 'twas fortunate that others were present. Had he and Llys been blessed with solitude he much doubted himself able to have tamed this fierce desire to claim all that the irresistible enchantress had once offered.

"Now that you are near mended," Wulf began, sensing the growing tension between the wounded man and the woman tending him and purposefully slicing through it, "I repeat my invitation."

Wulf paused and patiently waited until Llys finished tying her patient's new bandage before again posing a matter of great import to him. Then, holding his guest's complete attention, he spoke. "If you are willing to overlook potential perils lurking near, you are welcome to remain here until you find the grave you seek . . . and your assailants."

Llys had heard Adam tell Wulf in a single terse sentence during the early days of his treatment that his brother, a monk at Winbury Abbey, was dead. But this was the first she'd heard of a lost grave, and she wondered how that could be so. As the two men resumed their talk, Llys rose, gathered her supplies, and slipped silently into the shadowed corner containing Brynna's medicinal goods. Yet all the while she listened intently for further morsels of information about Adam and for possible clues to his strange enmity toward her.

Adam, confident that he'd left his own lands in competent hands, was quick to respond. "Gratefully will I accept your hospitality if in return you will permit me to join *your* search for an explanation of why these strange interlopers are stealing across Throckenholt. I suspect that either they and my assailants share a common conspiracy or they are one and the same."

Wulf nodded with a smile, yet his expression held not humor but relief that the two of them viewed looming threats in the same serious vein and that Adam would linger on at Throckenholt to help in seeking the peril's source. Firelight gleamed on the pair of blond heads as they continued weighing probable threats and the possible aggressors behind them as well as promising defensive responses.

Knowing her presence had been forgotten, the woman trained to patience was free to listen. From their words she initially gleaned little more about Adam but discovered much regarding Wulf's seldom spoken yet clearly increasing alarm. He suspected that danger hovered in the forests bordering the rolling hills of Throckenholt's fertile fields. And moreover, these foes who had yet to be seen had lingered too long to bear aught but ill intent for his people and lands. That they numbered more than a few seemed certain when judged by the count of deer, rabbit, and bird carcasses found stripped clean of meat each day.

Delicate brows knit in growing concern. Lost in a maze of worries, Llys understood almost nothing that was said in the following minutes until Adam's voice, deepened to fierce thunder, drove its way through the tangle.

"Whatever may come, never will I believe that my young brother's end came by his own hand. Never!"

This was the first time Adam had admitted to any why Aelfric's grave had come to be lost, yet he refused to declare the bishop a liar. Son of one monk, brother to another, and raised to venerate both the church and its leaders, Adam shied away from accusing a bishop. For this reason he chose to speak no allegations now against Bishop Wilfrid, nor would he do so without solid proof to back his words.

"And, by your leave," Adam added, "I will continue my quest to find and mark the grave of the one whose untimely death leaves me the last of our line."

With a soul attuned to the emotions of others, Llys heard the depth of Adam's pain. Despite the antagonism he harbored toward her, the faint first glimmer of a plan to solve his dilemma and ease the ache of his loss began to glow.

Chapter
4

Unrecognizable words of ethereal loveliness held Adam spellbound. Having shaken off the bonds too long enforced by his wound, he'd escaped Wulf's home while only the house thralls were about. Now the fragrance of wildflowers surrounded him where he stood in the shadows at forest's edge, every sense heightened by the tantalizing tune's pure notes. Beneath dawn's glowing hues and in the center of a triangle formed by three mighty oaks a dainty figure moved, lavender mists billowing about her feet.

Her delicate face and slender arms lifted to a sky shifting from bright pastels into the pale azure of early morning, she seemed an elusive fantasy come to life, one whose bewitching spell Adam fought. He shook his head in a futile attempt to make the image disperse like moonbeams. It didn't. Instead, as if in answer to a mystical summons, all manner of untamed creatures joined her in the glade—the shy does with their speckled fawns, long-eared rabbits, even their natural predator the wolf, and the normally reclusive badger.

Slowly spinning at the start, Llys gracefully twirled ever faster. Masses of shiny black hair danced on the breeze and twined about a figure of unearthly beauty until her song rose in a crescendo of wild sweetness and power.

"What is this strange dominion you wield over the beasts of the forest?"

It wasn't the question he'd meant to ask. Indeed, Adam hadn't meant to speak at all. But, uncomfortable in the role of spy, he boldly stepped from the shadows, scattering the startled animals. He had journeyed from Oaklea on a quest to seek the truth behind his brother's odd condemnation of a bishop and instead had fallen into the role of secret observer of a beguiling sorceress's haunting rites.

For Llys the intruder's rude end to the spell of chanting completely sundered an aura of peace. She whirled to face the cynical but potent smile of the far too attractive visitor who by rights should have been safe abed in the lord of Throckenholt's home. Topaz gaze locked with sapphire. Although thick lashes half descended, Llys lost the battle she'd no experience to fight and again found it impossible to look away. She only wished she dared explain that 'twas not her authority over but rather her empathy with the creatures of the wild that drew them to her.

Alone with the mysterious beauty, Adam mistook her steady, slumbrous expression for another of the wanton invitations she'd wordlessly issued in Winbury Abbey. Using his contempt as an excuse, he strode forward to accept.

Suddenly swept full against a broad, muscular frame and held there by bands of flame-forged iron, for the first time in her life Llys was wrapped in a male embrace utterly lacking the platonic nature of that of brother, friend, or mentor. The powerful man's nearness was overwhelming, and Llys went disgustingly weak. Trembling under a barrage of unruly sensations, she looked up only to discover herself drowning in an amber sea of fire.

As Adam watched, shocked awareness tinted a delicate face with soft rose. The sight diluted the strength of his scorn and diminished his ability to transform his desire into the punishment he'd intended to inflict. When a low moan escaped her tight throat, Adam bent to take what he wanted. But a kiss rough at the outset gentled into a persuasion that stole Llys's breath. His mouth brushed across tender lips once and once again until they grew pliant.

A fiery excitement Llys hadn't known existed throbbed through her veins. Driven by instinct and seeking a steady anchor in this shifting sea, she wrapped her arms about broad shoulders, twined her fingers into the cool golden strands of his hair.

Lost to thoughts of blame or guilt, Adam tangled his hands into a lustrous ebony mane and crushed the tender, deliciously curved maid nearer still. He surrendered to her silent entreaty and parted petal-soft lips, claiming the deep, devastating kiss she naively demanded.

Naively?

Shocked by what he could near have sworn was the honeyed nectar of innocence on her lips, Adam released her mouth and stared down into a blue gaze gone smoky with mingled desire and confusion. Naive? Innocent? These words could never be applied to this treacherous female whose nature he knew. Its despicable truth he'd seen with his own eyes and heard in her cruel laughter.

He smiled with bitter scorn for both himself and

her. Llys's training as sorceress must have honed to
incredible sharpness her talent for seeming to be what
she was not. Having long prided himself on his skill at
accurately reading the character of others, he was
vexed by his inability to delve beyond her sweet
surface to what must be a sour core. Ruthlessly he
quashed lingering tendrils of self-blame for having
initiated a chaste maid into passion. To further waylay
the flow of that worthless emotion, he let his arms fall
away and took a step back from the clearly dangerous
woman.

"What manner of fool would you play me for? Do
you think me so simple-witted I can be easily misled,
so weak and maneuverable I might forget your cruel
mirth over Aelfric's death?"

Feeling roughly set adrift on a troubled ocean beset
by dense mists, Llys lowered her fine dark brows in
puzzlement. "Who is Aelfric?"

Adam growled his disgust. "Next you will claim
never to have visited Winbury Abbey."

"But never have I done so." With these words Llys
spread her hands, vulnerable palms turned upward in
wordless entreaty for clarity amid the haze of her own
tangled emotions and Adam's strange accusations.

Long moments passed as Adam studied the maid's
apparent sincerity. Vivid memories would prevent
him from ever accepting her as a guileless innocent,
but plainly she would never confess to her part in that
dreadful scene. That fact acknowledged, he could only
deem it squandered time to further question her
statement.

"What strange rite were you performing?" Adam's
gaze was as impenetrable as cloudy amber.

Although she knew that asking such a question was
Glyndor's favorite trick to knock an opponent off his

stride, Adam's abrupt shift in subject so startled Llys that she answered without hesitation.

"I beseeched the forces of nature to grant Anya the boon of a hasty recovery." Seeing skepticism raise his dark gold brows, she quickly added, "Busy tending her daughter with a tisane of tansy, woodbane, and a few herbs more, Brynna begged me to seek healing for the child by chanting the dawn in her stead."

The next moment Llys could've bitten her tongue with annoyance. In her flustered state, she'd broken a rule of great importance. She'd spoken to an outsider of powers unknown to men untaught, powers more like to frighten strangers—those who were unwilling to accept or incapable of understanding—into violence against those able to commune with the forces embodied in all natural elements.

Determined to turn back the tide of her wrong, Llys resurrected the subject he'd abandoned. "Who is it you've mistaken me for? And what has that woman to do with the chaste men of the abbey?"

What game did the mercurial sorceress play? Adam refused to reassure her by voicing answers already known to them both.

Though never lacking in courage, it required every shred of Llys's bravery to stand undaunted before the man gone motionless as stone while bolts of golden lightning seemed to flash from his remarkable eyes.

Glaring into the dark beauty's unflinching gaze, Adam wondered what motive lay behind her questions. Did she think that by challenging his memory with bald-faced lies she might deflect his disapproval, weaken his certainty of what he had seen?

And yet to Adam she appeared in this new role as neither the wanton siren of Winbury Abbey nor the shy and quiet maiden of Wulfayne's abode. Was this resolute maid nearer to the true core of her being? Whatever the query's answer, with this fresh demonstration of her ability to switch between vastly different poses Adam grew more positive that he could never dare trust the devious beauty. His frown deepened in disgust over thoughts suggesting even the possibility of such a traitorous emotion.

Llys saw Adam's firm mouth twist down with derision. It was clear he would give no answer, yet beneath his steady gaze she refused to falter for so much as the briefest of instants. The banked fires of her carefully restrained nature lit sparks in sapphire eyes and tilted a dainty chin upward.

Thus they remained, each determined the other would give way and in so doing emerge as the one in error.

"Adam! Llys?"

At the call, the pair turned in unison to meet the quizzical scrutiny of Wulfayne come to summon them home for a discussion of strange matters recently exposed.

Unshuttered windows on one wall invited the light of midmorn into a dark room further brightened by sunbeams falling through a door opened on the one opposite to welcome an elderly farmer leaning heavily on a crooked staff. The four seated along a single side of the lord of Throckenholt's table waited on the hobbling man's slow progress.

Llys sat beside Adam while Brynna had taken her customary place at Wulf's right. Quietly nibbling her lip, Llys wondered what could be of such consequence that not only had she and Adam been summoned home but Brynna had been drawn away from her daughter. Thankfully after Llys's chanting of the dawn

Anya had roused from her unnatural slumber, although she was delirious and only awake for a few brief moments.

To waylay thoughts hovering between worry and puzzlement, Llys scrutinized her surroundings. She had been a visitor to her foster parents' home many times in recent years, leaving her familiar with the keep's layout—the long rectangular hall and off the south end, behind the table built atop a dais, a sizable bedchamber for the lord and lady and a smaller one for their children. Out from the northern end two chambers had later been added. Of equally modest size, they'd been intended to shelter the steady flow of patients come seeking Brynna's curative powers. But now one had been given over for Llys's use while the other was occupied by the visiting lord of Oaklea. The patients' needs were presently filled by simple straw-stuffed pallets stacked in the corner between Adam's chamber and the windowed wall while the herb corner's table jutted out from the wall of Llys's chamber.

Feeling the pull of the handsome visitor too near, Llys purposefully focused her attention on insignificant details which, though she'd taken up residence somewhat less than three weeks past, she hadn't earlier given particular notice. Such things as the shelving built between windows to hold baskets of foodstuffs and the barrels resting below. And pegs were driven into the wall beside the outer door to hold the family's cloaks—sometimes needed even in summer.

Wulf's deep voice broke Llys's visual survey of his well-tended and comfortably furnished abode. And it was a most welcome distraction for the woman fearing herself about to lose the battle in holding her face averted from the summons of a steady amber gaze.

"Ulford, here meet the famed warrior Adam Brachtward, Ealdorman of Oaklea." Wulf waved the age-bent farmer's attention toward a man as golden and plainly as powerful as himself.

Soft cap crushed betwixt gnarled hands, Ulford nervously smiled at the visitor about whom he and all of Northumbria had heard endless praises sung.

Wulf saw the awe in age-dulled eyes and heard the abnormal stillness in his hall. Several thralls ostensibly busy at their daily tasks barely moved while straining to hear every nuance of whatever might be said. Plainly they meant to glean every kernel of information they could from this strangely timed meeting between an odd assortment of two ealdormen, a pair of sorceresses, and an elderly farmer. There was no doubt but that before dusk darkened the sky every word here spoken would become a freshly sown seed sprouting to add a new vine to ever-thriving crops of rumor and gossip.

"On his journey to Throckenholt a fortnight and two days past, Lord Adam and his men made camp in the forest." As Wulf spoke he nodded toward Cedric and Pip.

Llys studied Adam's supporters. Since the day of their coming, she'd seen little of the pair. Yet she had learned enough to know the stocky, barrel-chested older one was stern and gruff while the cheery, oversized younger one could barely contain either his lively curiosity or his stream of banter. She'd been surprised when they earlier stepped into the hall. Now they stood to one side of the door amid shadows increased by the brilliance falling through the still open portal.

"Oh, nay." Ulford was not loath to show his poor opinion of this purportedly sharp-witted warrior's action, and though he sorrowfully shook a grizzled head his words were a reproof. "The forest hereabouts be dangerous, dangerous."

The corners of Wulf's mouth threatened to lift in a grin at the aging man's poorly hidden reproach. "So we've found, have we not, Ulford?" Wulf glanced to the side and was relieved. The glow in amber eyes proved Adam as amused as he.

"'Tis a lesson Lord Adam learned when, during the darkest hours of that night, he was attacked. But his pigeonhearted assailants learned one more valuable still. The fools fled once faced with his might."

Unfamiliar with the concept and lacking the experience that would prompt an exercise of tact, Ulford had no notion of how close he'd come to offending a man he admired. Thus he was free to mentally cast in the role of Lord Adam's assailants the strutting, beardless boy and followers he himself had come against. Ulford clutched his walking stick and let his head fall back while he cackled with glee at the image of that nasty group put to flight by an unexpectedly powerful foe.

Wulf waited for calm before continuing with his reason for summoning the ceorl. "Believing the elusive trespassers on my lands may've also been his assailants, Lord Adam has consented—for a time— to lend his strong arm and sharp mind to the goal of ridding Throckenholt of their ilk."

As open with his approval as with his reproof, Ulford enthusiastically nodded and grinned, more clearly revealing the loss of a goodly number of teeth.

"Because you are the first of my people to have seen them in the flesh, I ask that you repeat for Lord Adam all you've told me."

Proud to have been given so important a role,

Ulford beamed. While he bobbed his head in agreement, he paused to marshal his thoughts into coherent words.

"Seems as the night do be their time. 'Twere as I was a-comin' home in the dusk last evening that I stumbled over a new-killed buck. Arrow what brought him low were driven straight through his heart. I were a-marvelin' at the clean shot when sudden-like I were ringed 'round by strangers." Ulford grunted in disgust. "Certain they be forest outlaws, I 'spected I be next to die. What queered the whole were that the youngest amongst 'em were their leader. And don't you know he opened his pouch and offered a coin to see that I bridle my tongue."

Pausing, Ulford held tight to staff and cap with one hand while digging the other into a bag hung crosswise over his bony chest. At last what he sought was found, and slowly he hobbled forward to place a shiny gold coin on the table's bare planks between the two ealdormen.

"Striplin' lad's elders weren't best pleased, but afore they could alter his intent, I snatched up his gold." Ulford nodded toward the disk so bright it nearly glowed against the dark tabletop. His gaze then shifted to directly meet his lord's. "But you know as I brung it right here soon as the sun reappeared."

Ulford puffed, waiting for praise surely owed. The four at the table were quick to respond with the expected and earned appreciation. While Adam lifted and carefully examined the gold piece, Wulf urged Ulford to continue. "The fallen deer and that coin are not the only curious details you saw."

The most important bit of news had been omitted from the ceorl's colorful tale. Although Ulford could be forgiven for omitting something whose value he plainly hadn't recognized, that point more than any other must be shared. Wulf urged him on. "Tell us . . ."

"The ring, I ken?" Ulford was patently disgusted by his lord's insistence that he mention the bleedin' thing he hadn't included in his tale as 'twere the sort of useless detail what mucked up a tidy story. Though pretty enough, the ring hadn't any gems and weren't even purely gold. Hah! The coin contained more gold than that snippet of jewelry.

Adam's attention was immediately caught by the mention of a ring. He watched closely while Wulf nodded to prod the disgruntled man into explaining.

Ulford shrugged. "The striplin' in their lead wore 'bout the smallest finger of one hand an odd bit of twined metal strands—gold, silver, and bronze."

Sensing important answers hovering just beyond his reach, Adam chaffed at this unnecessarily slow path of revelation but reined in his impatience to ask, "Into what shape were these metal strands twisted? And which metal lay on top?"

"The bronze." Ulford promptly answered, watery eyes narrowing as he began to comprehend that the item he'd dismissed held the key to a riddle whose solution these lords sought. "I ken it were bent into one of them marks what scribes scratch on parchment, but I don't know their names and can't tell you which."

Instantly reaching inside his tunic, Adam brought forth the last letter he had received from Aelfric. "Pip," he called out, "fetch one of the coals gone cold on the fire's outer edge so that our friend Ulford may draw for us what he saw."

Adam had no patience to wait for a quill and ink to be fetched, nor was it likely the ceorl would be better able to employ a scribe's tools. While Pip hastened to do as his leader bade him and rummaged through the ash for a usable coal, Adam spread the parchment face down on the thick oak planks. He deemed it appropriate that Aelfric's last plea for help be used to trap the perpetrators of the wrong done him . . . or leastwise to point the way.

Anxious to atone for his lapse in not telling the whole tale at the first, once the coal was in his shaking hand Ulford bent to do as directed.

Brows meeting in a frown, Adam watched while the man laboriously created the rough likeness of a stylized "S." It was of the sort both his father and brother had skillfully drawn as the first letter on a manuscript page, the sort metalworkers used in creating fine ornaments for those in influential positions. This letter confirmed what the bronze strand's position had suggested.

Adam's attention shifted to Wulf. In silence the two men communicated a common conclusion. Ulford's contribution provided support for all that Wulf had initially feared, and more, and yet it explained nothing of the motivation at its back. Each man knew that a secondhand account of the ring, sketched by a ceorl, failed to provide proof weighty enough to wield in making serious accusations against a highborn miscreant. 'Twas deeply unfortunate, as without such intervention the "stripling lad" would doubtless continue his treacherous course, and his unrestrained menace would continue hovering near. If only they knew why and for what purpose . . .

Staring blindly down at hands pressed flat on either side of the letter and its drawing, Adam's fingertips went white with the pressure exerted. Below his pleasure at progress made, deeper than the unhappy need for further proof, lay dark disappointment that Ulford's report offered nothing either to verify or to ease his suspicion of the bishop, nothing to prove Aelfric innocent of a sin mortal to the soul of a Christian.

Llys watched, sensing Adam's bleak thoughts while he sat unaware as Wulf laid the golden coin in Ulford's callused palm.

Puffed up with pride, the elderly farmer departed with that bounty along with his lord's appreciation and the pleasing certainty that by nightfall the whole of Throckenholt would have heard the tale of his honorable deed. Aye, well rewarded he was.

As Adam's two supporters departed to resume the tasks they'd taken on to aid Maelvyn, Brynna gathered up her infant son who was beginning to howl his demand to be fed. She disappeared into the room where Anya lay while Llys slipped into the corner of the hall purposely left in shadow.

Llys settled on a three-legged stool drawn near the table covered with medicinal supplies requiring further attention. Her hands absently began to blend an herbal concoction to lend healing sleep to those in pain while wandering thoughts pieced together the previous day's revelations and this morning's obliquely hinted and unspoken suggestions. Seemed the two Saxon lords now suspected they knew the identity of those behind lurking dangers. It was their silence on the matter that left Llys wondering why she and Brynna had been included in the odd meeting.

From beneath thick lashes Llys's blue eyes surreptitiously studied two much lauded heroes. Though physically much alike—both golden, tall, and powerfully formed—they were different as well. That difference involved more than the fact that while Wulf's age was two score and a wee bit more, Adam was a decade younger. Each was a justly renowned warrior, but where Wulf was at core calm and gentle, Adam, despite his amazing gentleness with Cub, seemed outwardly stern even as the blaze of an inner battle raged. She had been scorched by the fire of his contempt and by the infinitely more dangerous heat of his arms.

Aye, two heroes—one her foster father and the other a man so dangerously attractive that Llys could almost be glad of his hostility to her . . . almost. Leastways she wished it were so.

While Llys watched, King Ecgferth's two ealdormen rose and, intent on their plans to track and end dangers of uncertain origin, departed the keep without further words spoken.

Chapter
5

Throckenholt keep's four well-born inhabitants returned to the evening's white linen–draped table as
the setting sun's last brilliant rays faded into the
monochromatic shades of dusk. Wasting no moment's
thought they settled into the same seats they'd occupied during Ulford's visit. Neither of the golden lords
offered any word on their afternoon's quest. As a
tangle of problems without answers held the full
attention of all, silence reigned throughout the first
course, of rabbit stew, and near to the end of the next,
of trout in verjuice and spices.

Ever too aware of the golden warrior at her side,
Llys felt she could bear little more. How, she wondered, was it possible that the man who looked at her
with such scorn could at the same time, doubtless
unintentionally, wrap her in the aura of his attraction?
The hearth's fire roared, and resin-soaked torches
flamed at intervals along the walls, but it was the
reflection of many candles amassed on a single brass
platter at table center that glowed on bright hair like a
beacon demanding her attention. Fearing to meet

piercing amber eyes seemingly able to probe her very soul for secrets that she dared not reveal, she kept her gaze trained on her platter and the remnants of a fish more mangled than eaten. The mere fact that Adam could so easily summon her response proved how great a peril he was.

As if in demonstration of that peril, under the lure of his nearness Llys's own thoughts betrayed her by soaring back to the dawn's forest encounter. Although on the one side it seemed to have happened a lifetime ago, on the other, it could as well have been but moments past, so tangibly did she feel his steely arms about her. Llys's eyes went the hazy blue of woodsmoke while vividly she recalled the pleasure of having her soft curves crushed against the solid wall of his hard chest, of tasting the passion in his kiss. *Dangerous, too dangerous!*

Seeking a distraction from her wrongful awareness of him, Llys leaned forward to look past Adam, past Wulf, and down to where Brynna sat at the table's far end. Never mind her own inability to enjoy the meal, it worried Llys to find the other woman simply pushing her food from one side to another on the wooden trencher she shared with her husband. Wulf, too, was watching his wife with concern. Clearly another layer had been added to the many burdens he already bore.

Sighing, Llys fervently wished she could lift even one. If only, she wished as she had before, she could spin a spell to restore the much loved Anya to laughing health. Once that was done, Brynna would surely recover from a deepening gloom of the sort she hadn't suffered since the loss two years past of a babe too early born. A disheartening memory and unpleasant comparison, that. Certain she could do no more to heal the child now than she'd been able to do then to lessen Brynna's grief, a downward curl came to the berry-bright lips Llys fell to nibbling.

Adam had unwillingly fallen time and again into watching the enchantress who seemed such a tender, timid doe, and he wanted not to do so now. Yet he couldn't help but see her forlorn expression as she peered around him. The small white teeth tugging at a soft lower lip seemed too natural a sign of distress to be feigned. He fought an inward battle to subdue an unwelcome but powerful desire to cradle the dainty figure and comfort her in her unhappiness. The contest was won by self-disgust, which curled his hands into fists. He loathed himself for even momentarily caring what ill plagued the wicked sorceress who assuredly deserved this punishment and more!

Deep blue eyes caught the abrupt clenching of strong hands. What wicked imp, she wondered, had of a sudden roused such mute rage in the famed warrior? The prospect of unseen foes? Nay, his anger was too deeply felt to be else than a personal blow. The death of his brother? Llys had seen Adam's anger over the claimed manner of his brother's end. It grieved her that no balm could be brewed of herbs to heal his inner wound. But mayhap there was hope for easing the pain doubtless aggravated by the frustration of his fruitless search for a hidden grave.

Llys straightened while a shy smile bloomed. Of all the difficulties faced by the table's occupants, this was the single trouble for which she possessed a likely cure—if two requirements could be met. First it would be necessary to overcome Adam's near certain rcsistance and persuade him to allow an attempt to be made by a woman he despised. And then . . .

"Have you any personal item that once belonged to

your brother?" Mentioning the second requirement with a fine show of bravado, difficult to maintain, Llys ignored both the initial shock on Adam's handsome face and the dark scowl that almost instantly replaced it. "Something he kept close to his person?"

Adam's fists tightened until his knuckles shone white. He refused to respond to a question whose answer she knew. This unscrupulous sorceress had watched him force Bishop Wilfrid to forfeit the pearl and ruby rosary. Did she dare dream he would permit her guilty hands to besmirch the sacred relic?

Brushing back a glory of flowing black locks, Llys braved both the darkening storm of his expression and the golden fires flashing in the depths of his eyes to explain her purpose. "A possession once treasured by your brother would aid me in locating the place where his mortal form rests."

"Oh-h-h!" Brynna gasped, straightening under a startled pang of remorse for not having earlier suggested this answer. Leaning forward to peer down the table, she met the entreaty in Llys's blue eyes.

Looking between his wife and his foster daughter, Wulfayne instantly accepted the feat's plausibility. Since the wild journey he'd once shared with his Druid "family," during which they'd repeatedly exerted their influence over nature to good purpose, he had come to respect their ways. Now, with the experience of years in their company, he acknowledged that their abilities went far beyond the limited understanding he and his Saxon brethren held of nature. Say they a thing could be done, it could be. However, one glance toward their guest raised the specter of failure for wont of opportunity.

Adam's half-lowered lashes guarded his gaze. He had already made his decision to reject the proposal.

Yet as the meaning behind his host and hostess's reaction to Llys's words was unclear to him, he politely waited for their explanation.

"I realize 'tis a concept alien to you, Adam," Wulf began slowly, weighing each word he spoke to this man whose close family bonds with the church doubtless would make it all the harder for him to yield even so far as to consider Llys's suggestion. "I pray you to not be overhasty in rejecting this openly offered gift. I deem it likely to be your best if not your only chance to find one small site amid an immense forest."

In the silence that followed, Adam appeared frozen in place, but though his body was immobile, his mind raced. Doubtless during the past fortnight and more the trail had gone cold. He feared Wulf spoke true of the difficulty in locating Aelfric's grave.

When he made no response, Wulf continued, exercising the persistence with which warriors ofttimes won where even might had failed. "I don't doubt but that frequently you've heard our tale repeated. And you may, as do many who were not there, doubt its veracity." A pale green gaze steadily met amber eyes. "I give you my oath that 'tis the truth. However, while I have many times been *blessed*"—he emphasized that purposefully chosen word—"with aid whose source I cannot explain, I am now, as I have always been, a Christian. There *are* powers beyond a priest's ken. I've seen them at work. These are powers which, I believe, emanate from the same divinity we both worship."

Though mentally sorting through alternative plans, Adam heard all that had been said. His jaw firmed against what was surely blasphemy spoken by this man he'd long admired.

Wulf shook his head in regret for the other's apparent inflexibility, the missed opportunity it meant. He made a final plea. "Trust me, if not Llys, and I swear we three will find Aelfric's grave."

"Aelfric?" Llys asked. Here was the name Adam had accused her of knowing only this morning. She glanced up into the handsome face turned toward her in response to the startled question yet closed against her.

Again Adam refused to state what he knew she'd learned in the abbey. It was left to Wulf to tell her that Aelfric was his younger brother.

Brynna unexpectedly joined the discussion and by so doing lessened the tension growing among the other three. "If you will trust me with the item, I will aid Llys in preparing for the task." Knowing the strange enmity Adam felt toward Llys might well be his reason for rejecting her assistance, Brynna sought to temper his opposition. "I've responsibilities that keep me here. Elsewise I also would journey with you on the morrow. And though I cannot, I'll offer up the most powerful triads I know, beseeching the powers of nature to grant you success."

Adam's first decision had already been weakened, and Lady Brynna's offer eased the way for him to act. Scraping his chair across the thick plank floor, he rose to his feet. His initial refusal to allow Druid hands to touch Aelfric's rosary yielded—not to an acceptance of pagan rites but to the sharp wits of a successful military tactician's mind.

Mouth compressed with regret, Llys watched the powerful man striding away from the table with amazing grace for one of his size. Had her proffered help driven him from their company? The answer seemed too clear when he disappeared into the bedchamber allotted him and almost immediately returned with saddle pouches slung over his shoulder. Her heart sank. Must be that he meant to leave more than the table.

Adam was deeply aware that Llys's forlorn attention had never wavered from him. Her wistfulness refused to fit the opinion he'd formed of her in the abbey, as an immoral, heartless sorceress. And worse, under the current sweetness of her expression that distasteful impression was losing form in his memory. He felt himself falling victim to a pagan enchantress's feigned innocence—and it was this seeming innocence that threatened to pierce the armor about his heart, for in her initial guise as seductress she'd left him unmoved.

Once he'd set sturdy pouches connected with long leather straps atop one end of the table, Adam clenched his eyes shut. He refused to fall victim to this further attempt to trick him into believing her false face, and he forcefully rejected this probing for the weak link in the armor of his certainty in her wickedness.

Llys's troubled heart cast off the heavy bonds of anxiety when the golden man began rummaging through one of the bags and eased from it an article wrapped in fine cloth. The care with which his strong hands cradled the small bundle made it clear he deemed its contents precious.

While placing his treasure on the table between Wulf and his wife, Adam reminded himself that as Llys had been in the abbey at the time of his brother's death, she likely knew where the boy was buried. If now to see the grave revealed he must outwardly accept her facade for reality, so be it. While Lady Brynna remained in Throckenholt Keep singing the sort of peculiarly haunting chants he'd heard soar

from Llys's lips, he would silently beg God's merciful
forgiveness for allowing a heathen to defile the crucifix, a treasure beyond price.

Facing those seated at the table and holding the
breathless attention of the hall's company, from lord
to thrall, Adam carefully lifted soft cloth aside. Thus
he revealed the glowing pearls and glittering rubies of
a gold rosary of great beauty. It was in truth a prize of
immense value, but to him its worth went far beyond
the base reckoning of mankind.

In the pale light preceding dawn three riders rode
out through the palisade gates of the village of
Throckenholt while, in respect for the all-important
privacy required by Druidic rites, Adam's two supporters remained behind to guard Wulf's family and
home. The party's two men and one woman steadily
advanced in single file into the tangled undergrowth of
a forest blessed with thick-grown trees and lush greenery.

The journey having begun in earnest, Llys attempted to shift her attention from the man directly
ahead. However, nature ever before her friend seemed
to conspire against her. Errant beams from a sun just
cresting the horizon wended their way through even
the leafy branches near joined over their path. They
defeated her purpose by glowing on the bright hair
flowing to a point betwixt broad shoulders and glint-
ing on the large metal links attached to Adam's jerkin.
Recognizing the action as her only hope for reprieve
from a dangerously potent lure, she closed her eyes
against the sight. An unmarked time passed during
which two experienced warriors constantly surveyed
their surroundings for danger while Llys was slowly

calmed by the bright melodies and delicate fragrances of her surroundings.

These past few weeks since descending from the hill home she shared with her brother and Glyndor in Talacharn were the longest Llys had ever spent separated by man-made barriers from the powers flowing through natural forms. She had missed her daily communion with the voices of nature and wondered how Brynna could bear so constant a severance. A tiny smile quickly curved cherry-red lips. Hers had been a foolish query. 'Twas the love shared between her foster parents that made all things possible and right. Giving full attention to the verdant loveliness revealing itself on every side, Llys silently chanted triads of appreciation for its welcome of her and others more of reverent awe.

A long, quiet time later humor momentarily flashed in deep blue eyes. Though fond of her placid little mare, Llys was amused by the sight of its compact gray form diminished and far outshone by the gleaming black hides of the two mighty war-horses.

She sobered the next instant, struck with a harsh reminder of the reason for her position of safety behind Adam, who retraced his trip into Throckenholt, and in front of Wulf while they continued down a narrow trail cast in shadow by densely grown trees. Never would she fear nature—neither its shadows nor its storms—but the ominous possibility of hostile men lurking near was another matter entirely. As with every threat to emotional serenity, fear was shameful for one of her heritage. Llys fought to subdue growing apprehensions, gripping the reins so tightly they bit into soft palms. It was frustrating to admit the difficulty she found in controlling her response to unseen foes, unfamiliar specimens of humankind willing to abuse the earth's haven for their own ill intent.

From that moment on, neither the melodious trill of songbirds nor the beauty of shy wildflowers peeking pastel heads through dense foliage could summon her attention from bleak thoughts. Once roused by skulking dangers, like unruly weeds her anxieties only grew and spread to new areas.

Had she learned enough to cast the spell of finding alone? Rarely and only to meet small challenges had she found reason to work a serious charm without the support of her mentor or leastways Evain. The thought brought a faint smile of pride for the brother who was now a sorcerer, too, and near as powerful as Glyndor.

Her attention returned to a somber question beyond the last. Would the pearl and ruby symbol of Christian belief in a God of the heavens allow for communion with the powers of the earth? Though Llys knew Wulf believed all powers above and below shared the same source, her anxiety was too deep to be easily soothed. Once again biting her lip in the oft repeated sign of uncertainty—shameful in a Druid— Llys decided 'twould not go amiss were she to also seek the aid of the Christians' God. After years of visiting Wulf's home, she knew enough of such prayers to offer one of her own and closed her eyes while joining her hands palm to palm, reins between.

"Dear God of the heavens," she soundlessly whispered. "I beseech you to grant me the boon I seek. Permit me to ease your follower's unhappiness. Allow me to lead him to his fallen brother."

"You looked as if you were praying." Adam spoke softly to the maid who obviously hadn't realized her mare had followed his stallion's lead in halting beneath the oak where he'd been assaulted.

"I was." Llys's eyes flew open. Alarmed to find Adam so near, she'd answered without forethought. That lapse of right reasoning tinted creamy cheeks a shade bright enough to near match cherry-sweet lips.

Golden eyes narrowed to examine the embarrassed confusion in startled sapphire eyes outlined by thick lashes as dark as the mane framing delicately rosed cheeks. His jaw clenched against this near-convincing image of naïveté. Here, he told himself, sat the finest mummer in all the world, one able to appear sincere in a role of deepest deceit.

All too well Llys sensed waves of disapproval washing over her. After weeks under its weight, she ought to have grown used to his disdain, but she felt certain that in this instance his resentment was for her supplication to his god. Her chin tilted defiantly. She wouldn't repent the deed so long as the goal was won.

"Llys," Wulf broke into the wordless confrontation. "As you requested, we've brought you to the place where Adam's wound was inflicted."

Nodding, Llys felt her cheeks burn even brighter for having been caught mutely staring at Adam. Awaiting neither man's aid, she promptly slipped from the saddle and fastened her mare's reins to one of the towering tree's lower branches. Under other circumstance never would she willingly perform the rite she was about to attempt before the eyes of an unbeliever. However, during the darkest hours of the night past she and Brynna had taken the crucifix into the moonlight. There amid the circle of young oaks Wulf had planted years ago at Brynna's behest, together they'd sought nature's consent.

All too aware of the men still ahorse, Llys sank to

her knees with less grace than was her wont. Delving into a small kidskin bag attached to the belt riding low on her hips, she carefully withdrew Adam's precious rosary. This she laid amid a patch of rich, soft grass. Next pulling forth a smooth white crystal, she rose while beginning to roll it between her palms as in a quiet voice of haunting sweetness she began chanting strange words unknown to men untaught.

Adam tried but found he could no more look away now than he'd been able to during their dawn encounter. Caught in an elusive net of speechless awe, he was held spellbound by the eerie music as this figure of ethereal beauty began to twirl. Like jeweled raindrops halted in midair, time seemed suspended while the purity of wondrous notes soared and grew, twining through and about the forest and all creatures within. Abruptly the song ended. Silence reigned. Yet the crystal nestled in one dainty palm glowed with a mysterious inner radiance. Llys sank again to her knees and gently placed it atop the rosary, then rested her hand over both.

Unnatural quiet held sway as Llys rose, the stone still aglow in one cupped palm and crucifix in the other. She turned toward Adam. Though no word was spoken, he instinctively extended an upraised palm.

The mystical deeds to which Adam had been witness were unsettling. He wouldn't, couldn't allow himself to believe the evidence of his own eyes. At the same time he found it impossible to reconcile this image of purity and light with the abbey's dark and wanton sorceress.

Llys carefully placed the heavy gold chain in his open hand. "Feeling safe among men he trusted, Aelfric met his end."

Just as he'd begun to question his opinion of the

maid, the freezing waters of unpleasant reality crashed over Adam. By callously wielding her first-hand knowledge of his brother's murder at the hands of faithless friends, she had wrenched open a painful wound only beginning to heal. Finding an error in trusting his own judgment deepened his disgust for both himself and her.

Seeing Adam go as cold and unyielding as solid ice, Llys realized that hearing this kernel of crystal-revealed knowledge from her had deeply offended him. Sorrow darkened blue eyes near to onyx as Llys turned aside. She forced herself to focus on the goal yet to be reached and led the way through a green wall of trees, then along the path of white light laid down by her still glowing crystal.

Wulf motioned Adam to also tether his horse and join him in following the unhesitating maid already threatening to be swallowed by the woodland's thick undergrowth and low-hanging branches. Adam nodded and did as directed. However, before joining the trail of crushed ferns and broken twigs, he took the additional moments required to remove saddle pouches from the ebony stallion and swing them over his shoulder.

After some little time spent traveling parallel to the brow of a gentle hill, Llys stepped into a glade. A strip down the center of its lush green carpet studded with tiny blooms had been rudely disturbed, first by human-wielded shovels and then, less successfully, by foraging animals.

Entering the glade behind Wulf, Adam was surprised to find Llys gazing sorrowfully at the soft ground he accepted without pause as Aelfric's final resting place. Rather than questioning his easy belief, he reminded himself to not be again misled by her false show of tender emotion. Pushing unsettling thoughts aside, he focused instead on the task he'd sworn to perform and for whose doing he'd endured Llys's games. Adam lowered the saddle pouches from his shoulder and laid them aside, relieved that no animal had yet been persistent enough to succeed in desecrating the grave. A narrowed amber gaze closely surveyed the surroundings, searching for sizable rocks which could be gathered without the aid of pickax and shovel.

Well aware of the golden gaze moving over her with undiminished disdain, Llys had refused to glance up until she sensed his attention turning away. And then it was the thud of a massive rock finding its new home in soft soil that caught her attention. Both men were busy unearthing and hauling large stones to create a sturdy base layer over disturbed ground, but her unconsciously caressing gaze never shifted from Adam. So intent was her scrutiny that she glimpsed the spreading of a faint dark stain and quietly gasped. He was bleeding anew. Plainly this strenuous work had reopened his wound.

Llys wanted to rush forward and beg him to cease before greater damage was done the healing process. But she'd the wisdom to realize her well-meant concern would be ill received. Indeed, it likely would drive him the harder. That fact left her no option but to resolutely dare the golden glare intended to restrain her and add her efforts to see the task completed the sooner. With labor shared by three sets of hands, a mound of stones was constructed, one able to protect the young man's final resting place from further marauding animals.

Grave secure, Adam moved to the bags deposited in the shade of a flowering bush. From one he took out two uneven lengths of carefully hewn wood and a long leather strip. Laying the short piece of wood across another that was longer and sharply pointed at one end, he began lashing them together. Next he drove his makeshift cross deep into the ground at one end of the grave, bracing it with carefully laid rocks. When Adam rose to stand just behind the cross, head bowed, Wulf took up the same position on the far side.

"God, I pray you will open your arms in welcome of Aelfric." Adam paused. Refusing to weep before the Druidess who had laughed over his brother's death, he gritted his teeth until he regained control. "And I pray you will give him an honored place at your table beside your devout servant, our father."

Seeking solitude as a shield for the sorrow and anger roused by this waste of a harmless young life, Adam turned away from the others and began climbing. At the top of the hill, he halted. Sweeping aside hanging tendrils of ivy that thickly covered an old tree's thick trunk and had grown to drape over its lower limbs, he found a sight he'd expected and another ominous one he had not.

"Wulf." The single word was not loud but well able to carry an unmistakable urgency to the man lingering in the glade. In an amazingly brief time his companions joined him to gaze down at Winbury Abbey . . . and around it the encampment overflowing once fertile fields now trampled by a multitude of booted feet and massive steeds.

"What vile demon dares lay siege upon so hallowed a site?" Wulf asked in a voice deepened by disgust.

"Initially I also viewed these armed men as aggressors." Amber eyes gone hard turned to meet Wulf's puzzled expression. Adam motioned toward the scene in the valley below. "Look. Note with what ease people move through the abbey gates—soldiers and monks alike." He paused for other gazes to narrow on the portal before adding, "They are not foes."

As if to confirm Adam's assertion, Bishop Wilfrid's unmistakable figure appeared. He slowly walked through fields laid waste, in close conversation with a man heavily armed. The latter was treated with such deference by the warriors they passed that his position as their leader was clear.

"Best we send a message to our king, asking if 'tis fear of invasion that lies behind this arming of abbeys." Even as he spoke, Adam exchanged with Wulf a silent look that said a great deal more. They both knew how extremely unlikely it was that Ecgferth would equip such minor monastic sites for war while at the same time leaving his ealdormen—military leaders all—uninformed and ill prepared. Further, those men were all aware of the growing resentment the bishop felt toward their king, who over the years had begun to limit the powers of the church and specifically Wilfrid's personal wealth.

"Let us hasten back to Throckenholt, from whence I'll dispatch a courier with that question," Wulf agreed. "And, too, I will mention my regret that though King Ecgferth's youngest son, Saexbo, tarries so near, he has yet to permit me the privilege of hosting him in my home."

A rare full smile warmed the sharply chiseled lines of Adam's handsome face. This message offered the prospect of ease to his growing alarm over apparent dangers to his king and to his fellow ealdormen. Still, because his own lands lay in peace and protected near Ecgferth's base of Northumbrian power, Adam felt honor-bound to remain and lend his strong arm in support of a Throckenholt menaced by lurking foes.

Moreover, though he had fulfilled his intent to see Aelfric's grave marked and protected, his self-given oath was only half complete. His brother's killers had yet to be found. The determination to continue that quest was not weakened but rather strengthened by the desire to seek out and lay bare the agents behind this building up of sinister forces . . . and their purpose.

Chapter 6

Gazing down at a platter purposely rubbed to a smooth finish, with one fingertip Llys carefully nudged into a small pile the proper number of seeds to be steeped in a tincture of herbs. Though she honestly desired to learn more of Brynna's healing secrets and to lend her worried foster mother all possible aid, Llys found it difficult to bear the prolonged separation from nature's restoring spirits enforced by her stay in this man-built home.

The scattered clouds of morning had provided an appropriate cover for the day poorly begun with a glimpse of fragile Anya. Despite Llys's best efforts at chanting the dawn, the child had again fallen into a peculiar sleep. Indeed the alarming condition had deepened, taking the frail girl even further from the waking world. That Anya hadn't responded more favorably to her daybreak chants left Llys fearful that her link in the chain of Druidic powers was seriously eroding . . . from confinement within man-made walls or from the disruptive influence of an unbeliever?

The half-gone day was not improved by the nearness of a towering man whose pent-up energy threatened to explode. Brynna had entreated Adam to surrender himself to at least a few days' additional rest for the sake of repairing damage done his healing wound while toiling to protect his brother's resting place. Adam had politely acquiesced to his hostess, but the lingering glitter in topaz eyes made his frustration clear. As he paced from hearth to door and back, his sheer size seemed to shrink the large hall to the proportions of a meager hut. To Llys, already full of self-doubts over her inability to achieve inner peace, his actions seemed those of a stalking predator and endangered her taut nerves.

"Llys," Brynna softly called to the young woman dutifully laboring over tasks an ailing daughter's care had left her no time to perform. Taking pity on the jumbled emotions she sensed troubling Llys, Brynna offered an escape into nature's soothing balm. "The precious blooms Anya was to fetch the day she was overcome by the strange illness have yet to be recovered. If not soon done, they'll be of little use to us."

Thankful for Brynna's sundering of the invisible cord binding her attention to the devastating man, Llys instantly nodded her willingness to finish Anya's task.

She promptly rose. However, 'twould have been irresponsible to leave everything as it was. Restraining a fervent desire to be immediately gone, she added the chosen seeds to the steeping tincture, returned the rest to their pottery jar, and tilted the platter up to sit beside it. Finally free, Llys scooped a basket made of carefully woven vines up from its position beneath the table and crossed to the door.

Throughout the procedure Llys had been well aware

of the unswerving amber gaze upon her. She could easily understand and even empathize with Adam's impatience over unaccustomed constraints. But the burning dislike in golden eyes remained as incomprehensible as it had from the first, and it was that which drove her from his company. She welcomed the fine excuse curing blossoms lent for being quit of the house and the man who unaccountably resented rather than appreciated her aid in finding his brother's resting place.

Once safely outside, she drew a deep breath of fresh air absent in the building's faint smoky haze. Hoping clear air would bring clear thoughts and revive bright spirits, she skirted the house and spring at its back. Then, crossing fertile fields, she slipped through the hidden rear gate in the palisade and moved toward the green shadowed forest.

Llys's hopes for lightened spirits were not blessed with reality. Despite the cheerful sunshine's victory over morning clouds, her thoughts were darkened by relentless visions of Adam's grim reaction to her attempted and, aye, successfully rendered aid. For the first time in memory, when she entered the woodland absent was the awed pleasure its beauties had ever lent her. Unaware that she had reached the oak grove that was her destination, Llys was blind to the beams slanting through abundant leaves to reveal shy daisies half hidden amid thick undergrowth, oblivious to the joyous calls of larks flitting from branch to branch . . . and deaf to the snapping of twigs as strangers approached.

A thick hand curled about Llys's mouth just as a burly arm wrapped its inflexible restraint around her midriff. Flooded with the desperation of a panic never before experienced, she dropped the basket and struggled valiantly. But to the man against whose short, sturdy frame she was pressed, her efforts were no more significant than the annoyance of a pesky fly.

Bound in a brawny grasp unaffected by her frantic resistance, Llys purposely went limp, striving to slow her pounding heart and summon the emotional control required of a Druid seeking the aid of nature's powers. Her honest attempt at serenity was knocked askew by the sight of a second man—tall and angular —swaggering near while intimately ogling her bounty. She felt soiled by his loathsome gaze.

"What a fine prize we've seized." The words opened thick lips, revealing a mouth filled with overabundant crooked teeth. "And afore we gives it away, I ken we've earned the reward of dallying with it awhile."

As the lanky man reached out a filthy, clawlike hand, Llys lost her tenuous hold on a fragile serenity. Her struggles increased fourfold . . . to no good purpose.

When a despondent Llys, looking like a frost-blighted flower, slipped quietly from the building, Adam was struck with guilt. He vehemently assured himself that the emotion was unjustified. It was the stance he had carefully reinforced since the unexplainable rite and her glowing stone had led the way to his goal, threatening to further weaken his certainty of her wicked nature. Despite outward appearances, his attempts to find naught but ill traits in the woman had met with woefully limited success. Moreover, he discovered the impossibility of restraining a powerful urge to again follow her.

Casting darkling glances at the female thralls watching with sly grins and knowing eyes, he passed through the portal, only absently aware of the rare pleasure in not being forced to dip his head to do so. Few doorways were created for men of his height, but as he and Wulf shared a lofty size, this house, like Adam's own, had been constructed to meet such needs.

Light as the slender maid was, Adam's experience in tracking as warrior and hunter allowed him to follow the path of dainty feet. It led him past the spring behind Wulf's home and beyond the point where she'd left soft, cultivated ground to move through a gate he'd not have seen without her footprints to lead the way. Outside the palisade, he followed their trail over long blades of hardy grass and ferns flourishing in the damp earth beneath towering trees.

Unfamiliar voices broke into Adam's thoughts. Ignoring a suddenly useless trail, he dove into a thicket of trees and dashed straight through dense undergrowth toward the source.

"Never tasted no Cymry maid afore, but hold her still, Johnny, and I will!" A foul cackle punctuated gleeful words. "I wager 'tis sweet."

Adam's broadsword sang as he unsheathed it. Its warning of peril was distinctive enough to freeze crude laughter and paralyze groping hands.

Abruptly released, Llys landed hard atop ground padded with rich vegetation. Stunned by rapidly changing circumstances, she lay unmoving while her tormentors fled, stumbling in their haste to escape the impressive warrior with his bared blade glittering a deadly threat.

Wasting no moment to wonder if these craven men were the same cowards who had attacked him while he slumbered, Adam slid his weapon into its scabbard and bent to lift the fallen maid into the strong circle of his arms.

"Were you harmed?" The question was a harsh velvet rumble deepened by his anger with her assailants and his anxiety for her well-being. Holding her close, he gently brushed aside the ebony hair her struggle had tangled and whipped across a delicate face.

"No." Llys's soft whisper could only have been heard by the one a mere breath distant. Shaken by the succession of wild events, she looked up into an amber gaze concern-warmed to dark honey. She trembled the more under this rare contact both free of scorn and filled with a gentleness that doubtless increased its danger.

Thinking Llys's distress to have been born solely of the violent experience just past and impervious to his wound, Adam cradled her near while settling atop a thick tussock of grass. He then laid the shivering girl across the hard muscles of his thighs.

Despite instinctively curled hands pressed against him in mute resistance to his likely unintentional lure, Llys buried her face in Adam's strength. For long moments she rested quiescent against his broad chest while her fear slowly subsided. But rather than easing, her heart's rapid beat accelerated. With an ear pressed to the fine wool of Adam's brown tunic Llys could hear his heart pounding a cadence to match her own. Firmly caught in the golden mesh of his attraction and drawn deeper by the power of her own longings, Llys uncurled her dainty fingers. Initially lying motionless, soon they tentatively moved a brief distance over the powerful form remembered too vividly.

Now it was Adam who shuddered. One strong hand burrowed into a too well remembered ebony cloud of luxuriant curls while the other gently trailed fire up her throat to lift a pointed chin, easing his claim of a beguiling mouth. He brushed short, teasing kisses against its corners and moved enticingly across her lips, ever tempting but never satisfying the hunger his caresses roused.

Thoughts filled with the memory of their last embrace, searing, exciting, and a goad driving her far beyond the safe haven of serenity, Llys blocked warnings of danger. She yearned toward pleasures withheld until under his sweet torment of light, tantalizing kisses a soft whimper escaped her tight throat.

Adam's restraint, too, broke under the aching sound. His mouth closed over her parted lips. 'Twas a petal-soft delicacy his dreams had first promised and then kept fresh in his memory. He learned anew that in reality it was an ambrosia infinitely more powerful. The deep kiss he craved grew and burned like a wind-fanned wildfire.

Logical thought was lost, unmourned beneath the devastating melding of lips. Llys recklessly twisted to twine her arms about wide shoulders and press fully against this source of the fiery sensations igniting a burning hunger she feared could never be eased.

Reacting to the feel of her soft flesh melting into the hard muscle of his body, beneath a wealth of black silk curls Adam swept the large hands spanning her tiny waist slowly upward, urging her luscious curves closer still. Llys arched beneath the caress searing her with flames of wicked excitement.

A deep groan rumbled from Adam's chest. In unthinking impatience, he shifted the vulnerable beauty to lie against a soft layer of summer-thick grass and her mane's dark glory. Rising above her, his amber eyes gone to velvet brown, he gazed down into hunger-dazed eyes and studied lips rosed by their yielding to his passionate demands. Once again he found not the face of the abbey siren with her practiced wiles but the expression of an innocent, untamed creature yielding to an experienced predator's lures. Adam was struck by a lance of guilt dual barbed and just as painful on either side. Whether he was threatening the chastity of a virgin or falling to a harlot's well-versed lures this near taking of Llys was purely wrong!

Had he saved Llys from the ill use of other men only to abuse her himself? Dishonor lay in his actions—no matter the nature of hers. Jaw firming with self-disgust, he forced himself to pull a safe distance away from her tempting curves and stretched his hungry body face down against cool sod.

Even if the delicious enchantress of his night dreams was not also the wicked sorceress of abbey memories, an impenetrable barrier lay between them. One fact she had never denied; one fact he could never accept; she was a Druidess; he was a Christian. And never could he believe God would find acceptable the kind of concessions Wulf had made to wed his Brynna.

Silence expanded until Llys felt her beloved forest aching with it. Was it the source of the quiet voice she heard inside her? Ought she to act now when surely his guard was as low as her own? Was this the opportunity she'd craved, the opportunity to learn what unwitting wrong she had committed that lay behind his distrust of her? Rolling to her side, she faced the intimidating length and breadth of his prone body. In a tremulous voice she deemed disgustingly weak Llys spoke.

"What wrong have I done that you harbor such contempt for me? Whatever it may be, I would forfeit much to undo it."

While tension grew to overwhelming heights, Llys sought to bolster her wavering courage enough to enable her to withstand Adam's response. But her best efforts were unequal to preparing her for the heat of fierce scorn burning in the depths of the gaze he turned upon her. She gasped, and her eyes went wide.

Adam rose without voicing a response, and Llys began scrambling to her feet. Her intent was forestalled by once gentle arms turned to inflexible steel swinging her up into their cradle. Adam hardened himself against the certainty that he was responsible for so disheartening the maid, yet he acknowledged the fact that Llys had suffered two harms—the one rendered by her assailants compounded by that of her rescuer—and deemed this single boon owed.

Still he refused to give her question a spoken answer. What point would there be in speaking of a thing she would assuredly deny, a denial he dared not accept? Thus merely would they embark upon a useless round of refuted accusations.

Although carried in powerful arms, Llys held herself as stiff and distant as possible under such intimate circumstances. It hurt to discover that the man who so easily scattered the emotional control she'd practiced for years to maintain could just as quickly shift from tender, fiery caresses to cold, unyielding contempt. She sternly admonished herself to be thankful for Adam's unfeeling talent. It would prevent her from further humbling herself by ever again seeking the answer he withheld.

Neither had a thought to spare for the abandoned basket or the blossoms left ungathered while the tall man's long strides took them from the forest's concealment. As they passed through the hidden gate and entered the cultivated field's harsh sunlight, Adam could hardly help but see the gleaming tracks laid down emotion-rosed cheeks by silent tears.

"Pip!" Waning daylight slid over Maelvyn's gray hair as he shook his head in teasing disgust at the good-natured guest who'd won his respect during the weeks they'd shared his cottage. "What wicked imp so bestirred your wits as to land you on the ground, helpless as a newborn calf?"

This opportunity to gaze down at the huge Pip was an unusual circumstance for Maelvyn. Though possessing the muscle and might necessary for one of his calling, the smithy was half the russet-haired lad's size and twice his age. And he took merry delight in this rare chance to stand over him.

Pip's meaty hands gripped a painfully twisted knee, but still he lightly returned the other's baiting. "Take care I don't bring you down to share my uncomfortable perch."

"Perch, you say? Hah! 'Tis a trap." Maelvyn barked his laughter while rubbing his palms together in glee. "One advantage I have over so lofty a person as you is being near enough to the earth that I see and can avoid stumble holes meant to trip unwary prey. Most humans hereabouts are wise enough not to wander far from use-laid paths."

Pip growled and made a wild swipe for his companion's knees. Maelvyn danced to the side and shook a cautionary finger at the one fallen low.

"Only see what a fine mess a big hulk like you has made of a poor hunter's now wasted labors."

"Poor hunter?" Pip groaned with mock outrage. "What of me—the newborn calf?"

"Share with me what strange enticement summoned you to this fate so that I may avoid a like blow. Mayhap then I'll see you set right."

"Many a time have I been warned my imagination would bring me to grief. Guess it has." Pip blushed. His ruddy complexion rarely allowed him to hide his embarrassment, and he could only be relieved that Cedric was busy with duties elsewhere, leaving some slim hope that on their return, this story would not spread throughout Oaklea as well. Sheepishly grimacing, he shrugged and admitted to a foolish deed. "Would've given my oath that someone was here—and weeping. Wasting no moment to ponder the ill judgment of my course I rushed to lend aid I thought clearly needed."

"And instead you found a trip-hole scooped out and covered to catch unwary creatures . . . plainly a success." Maelvyn mournfully shook a shaggy gray head but grinned. Yet behind the jovial expression, he wondered if the strapping boy had truly been the victim of otherworldly powers. Who knew what strange forces might linger near to play tricks on mortal man? Oh, he thought much of his lady and had naught but praises to sing of her healing powers, but of the others—particularly the old sorcerer? Well, never had he quite trusted or been comfortable with them about.

When Maelvyn's grin faded into a frown, Pip was certain this folly committed as daylight began to fade had forced a man he liked into an unwelcome deviation from his plans. Firmly gritting his teeth, Pip tried to stand. His wrenched knee refused to cooperate in his intent, and he crumpled back against the nearest tree.

"Hah! Stay put, lad. I'll go and fetch your lord . . . and mine, for I fear 'twill take all three of us to haul one as big as an ox back to the keep and Lady Brynna's care."

When Pip looked less than comforted, Maelvyn hastened to reassure him of the certainty of a cure. "Throckenholt's lady has wondrous talents to heal. Only think how quickly Lord Adam's wound has mended, and it was more like to kill."

Pip smiled broadly into the other's earnest face. "I have no doubt of Lady Brynna's marvelous ability to heal any ailment or wound. Merely do I regret the unwise action that requires you to waste time on my behalf."

"Hah!" Maelvyn barked again as he waved the hurting one's apology aside and set off to do as he'd pledged.

Pip watched the bowlegged man's back until he disappeared into undergrowth and trees. Only a man with Maelvyn's confidence would persist in describing another at least twice his size as a "lad," and Pip thought the better of him for it.

Soon Maelvyn was out of sight, but still Pip felt that he was not alone. Had he truly heard someone crying? Was that someone close? Despite an awareness that he sounded like a fool babbling to himself, he spoke to that sensed presence, a gentleness nearby.

"I truly came to help, you ken?" he crooned. "Though 'struth I am as big as an ox, you needn't hide in fear of me."

Silence was his answer, yet he repeated his reassurances again and again. At length he thought he heard a tiny sob. Or was it the sound of some woodland creature foraging nearby? There was a definite rustling in the bushes at his back just as Adam's steed broke the forest wall he faced. Pip's master immediately dismounted and began striding toward him.

"I much doubt the hunter who caught you would consider you either worthy quarry or just reward for his mangled trap." Adam sank to his knees beside the impetuous youth he had hesitated to bring on this journey. Pip's parents were Adam's particular friends and had urged him to bring the overgrown boy who was not merely strong but skilled at arms as well. Besides, like Cedric, Pip was unwed, and therefore this absence from home would be no trial to wife and children. Moreover, Adam was fond of this injured supporter.

While Adam carefully probed the twisted limb, Pip held his face impassive to the pain, relieved that his lord had not reproached him for the foolishness that had laid him low. But then Lord Adam was a just man and had never taken his frustrations out on those in his charge. One of many reasons he was so well regarded by both his own people and those who met him as a powerful but fair-dealing warrior. Pip was proud of his leader, even prouder to have been given the honor of serving as personal guardsman.

"We'll take no risk and splint your leg." As Adam spoke, a cart driven by Wulf followed Adam's path through the trees. Once in sight of their destination, Maelvyn leapt from its bed to approach Pip with two long pieces of neatly split firewood in his grip.

Reining the cart to a halt, Wulf smiled at the injured

man. "Knowing it impossible to mount a horse wearing the hindrance planned, we'll load you in the wagon and haul you back to the keep." He swung down, offering further encouragement. "Brynna will test to see if your leg is broken and, if it is, will set it aright so as to ensure it heals straight and strong."

Quiet reigned while proposed actions were taken, but during their return journey Pip reluctantly shared his tale of the apparently disembodied weeping. He knew it sounded like a witling's tale, yet also knew it to be his duty to tell. For long moments after the story's conclusion neither lord spoke, but the two lords exchanged a speaking glance.

"Another foe to add to our list?" Adam slowly shook a bright head, vexed by the constantly growing list of oddly mated forces. "Surely not another."

"Aye," Wulf's green gaze steadily met one of amber. "With Saexbo on one side and on the other the strange armed camp amid the peace of an abbey, the mystery of another opponent we do not need."

The glance exchanged between two golden men was full of meaning. They could only pray for aid in uncovering some hint as to what relationship men so seemingly dissimilar bore to one another.

"I swear, Bishop Wilfrid, we had her in our hands." The tall, ungainly speaker's whine sharpened into a desperate plea. "Like I said afore, it were the interfering golden warrior what stole her from us."

"A golden warrior, hmmm?" There was a sneer in the words. "Were you so surprised to find such a man on Lord Wulfayne's lands?" Had the bishop not been so irritated he would've been amused by the ridiculous sight of a much broader oaf uselessly huddling behind the gangling speaker's questionable protection.

"But it weren't Lord Wulfayne. We swear it weren't!" The speaker lacked courage enough to tell his already angry master that the maid had been rescued by the man they'd earlier failed to kill.

Such a confession was unnecessary. Wilfrid assumed as much, and as his minions had feared, the fact did indeed deepen his fury.

"Would you have me believe the rescue was effected after a mighty battle?" Wilfrid made no attempt to hide his disbelief and his thick hands, ever resting atop the shelf of his belly, clenched. "And, even more, would you ask me to accept your claim while it is plain that you've returned without a scratch upon your worthless hides?"

The two hapless men before him blustered unintelligible excuses for their miraculous escape from injury —but none worth the time wasted in speaking them. Wilfrid growled his disgust and waved them toward the door of his chamber, much larger and infinitely more opulently furnished than the tiny cells of the abbey's monks.

"But what of our pay?" The taller stood his ground although his feet shuffled nervously as he whined his foolish demand. "You owe us, you do."

"*Pay* you?" At the ferocious snarl, unworthy of a bishop, the pair cringed. "I pay no one for invisible goods or for broken oaths. You ought know that by now. You've experience enough in failing me."

As the bishop snatched up a flagellate's whip and approached, his erstwhile employees tripped over each other in scrambling from his presence.

"I think little of your choice for hirelings." From a door hidden in the shadows of one corner stepped a bearded man of near the bishop's own height and age but in much better physical condition.

Vexed by this further criticism from a man who had been a thorn in his side for weeks, Wilfrid shrugged and turned away to replace the whip atop a chest near the entry.

Hordath enjoyed annoying the prelate and never let pass an opportunity to prick the bubble of his self-righteous attitudes. Only to claim the ultimate prize did he put up with either this supercilious bishop or the insolent boy who thought himself a man.

"And curious, too, is a celibate's alliance with two women." Hordath sneered as with perverse glee he prodded the edges of the other's discomfort. "More so given the nature of their calling."

Wilfrid puffed with injured pride. "You offered no ploy, even less a viable scheme to win what we must have of the Welsh." He soothed his wound with a recrimination of his own. "Besides, your actions certainly demonstrated no dissatisfaction with the younger woman when I came upon the two of you here in *my* chamber."

Over Hordath's broad face spread a grin so wide even his thick mustache could not hide it. Few experiences had given him the kind of amusement that he'd received when the Ealdorman of Oaklea unexpectedly appeared that first day. He'd been near enough to the hidden door to slip out unseen when the "golden warrior" had unexpectedly appeared. The door he'd left slightly ajar, enabling him to listen while the overconfident bishop—caught in a compromising position and badly ruffled—had floundered adrift on a sea of dubious explanations for the half-nude beauty in his bedchamber.

Hordath's nasty grin made it clear to Wilfrid that

his intended censure of a coarse collaborator had merely revived the pleasure Hordath had taken in the uncomfortable scene.

"You believe the men I dispatched to do the necessary deed were unequal to the challenge?"

Hordath knew enough of the questioner to realize that when his voice softened it was in direct relationship to the degree of his anger.

"No doubt you are right." Wilfrid immediately went on to make a sarcastic suggestion he was certain would win the agreement of his less than sharp-witted cohort. "Alas, I have no army close to hand and none I can summon without alerting those whose curiosity we had best not rouse."

Suspicion furrowed Hordath's heavy brows.

Wilfrid's voice slid into the cloying honey of false flattery. "But your army lies just beyond the door, and as you doubtless have a variety of better choices, I feel safe in leaving the important task's completion to you and your warriors."

Offended by the rotund man's ill-hidden contempt, Hordath instantly gave his vehement acceptance. "Happily do I accept the challenge you and yours have failed to meet!"

A contented Wilfrid rocked on his toes, watching his irritating cohort stride across a bare wood floor, heavy boots thumping an emphatic beat. Hordath departed and slammed the door behind him.

Chapter
7

Two powerful men sat in close conversation beside the hearth while the sun spread its final glory across the western horizon. On the far side of the fire's enclosing ring of stones Pip lay sleeping. Brynna had earlier moved Cub's cradle into Anya's tiny chamber, allowing her to care for her baby while still remaining with the ailing girl. She had examined the strapping guardsman and assured them all that his knee was merely strained. After wrapping it tightly with strips of cloth soaked in an herbal solution, she'd given Pip a tisane to lessen his pain before returning to her children. Llys was seated on a bench at the table in the herb corner's shadows quietly working and leaving the two ealdormen to speak in privacy.

Adam and Wulf seemed unaware of the savory aroma of stew bubbling in a huge pot suspended from an iron tripod over the low-burning fire. The ominous event that had befallen Llys too firmly held their attention for either to realize the time had come and passed for increasingly nervous thralls to serve the meal.

"My foster daughter is not well known hereabouts, having spent most of recent years in Talacharn with visits to Throckenholt both brief and rare." Flame light gilded even the silver strands in Wulf's mane as he shook his head in further denial of the possibility that Llys had been the planned target of an abduction attempt.

Listening in silence, Adam leaned forward to rest forearms on powerful thighs and stare unseeing at floor rushes recently changed and scattered with fragrant herbs. Wulf's words reminded Adam how nearly he'd missed saving Llys from greedy hands and a cruel taking. Had his pride prevented him from following her or had he tarried even a short while longer . . . A muscle jerked in his clenched jaw.

"Garbed as she was for the day's work much like a thrall," Wulf continued, unaware of the other's inner storm, "'tis probable Llys's assailants believed her to be one and were themselves merely attempting another theft of what is mine. A likelihood which assuredly does nothing to excuse the seriousness of their misdeed."

Though he chose not to argue the point, Adam couldn't agree that the foiled abductors had mistaken Llys for a slave. Adam understood Wulf's fervent hope that those he loved had not been singled out as quarry. Yet surely Wulf must be conscious of the oddity in both daughter and foster daughter coming to harm—at the same location. A coincidence? Mayhap. However, Adam strongly suspected that once the whole was known, this "coincidence" would prove to be an important link in a dangerous chain.

A soft knock at the door interrupted the brooding men's concentration.

"Enter," Wulf called out, striving to keep irritation from his voice.

Heavy oak planks moved but only a short distance. In that narrow opening, silhouetted against the purple shades of dusk, stood a small feminine figure.

Closest to the portal, Llys hastened from the shadows to draw the visitor fully inside. Once subjected to the firelight's pitiless glare, the figure was shown to be a silently weeping girl clutching a tiny bundle to her breast.

"My babe's been taken sore ill." The words came out in hoarse gasps. "Lady Brynna, I beg you will save her." In emphasis of the desperate plea, a fresh flood of tears welled from dark eyes dominating a wraithlike face.

"Lady Brynna is caring for another," Llys quietly told the supplicant, whose response was a fresh flood of tears. "But I'll help if you permit?"

Tangled brown hair fell forward with the nod of her response, and Llys gently took from the frail girl's arms the baby wrapped in rags. In doing so, she realized life had already departed the little body. With a brief shake of her head, Llys immediately transferred the pathetic burden to Wulf, who had come to stand just behind her. Then Llys returned her attention to the supplicant, who looked too young to be a mother. The tearstained blotches on her face did nothing to hide a patchwork of old and fresh multihued bruises and scrapes. Aching with compassion, Llys pulled the one softly weeping into comforting arms and whispered the unhappy news that her babe was dead.

Eyes narrowed, Wulf also studied the sobbing girl wrapped in Llys's arms. He prided himself on personally knowing every native of Throckenholt, his people all . . . and never had he seen this maid before. Her pain he believed sincere, but who was she and from whence had she come?

Wulf moved to tenderly lay the lost baby atop the stack of clean cloth strips Brynna kept in a basket on one side of her worktable to await burial preparations. As he did so, the towering man caught the new arrival's attention for the first time. She cringed and desperately backed away into the herb corner's shadows.

Llys realized this visitor was terrified of Wulf, possibly of all men. Yet slowly she coaxed the girl, unnaturally chilled by sorrow, from the darkness and into the chair Wulf had abandoned within the fire's ring of warmth. Sinking down to kneel at the woefully thin girl's side, Llys attempted to rub warmth into limp hands while murmuring consoling words.

From the neighboring seat, motionless and unnoticed by the grieving girl, Adam watched and listened to Llys. Her empathy with the other's grief seemed so sincere it was difficult to believe that this same woman had once cruelly laughed over talk of Aelfric's death. A slow smile stole across firm masculine lips. Her care of the one hurting, added to gentle care for Cub, easy friendship with the house thralls, and cheerful toil on every task assigned made it even more unlikely that the Llys before him was merely a disguise assumed by the abbey's heartless sorceress.

Adam's smile was lent further warmth by these flickering lights of hope that the woman who'd wound her way into his near every thought and dream was as pure as she seemed. A chill flood of distrust abruptly extinguished them. What did he know of an enchantress's mind? Hadn't he heard it said that

Druids, leastwise Glyndor, reveled in the ability to unsettle foes with mercurial moods? Golden eyes went dark. Besides, long had he known the perfidy of all women, a trait likely intensified by a sorceress's powers. He refused to consider the paradox implied in thinking her a sorceress on one side while continuing to deny the existence of Druidic powers on the other, never mind the rites and wonders he had seen.

Though sensing the weight of attention again resting upon her, Llys was deeply concerned for the one in her care. Fearing the girl would be equally terrified of Adam, she gave the grieving mother her full attention.

The day's last meal eventually was served, but 'twas a haphazard affair. The two ealdormen sat alone at table. Llys took a bowl of stew to Brynna in the ailing Anya's tiny chamber before returning to her charge, who'd slipped again to the shadows she preferred. Willing to cater to the girl's fears in hopes of easing them, Llys laid in the dark corner another of the pallets ever prepared and stacked in readiness for the inevitable flow of patients come to seek Brynna's healing gifts. Llys urged the unhappy mother to nibble a crust of fresh bread and drink a warm, calming tisane between renewed bouts of tears. Finally the girl slept, although her rest was troubled and punctuated by soft sobs.

Unnoticed by either the men at table or women in the corner, Pip awakened. His russet head turned toward a familiar sound—the one he'd heard in the forest, the whimpering that had drawn him into a hunter's snare.

"Drink, Maida. One swallow more," Llys again urged, kneeling beside the pallet settled on the floor among the herb corner's shadows. She held a steaming mug to the lips of the girl only recently roused from a night's fitful sleep.

"What is this sweet liquid?" With the question Maida sought to prove herself improving under this gentle stranger's good care. Throughout the long hours of darkness dreams of vicious deeds had repeatedly awakened her to renewed awareness of sorrow's reality, but Llys had remained close, providing comfort. The memory of a compassion rare in Maida's life put an unsteady smile of gratitude on her lips.

Llys was as heartened by the smile as by hoarse words, the first spoken since the previous night when she'd coaxed her charge into revealing her name.

"A mild tisane of chamomile, springwater, and honey—the same beverage I gave you last evening." Llys returned the other's smile. "It will calm and bless you with a peaceful rest, so I pray you will take a wee bit more."

Maida nodded, lank, dust-brown hair brushing narrow shoulders before she took the mug into her own hands and obediently sipped the warm liquid.

"Ought we contact the babe's father?" Llys quietly probed, having learned from Wulf that Maida was not one of Throckenholt's own.

Sheer terror widened dark eyes almost immediately flooded with tears. Maida shrank back, spilling tisane over fingers gone white with the sudden strength of their hold.

"Forgive me." Easing the mug from the girl's hand and carefully setting it aside, Llys gently urged Maida to lie back. "You've nothing here to fear and need tell nothing you had rather hold private."

Maida clutched desperately at Llys's hands. "Do you swear it? Swear it on the holy cross?"

"I swear it on your cross." Her smile slid awry at the uselessness of one holding her beliefs doing so. Then, to lend the oath credence in her own mind, she silently added, *Swear also do I upon my white crystal.* The latter was a solemn promise, for a broken oath would shatter the stone—which was to her a most precious possession, her personal link to the power of nature.

The spoken promise proved effective. Maida relaxed enough to drift into untroubled dreams.

Except for the brief time required to prepare the tisane, Llys had spent the night either kneeling or lying curled up beside Maida's pallet. She was stiff when she rose from the cramped position. Before dawn had fully broken, two golden warriors had departed for another day's search through forestlands for skulking brigands. But Pip, the injured guardsman, still slept, apparently more susceptible to Brynna's sleeping potion than would've been expected of a man his size.

Having watched with interest when Adam accompanied his hurting supporter to the hall for Brynna's treatment, Llys had been impressed by both his honest concern and his fondness for the younger man. In her time at King Ecgferth's court as a child and in visits to Throckenholt while others were present, she'd seen enough of Saxon lords to know these were not common traits. The care Adam had shown Pip, added to his gentleness with Cub left her able only to admire the famed fierce warrior the more.

Taking with her a basin of water warmed over the fire for morning ablutions, Llys sought privacy in the bedchamber allotted her—the chamber, she'd become increasingly aware, that was separated from where Adam slept by naught but a thin wall. Once freshened by the reviving liquid, she pulled the comb through black locks near identical to those of a beautiful mother only hazily remembered. Next, she exchanged the heavily creased gown in which she'd slept for another simple homespun gown. It was a favorite among her meager wardrobe and painstakingly dyed a deep blue, yet Llys had little attention to spare for it.

As she thrust her arms into sleeves, her thoughts were occupied by unhappy news. Not long before Maida had awakened, Brynna had slipped away from her daughter's side and come to the herbal corner to prepare a fresh elixir. Upon her appearance, Llys had related the tale of a dead babe and sorrowing mother. Brynna had listened with a sympathy deepened by her own ailing daughter's plight. Then, after assuring Llys she'd provided their newest patient the best response and care, in a tone of quiet desperation Brynna had spoken of a growing fear that Anya's deep sleep would soon see her, too, descend into death's cold grasp.

Thoughts of the child's tenuous hold on life increased Llys's guilt over her failure of the previous day. The flowers harvested but waiting uncollected beyond forest edge were rare and most potent. In truth, they might well be the single ingredient able to revive the wee golden maid.

Having returned without the blooms, although once rescued she certainly should have gathered them up, Llys felt responsible for Anya's decline. Moreover, where Anya had once failed to collect the blossoms, Llys had failed not once but twice—first in being waylaid by the attack, and second, more guiltily still, by falling victim to Adam's seductive charms.

Her sad lack of a Druid's emotional control was at

the root of both failures. Distracted while entering the forest by thoughts of the fascinating man who despised her, she hadn't sensed danger as she should have. Then, worse, having lost a necessary serenity, she'd been unable to exercise her abilities to even the negligible extent needed to thwart such fools as the men who had captured her. Foolish errors, yet they were as nothing compared to the mistake she'd made in Adam's arms by completely surrendering her touch with reality. That had been the most dangerous wrong of all.

Determination glittered in sapphire eyes as Llys sharply shook her head, setting the mass of newly combed and lustrous curls to rippling like a cascade of liquid ebony. No matter the past, she could not, would not, allow the previous day's assault to restrain her from fetching the flowers now.

Llys wrapped a belt of intricately plaited reeds about her waist. Believing items of clothing animals had died to provide would weaken her bond with all living things, Llys seldom wore them. As was her wont, to the reed belt she added a small cloth bag containing the barest minimum of necessary items—a vial of liquid with many healing uses, a shard of flint from which to strike fire, and, most important, her white crystal.

If the delicate blossoms—her goal in this quest—failed to bring Anya back to health, then Llys would journey to Talacharn and return with Glyndor and Evain. Never would they have left if they'd had any notion that the child's illness could not be healed by Brynna's curative skills, amazing skills they'd seen consistently produce desired results. Though no Druid had control over death, Llys was certain that where she and Brynna had failed with potions and even with chants, two powerful sorcerers would succeed. Restoring the little maid was a feat she knew they would find of great import. She suspected that even the taciturn Glyndor was particularly fond of Anya, and Evain doted on the child, who adored him.

Aware that the basket she'd taken the day before must still lie unused beside waiting flowers, while two patients slept, Llys left the house empty-handed and so quietly that the two house thralls laboring to spit a fat pig failed to notice her departure.

Following a trail hard-packed by the passing of many feet, Llys circled the house and skirted the spring, giving little thought to the gentle song of water bubbling upward to ripple down the brook it spawned. She passed through the hidden gate—wishing but failing to still an anxious desire to accomplish the task and be quit of the deed—and for the first time in many years, she entered the forest's green shadows with fear.

Llys hastened over the path lightly marked through the woodland's verdant foliage. Sensing the coming of a storm brewed by summer's heat, her apprehension grew. She instantly chided herself for it by silently restating a fact taught from earliest childhood: as a Druid she had no reason to dread nature's fury. *Now, in truth, you are a fool!* Disgusted by a likely self-delusion, Llys acknowledged that, while she need not be alarmed by storms, too oft they portended events well to be feared.

At length Llys stepped again into the small glade where precious blooms lay, just as gentle hands had placed them weeks past. Her prettily woven basket, upended and forlorn, was not far distant. With a smile for her foolish misgivings, she bent to retrieve it . . . and tumbled to the ground unconscious.

Pip had been awakened by the house thralls as they readjusted the fireplace's metal rods. First they'd straightened the two that were forked at the top; then they had braced them to stand firmly and support a spitted pig. Once that chore was done, they'd moved away, and Pip had struggled to sit up. Leaning against the hearth's high and sturdy stone ledge, he'd peered through the gloom toward the now sleeping source of the previous afternoon's crying, the sound that had summoned him from a safe path into the folly ending in an injury.

At length under his steady gaze, she stirred and made to also sit up, a fragile figure indistinct amid shadows.

Irritated with himself for his unwary dash into the forest and not pausing to consider his words, Pip spoke a wish that would've excused his deed. "You ought to have allowed me to provide aid when I came thrashing through the woodland to lend it to you."

When the girl cowered deeper into shadows, he felt like a clumsy oaf and fumbled to justify the awkward words, inadvertently sounding like a vexed rebuke rather than the confession of his own wrong that they should've been. "Had you done so, I'd have brought you to Lady Brynna in a trice. Might be, we'd have arrived in time to save your child."

A fresh burst of aching sobs smote Pip with guilt. He'd muddled his meaning the more with words intended as comfort but sounding like an accusation —as if by her failure to welcome him, she had been responsible for the babe's demise.

The house thralls departed on some errand at bakehouse or spring, leaving Pip and Maida alone. And again he instinctively tried to answer the unspoken call of her anguish, scooting closer without rising on his injured limb.

Maida buried a tear-flooded face in painfully thin hands and pushed herself farther away from the advancing giant until her back came flat against the wall. Feeling well and truly trapped, she shook with fear.

"I mean you no harm. . . ." Pip's gentle words trailed into silence when she lifted her face. For the first time he saw evidence of another's brutality in the purple bruises and deep red cuts marring skin otherwise too pale.

The soft thud of a closing door broke the visual bond between huge, amiable guardsman and frail, frightened girl. Turning as one, they found Brynna quietly approaching.

Their hostess first checked Pip's injured knee and was pleased that the swelling had abated. Next she applied a fresh layer of unguent to Maida's abused face, leaving more for her to later use wherever it was needed. Then she encouraged the grieving mother to join her in bathing and swaddling her babe a last time before the tiny body was laid down for its final sleep—an event planned after the golden warriors returned later in the day.

Through thick leaves slipped a ray of sunlight to glint over metal rings interlaced and attached to a leather jerkin whose wearer moved nearer the maid fallen beneath his man's comparatively gentle blow. Braced by a spear that was his considerable height and half again more, Hordath leaned forward to study the slender figure crumpled atop lush grass and beside flowers laid in neat rows. Masses of black curls provided a perfect contrast for the ivory fairness of her dainty face. A beauty she was. Restraining the useless urge to bend down and touch her cheek to test if 'twas as petal-soft as it looked, he shrugged and spoke of a far different woman.

"The old witch had the right of it." As he shook his head in disgust, the thick gray hair flowing beneath a half-helm brushed his brawny shoulders. "The foolish maid came back for these flowers." He straightened and stirred the blooms with his spear, bruising petals amazingly fresh for having been uprooted.

In the next instant Hordath slowly turned, peering hopefully into the shadowy forest.

"Stand prepared lest her rescuer again appear." The laughter accompanying Hordath's words held no humor. "And I pray that he will . . . giving us the opportunity to repair yet another of the bishop's failed attempts."

Hordath's armed contingent, five men strong, crowded the small glade. They joined in their leader's laughter while at the same time creating a loose ring about him and their captive. Facing different directions, they peered into a forest filled with the ominous stillness that often preceded a storm.

"Aye." A young but proven soldier broke the suddenly tense silence by adding his disgust to Hordath's. "'Twould render further proof to the bishop of what poor choice he made in sending ceorls inexperienced with military deeds to do a warrior's work."

The comment earned a nod and a cynical smile from Hordath. He and his men had little respect for Bishop Wilfrid, their less than competent ally.

"We can but hope the bishop will retire the pair

from the fray afore they muck up the more important tasks that lie ahead," another of Hordath's men sneered.

"Halt!" A slight cowled figure slipped from green shadows, eliciting Hordath's immediate challenge.

Instantly surrounded by drawn swords, the monk remained motionless as the demand was followed by a curt question. "What business have you here?"

In answer of sorts, a hood was brushed back to reveal masses of black curls surrounding another uncommonly lovely feminine face and sapphire eyes gleaming with a strange power able to intimidate the men into silence.

Without pause she passed between the wall of armed men to slowly circle the unconscious maid, pleased that even the early stages of a storm she'd begun to brew hours past had been enough to muddle the Druídess's sense of nearing foes and imminent danger.

"Stand firm," her low voice commanded, "and do not be alarmed when you see neither her nor me. 'Twill pass, and once again she'll lie before you, but she will be garbed as I am now."

The last of these enigmatic words trailed into an eerie chant. Rough homespun fell back from slender alabaster arms lifting to the sky. The song, if that it was, deepened in intensity and power until a sudden blinding flash of lightning struck nearby.

Hordath and his men were momentarily robbed of vision. When fading brilliance restored their sight, the women were gone.

Confusion reigned in muttered curses and whispered dread of the unknown forces at work among them. In vain Hordath called for a calm not restored until a second bolt of lightning pierced the sky to strike so close they could smell its singeing odor. As foretold, the still unconscious maid again lay in their midst, but now she was garbed in a monk's humble robes.

Hordath was nearly as vexed as awed by these inexplicable doings and irritably waved his stunned men on to the next task.

"See her placed across my steed." Between thunder and an abruptly risen wind, Hordath was forced to bellow his command and the added direction for a further deed that would demonstrate his triumph over a disesteemed ally. "Then let us be off to see our booty laid in a 'holy' celibate's cell—physical evidence of our skill."

Watching men hasten to do his bidding, Hordath's stern expression was a fine mixture of annoyance with what had just passed and defiance of what was to come. Bishop Wilfrid, who would wonder at how the beauty had come to be thus attired, could interpret it any way he chose. Hordath would refuse comment. And Hordath would most certainly not speak of a mystical appearance by the captive's living reflection.

Unabated thunder shook the forest while lightning streaked a sky so heavy that it seemed to reach down with fierce winds that howled through trees groaning in protest. The party struggled between wildly whipping branches and saplings bending near to the ground, determined to succeed in their task and return to Winbury Abbey.

Chapter
8

Something strange was afoot.

Although those within the house were taut with the tension of growing alarm over a mysterious illness, an assault, and lurking strangers, everything had been as expected when Adam departed in predawn hours. However, that had changed by the time he and Wulf came through nature's unleashed fury to enter the keep's shelter. Changed, aye. And Adam didn't like it!

He took a long draft of ale before carefully replacing the sturdy pottery mug atop the white tablecloth. Staring blindly at the blank view of a window shuttered against gusting winds, he ignored the wordless call of a woman suddenly become stranger yet not a stranger—Llys but not Llys. His powerful hand curled dangerously tight about a sharp dagger ostensibly bared to carve a slice from the slab of roasted meat waiting on his platter.

Upon joining his host at table for the evening's repast, he'd been surprised by Llys immediately slipping into the seat beside him and then constantly leaning too near. Between Maida's appearance the night past and the moment he'd departed for the day's search, Llys had solicitously hovered near the sorrowing young mother. But even during the weatherabbreviated ceremony of laying the dead babe in the small grave Maelvyn and Cedric had prepared, Llys had hardly glanced Maida's way and had offered her no comfort at all. That the apprehensions of a girl already fearful had increased in the face of her protectress's abrupt shift in temperament was no surprise, but Adam was at a loss to understand the change in Llys—an inability that vexed him.

Throughout the remainder of the meal, Adam was aware that sapphire eyes seldom shifted from him. And this was not the shy, surreptitious glance he'd come to expect, even to enjoy, but the bold gaze of the wanton he'd encountered in the abbey. 'Twas as if this afternoon's violent storm had washed away a facade of shy purity to leave Llys truly the temptress of cruel laughter. The change annoyed Adam no end. And that fact worried him as well, for it revealed how thoroughly the sweet enchantress, now proven as false as all other women, had pierced the armor he'd thought impervious to such assaults.

"In my determination to weed out the human tares threatening my fields, have I driven you too hard?" Wulf questioned the man who, though seeming to vibrate with renewed health, had barely touched the savory meal.

Adam scowled at the platter, further irritated to discover it still bore the major portion of each tasty dish he'd been served.

"Does your wound pain you?" A worried Wulf probed deeper. "Or are you, too, falling prey to Anya's mysterious illness?"

Forcing a smile he didn't feel, Adam promptly

turned to reassure a host already shouldering too many troubles, from a tiny daughter hovering near death despite her mother's unceasing ministrations, to the nameless, faceless foes of the forest. "I am as healthy as any stallion in yon stable."

The claim won a short bark of laughter from the older man. That laughter lent Adam an honest grin and bolstered his determination to speak frankly of at least one matter he hadn't earlier raised.

"Merely was I pondering what direction we ought next to patrol. You, of course, are more familiar with coverts and caves able to shelter those wishing to remain unseen, but . . ." His deliberate pause lent emphasis to a proposal not earlier suggested in deference to Wulf as ealdorman of these lands. "I suggest the importance of searching the area where two have fallen to harm."

Adam saw Wulf's lips firm against the bleak visions roused by his words, yet he knew the man's instincts as a warrior would win out.

"Aye." Wulf nodded. "On the morrow best we follow that path."

Though relieved to have shifted Wulf's attention from his own growing tension, Adam would rather it had not been accomplished at the cost of reminding a friend of loved ones falling prey to vile forces at work . . . and still beyond their control. This thought brought Adam renewed awareness of the loss of leastways the facade of a bright presence whose sweetness he hadn't sufficiently appreciated until it had gone, replaced with a darkness he despised.

Beneath the golden fire of a narrowed gaze, Elesa blinked once but then boldly returned the stare. It seemed that softhearted Llys had little talent in the lures of a sorceress. Elesa was amused. First, by her double's inability, and second, by the apparent fact that this stunningly handsome man meant to resist her wiles. Such a battle could but add heated pleasures to her success once she'd won. And she'd no doubt but that win she would. His resistance boded nothing more serious than a minor setback to her desires. She wanted him, and in time, whatever she wanted had always been hers. Deep red lips curled in a self-satisfied smile. Simply put, it was the character of her dark powers that they inevitably overcame any impediment to her goals.

Despite his best intent to avoid a visual bond, Adam's attention was captured by a blue gaze gone sultry, enticing him with dangerous secrets waiting to be explored. But when she began stroking his forearm, he tensed, then jerked free of her touch.

"Surely you ought have taken supper to your charge." Adam nodded toward the huddled shape of Maida, who watched from the shadowed corner with trepidation.

His words were a rebuke. And although it was a thing rarely spoken to her, Elesa recognized it as such. Was Llys so weak that she bent to the man's will? The thought deepened Elesa's disdain for the duplicate she'd never met and had seen only briefly during the time spent exchanging clothes with the other's unconscious form.

Elesa glanced toward the sorry child-woman apparently in her care, and vexation momentarily furrowed her brow. She'd seen the girl before—days past and while Maida was cringing from her master.

Although 'twas quickly smoothed away, Adam caught the distaste in his table companion's expression. Still, this woman turned stranger shrugged and rose to do as he'd suggested.

It was with ill grace that Elesa placed a bowl of soup, a chunk of bread, and another of deep yellow cheese on a small wooden platter. Then she approached the ragged figure and knelt to place her offering on the floor within reach of a bony hand.

"Speak of me," Elesa hissed, "and I'll see you returned to your master to suffer under his blows for the deed."

The already small Maida seemed to shrink, but her reaction was hidden from the view of those at table by the figure of the woman who spoke.

However, the exchange did not pass unnoticed by one whose presence the others had forgotten. With breadcrust half lifted to his mouth, Pip had frozen at the older girl's approach to the hurting younger maid. And so he remained, afraid that any movement would cause Maida greater woe. The cryptic warning Pip wished he understood. How could it of a sudden appear that Llys knew Maida's past so well? Plainly the master Maida had been threatened with was responsible for her wounds, but who was he? And where was he? Of more consequence, would it be a betrayal of secrets Maida must keep if he spoke of this threat to Lord Adam?

Although Adam neither heard the server's words nor saw the recipient cringe, he deemed Llys's ungracious actions of the entire evening a further demonstration of her vast and inexplicable change of heart. He, too, was filled with questions and glanced toward Wulf, but the other man was clearly so preoccupied with thoughts of the ailing Anya and the looming threat to Throckenholt that he'd failed to note his foster daughter's odd deeds and responses. Adam chose not to draw the hurting man's attention to this further mystery, particularly as, to one more familiar with Druidic ways, it might be no mystery at all but merely a common occurrence. Instead, as Llys rose again, Adam shifted his attention to Maida.

When he first became aware that Llys had lost interest in comforting Maida, Adam had tried to speak with the girl. But, shaking in fear, she had cringed from him. Her battered face gave evidence of what manner of wrong lay at the core of her terror. But as Wulf assured him she was not of Throckenholt, who was the perpetrator? He wanted to help, but as so many problems already clamored for answers, little time could be spared. . . . Nor, in honesty, was Maida likely to speak with frankness to any save the one who had welcomed her with gentle sympathy—if only she would.

This renewed the question of what had caused such a complete change in that once sympathetic person and returned Adam to his own initial confusion. He was further irritated by his inability to quell a guilty sense of loss for the gentle female who, as a Druidess, could never have been compatible with the Christian he was. Indeed, even the threat of such an emotion made him traitor to all for which his father and brother had stood.

While Adam wandered through a maze of tangled thoughts and unsettled emotions, Elesa carried the platter she'd haphazardly arranged into a dark corner. Once done with the deed she'd found an annoying interruption to her intents, she hastened back to the table and the golden lord watching with a disgust quite unlike the response she was accustomed to receiving from men. But no matter. Her lips curved into the smirk of a cat presented with a bowl of cream.

Tonight she would weave her spell, and the wickedly handsome warrior would be hers.

A steady pounding in her head slowly drove Llys to wakefulness. She forced reluctant eyelids to lift, if only a slight distance. Then, struggling to sit up on a pile of fresh straw, she found herself in a barren chamber, alone in a prison with no window and only a small arched portal. By the light of a single foul-smelling tallow taper she studied the thick iron-bound planks of a door so low even someone of average height, like her, would be required to bend nearly in two to pass through.

While azure eyes focused on that door, it swung open. A woman ducked inside. A score of years, likely more, older than Llys, she was tall with thick streaks of white running through unrestrained tangles of black hair. Her penetrating iron-gray gaze scrutinized the prisoner as if searching for flaws.

Llys's chin tilted in proud defiance of this wordless examination by a woman whose sneer soon proclaimed her inferior. Even as the stranger's opinion rankled, Llys was struck with a sense of something oddly familiar about her denigrator's strong jaw and penetrating eyes. Certain they'd never before met, Llys attempted to thrust aside the unpleasant sensation only to discover it clung like pitch to unwary fingers brushing against a tree trunk.

When the woman bent to place a mug within reach, Llys's attention was caught by her odd pendant. Formed not of the brightness offered by either gold or silver but rather of dull black metal, it was a circle containing an inverted triangle. The pendant was singularly ugly, but Llys found it more than that. To her it was repellent.

Then as abruptly as the woman had come, she was gone. Under the metallic thud of a bar falling into place on the far side of the chamber, Llys's heart sank. There was no handle on the thick plank door. Plainly it could be opened only from the outside and was barred to prevent her from making an escape. Attempting to ward off a hopelessness threatening to overwhelm her, Llys looked about her prison more closely and found reason not for hope but for greater apprehension. The walls were stone! All of stone and not the natural rough rock of her hill home in Talacharn but stone smoothly cut and laid by human hands.

No matter who had brought her here or why, they'd chosen the most secure jail in which to hold her. The cutting of stone by human hands robbed it of spirit, leaving it silent and dead. Such walls placed an impenetrable barrier between Llys and nature. Thus she was bereft of the ability to call upon such powers, left helpless either to defend herself or to win her freedom. She nearly wept in frustration and despair.

Pull your wits about yourself, an inner voice warned, years of training coming to Llys's aid in this darkest of hours. *Nowise can anyone be your liberator here in this place save you.* Pushing aside the distracting pain of a relentless throbbing in her head, she put the wall to its single good use by leaning against the reviving chill of stone, cold even in summer.

Absently lifting the mug left within reach, she drank the full measure of its cool, fresh water while her mind began to free itself of fainthearted fear and useless regret. A fine goal but one that also opened the path for additional disheartening facts to come into focus. The single structure she knew to be built of such stones as those at her back was part of the abbey—the same abbey Adam was so certain she'd visited in past, the abbey where his brother had met a violent death. In that instant it became plain to her that between her abduction and the death of Aelfric lay a link, though a link so oblique she could not see it clearly. For aid in piercing the mists of this confusion, Llys instinctively reached for the crystal contained in the bag ever at her waist.

Saint's tears! Without forethought Llys invoked her foster father's favorite expletive. Her bag had been taken! Moreover, she was garbed in a monk's robe—and naught else. While horrified to think that the vile deed had been done as she lay unconscious, it was the loss of the white crystal that Llys mourned most fervently. Yet, this further blow, rather than driving her deeper into hopelessness, burned to cinders the cords restraining her temper and fired her determination to defeat whatever wicked knave had sought to tame a sorceress.

Stoking ever higher the flames of that decision was the realization that this taking of her played an important role in the danger threatening her foster family . . . the danger that had already assaulted Adam once and, given the opportunity, doubtless would again.

Not long after Adam had surrendered to sleep, the recurring image of the gentle enchantress yielding in his arms returned, slipping into his dreams. But this time it changed, and soon the refreshing taste of spring wine became the thick, dark liqueur of twice-brewed and heavily sweetened wine that he found too cloying. He pulled away . . . or tried. The woman playing Delilah to his Samson followed, twining herself about him until he abruptly awoke. Sitting up,

Adam thrust aside a half-clad siren too free with her voluptuous charms.

Every past kiss exchanged had been at his instigation and seemingly taken from one innocent in such games. Now to find her to be a clearly experienced wanton rudely crushed the gauzy fantasies he'd unwillingly woven about the sweet enchantress. The unpleasantness of the scene washed over him with a reality as chill as the icy northern sea. He glanced from her sultry eyes to the body arching bared breasts toward him while from the midst of a ring of candles placed on the floor about the head of his pallet, he saw smoke rising from a brazier. Its musky odor he found repellent.

Had this creature—his thoughts instinctively refused to name her Llys—cast some spell about him? His glance shifted again to the reclining woman, draped seductively across his pallet. She extended a languid arm to entice his return to her overabundant charms.

Candlelight glanced over blond hair like warning beacons as Adam shook his head in an attempt to free himself of the dangerous siren's wiles. Never would he fall to a pagan's spell! Hah! Adam silently scoffed at his own claim. Had Llys remained the gentle sorceress, he suspected even his renowned iron control might have melted beneath her tender fires. But yield to this blatant she-devil who had laughed at Aelfric's death—*never!* Indeed, as soon as he realized whom he held in his arms, his fevered blood had gone cold.

He left the furious woman in possession of his bed while he slipped from the house to share his great destrier's clean straw. But when he had settled in a darkness disturbed by no more than the huge horse's occasional movements, thoughts of Llys reigned in his mind. Although but one body she seemed to host two distinctly different souls. Adam fervently wished he could seek answers from someone familiar with the mysteries of Druids, but he knew only a single person possessing such knowledge, and Wulf already had enough with which to deal.

He cautioned himself to clear his mind and seek the rest doubtless needed for another day's search, but the effort was useless. Adam could do naught but lie staring blindly into the lean-to stable's dimly seen rafters while contrasting Llys's two personalities.

The first he'd met in the abbey, then again today, and tonight in his bed. She was a brazen seductress of direct stare and voluptuous form boldly flaunted. The second had forced him from unnatural slumber with a cold-water caress but shied away from him every day since. She seemed as timid as any untamed forest creature with her sidelong azure gaze clearly fascinated but just as clearly fearful of him. Not that he hadn't seen defiant blue flames flare in those eyes on more than one occasion. The memory put a wry smile on firm lips.

Thick bronze lashes half hid the glow of dark amber as Adam's thoughts relentlessly pursued the comparison. While the first Llys stank of musk, the second's scent was of fresh wildflowers. Yet, surely most telling of all, the flaunted breasts of the abbey's Llys were overly lush while the curves of Throckenholt's Llys, though a generous bounty, he was certain were more delicate and finely formed . . . and to him infinitely more tempting. Expressions and deeds could be given false faces, but surely such physical differences could not be so easily altered.

Adam abruptly sat upright. Could there be, in truth,

not one Llys but two? *Nay,* he told himself, *'tis naught but your forlorn wish to breathe life into a forbidden fantasy of either your own devising or a sorceress's design.* He clenched his jaw tightly against an illusion whose price was like to be his sanity—and his Christian soul.

Chapter 9

Llys abruptly awoke. How could she have fallen asleep amid such desperate circumstances? Had the cup contained something more than water? Scowling, she glanced toward a guttering candle. Judging by the flame near swallowed in puddled tallow, she'd lost a considerable amount of time. Llys wished that the windowless chamber could provide some clue to whether 'twas night or day. For someone accustomed to a life lived within nature's gentle embrace, being completely cut off from so much as the faintest hint of the heaven's natural light was distressing . . . and now even feeble candlelight threatened to fail her.

Still Llys refused to yield to the greater darkness of despair looming above her with its daunting lists of what difficulties awaited and of all the weapons denied her. The determination glowing in sapphire eyes was infinitely brighter than the taper's faintly flickering light. To defeat sinister shadows Llys began counting the blessings at hand.

First, the pounding in her head had eased. Second, sleep-refreshed wits were assuredly sharp enough to carve from her long marinated predicament some method of winning her freedom. Third, well, no matter . . . It was more important to waste no further moment. She must launch herself into the search for a possible method of escape.

A closer examination of her cell revealed two oddly shaped objects lying on the floor's unevenly laid stones to one side of the door. Peering through the deepening gloom, she recognized a spoon of sorts and a small pottery bowl that emitted a foul odor. She leaned forward and discovered that the latter contained a congealed lump of something gray covered with once white liquid beginning to clot. Either it had been put there to serve a previous occupant of this cell or had been served with milk already gone sour. Whatever its source, a less appetizing dish Llys had never seen.

Llys's attention moved on to the door without a handle . . . then returned to the revolting meal. The thin, flat wooden utensil was a poor excuse for a spoon . . . but it might well be as valuable to her as a golden key.

Upon making to rise, she discovered that sleeping on cold stone, despite its thin covering of straw, had left her stiff and sore. But, wasting no moment to rue her discomfort, she moved toward the door. Sweet lips instinctively turned down with distaste as she approached the unpleasant offering. She tugged the spoon free of the sticky gray mess. The sucking sound made by the spoon's withdrawal was disgusting but of little interest compared to the important task for which she intended to use the utensil.

With a handful of straw, she cleansed the spoon of as much muck as possible. Then she turned to kneel facing the small door. Placing the spoon's flat end against a crack between the sturdy door and its stone frame, she cautiously pushed, fearing to hear the crack of splintering wood. The smoothness with which the spoon was inserted merely increased her fear that the next and most important step might fail. Pausing, she softly chanted a simple litany imploring natural powers to lend her the favor of aid in this deed and success in eluding her captors thereafter.

"Spirits of earth and stone, of flower and tree, of river and sea, thrice bless me—once to set me free, twice to find my path, and thrice to guard my way."

That she was surrounded by man-laid walls likely blocked the plea from its intended recipients, but she felt better for having offered it. Cautiously, slowly, she moved the spoon upward until she felt it meet strong resistance. Still she persisted, exerting more strength to push it higher.

Thick lashes fluttered as the obstruction abruptly gave way. The spoon flew out of her hand, and a clatter sounded on the door's far side. Llys froze. Had the dislodged bar attracted unwelcome attention? Breath painfully halted in a tight throat, she waited for the sound of feet approaching . . . though it seemed doubtful that any noise could be heard over the thundering of her heart. Gradually its pounding eased enough to reassure her that silence still reigned. Placing her hands, palms flat, against the door's rough surface, she pushed. Thick oak planks slowly swung outward. Llys scrambled to her feet but was forced to crouch in order to leave her tiny cell. Taking care, she quietly pulled the door closed and replaced the heavy metal bar atop iron brackets driven into stone on either side.

Standing upright in a narrow hall, Llys caught a glimpse of sunlight slanting through a window at the far end. However, as she was unsure of her prison's position, she couldn't tell whether the sun was half-way between the eastern horizon and its zenith or half descended toward the western skyline. No matter, she must find her way free of the abbey and elude her captors.

Llys slipped quietly down the corridor toward the window, hoping it would not be so high as to make it useless in her escape. Nearing the end, she realized a stairway branched off to the left . . . one that provided the odd attribute of serving as a conduit for unpleasant words spoken below. Listening to three strange voices, Llys soon moved to lean flat against a wall whose cold support was a welcome reinforcement for disgustingly weak knees in danger of buckling while there raged below an intense discussion of what should be done with her!

"You're a fool! Why waste time and strength upon a useless captive who can only be a danger to us?" Llys could nearly see the woman with white-streaked hair drawing her imposing self up to deliver this condemnation. "You should've killed the girl instead of carrying her here."

"You're the fool, Gytha. If you speak the truth of a Druid's powers"—the speaker's voice held such derision it was clear he'd no faith in the woman's claim—"no grave could be deep enough to hide her body. And if found, then what use your precious Elesa?"

"So kill the girl now, Hordath. Bury her in cut stone, which even the famous Glyndor cannot penetrate." The woman's words were filled with contempt for her antagonist. "Such would lend a permanent solution to a problem too likely to plague our intent."

Llys's sapphire eyes widened. This Gytha was obviously of the same heritage as she. Only one trained in secret truths could know the ghastly end of a Druid's soul to which she'd advised Llys be subjected.

A third voice flatly interrupted the verbal fray. "The choice belonged to the pair of you neither then nor now. 'Tis mine, and I choose not to employ a method that goes against my sacred calling."

Fine brows knit as Llys realized, at the mention of a sacred calling, that the speaker must be Bishop Wilfrid.

"Hah!" The woman scorned the bishop's statement. "'Tis too late for such a noble sentiment. Though not by your own hand, already you are guilty of that dark deed. And were your minions not so pigeonhearted that they failed to finish the task, you would've been again. That their attempt to put a permanent end to the Ealdorman of Oaklea's intrusion into our plans was fruitless only means you must strive harder to see the deed successfully accomplished."

This boldly stated threat against the life of the golden warrior who had once saved her from a similar plot curled Llys's hands into impotent fists. Though she couldn't see the participants' expressions, the silence that followed proved Gytha's blow had hit its mark, increasing the danger to Adam. It added strength to Llys's determination to win free. She must, she *would*, escape and warn Adam to beware of dangers no longer faceless but very, very real!

"I have had enough of such criticisms from unworthy cohorts and will not linger to be further abused," the bishop flatly stated.

The sound of wood scraping over stone and the thud of heavy footsteps approaching the stairwell sent Llys dashing toward the open window. No time now to consider the wisdom of the deed! She pulled herself up to the sill, swung her legs over, and pushed away. After a short drop, she landed on a sloping thatched roof. Momentum carried her downward and over the edge to sprawl atop a mound of hay.

After a moment lying flat, half buried in sweet-smelling straw, Llys struggled to sit up and determine her whereabouts. Clearly she'd come to rest beside a large lean-to barn. Taking care to remain as well hidden as possible, she peered through interlaced blades of hay and found herself to be more fortunately placed than she could've hoped. It seemed the window of her escape was in the back wall, out from either side of which extended the wooden palisade meant to guard the abbey.

This barn, built outside the wall, was plainly intended for the farm animals she could hear restively moving about inside. In the other direction stretched fields . . . bearing the strange crop of tents and armed men she had seen with Adam and Wulf. Among the warriors walked monks with heads lowered and arms apparently folded inside the wide sleeves of their habits. Suddenly Llys was most thankful for the strange garb in which she'd been clothed after her own garments had been taken.

Llys faced a fact that was unpleasant but true: she must risk drawing attention by flailing about in order to descend the haystack. Bare and shapely legs flashed as she kicked free and slid to the ground, only to find herself in an awkward heap, hood fallen back and the sad garment's hem well above her knees.

Disconcerted by her own disarray, Llys glanced up, black curls tangled about an undeniably feminine visage. A cowled figure stood not two paces distant, staring at her with unshielded contempt. Yet, to her astonishment, the man merely averted a cold face and continued his slow progress toward the refectory.

Rising, she pushed down the coarse brown folds of the monk's habit to settle sedately about her feet although the robe was so long that its hem hung on the ground in folds. Around her hips she retied the crude cincture, which had come loose in the descent and then arranged the too abundant homespun cloth to billow over the belt, leaving the hem at a proper length. Pulling the cowl forward to shield her face in shadows, she copied the monk's method of wrapping her forearms together, allowing the cuffs to meet, thus hiding the arms and hands of a maiden.

The sun's changing position left Llys in no doubt as to which direction to travel in order to enter the western forest. Having recognized the newness of the day, she composed herself to walk through the encampment of armed foes with the measured steps of the monk who had passed her by. Then, slowly and steadily, she set off for the welcome surely awaiting her in the woodland's cool and comforting arms.

Adam strode from the barn, irritably brushing away blades of hay caught in the russet-hued wool of his tunic and even in the cloth trousers molded to strong calves by long leather bands crossed and wound to his knees. So long past had the sun risen that the colors of dawn had fled to leave the sky washed with palest blue. He was annoyed at having slept so late. In truth his anger-delayed slumber had been brief. After the sorceress's uninvited invasion of his bed in Wulf's abode, Adam had found it difficult to calm chaotic emotions and drift back into dreams.

Twisting to pull a particularly recalcitrant straw from the back of one broad shoulder, Adam nearly overtook a pair just entering the hall before noticing them. He paused to watch an aged but unbent figure, with white flowing mane and long beard, walking with the aid of a curiously topped staff and accompanied by a much younger man—judged by the locks brushing his shoulders, as deep an ebony as Llys's. Both men were strangers to Adam, but the warm greeting elicited by their appearance suggested they were more than familiar to the woman within.

Adam slowly ascended two wooden steps and stepped through the doorway. Not wishing to intrude, he moved into the shadows to one side. As his hostess began to speak, he was, for the first time in his life, grateful for his father's insistence that the willful child he had been—reluctant and unconvinced of the deed's usefulness—must learn the Cymry tongue.

"You are welcome and more!" Brynna gently urged the odd matched pair of age and youth into the comfortable hearthside seats. Then before she could relate the unhappy news plainly burning on her lips, the dark-haired visitor spoke.

"Where is Llys?"

Mind hazed by lack of sufficient rest and attention held by the black-cloaked guests, Adam had failed to wonder the same. Now amber eyes peered into each shadowed corner but found neither the shy enchantress nor the immoral siren known as Llys to the inhabitants of Throckenholt. Bronze brows came together in a frown while he, too, anxiously awaited the answer.

"Fetching water from the spring." Brynna fought to subdue a wrongful resentment of Evain, the younger visitor, for throwing this impediment into the path toward a desperate plea to come to Anya's aid. "She'll be back anon."

Evain nodded, apparently finding nothing unusual in a sorceress performing tasks a Saxon lady born would have left to thralls.

Brynna, having answered Llys's twin, hastily continued with the next question that must be asked before she could beg their aid for Anya's sake. "What brings you back to Throckenholt so soon?"

"Well you may question the reason for our return, granddaughter." Firelight stroked the snow-white hair of a nodding head, lending it the appearance of an inner glow.

Granddaughter? Here then, Adam realized, was the famous Glyndor—the sorcerer who had been party to feats that had so complicated his own father's task in keeping the record of passing years. Adam's thoughts were shattered by an unexpected cackle of dry laughter breaking into words.

"Important it is or here we would not be."

Lifelong familiarity enabled Brynna to see grave concern beneath the glitter of false mirth in her grandsire's black eyes, and she knelt at his side. Had he been spirit-warned of Anya's fate? Or of his own? She clasped between her palms a hand whose frailty frightened her, but it was his companion who next spoke.

"Dark powers are rising from the earth," Evain said. "Others descend from the sky. Together they crash and meld into an ever more ominous whirlwind of increasing peril."

With the low rumble of these eerie words echoing in his ears, Adam realized Wulf had come to stand and block sunlight from falling through the open door. But neither of the golden Saxon warriors possessed the power or the desire to interrupt the solemn conversation.

Brynna's dove-gray gaze darkened to charcoal as she met Evain's unwavering stare. Sparks seemed to have been struck off the flint at the center of his sapphire eyes, and she realized the time had come for her to acknowledge the status of this foster son new come to manhood. It was clear he had earned the right to speak as a sorcerer equal to his mentor. While she—and to a growing degree Llys—possessed talent at working *with* natural powers, her grandsire and Evain had mastered the ways of *controlling* those forces.

"Do these powers bode ill?" In a vain attempt to hide nerves sorely strained, Brynna released her grandfather's hand to tighten and then methodically smooth an intricately embroidered cloth belt riding low on her hips.

"Others able to converse with voiceless spirits are near . . . very near." Evain's voice had matured to a depth that matched the thunder of Glyndor's, but it softened into deep velvet with this bearing of unpleasant tidings to a woman admired and beloved. "But where we commune with the dawn and the dusk, the sun and the moon, they call to midnight terrors and to the eye of the tempest."

An unaccustomed dread of disaster, of tragedy surpassing even deadly harm to family and friends, bleached color from Brynna's face. She'd been told of such wielders of Druidic powers pulled inside out by perverting benign energies to achieve vile ends. But her grandfather had been quite certain that over passing centuries their vicious strain had dwindled into the dark and silent void.

"Near?" She asked the question that had to be asked. "How near?"

Evain's eyes went as black as Glyndor's own.

"Throckenholt lies in the vortex of their brewing storm."

The older sorcerer took up the ominous warning to heighten her awareness of looming hazards. "The threat is made the more menacing still by the fact that it builds at so important a moment during nature's cycle of flowing energy." Glyndor's deep voice reverberated with unspoken danger.

Brynna's frown deepened while she earnestly strove to align this date with the secret answers to mysteries she'd learned. But having been caught for what seemed an eternity in constant care of her ailing daughter and infant son she'd lost count of the days. Now she found herself adrift in an unfamiliar sea of time. It was a shameful admission for one of the chosen few.

"Hrumph," Glyndor growled. "Will you have me believe I left you so ill tutored that you've dared forget an astral event both rare and momentous? That much of the debt all Druids owe the past you *must* pay to the future!"

Her grandfather's rebuke rumbled over Brynna and broke through the clouds fogging her memory with a blinding flash. As he proclaimed, the coming event was one most rare. And, if ignored, could cause dreadful consequences to befall them—particularly if others lacked reverence for its power to disturb natural currents.

"I'm sorry, Grandsire. The illness that brought Anya low as your last visit ended has yet to release its grip upon her. Indeed I fear that even now the candle of her life hovers a faint whisper from extinction."

Thick white brows drew together to form a straight line that lent his visage a fearsome cast. Though he would have denied it, he harbored a special fondness for the tiny girl-child so like a dainty flower ever daring to turn its face toward even the fiercest elements nature could unleash.

But where Glyndor was fond of Anya, Evain fair doted on the child who clung to him whenever he was near. News of an illness so serious it had lingered this long roused in him a fierce concern.

Evain leapt to his feet. "Where is Anya?" The question radiated a burning impatience ignited by fear.

Brynna wordlessly led the darkly handsome young man to the small chamber where her daughter lay so near to yielding to the beckoning arms of death.

The sweet resonance of church bells tolled the hour of terce across the armed camp filling the abbey's fields and reverberating in deep tones through the stone church. But their call to peace was alien to the conflict exploding in the bishop's chamber.

"Vanished?" A near purple-faced Wilfrid snarled the word. Gytha's complacent grin grew only broader, kindling his temper to a brighter flame. "You told me that even a Druidess could not escape man-laid stone!" He was furious! Never would he elsewise have desecrated his abbey by using it to hold a pagan prisoner.

What faint light of midmorning forced its way through the cracks in a shuttered window glinted on the broad bands of white in Gytha's black hair as she shook her head in mock regret.

"Nay, Wilfrid." She had never, would never, address him by the title of a religion she considered patently unworthy of respect. A fact she felt had been established by how easily its leader betrayed the beliefs of his creed.

"You misstate me. I urged you to *bury* her in stone."
A grinning Gytha remained motionless while her
pudgy antagonist strode from one side of the small
room to the other, succeeding merely in robbing
himself of steady breath and further deepening the
unhealthy hue of his countenance. She'd have preferred to thwart the girl's escape at the outset, but her
irritation was soothed by a pleasing opportunity to
gloat over Wilfrid's foolishness.

"Had you followed my counsel, this threat to your
dreams of power would have been averted." Though
Llys's disappearance constituted a threat to her
dreams as well, she was confident of her ability to win
her goal in the end—a goal far different from the
bishop's.

"Possess you no incantation to plague her path? No
spell to weave and tangle her fleeing feet?" The
desperation behind this plea overcame even his distaste for the imperious woman's pagan rites.

Gytha's glee deepened. Wilfrid was a sorry creature
and truly miswitted if he thought she might fail in a
need so clear, when Elesa's position in Throckenholt
was endangered by the prospect of a double's sudden
appearance.

"'Tis already a deed done." With the statement she
abruptly turned, causing her voluminous skirts to
swirl about the feet that carried her from the bishop's
presence.

Chapter
10

As Evain strode toward the forest's deep green shadows he cradled the dainty elfling child in the crook of one strong arm. His other hand grasped the staff topped by a crystal held in a bronze claw. Once deep into the woodland's privacy and peace, the young man paused while a low, eerie chant rumbled from his chest. The crystal began to glow. Its luster intensified as thrice he repeated poetic triads of veneration twined with pleas for guidance.

While low notes faded into the depths of nature's silence, a wordless answer wafted to him on gentle breezes. This Evain followed through the wildwood's densely grown trees and thick undergrowth until the wall of vegetation abruptly opened. Evain sank to his knees here in the same sacred oak grove where weeks past he'd found the unconscious child—suffering, he'd thought, from an illness easily cured by Brynna. It was no surprise that silent powers had led him to the site where precious blooms, long since reaped but still waiting to be gathered, lay upon the carpet of rich grass.

Evain gently settled Anya atop lush blades the deep emerald of advancing summer, confident that 'twas the softest pillow in all creation. Lying there, Anya was the image of helplessness with her fine hair so fair 'twas almost white spread out in sharp contrast across the verdant background. The sight of the already delicate child, weeks without eating and grown even more fragile, lying helpless heightened his fury with the faceless powers assuredly responsible and deepened the guilt gnawing at him for having departed from Throckenholt before being certain she was well.

Evain rose and lifted the odd staff toward the sky's blue dome while his low chanting began anew, although this time 'twas a litany of potent triads that descended into shivering depths. Each demanded the powers of invisible wind and the strength of rushing torrents to blow the mysterious illness into infinity and wash the innocent child clean of malignant influences. It was a forceful rite that did not waver until the lyrical tones of another's voice slipped like quicksilver through the deep notes of his own.

"Have you come to help me gather the flowers?" Anya's leaf-green eyes gazed up at the one both hero and friend for all her tender years.

Pausing only long enough to utter a brief avowal of gratitude, Evain dropped to his knees and held his arms out wide for the little creature who hurtled into their ever welcome shelter.

After a tight hug whose fervor Anya didn't understand yet appreciated all the same, she leaned back a brief distance. "You said you must leave for Talacharn, but I prayed you'd come." Her dimpled grin was enchanting. "And now you're here." Raised in her father's Christian beliefs but daughter of a

Druid sorceress, Anya didn't understand the possible conflict between two religions both worshiping the source of nature's powers.

Evain realized the abruptly awakened child had no notion of the hours and days that had inexorably rolled into the past between the moment she'd entered this sacred oak grove and the present. His relieved expression faded first into one of mournful regret for time lost and then hardened again into a mask of tightly restrained fury against the forces behind the tiny maid's near demise.

Seeing both the sorrow and the banked fire of his temper in Evain's steady blue gaze, Anya assumed she was the cause. Seemed of a sudden clear that Evain's coming had been less an answer to prayer than a concession to a request that he fetch an erring daughter late in returning home.

"Is Mama very unhappy with me for tarrying too long?" It was far less a question than a rueful statement of expected fact. That she was too willful Anya knew, but truly she hadn't meant to be late. "Guess I must have fallen asleep after eating more of the sweet berries than I ought."

"What berries?" With the sharp question, Evain scooped the small figure again into the cradle of his arms and moved to sit beneath a towering oak's spreading branches. Holding Anya in his lap, a mask of mild interest firmly over his features, he listened to her tale and interrupted with neither praise nor rebuke, indeed without a comment of any making.

"Will Mama be upset with me?" Though Evain's hold was as gentle as it had always been, his impassivity alarmed the little maid accustomed to his full attention and support.

"Mayhap," Evain answered, brushing from her delicate face a golden lock completely the reverse of his own black hair. "But 'tis more likely she'll be too relieved to have you home and healthy to chastise you overmuch. Still, you must confess all you've told me to those awaiting your return."

Anya smiled sweetly but did not speak. Well acquainted with the independent child's habit of listening attentively only to do as she pleased, Evain was not so foolish as to leave the matter there.

"Will you give me your oath"—he paused and withdrew an object from the bag attached to his belt—"on the white stone?"

For a brief moment Anya's eyes glowed with emerald rebellion. Despite the fewness of her years, she knew right enough the dangers attendant upon breaking any oath sworn on a Druid's revered crystal. But little choice had she. Besides, Anya would have done near anything to please Evain.

As if to bless her action, a beam of sunlight slanted through the thickly leafed branches overhead and rippled over Anya's fair head as she nodded and placed her hand over the crystal in Evain's palm. It began to vibrate when she gravely spoke the words he demanded, the first of which she'd heard in solemn oaths given before.

"I swear by the power of the white stone to confess to Mama, and to any other who wishes to hear it, the wrong behind my delay in returning home." Anya's dimpled smile flashed again.

That deed complete, she was anxious to have done with the deed promised and pulled free to hastily recover the reed basket from a strangely trampled patch of grass. Although definitely not where she'd left it neatly placed beneath a bush's shiny leaves, the odd detail was of little importance. It was likely that during her slumbers a gust of wind had blown the lightweight container about. Anya did worry that the precious blooms she quickly began gathering up were fading and some were bruised. Was her laggard's pace responsible?

Evain saw growing concern knit a youthful brow and knew the reason. Yet he deemed the truth so complicated and the burden of its dreadful purport too heavy for the beloved imp's tender shoulders.

"Don't fret." To waylay Anya's fears, Evain tapped her small nose with the last of the retrieved flowers before dropping it into the basket. "Now we must please your worried family by hastening back to the keep."

Anya thought her mama more likely to be upset than pleased with a late-returning daughter, but she happily put her hand into Evain's outstretched palm. He smiled and reached down to sweep both her and the basket in her hold up into the circle of his arms. They'd travel easier and with greater speed if they both depended on his strength and the length of stride. Evain's heart, already brightened by Llys's restored health, was further lightened by the prospect of his foster mother's certain joy. He turned to face the point at which he'd entered the grove . . . and froze.

The path was blocked by a replica of Llys but only a replica. Not for an instant did Evain mistake the woman standing before him for his twin. Indeed, whether the likeness was born of nature or of sorcery, this creature was as certainly a product of the dark Druidic powers that had brought him and Glyndor back to Throckenholt, as was the curse put upon Anya.

Elesa's escape from the growing danger of exposure in Throckenholt had met an unexpected complication. Another's call to the powers of the wind and the storm, powers over which she considered herself the master, had been a jarring offense that had forced her to veer away from the direct route to the abbey. Following bestirred currents of energy, she'd deliberately come to face this man who would oppose her command of the elements—only to find a child who should be dead fully revived and in his embrace.

"She frightens me." Anya pressed back, deeper into her hero's comforting arms.

Inwardly Evain smiled. Seemed Anya was no more fooled by this false Llys than he. He recognized in this stranger an ill omen, one he would discuss with Glyndor as soon as private moments could be arranged. He would not raise others' fear by speaking of it until the two of them had considered all probabilities and sought guidance from the forces of nature. By using the powers of a sorcerer, he not only kept his face emotionless but blocked another Druid from sensing his thoughts.

Evain had steadily met the woman's glare, but now, as if her challenging look was of no import, he turned his attention to soothing Anya's distress.

"This stranger possesses no power able to defeat those I wield," he said.

Elesa was furious. Yet while the young sorcerer spoke his defiance of her abilities she melted into green shadows, choosing to await a more propitious moment to see their confrontation reach its inevitable clash and likely fearsome end.

* * *

Llys wearily sank to her knees amid a dense thicket, little caring that in doing so she brushed the short but sharp thorns of a wild rosebush. Concealed by the limber branches of saplings and thickly leafed shrubbery, she gasped for air. After breathing heavily for what must have been hours, her throat was so dry it hurt. By the time Llys had sedately crossed open fields under the gazes of too many warriors watching too closely, she'd been filled with terror, and since entering the forest had kept up a merciless pace. Now a pain pierced her side and she was exhausted.

Fool! Llys berated herself for faltering. *Wrapped in nature's embrace, no Druid has reason to fear.* That was assuredly so . . . but again, as the last time she had reminded herself of this truth, it was also of limited comfort. Her alarm had not been roused by nature. 'Twas the likelihood of humankind's relentless pursuit that set her to trembling.

Too clearly in her memory rang words she wished to forget: "Kill the girl now. . . . Bury her in cut stone, which even the famous Glyndor cannot penetrate." Were such a deed done to her, it would truly be the end of her. Buried in man-hewed stone even her spirit could never escape to pass through the door into a better sphere. She would simply cease to exist at any level.

Melancholy thoughts of the sorrow and confusion her disappearance would bring those Llys loved joined with her dread that she might fail to deliver the crucial warning to Adam in time. An inability to stanch the flow of trepidation was bad enough, but she worried the danger was made infinitely worse by her inability to resist a wrongful fascination with the wounded Saxon—forbidden to her first by his misliking of her and, of greater consequence, by her Druid destiny foreordained. All jumbled together in a single stew, the latter rose to the top and increased her concern. Was it true that Adam's appearance and devastating presence had been but the start to a weakening of her link in the chain that must never be broken? These ponderings left Llys feeling as utterly weighted down as if she were already buried in the dreaded man-hewed stones.

In an earnest attempt to deflect further assaults on her confidence, Llys pressed her fingertips together and extended her thumbs to meet below, forming the three points of a sacred triangle. This done, she let her thick lashes drift down to rest in dark crescents against creamy cheeks as she offered a plea for comfort and aid to the spirits renewed in young trees and bushes already providing her their shield.

Moments later a serene smile curved rose lips while a sense of contentment bred new courage. Apprehensions set firmly aside, she cleared her mind to hear what nature would reveal and peered through her prickly haven's green tangle to find that, though it seemed a lifetime had passed, the sun was barely half done with the journey to its zenith.

Looking behind her in the direction from which she'd come, Llys scrutinized each of the nearest trees and probed the shadows between them. A linnet sang its sweet song in the branches of one while from another came the discordant caw of a raven that had plainly veered far from its mountain home. Beyond the displaced bird, she found nothing more dangerous than a pair of chittering squirrels vying for a particularly fat acorn. Reassured to hear only these normal sounds of a forest undisturbed by human interlopers, Llys next turned her attention to the view ahead. This held the expected plethora of oak, ash, and elder trees—and another that caught her attention as thoroughly as the homespun habit had been snagged by rose thorns.

Many a time during journeys with her brother and Glyndor they'd sought shelter and protection from the elements beneath the gracefully draped branches of a willow—like the one not far distant. Watching intently, she saw a faint glow slipping between curved boughs bending down to trail across thick grass. It beckoned her with warm memories of other such retreats. She answered its welcoming call . . . but not without taking precautions.

Thorns reluctant to release their hold on her garb were her first challenge, but easily met. She stepped from the thicket and hastened into the gloom behind the closest oak, grateful for the sturdy shoes she'd found herself wearing upon first waking in the abbey. They were of thick leather, laced from toe to ankle, and a fine protection as she dodged from one towering tree to another until she stood next to the willow's drooping boughs.

Llys parted the green curtain and inside found what she had expected. 'Twas a cook fire's banked coals that had invited her into this presently empty but plainly inhabited haven. The tended fire with utensils laid alongside it was proof enough, but additionally there was a pair of neatly rolled bed furs—one dark and one light—accompanied by large satchels with long straps to allow for easy carrying across shoulder and chest. Aye, this haven sheltered two.

Moving farther into the shadowed retreat, Llys came to an abrupt halt. Draped across the roll of strangely light-toned furs lay an item of jewelry all too unpleasantly familiar—the inverted triangle. Free of both the thought-muddling restraints of the stone cell and the confusion brought by fear-engendered loss of tranquillity, Llys recognized the perversion of a Druid's faith that the pendant symbolized. This piece wrought in dark metal had been worn by the woman with white-streaked hair who'd provided Llys with a refreshing drink of water . . . water near certainly responsible for an unnatural sleep. From words overheard as she escaped, Llys knew that the sorceress's name was Gytha. Moreover, she clearly remembered Gytha as source of both a threat to kill and bury her in stone and a danger to Adam's survival.

A surge of twined dread and anger threatened Llys's serenity. These emotions joined with the image of Adam to call forth memories that were a danger all of their own. Any thoughts of the disturbingly handsome man were devastating to Llys's control. She struggled to halt thoughts of the towering golden warrior, sword drawn in her defense; memories of the heated moments following her rescue when he'd become the tender lover of amber fires, searing kisses, and pleasures near beyond bearing.

That even in the midst of mortal danger he could divert her thoughts from the task at hand proved what a wicked danger he was. Scowling, Llys turned away from the rolled fur bearing a pendant and the satchel resting against it to earnestly chant a triad begging for inner calm. To this she added the powerful chant she'd softly sung in the abbey.

The gentle flood of peace that swept over Llys left in its wake an urge to hasten onward. As a first step toward that goal, she bent to carefully rummage through the other satchel resting against a roll of dark fur. She was certain her pursuers were searching for a slight figure in a monk's habit. Thus she was relieved to find a gown. Though deep crimson was not a hue she'd have chosen for fleeing through the forest, it was far nearer her size than any the sturdy Gytha could wear.

Shedding her homespun garb, Llys quickly donned the crimson gown and found it fit . . . all too well. Never had she worn anything that so closely conformed to her figure. After pulling front laces tight enough to modestly cover bare skin, Llys was disconcerted to find its snug fit revealed far more than she'd willingly have permitted. Adam would assuredly deem her a true wanton were he to see her thus garbed! Again she thrust persistent thoughts of the man aside. No matter her discomfort or his distaste, what must be, must be.

Forcing her sense of immodesty into abeyance with the fact that it meant nothing laid against the need to be quit of this harbor of foes, Llys dug deeper into the satchel. She was rewarded by the discovery of a small cloth pouch much like the one her abductors had taken from her. Llys's serenity slipped, but this time with excitement. Feeling as if she were on the verge of uncovering a king's treasure hoard, she fumbled as she loosened the cord cinching the pouch closed. At last it opened wide.

Llys's white teeth nibbled at a tender lower lip, and her breath was trapped in a tight throat as she upended the pouch above the dark furs supporting a looted satchel. Out tumbled a flint, two small vials . . . and a white crystal—very much the same as the contents of her own pouch. The dim refuge was suddenly lit by a smile holding near the brightness of the summer sun. Here was proof her bond with natural powers remained strong enough to see her pleas gifted with benevolent answers. That reassurance was almost as welcome as the precious white crystal, not her own but one which she could hope would answer her call when needed.

With gentle care she returned the crystal to the pouch and added the practical flint. What potions the two vials held was a mystery and, considering the sleeping elixir she'd been given, one whose beneficence she doubted. Leaving them where they lay, Llys dug deeper into the satchel until she at last found a belt. Never having worn anything finer than plaited twine, Llys found this one—formed of hinged bronze disks, each worked with a swirling design—unfamiliar. Yet it seemed simple enough to work with the hinge of the last disk open to hook into the loop of any other. Of most import, the pouch could be easily and firmly attached to such a belt.

After wrapping the length of metal disks above her hips and affixing the pouch, she folded the discarded habit and placed it neatly atop the satchel now missing several items. Then, as she turned to depart the shadowed haven, her attention was again caught by the gleam of banked coals. However, this time their glow slipped over the odd pendant, lending its dull, dark surface a bright sheen.

The pendant repelled her, but knowing that Gytha's powers were being wielded against those she loved, Llys reached down and picked it up. Likely Glyndor could use the loathsome thing to help deflect threatening dangers. Despite this possible good use of a wicked object, she was quick to thrust it from her sight.

As if 'twere a poisonous insect, she buried the ugly black charm in the pouch next to the welcome white crystal.

Llys stepped beyond the willow's green wall on the side opposite from where she'd entered and was immediately aware that here the grassy surface beneath her feet had half given way to moss. Flowing water must be close. She stood silent and perfectly still. The silvery murmur of a stream could be heard. It forcefully reminded her that the thirst caused by her long, desperate flight had yet to be quenched. Llys followed the sound, which became a soft roar the nearer she drew to its source, until she stood on the edge of a narrow ribbon of rushing water. Dipping down, with cupped hands she thankfully scooped up handfuls of refreshing liquid to drink.

Revived, she offered a brief triad of gratitude to the brook—gratitude for more than the easing of thirst. She meant to follow it upstream, certain that by climbing to retrace its route she would come to the ridge from which Adam, Wulf, and she had seen the fortified abbey. From there she believed it would be a simple matter to find her way back to Throckenholt. Confident of her plan's soundness, she set off with a light heart to see it fulfilled.

Her confidence seemed justified when by the nooning hour she'd reached the brow of the hill and looked down to find the expected view of the abbey and its encampment. Believing she'd found the right course —yet not so miswitted she failed to remember that she was the quarry of a deadly hunt—Llys set off through the trackless undergrowth and natural gloom beneath the towering trees of the forest.

* * *

"Impossible! I tell you it was impossible for me to remain in Throckenholt!" Arms wildly swinging in time with her agitation, Elesa stormed from one side of the willow cavern to the other while her impassive aunt watched.

When at last the girl's fervent explanations began to wane, Gytha rose, voluminous black skirts swirling and then folding about her feet like the wings of a raven. "You have not failed. Merely is your unplanned return a further demonstration of protection lent by the source of our powers, the import of the destiny they shield."

Not a little surprised by Gytha's easy acceptance of a fumbled scheme, Elesa brushed tangled dark hair from her face to peer suspiciously through the green gloom at the speaker.

Ever amused by the discomfort of others and best pleased by their deepest distress, Gytha allowed her lips to curl into a sneer that passed for a smile.

"Had you remained, your situation would in truth have been impossible. When faced with your double, what explanation could you have given?"

"She is free?" Elesa gasped.

Firelight rippled over the white streaks in Gytha's hair as she nodded. "Early this morning she slipped from the abbey." The acid of her disgust burned in the words. "I warned them to see her dead, but the bishop has grown squeamish about breaking his vows! Hah! As if his greed hadn't ground them to dust long years past."

"Even without my double's appearance, staying would have been impossible." Elesa paused for an instant before adding the one excuse which, wary of her aunt's response, she'd hesitated to earlier give.

"Had I stayed I'd have had to trick *two* sorcerers, who know her very well, into believing that I was she."

"Glyndor?" Disregarding issues of lesser consequence, Gytha leapt straight to the single fact that mattered most to her.

"Aye." Elesa was quick to respond but couldn't leave it there. "And another one who is younger— but, I think, as powerful."

Gytha refused to hear a suggestion that one younger might be equal in power to any elder. Moreover, whether 'twas true mattered to her not at all. It was for Glyndor she had come; for the sake of challenging Glyndor she had offered their services to covetous, squabbling Saxons.

The sight of charcoal eyes going black told Elesa her aunt's attention was focused, consumed, by her objective. Yet, still Elesa sought answers to her own concerns.

"As our ploy to place a foe in their midst has gone awry, what now shall we do to win information we must have? And, more important, what can we do to prevent Llys from revealing our intent not merely toward two famous warriors but also toward two sorcerers likely more able to put our plans in jeopardy?"

Gytha was disgusted by the hint of panic in Elesa's queries. "The warriors we leave to the bishop and a spoiled prince but the sorcerers I'll take joy in personally defeating by wielding greater powers than they will never hold.

"As for your double, against her possible escape I laid and baited a trap." Gytha unthinkingly moved her meaty hand to the point on her chest where ever before the pendant had resided.

Elesa blinked at the abrupt realization of the prized emblem's amazing absence while her aunt continued in a gloating tone.

"Already has she made a choice that shall see her fall—a matter to which our foolish cohorts failed to attend."

Chapter
11

"I know I shouldn't have eaten the white berries you warned me not even to taste, Mama." Anya sat on Brynna's lap in a hearthside chair. Evain had set her on her feet the moment they entered the hall, and she'd run into her mother's arms for a loving hug. However, soon Evain's unswerving gaze impelled her to keep her promise by explaining her delay.

"But the lady swore they were the sweetest in all the world, and she dared me to try just one." Tiny fingers indicated a single wee berry while green eyes soft as summer mists pled for understanding. "It was sweeter than the honey cakes that sometimes you make. Truly it was."

Brynna's gray eyes darkened to charcoal as they lifted to meet the steady gaze of the young sorcerer standing at her side. That Anya had accepted a dare was no surprise. 'Twould have been more a surprise had she not, but the remainder of her statement held the shock of impossibility. The flavor of white berries contained a bitterness to rightly match the vile poison they were. Only magic of ill intent could have convinced the child elsewise.

"Did you eat only the one?" Evain gently prodded the small girl to tell the whole.

Mutiny briefly flashed through green eyes, but Anya honored her oath to confess the full tale. "Nay. They were so tasty I gobbled many and then many more." Squaring dainty shoulders, she defensively added, "It was wrong but only the same as most big people do after eating too much. I got sleepy and took a little nap. And that's why I'm late." Silky-fine curls of the palest gold lent Anya's face a glowing frame as she gazed up into her mother's solemn eyes to make a tiny plea. "Forgive me?"

Again Brynna tightly hugged her small daughter. A single berry could kill. After consuming so large a quantity of their virulent poison, Anya assuredly ought to be dead. Brynna looked up to meet the deep blue gaze of the one responsible for the miracle of her child's recovery. While Brynna's own elixirs had delayed the inevitable, plainly Anya's life had been saved by the powers Evain wielded.

While Wulf conducted a brief meeting with his villagers in the square and the house thralls toiled in the bakehouse, Adam had waited at the table in the hall, which at midday hosted a remarkable group of people—a quietly grieving child-mother, a wounded but curiously watching guardsman, two sorcerers, a sorceress, and a newly revived little maid. From his vantage point facing the large chamber, he had watched the young Welshman return with a miraculously cured child and, too, had heard everything that was said. Although he hadn't the knowledge of nature that the Druids claimed to possess, he and all of his acquaintance were aware of the baneful character of any white berry.

Despite a reluctance to interrupt so personal a moment, Adam felt there was a question whose urgency justified the deed, particularly as Llys had never returned from the spring.

"What did the lady who gave you the berries look like?"

Although startled by the unfamiliar deep voice rumbling from an unnoticed Saxon stranger at Wulf's table, Evain recognized this as the sort of question he had warned his young friend she must answer.

Childish lips pursed in a moment of concentration before the precocious Anya gave a remarkably concise description. "She was older than Mama and kind of fat. Her hair was as black as Evain's and had in it wide stripes of white."

Steadily scrutinizing the stranger, Evain saw his disappointment. The golden man's reaction, joined with the abrupt realization that he'd yet to see his twin, struck Evain with a deeply disturbing possibility. Concern overcame his discomfort with speaking of such matters before a Saxon unbeliever, and he related a recent confrontation with the intention of testing a most unpleasant supposition.

"As Anya and I made to return here, we met a strange figure." He looked from Adam to Brynna and back. "She was the image of my sister, but 'twas as if I were gazing through a glass clouded by dark desires and hate." He shook his black hair as if to dissipate the image. "Anxious to return a healthy Anya to you, I chose not to linger long enough to work the rites that would reveal where she came from and what put her so near Throckenholt."

"She was here." From a shadowed corner came a timid voice, barely above a whisper, yet clearly heard. "Thought she that everyone would believe her to be Llys—not recognize the differences betwixt them." Although silently given courage to speak by the steady, encouraging gaze of the gentle giant named Pip, it was disgust that lent Maida's words strength.

"Two!" Feeling as if a great weight had been lifted from his shoulders, Adam spoke without pausing to consider the revelation his words might be. "I was right. There are two of them!"

Adam was jubilant. The sharpness of his wits was not in danger. Yet beneath that soaring note of joy sounded the deeper, stronger tone of warm relief at this confirmation that the sweet Llys of Throckenholt and the wicked siren of the abbey were truly not the same woman. Beyond that happy thought he refused to look, unwilling to quash it by acknowledging how useless was delight over a single fact that was unable to alter others that remained to keep them forever apart.

"I thought Llys had greatly changed this last day and more, and I wondered . . ." Brynna mused while at the same time startled that the Saxon, lacking any link with the powers of nature, had sensed something she as a Druid had failed to note.

A tilted head sent her swath of black hair tumbling to one side in stark contrast to the fair curls of the big-eyed child quietly watching the odd scene from her lap. As she studied the golden man, unable to hide his pleasure at this confirmation of suspicion, Brynna's gray gaze softened to smoke. The only explanation for his perceptiveness and his satisfaction —nay, his relief—at its accuracy would be the existence of a stronger bond between the pair than she had thought possible—or could now deem likely to bring happiness to either.

Unbeknownst to his hostess, Adam chose not to speak of the scene in the abbey. He justified the decision by telling himself that now the impostor had been revealed, the tale could only add to the confusion.

Before Brynna could remark upon Adam's perception, from the shadows came the voice of another whose presence had been forgotten in the joy of her daughter's restored health.

"Two?" The aging sorcerer echoed Adam's first word as he moved toward flames that lent an unnatural brilliance to his pristine hair and beard. "Curious. A second Llys and an older woman able to make bitter berries taste sweet?" A crack of laughter, inappropriate from any other, punctuated his observation. "Curious indeed."

While Evain directly met his mentor's black gaze the two of them wordlessly communicated an awareness of the second Llys's recent presence in this place.

Evain ignored the Saxon lord as completely as he ignored the bruised maid and the injured guardsman. In the usual way of things none of them should have been privy to talk of Druidic mysteries, but dangerous circumstances demanded that risks be taken.

"Shapeshifter?" Evain asked.

The sharp shake of a flowing white mane served as an answer as cryptic as the question.

"Aye, 'twould require immense powers to hold a shape so long."

"No matter." Glyndor sharply waved his hand, brushing such inconsequentials aside. "They are the

Druids whose coming we foretold, those whose disturbance of natural powers has begun to spread a poison of its own."

Adam's initial relief had been tamed by the whip of a very literal and immediate peril. It was a peril that left him irritated by the wizards' waste of time in enigmatic talk of prophecies and eerie powers.

"Surely the identity of these two unknown strangers is nothing laid beside the only question of any importance." Like a hunter's loosed hawk sighting prey, Adam's attention had focused on the single issue of greatest concern to him. "Rather we must immediately set out to discover where *our* Llys has been taken."

His unthinking emphasis on "our" put a curious smile on Brynna's lips and confusion on the faces of two who'd been justly rebuked.

"Long have I respected your prowess in battle, Adam, and your ability to devise winning strategies." Wulf had been standing in the open door long enough to overhear Evain's talk of his sister's double—and all that since had passed between the hall's occupants. "But this demonstration of your talent for striding clean through walls of distractions to the maze's core provides reason for greater admiration."

Although Wulf's imminent return had been expected, his interjection startled most in the hall, but Adam gave a slight nod of appreciation to the man.

"That you," Wulf continued, "who spent but a fortnight in Llys's company, were first to recognize the deception lays bare the failure of those of us who should've realized the truth immediately. Your clear sight proves both how keen-witted you are and how we have wrongly permitted our worries to blind us. 'Tis we who are responsible for the ominous length of time wasted by an impostor."

"Hrumph," Glyndor growled, puffed up with vexation. "Speak for yourself, Saxon." Coal-black eyes swept over Wulf, leaving no question as to which Saxon he meant. "As Evain and I are so recently arrived, we cannot be blamed for your past oversights. In plain truth, 'twas Evain's one glimpse of the impostor that confirmed your companion's suspicion."

"I meant no word of blame to you." Wulf repressed a smile too likely to insult the aging sorcerer who could rarely bring himself to call his grandson-in-law anything more personal than "Saxon"—even in a land where near everyone was the same. "Only did I intend to praise Adam for compensating for the weaknesses to which I must own."

Adam watched the curious exchange between a prickly sorcerer and the patient Wulf. Though too late to prevent his host from shouldering the full burden of guilt, when Brynna straightened and opened her mouth to speak, he intervened to prevent Anya's worried mother from claiming a share of the wrong.

"Stray no further along the road of guilt. Remorse can be but a hindrance while we seek the path that will lead us to Llys. To tarry now . . ."

The gazes of two famous warriors met as they silently acknowledged grim realities. Choosing not to exacerbate their listeners' dark fears, neither raised the unpleasant question of what dastardly deeds might have been wreaked upon Llys.

Wulf motioned the hall's healthy men to join him at the high table. At the same time, Brynna lifted the stirring Cub preparing to howl for his next feeding. She led wide-eyed Anya into the shadows of her herb corner and asked the apprehensive Maida to watch over her daughter. It was a ploy aimed as much at preventing the visitor from sinking back into tense gloom as to guard the blond child.

Already filling the seat he'd become accustomed to occupying at his host's table, Adam was tormented by bleak visions of Llys subjected to any of the many cruelties he'd seen done, as had every warrior he knew. Confidence in his physical strength and military skills enabled Adam to subdue his trepidation for Llys with a determination to rescue her as he had once before.

The midday sun lent its brightest gleams to inspire the odd collaboration between a pair of golden Saxon lords and two dark Druid sorcerers deep in solemn consultation over a challenge to be met and best means to attain their goal. It was accepted as obvious fact that a search must begin without delay. Further, Wulf made the decision to summon his fyrd to stand guard in a double ring, first atop the village of Throckenholt's palisade and second in the forests beyond its open fields. But which direction to take and who would do what task could not be so quickly decided.

After an earnest and at times heated discussion it was agreed that to prevent a potential loss of time— and to end a disagreement over the best course—they should avoid searching as one unit covering a single direction. Rather, while Pip would be left as armed protector for Wulf's family, each of the two warriors would choose a man to accompany him in pursuing the different tracks they believed to be the most promising.

Because Saexbo had been seen in the southern forest, Wulf would take Maelvyn and go forth to search there. Adam, deeming the danger more likely to radiate from the abbey and its bishop, chose to travel with Cedric in that northerly direction.

The Saxons were content with their compromise, but Glyndor and Evain remained adamant about a proposed return to the forest. By their mystical reasoning, time spent on a physical search was wasted when, amid a sacred oak grove they could perform the rites Evain had earlier forgone for the sake of seeing Anya returned home the sooner. This, they claimed, would tell them the alien Druids' position and likely their purpose for coming.

The apparent obsession of these wizards with other Druids disgusted Adam. How could Llys's brother and mentor let it so consume them that they would fail her?

"Surely if your magic can locate the 'alien' two, it should be a simple matter to seek an answer for the more important question of Llys's whereabouts?" Bright sunlight flooded the table at which they sat and left Adam's scorn abundantly clear. "And might you not thereby save Wulf and me from wasting precious time in searching for a path whose shroud you claim an ability to easily pierce?"

"Precisely!" Blue sparks of deep resentment flashed in the eyes Evain turned toward the Saxon, a stranger to him and plainly one woefully ill informed of the dangers in tempting a sorcerer's ire. The suggestion that he would do less than everything possible for the sake of his sister infuriated him. He spit out deep words that rolled like thunder.

"You understand nothing! All that we have proposed to do will be done for the sake of finding Llys. The two we seek have cast a spell of concealment about Llys. To find her we must first find them. Only then can we reverse their hold upon her."

"I thank you, Evain." Wulf smoothly intervened to pour calming oil on waters beginning to boil. "Knowing that you will do all possible to reverse the spell eases my worry." Although his own irritation with Druidic mysteries had long since been tamed by close acquaintance with inexplicable events, he well understood Adam's difficulty in accepting the reality of such powers. "Pray forgive Adam, my friends. He was not present to observe the wonders you performed to save King Ecgferth's crown. In truth, he possesses no experience to lend him belief in the invisible powers you wield."

"Neither will he now," groused Glyndor. "Nor should he or any other not of our heritage be privy to such secrets!" With those words the old sorcerer turned a wrathful glare upon the younger, who shouldn't have spoken. Indeed, after years of concentrated training, Evain's emotions should have been so well controlled as to remain impervious to the Saxon's insult.

Adam refused to break the bond between his gaze and the young sorcerer's, but for Wulf's sake he forced a faint smile. By both religious training and his Saxon heritage, Adam was less impressed than Wulf. And yet . . . Wulf had spoken the truth insofar as he knew it but Adam had seen enough of inexplicable events that he couldn't completely discount the wizards' offer of assistance. Moreover, he feared their task might require all the aid they could secure.

Llys continued to follow the route she'd set, traveling steadily southward. Her certainty of its rightness held firm from midday, when the sun reigned supreme in the apex of the sky's blue dome, to late afternoon. But by the time the bright orb rested atop the dark, ragged line of treetops silhouetted on the western horizon, she knew something had gone desperately wrong.

Though not daring to stop, she took care to note her path. By the time the last rays of the setting sun had fallen, conquered by dusk's color-robbing powers, she realized that no matter the care she had given to holding a southern path she'd wandered far afield.

Her self-confidence faltered and discouragement grew when, in the full darkness preceding a moon's rising, she acknowledged having thrice passed the same distinctively misshapen tree.

A spell had been cast. There could be no doubt. While the abbot's warriors had for a certainty mounted a physical search, Gytha possessed methods of her own. Aye, a spell the wicked sorceress had spun to muddle Llys's way and lead her ever deeper into its web.

Refusing to easily surrender, particularly to one she suspected was an exponent of unnatural practices and a wielder of perverted powers, Llys reached into the bag at her waist. She sought the white stone, but it was the pendant's inverted triangle that caught at her fingers. Like a bright flash of lightning striking from storm-darkened sky came the certainty that 'twas the black talisman she carried that permitted Gytha to confuse her course.

Llys's hand closed about the wretched emblem. Jerking it free, she gazed down in disgust. The first faint glimmer of moonrise plainly revealed its dark shape against the fair skin of her palm. Her initial impulse was to throw it as far and as deep into the woods as her strength allowed. But . . .

'Twould be easily found and most probably used to strengthen the energies of one whose peril to all of

Throckenholt was fearfully real. And that person was as great a threat to Adam as to her. Only Glyndor—and mayhap Evain—commanded strength enough to defeat a dangerous foe of frightening powers. The possibility that this bit of black metal might be a vital component in a rite capable of securing peace and safety for those she loved was enough to convince Llys that she must keep the pendant in her possession.

As she turned the black object over in her hand it caught and reflected starshine into her eyes, momentarily blinding her. Aye, even the gleams flashing off its smooth surface seemed evil. The more Llys thought on it, the more convinced she became of the importance of seeing it reach Glyndor's hand.

Brynna and she were trained in working with natural laws and astral events, in the ways to call upon the forces inspiriting all of nature for aid in the healing arts and other beneficial uses. But only Glyndor, and now Evain, had mastered the art of controlling and wielding those forces in meeting the challenges of men's conflict and weapons of war. Brynna had once told Llys that she sensed the same degree of power in her. Llys hadn't believed it then and believed it even less now. In truth she feared her hold on even the most basic link with such powers was in jeopardy—making it all the more important that she get this strange charm to a sorcerer able to unlock its secrets and defeat its dark purposes. Aye, no matter the dangers possession of the pendant raised, she *would* see that task done!

Before taking obvious precautions, Llys took one that might mean nothing save the easing of her own apprehensions. She turned the pendant until its triangle pointed upward. Then she placed it atop the rough bark of a fallen tree trunk. Though not certain an unfamiliar crystal would answer her call, she withdrew the white stone from the pouch and rolled it between her palms until it glowed with the same pure beams as the new risen moon. Laying the shining stone over the dark pendant, she closed her eyes and formed a triangle with her hands. Llys chanted a plea to be freed from Gytha's spell and led to the path of safety.

Rising to her feet, she surrendered herself to the natural currents that had ever before been her ally. She lifted and cradled in one palm both the pendant and the glowing stone. Then she followed the glimmering white path that the crystal laid across dark earth. At length an unfamiliar yet surely sacred sight loomed up amidst a slowly whirling ground haze blanketing the hilltop ahead. 'Twas a cromlech—two huge stones lifted by the ancients toward the sky with another laid atop. She climbed to its base, fell to her knees, and offered homage to this venerable relic of the wise ones who had come before.

If there existed any well of strength deep enough to fight the dark sorceress's incantations, it was this. Llys had no doubt that she'd been led here for the purpose of chanting the power of this magical site, entreating its potent forces. Soft rose lips moved in an eerily beautiful chant too powerful to speak aloud while even the night animals went still in deference to her soundless song.

After Adam and Cedric departed Throckenholt, they'd stood facing the northern forest. It was then Adam had chosen to further expand their chances of locating Llys by commanding that they separate and circle around in opposite directions. He'd sent Cedric to the right to search the area where once he had rescued the enchantress from rough hands. Claiming the left path for himself, Adam had reined in his stallion to follow the same trail by which he'd first arrived from the abbey and later had used to return and find Aelfric's grave.

By the time daylight was near spent, Adam had climbed the hill he'd last stood atop with Llys and Wulf. The marks of their passing were still visible, and the view of an armed abbey had not changed. He wasted no time in turning his horse aside to travel back in a wide loop over a stream and across new ground.

Unfortunately, during the hours spent and distance covered in the journey through dense woods and over rough trails, never had he discovered a single clue to Llys's current whereabouts. That lack smote him with a sense of defeat. To the warrior he was, this emotion was as utterly alien as it was unwelcome, and it melded with his growing dread as he imagined what ghastly deeds might be perpetrated against an undeserving Llys, greatly increasing his frustrated anger.

Adam railed against fate, asked God why he must lose everyone he loved. Even the shock of this first admission of his love for Llys was instantly overwhelmed by guilt for having questioned God's will. Earnestly he begged God's forgiveness, but to that supplication he added another. Adam prayed that God would aid him in saving Llys from the danger he could feel hovering near.

No sooner had Adam concluded his plea for divine intervention than he heard a faint, elusive yet familiar sound. 'Twas a beguiling enchantment of sweet notes, each of such purity it seemed to brighten the light of glittering stars, and when mysteriously woven together, the sounds intensified the glow of the moon.

Even without direction from Adam, the great black beast he rode upon turned from the barely visible trail and broke through a wall of vegetation to answer the magical tune's summons. Moving safely through a night forest full of invisible stumble holes and likely hidden foes was a miracle of its own but one Adam wasted no thought to question. He peered intently between the dark shapes of towering trees until was seen a dim glow and, silhouetted against it, the dainty source of the enticing song.

Adam dismounted at the base of the rise. So filled with relief was he to find Llys free and unharmed that he gave little notice to the ancient structure of huge rocks she knelt below.

"I prayed to God, begging that he'd lead me to you. He answered, sending me near enough to hear your sweet singing."

Shocked first by the unexpected voice and second by the words it said, Llys abruptly stood up and turned to face the golden man dismounting—her rescuer once and apparently again.

Soft rose lips opened to tell him she hadn't sung aloud, but Adam bent to claim them in a devastating kiss. It instantly drove all sane thought into a void of nothingness while at the same time luring her toward a reckless response she'd no will to deny. Feeling stripped of bones, she clung to broad shoulders, wanting the heady closeness to go on and on. In that moment, while the kiss deepened to a hungry ferocity growing ever hotter, she would've counted even her precious bond with nature well lost if that must be the price for a single night in the arms of this man beloved.

Choosing to believe his answered prayer showed approval for his love of the elusive temptress, Adam felt the strong bonds of his control shatter. And yet, that tender emotion forced upon him a measure of control, at least enough to see she would be as deep into passion's consuming blaze as he before came the inevitable surrender to carry them both into the billowing smoke of satisfaction. Toward that end, he released her mouth and lifted his face toward the cool light of a new risen moon.

Feeling bereft as the fire of his mouth left hers, without conscious thought Llys touched her lips to the firm skin of a sun-bronzed throat and then, with insatiable curiosity, ventured farther.

Adam went still beneath the tentative brush of gentle lips against his throat. Untutored though she might be, the temptress proved herself able to return fire with fire as her caress moved down to skin bared by laces loosened at the neck of his tunic.

"Seeking again to caress me as you did in the days of my convalescence, hmm?" His soft laughter was deep and darkly textured as he shed his black cloak.

Llys started to deny his claim, but the words were strangled by breath caught in her throat at a stunning sight renewed after he suddenly withdrew his arms. Shedding a jerkin covered with metal rings, he pulled his tunic over a blond head. This he flung carelessly aside, leaving bare the temptation of a hard male chest—all strong muscle with a wedge of bronze curls tapering from below broad shoulders to disappear beneath chausses tied at narrow hips. Though not her first view, it had lost none of its power to speed the beat of her heart into an erratic race. She desperately wanted to stroke over tempting planes but curled her hands against the urge, afraid such an action would only confirm the low opinion of her suggested by his repeated taunt.

Adam recognized the source of her hesitation. Ruing his ill-thought jest, he lifted dainty hands to lay them above his own fiercely pounding heart before slipping his fingers beneath her black cloak of curls and wrapping them about slender shoulders.

"Despite the wall separating our bedchambers, I am so aware of you lying near that each night I dream of your touch. . . ." He had dreamed of that and a great deal more.

Past experience of the feel of his smooth skin and the firm thews beneath it only increased Llys's excitement and so sharply that she bit at her full lower lip. Here was her opportunity, likely the only one she'd ever have, to openly caress the man she loved. With remembered delight, her fingers flattened against burning flesh and journeyed through wiry curls. Nothing existed but the feel of him, and given the freedom to touch where she would, her caresses grew more daring.

A tension stretched taut was broken by the low velvet growl Adam could no longer restrain. With passion-glazed eyes Llys looked up into a gaze like molten honey. Her soft curves melted against him. Adam hungrily reclaimed her mouth while his hands swept down from fragile shoulders to the small of her back, then lower to cup her derriere and pull her tight against his desperate need.

As she instinctively arched into his embrace, wild shudders of excitement shook Llys. That response intensified when he stoked the fires of pleasure with repeated soft strokes from her hips up her sides to beneath the arms wrapped about him and then down again, ever moving closer to the center.

Llys's ability to easily breathe died unmourned under a nameless, dangerous wanting, and she'd have fallen had he not caught her in his strong arms. With a harsh groan he gently lifted and laid her luscious form atop a carpet of plush grass studded with fragrant blossoms whose white petals glowed in moonlight.

Adam leaned above Llys while the golden fire of his gaze moved over her in a burning caress, lingering where the bodice of a red gown laced in front permitted enticing glimpses of full breasts whose creamy satin skin he longed to touch . . . and taste. Drawn by a sweet temptation, Adam reached out to tenderly trace lush curves. Caressing fingers alternately stroked and loosened laces until the offensive red cloth lay unwanted at her waist. Leaning away, from beneath desire-heavy lids Adam studied the moon-kissed perfection of her against the rich backdrop of ebony curls.

Llys reveled in the admiration so clear in the glittering depths of Adam's eyes. Lifting her arms, she twined slender fingers into his thick golden mane, striving to tug him nearer even as his outspread hand glided over her with heady intimacy.

To Adam her breasts were like warm rose petals in his hands, hard tips branding his palms. He exalted in the sight of his fingers moving against the luminescent whiteness of her skin with exquisite gentleness. He stretched out at her side to nibble, kiss, and savor her tender flesh until she arched beneath his caresses, yearning for more and twisting her straining flesh nearer.

Llys's world spun with incredible, wicked sensations as, through the smoke of passion's fire, blue eyes gone near to black watched Adam lowering himself over her. He halted a slight distance above her to slowly move his chest back and forth, rubbing wiry curls across sensitive tips. Helpless pleasure sent yet another wild shudder through Llys, and heavy lashes drifted down on a soft moan when at last he allowed the pleasure of his broad chest to crush her bare skin. But still it wasn't enough.

Llys writhed against Adam's overpowering form while she dug the nails of one hand into the firm flesh of his neck and smoothed the other palm down his back to urge his body ever closer. Adam desperately wanted to be rid of every barrier betwixt hard muscle and silken flesh and gradually pushed her gown lower. His hand glided over each delicious inch of the path until she was free from unwelcome cloth encumbrances. For all the care he'd taken in disrobing her, he lost no moment in stripping his own garb away.

Again rising above her and slowly coming down to rest on his forearms, Adam let her feel the strong contours of his body. At the exquisite pleasure of being so intimately held against the complete length of her beloved's superbly masculine form, a breathless whimper escaped her tight throat. She felt herself drowning in the blazing sea of her own longings as Adam returned his mouth to hers and with seductive slowness fanned the potent flames of their voracious need until desire surged through their veins, uncontrollable, unstoppable.

With hands and mouth, Adam guided Llys's descent into delicious torment and shocking pleasures. His palms slid down to cup her derriere and tilt her hips upward to aid the merging of their bodies. Though smoldering blue eyes widened at the outset and Llys went still for a moment, with an instinct even more ancient than the mysterious stone monument so near, it was she who first surged against him. But it was Adam, with a passion-stiff smile, who taught her the delirious delights to be found in a wicked rhythm that grew ever wilder and carried them into a desperate abandon where, at last, raging fire exploded into a storm of sparks and unfathomable ecstasy.

The golden rose of dawn's light played over soft, translucent skin, lending it the sheen of a pearl.

"You didn't sing aloud?" Adam rose up on one elbow and gazed down at the beauty he'd so thoroughly claimed. "But I heard you."

With a shy smile Llys gazed up into the faint bronze frown of the man now proven as devastating as once she'd feared but feared no more. On first awakening, she had told him of the foes in Winbury Abbey and of the threat made against his life. Feeling greatly relieved to have accomplished that goal, she saw no cloud to darken their ride back to the keep and, in answer to his bemused question, slowly shook her head, stirring the black cloud of tangled curls pillowed on lush grasses. "Nay, but while you prayed, I silently chanted a powerful entreaty for aid—and you came."

Adam's frown deepened. He felt as if a friend had unexpectedly landed him the fierce blow of a foe. Her claim complicated matters in ways he couldn't accept. Thinking his discovery of her had been by the blessing of God, Adam had felt his love for and taking of Llys divinely sanctioned. But if it was the result of some unholy pagan magic, then he'd been as thoroughly tricked as ever he'd feared by a woman's wiles.

"Did you and your brother conspire in the deception that put your double in Throckenholt to mislead us all?" Adam's words were muffled and golden hair was ruffled as his head popped through the neck opening of his tunic. "Does a double really exist, or are you in truth two women in a single body?" He asked as he rose to tug on his chausses.

"Have you gone witless?" Llys sat up, stunned by

Adam's abrupt change of mood and bewildering questions. As he was rapidly dressing, she struggled to don the tight red gown that was likely to convince him the disdain he'd had for her from the first was justified. "What madness is this you speak of doubles and deceit?"

"Witless? Madness?" He finished crossing and tying narrow bands about his calves before rising to jerk her upright. "Aye, I think you'll drive me to witlessness. Here and in the keep's hall you are all sweet innocence while in the abbey and in my bed you were an experienced strumpet!"

Llys could make no sense of Adam's sudden ranting, save for the mention of another in his bed— apparently the same woman he'd met in the abbey and mistaken for her ever since.

Before Adam had finished his tirade, he glanced Llys's way and saw the confusion on her face. Her seeming innocence further muddled the morass of his own feelings. He was either guilty of a terrible wrong against her . . . or more the fool for permitting a wicked temptress to trick him into suspecting himself to blame. Of a sudden he reached out and pulled Llys into his arms for a passionate kiss, intending to prove his heart's armor intact despite having succumbed to an enchantress's lures the past night. It was an abysmal failure, a fact that deepened his irritated self-disgust.

Mounting his steed, face impassive, Adam used his great strength to impersonally sweep Llys up to sit in front of him. The quiet following his storm was more ominous still.

Adam's jaw was hard, as if carved of the stones that had earlier imprisoned her. Llys knew it would be impossible to win from him any explanation for his wild accusations. Yet, without understanding the charges against her, she couldn't defend herself against them and did not try.

The cromlech proved to have been much nearer to their destination than either expected, and it was in the colorless light between dawn and full daylight that they silently rode through Throckenholt's palisade gate.

Chapter
12

Pip took seriously his assignment to guard the inhabitants of Throckenholt Keep while others searched for Llys. It was the reason he'd spent the night dozing lightly. And now as the dull gray light preceding dawn began to fill the sky, he was fully awake and moved to resume the position that had become habit in the hours he'd spent as Lady Brynna's patient. He sat upright on his pallet and rested his back against the low stone wall encircling the central fire pit. Lightly running large hands over his injured knee, he was pleased to find the swelling gone. To further test its health, he rose gingerly to his feet. Although his leg was still tender, most of the pain had disappeared.

As the house thralls hadn't yet arrived to stir banked coals to renewed life, the hall was chilly. Feeling like a laggard and anxious to physically do some worthy deed, Pip lifted a metal rod and prodded ash-covered coals until tiny flames burst free. Atop these he judiciously laid several of the wood rounds stacked to one side for that purpose, never thinking of the noises made by the action.

"Good morrow," Maida called softly from the relative safety of the shadowed herb corner. To speak at all required every shred of courage she could muster. In past more oft than not such a deed had earned her vicious blows. But after even the little time she'd spent in this keep she'd begun to believe such actions might not be the wont of its inhabitants . . . other than the impostor who had threatened retribution if Maida revealed what the sorceress wanted hidden. That potent warning had easily bridled Maida's tongue.

Startled that the timid maid had spoken, Pip spun about—an action his knee protested. But his initial shock was eased by the gift of a cheery grin for these first words said by the maid directly to him.

"And good morrow to you, milady." He bowed as gallantly as if she were the queen. His playful action earned a shy smile from the thin woman whose bruises proclaimed her unused to gentleness.

Encouraged, Pip attempted to draw her into an actual conversation. "I pray your slumbers were more restful than mine."

Maida's slight smile disappeared, and her wan face returned to lines of worry. Pip rued the comment he'd foolishly thought safe, since she had, to his certain knowledge, slept heavily for most of the night. Thinking her deep slumbers proved his suspicion that either her ailing babe or her brutal master had prevented her from securing needed rest in weeks past, he'd believed this reminder of improved circumstances a warm opening to quiet talk. The glaring truth of how ill considered his words had been flooded him with embarrassment.

"I'm a clumsy oaf!" As was too oft the case for a man of his coloring, a ruddy shade burned his cheeks so brightly it could be seen even while he stood with back to fire and face lit only by dim predawn light. "Pray pardon my stumbling tongue for reminding you of what can only bring distress."

Amazed by the big man's shamed regret at causing her distress, Maida permitted another shy smile to creep across her face while she quietly answered his initial question.

"I woke only the one time when your friend Cedric appeared." Although this Pip was a huge man he seemed a gentle soul. And she had experience enough of the reverse to recognize how rare was this quality in a warrior. Aye, she'd long had too close an acquaintance with another man, considerably smaller . . . and brutal. The contrasts between them were sufficient to suggest that physical size and cruelty bore no relationship to one another.

Realizing of a sudden how long she'd stared at the man shuffling uneasily under her gaze, Maida rushed to ask an important question sure to divert his attention. "Have others returned with better news of Llys?"

The answer was a mournful frown and shake of Pip's russet mane. Of the six men who had gone out in search of Llys only Cedric had come back. In the darkest hours he'd arrived to knock at the door, hoping to find others more successful than he. All within Throckenholt village's palisade waited, initial worries for Llys expanding to include fears for those who had departed in full daylight but near the following sunrise had yet to reappear.

Pip glanced toward the cracks in shuttered windows revealing a growing brightness. The imminent arrival of dawn with no news could only increase Lady Brynna's fears for husband, foster children, and grandfather. That she slept now was a blessing as she had lingered in the hall until well after Cedric appeared and then retired to Maelvyn's abode.

"If there were trouble, how would you know?" Maida quietly asked a question that addressed one source of her alarm. She knew better than anyone within Throckenholt's walls that, snug though they were here, their safety was in serious jeopardy with danger inexorably creeping closer.

Pip saw the strain again take hold of his companion and forced a reassuring smile. "'Tis a matter of two hunting horns. Lord Wulfayne carries the larger, which emits sounds of deeper resonance. Lord Adam carries one somewhat smaller and with a higher tone. The men standing guard at forest edge, as well as those atop the palisade, are ever alert and listening. If three short blasts from either are heard, an armed force will immediately answer the call."

"And you would know if either had been heard already?" Maida asked.

"Aye, we all would know." Pip decided that the only way to lessen her concern was to divert her thoughts into a more pleasant path. After slowly approaching the girl so as not to frighten her, he held out his arm. "It's cold here in the corner, come warm yourself by the fire."

Maida hesitated, studying the proffered arm with apprehensive eyes. She had been the brunt of too many blows to easily trust even so simple a gesture.

Pip tamed his normal impatience and waited while the girl examined his arm as if suspecting that the moment her guard was lowered it would lash out to do her injury. In the end, he deemed it a victory that at least she didn't so fear him that she cringed.

Although still reticent, Maida laid her too thin hand atop his huge forearm and allowed him to lead her toward the fire. Next and with due courtesy, he settled her on the softness of his pallet.

While the flames whose strength he'd revived leapt in twining tongues of yellow and orange, he lowered himself to sit beside Maida within their circle of warmth. The maid said little, but the ever talkative Pip was at no loss for words. He laughingly related a number of rowdy adventures shared with his eight brothers and three sisters.

"Mum is a miracle worker." The love in his voice was as unshielded as it had been when he described his siblings. "No matter the hardships during years of poor harvest, she manages to burden our table with the huge meals required to appease so many healthy appetites. Of course"—Pip glanced down and winked at the maid who seemed enthralled by his homespun tales—"she ensures that her daughters toil as hard as she. During days of bounty they salt away barrels of meat and store all they can of grains and fruit against what lean days may follow."

Maida was warmed by the vision of a happy family full of a love such as she had never known, and she eagerly listened as the gentle giant continued.

"And my father has only one complaint." Pip grinned. "Albeit 'tis ever ongoing. He grumbles that his brood leaves only enough on the table to keep him barely alive. 'Tis truly a jest, for my father's appetite is as legendary as his size which, I swear, is near twice my own."

Even Pip's fund of idle talk eventually faded into silence. Having revealed so much of himself, he lost the battle to completely restrain his curiosity about the timid girl, but began with what he hoped Maida would recognize as honest concern for her.

"I heard what the one pretending to be Llys said to

you," Pip quietly stated. Maida remained mute, and Pip was afraid he'd frightened her back into the shell from which she'd just begun to emerge.

That dreadful memory so roused Maida's alarm that she was unaware of Pip's worry. Her attention rested heavily upon the fingers she smoothed over tattered skirts until, after long moments of silence, she was struck by the shabbiness of her garb. Shame twined with renewed fear to nudge her into a response given without thought of the betrayal it would be of her apprehensions. "I am glad she is gone. Only do I wish it could be forever."

"But she *is* gone and no longer able to do you harm." Pip wanted to soothe away the renewed fear he could see in trembling fingers nervously fumbling with a gown of the meanest quality.

Maida looked anxiously up into her companion's solemn face. "Nay. She can. Always she can."

"Who?" Pip's voice rose as he earnestly begged for an explanation he knew the girl was unlikely to give. "And how can she? How, when she is nowhere near, nor can she return with guards posted all about?"

"Oh." It was a sound of disappointment. "Pip . . . Maida . . ." Brynna stood in the door of the lord's bedchamber. She'd just fed Cub and rocked him into a sleep as peaceful as Anya's natural rest, when promising sounds came to her ears. "I heard voices and wanted to believe . . ."

"Nay, I am sorry we raised expectations that have yet to be met." Pip lumbered to his feet and turned to face Lady Brynna. The dark shadows under her eyes were an obvious sign of how little sleep she'd had either the previous night or during past weeks. He took several steps toward his hostess, but before he could reach her side, their attention was summoned

by the outer door's opening and held by strange
Cymry words neither Pip nor Maida could understand.

"The spell is broken." White hair glowed with the
dawn's first bright rays as Glyndor entered Throckenholt Keep.

"But not by any doings of ours." Stepping into the
hall behind his mentor, Evain met Brynna's mist-gray
gaze directly. "Plainly Llys, on her own, learned of the
binding spell and wielded power sufficient to sunder
its hold."

Brynna's somber expression lightened not only in
relief that the spell over Llys had been shattered but,
too, in delight that her own much earlier prediction
had proven true: Llys truly did possess a bond with
nature that was the equal of her brother's.

"Then doubtless Llys will find her way here." Even
as she spoke the reassurance, worry of another making
slipped over the lady of Throckenholt's lovely face.
"We can but hope the others are as fortunate."

"Nay, we can do more and we will." Evain instantly
made to turn back toward the doorway, anxious to
calm his foster mother's concern. A hand, amazingly
strong for one age-spotted and gaunt, restrained the
young sorcerer.

"Already have I sought aid for the searchers' safe
return." Glyndor had his own methods of distracting
his granddaughter. In truth this was more than a
distraction, it was a message that not only must be
shared but that promised him a long-anticipated
contentment. "I also have more to share—the proph-
ecy of my own end."

Evain and Brynna stood frozen by the words of the
clearly weary sorcerer settling into a hearthside chair.
He motioned his apprentices nearer, ignoring the pair

of Saxons already in the hall. Glyndor lent no more notice to the two figures just arrived at the doorway neither he nor Evain would willingly see closed betwixt themselves and nature. From there the missing one returned would hear and understand his words while they would mean little to the young golden warrior who he feared was as great a threat to Llys as Wulf had years past proven to be to his granddaughter.

"During hours spent communing with the forces of nature, I learned the reason why—after honorably fulfilling my duty to pass on the secret knowledge—I've lingered so long in life's vale."

Glyndor paused to draw a deep breath, an interruption that increased the tension of the two who'd come to kneel on either side of him. Evain wondered what awful thing his mentor had foreseen that prevented him from speaking of this momentous revelation as they journeyed back to the keep. During those same moments, Brynna could think only of the unavoidable truth that her grandsire's end was near.

Silence lay like a heavy shroud on the hall whose very walls seemed to ache in suspense, waiting for the sorcerer to continue.

"One more task I must perform." Glyndor's voice seemed to have deepened to the voice of doom. "One more mighty battle must be waged, and it is more important than any in my many years." Golden fires burned in the depths of the coal-black gaze he turned first to the granddaughter and then to his inheritor. "Only after its victory have I won can I be released from mortal coils."

"Whom must you battle?" Brynna asked, striving to suppress a sorrow already beginning to ache with the certainty that death was the release her grandfather longed to attain.

"When?" Even as his foster mother spoke, Evain questioned the issue he deemed most important. With a Druid's advanced training and ability to view all people and events with dispassionate objectivity, Evain saw clearly the link between Glyndor's mighty battle and the menacing danger of perverted Druidic powers. And, should preparations be needed, his was the only query of possible use.

Glyndor smiled serenely, leaned his head against the high chair back, and closed his eyes to compose himself for a sleep his apprentices knew better than to interrupt. And it was neither of them who did so.

From the open door where Adam stood with Llys close beside him, he had heard all that Glyndor said. Talk of a foretold demise and the passing of secret knowledge meant nothing to him, yet he wanted answers to questions the sorcerer's pupils had asked at least as much as they. To him the warning of a coming mighty battle was the only issue of significance.

"Nay, you cannot raise the prospect of deadly conflict and then calmly drift into dreams." As Adam strode forward his black cape swirled back from broad shoulders to float behind him like wings. Arms crossed over his broad chest, he towered above the seated man, much smaller than he seemed when boldly standing, and in the Cymry tongue protested Glyndor's intent. "Sleep may be appropriate for a Druid wizard, but I am a warrior trained to the literal deeds of battle, one experienced in the tactics and human price of war. And I *insist* on knowing more."

Thick white brows lowered over dark eyes, open and flashing with dangerous fire. Llys, seeing this ominous sign of Glyndor's growing fury, was too concerned by the ill-boding confrontation to wonder at the Saxon's easy use of a tongue none of them would've expected him to know. She rushed to Adam, pushed a delicate hand through an infinitesimal opening, and wrapped her restraining hold about the crook of one powerful arm. The gesture was for naught, as he seemed impervious to her touch.

"Insist all you please. Shout your demands to the heavens if you so desire." Glyndor found this Saxon as annoying as ever Wulf had been. "But never will I share the fruits of my gift with an arrogant unbeliever!"

The two stubborn men glared at one another, charging the air with the same danger as an imminent lightning strike.

Brynna swept through the tension to claim Llys in a tender welcoming hug. "I am so relieved that you've returned to Throckenholt unharmed."

While Llys fervently returned the affectionate embrace, she glanced over her foster mother's shoulder to meet the warm pleasure in her twin brother's gaze. They'd such a bond as made words unnecessary. She gave him a bright smile, knowing how pleased he was at her safe return.

"But where did you go?" Anya had awakened and come to the door of the tiny chamber she shared with her brother in time to hear her mother's words. Ever the quiet listener whose presence was forgotten, Anya had picked up most of what she'd missed during her berry-induced sleep, but not the reason for Llys's disappearance.

Thrilled to find the dainty girl at her feet, clearly restored to health, Llys swept Anya up into her arms. Llys had no doubt but that Evain had roused the child from her unnatural sleep—just as she'd been certain he could.

"Where did you get so bright a dress?" Anya pushed against Llys's shoulders to look down at the red cloth.

"Someone took mine," Llys quickly responded, "leaving me no choice but to wear what I could find."

That answer was easily given, but the answer to the child's first question, as with those unspoken by Brynna and likely Evain must wait. Llys was too well aware that the strain growing ever tauter between Glyndor and Adam had not flickered for a moment during her welcome. Thus she accepted the need for their conflict to be resolved before she could, if they wished, repeat all that she'd earlier told Adam of what had happened to her and what she'd learned.

It was into this conflict that an oblivious Cedric strode. Rarely sensitive to undercurrents of feeling and able to understand none of the words being spoken, he paused only long enough to locate Adam. So consumed was he by the ill tidings he bore that even the hall's thick tension failed to penetrate his single-minded determination to be soon quit of an unpleasant duty.

Once standing within a pace of his lord, Cedric began with characteristic bluntness. "The wife of a ceorl from an outlying farm came to report a blow to our cause."

Golden brows raised in question, Adam turned toward his gruff guardsman. "What had this farmer's wife to say?"

Cedric immediately answered. "The messenger sent by Lord Wulf to King Ecgferth was found hanging from an elm in the forest."

Llys had at first been relieved by the gruff guardsman's interruption, but his explanation filled her with guilt for even that initial glimmer of pleasure when the news was of a heartless end to a young man's life.

"He's been dead several days but was discovered only last eve. . . ." Cedric paused to pull a badly crumpled parchment from behind his wide leather belt. "This note was attached to the rope about his neck."

Rubbing the stubby fingers of one hand against the broad palm of the other, Cedric awkwardly attempted to smooth the worst wrinkles away before passing the missive to his waiting lord.

To Llys's surprise, and likely to the surprise of others as well, rather than immediately reading the note's message, Adam refolded it.

Amber eyes narrowed to peer closely at the broken seal realigned and then went dark. Plainly the imprint laid in melted wax was made by the ring that Ulford, the aged farmer, had sketched with a chunk of charcoal.

"Saexbo." That name held all the disgust Adam felt for King Ecgferth's youngest son, the one Ulford had described as a "stripling lad."

Llys had lowered Anya to her feet and turned again to stand quietly at Adam's side. She had seen the mark left in the wax and recognized it from the aged farmer's crude drawing. And although the name Saexbo was not one she'd heard mentioned while escaping the bishop's hold, she recognized it as one Adam and her foster father had listed as a foe while the three of them gazed down at an armed abbey.

That name also drew from Maida a quiet gasp unheard by any save the big man who'd followed her when at the arrival of others she'd scurried back into the shadowed corner. In response to her pained reaction, Pip gently pulled her into the protection of strong arms. She went stiff with fear, but as Pip lightly and repeatedly smoothed a huge hand over the tangled brown hair flowing down her back, she slowly relaxed against him.

"I won't let anyone hurt you again." Pip whispered into the cushion of hair atop her head. "And I'm big enough to ensure what I promise will be true."

"You don't understand." Maida's face tilted up, and she gave her head a brief shake.

"I may not know for certain sure, but I'd wager much that my suspicions are correct." Pip's reassuring smile hardened into determination. "And still I give you my promise as an oath I would die before surrendering."

"Don't say that." Maida's eyes filled with tears. "It doubles my fears! Once for myself but twice for you. I'm terrified that death is a price you might be called upon to pay. And I am not worthy of it. You don't know, you don't know. . . ." The words dissolved into silent tears.

Again Pip enfolded her in a tender embrace, disgusted with himself. He'd meant to console the hurting maid and instead had increased her woe.

What with the unresolved confrontation between Druid sorcerer and Saxon lord, closely followed by alarming news, the others in the hall had spared no attention for the pair's conversation. Rather Lady Brynna, her foster children, and her grandfather intently watched Cedric and his lord.

"What does the letter say?" Brynna moved forward as she questioned the man, a guest in her home.

Adam nodded toward the approaching woman. The lady of Throckenholt had every right to make this demand. Moreover, the missive would affect the welfare of all here, making it just that they hear its contents as well. The parchment crackled as he opened it and began to read.

"'Neither this messenger nor any other will live long enough to win you deliverance from soon-descending conquerors.'"

The hall's tension was in no way eased by this news. In truth it increased fourfold in the ominous quiet that followed. During this time, the two sorcerers slipped from the chamber, black robes swirling about them like a silent storm. They knew only the Saxon warrior would dare to challenge their leave-taking, and his opinion they disdained.

But Adam wasted no thought on their departure. To him it represented the welcome removal of an annoying distraction while he analyzed this day's many quickly falling layers of darkness, each adding greater peril to the looming menace that was growing ever more complex.

Llys remained quietly standing within a breath's distance of the one who had held her safe during their return to Throckenholt. Yet despite Adam's protective hold, he had been as unyielding and quiet as stone. How was it that the source of such fiery delights as they had shared could have become so unyielding to her? If her mentor and her brother learned what had passed between them only hours ago, likely they would denounce her for her love of this Saxon who would challenge a sorcerer. In truth it was likely a shameful deed she'd committed . . . yet she would not have it undone, not when it was so clearly the single experience she would ever have of such joy in her beloved's arms. Llys turned a gaze clouded with pain upon Adam. Surreptitiously, she studied the man whose close proximity enfolded her as surely as his arms so recently had, leaving her achingly aware of her loss at his denial of her.

She would have thought Adam could grow no colder, but his clenched jaw's hard curve proved it possible. He seemed carved of ice-layered granite.

Despite appearances to the contrary, Adam was now and had every moment of the day been intensely aware of Llys's tempting nearness. A sorceress of puzzling qualities though she might be, the prospect of renewed danger to her deepened both his disgust for the menacing words he'd read aloud and his determination to ensure that the author and his cohorts suffered defeat.

"I pray pardon, but the door was ajar." The uncomfortable silence that had descended once Adam's words faded, and that continued unabated once the sorcerers departed, was broken by the hesitant voice of an overfed villager hovering in the open portal. "The news is so urgent I thought I ought to bring it immediately."

More desperate news? Adam's frown deepened but no more so than those of the others in the hall.

Against this demonstration of how unwelcome he was, the speaker fell a step back and nearly turned craven enough to flee. He was a simple man who had never claimed to be brave. Only a greater fear of the price he might be called upon to pay if he failed to give his report lent him sufficient courage to perform the chore.

"From the southern forest came the low sound of a hunting horn in three strong blasts. After a time 'twas repeated and then yet again."

Weeks of growing apprehension over Anya's fading life and then worry for the missing Llys, followed by a long night of anxiety for Wulf, proved too much for even Brynna's strength. On hearing this dreaded news she slumped and would've fallen but for Adam, who took one long step and caught her.

While Adam laid his slight burden on the pallet earlier vacated by Pip, Llys rushed to soak a fresh cloth square in cool water. Under Llys's gentle ministrations, the older woman soon roused.

Ashamed and irritated with herself for the unaccustomed weakness, Brynna sat up and turned her attention to Lord Adam. "We must leave immediately to answer Wulf's call."

"Nay, milady." A mere pace distant and gazing down at the woman barely recovered from a faint, Adam formally rejected the lady of Throckenholt's proposed action. "Your husband would not likely forgive me were I to allow your participation in so dangerous a quest."

He saw Brynna straighten under the rejection and, convinced she meant to argue against his decision, laid out the alternate course he intended to follow. "Cedric and I will select a small force of Throckenholt's menfolk to join us in locating the source of the horn's plea. Once those we seek are found, with all possible haste we will carry the injured back to benefit from your healing care.

"Remember . . ." Adam recognized the determination tightening Brynna's gentle face but offered one more logical attempt to dissuade her. "Wulf is not alone, and there is no reason to believe 'tis he who is in need of assistance."

Brynna smiled ruefully at the man she suspected could nowise understand her certainty that it was Wulf whose life was in jeopardy. He would think her knowledge was lent by powers unfathomable to him. 'Twas not so, as she attempted to explain.

"I can feel Wulf's pain and *must* do all possible to see him restored."

Druid magic? Too much of death and battles foretold by sorcery had Adam heard. His lips firmed into a straight line against her supplication. With the clear sight of a Christian warrior he saw enough to know that permitting a woman so committed to preserving life to join a perilous quest would be the greater wrong.

"You would deny me as a sorceress, but 'tis not by such powers that I know Wulf's peril." Brynna laid a small hand atop her heart. "I know it here, by the love he and I share." The unblinking gaze of amber eyes seemed to prove Adam unmoved. "As Wulf's wife I claim the right to go to him."

Adam frowned.

By the love she bore the golden man Llys sensed in him a deepening conflict. Likely it sprang from his long established inability to accept the ways of a Druid. That his suspicion of Druidic skills was in this instance utterly unjust made it all the more regrettable. Plainly he found it difficult to believe this knowledge had been won without mystical powers. Again she dared to step too close to him. Bravely reaching toward the man who had refused even to glance her way since their return, Llys laid her hands palm-flat against his powerful chest, unconsciously savoring his strength.

"Brynna speaks true, Adam. For us as Druids to acquire such knowledge would require rites performed with the white crystal and chants seeking nature's powers. You know for certain sure that Brynna has worked no spells, yet still she knows."

Looking down into blue eyes so wide and full of emotion that he felt in danger of drowning in their soft depths, Adam did understand. He understood because he remembered how overswept by the sense of her danger he'd been less than a full day gone by. A lingering wildflower scent rose from the ebony hair so near as Adam shifted his attention to Lady Brynna and nodded a wordless compliance with her request.

"Remember, Adam," Brynna consoled her reluctant escort. "'Twill not be the first time I've come to Wulf's aid in the face of great danger. He cannot expect less of me now. And although you say you will bring him to me with all haste, there are injuries that would make such an action a greater danger to the patient than the wound itself. Against such a possibility I go prepared to remain at his side for as long as is required to restore his health."

Golden brows met in a renewed frown. "You believe Wulf is in such dire straits?"

Brynna gave the honestly concerned man a grim smile as she shook a mane of dark curls. "I do not know . . . but fear 'tis so."

Adam's nearness heartened Llys as did the breach she sensed in the wall of harshness he'd placed betwixt them. But even knowing she jeopardized both with the action, she made what he would assuredly deem a further unwelcome demand. "Because the treatments and, aye, the spells to treat wounds so extreme are like to respond better to two sets of hands and the twining of voices, I go as well."

Adam's concerned frown turned into a dark scowl. He hadn't wanted to see Lady Brynna, his hostess and Wulf's wife, subjected to the dangers of the journey, but the notion of Llys riding into their shadows was infinitely more repellent.

"I thank you, Llys," Brynna immediately responded, "and I welcome your aid in this task.

Though I wish it were unnecessary, I fear it may be just that. But only for the initial steps to see him on a steady upward course. Then you must return for the sake of the many who come to Throckenholt seeking care for their illnesses or hurts."

Having accepted Lady Brynna's demand, Adam realized that once she'd welcomed her foster daughter's company and assistance, there was nothing he could do to forestall this unwelcome addition to his doubtless odd little band of rescuers. Although his face was an impassive mask, the knotted muscles of his clenched jaw made clear the frustration felt by a powerful lord accustomed on his own lands to brooking no resistance.

With a wry smile, Brynna purposely misinterpreted his annoyance. "Don't fret that Wulf will blame you for any ill that befalls either me or Llys. Already he knows how headstrong we both are and would be more like to pity you for having been forced to bear the burden of our willfulness."

Irritably shrugging, Adam turned away. He intended to waste no further time in useless arguments and instead left the abode to initiate arrangements that must be made.

Llys retreated to her small chamber and hastily changed from the tight red garment she found so uncomfortably revealing into a sturdy yet pleasing gown of deep green. After pulling a brush through tangled locks, dislodging more than one fragrant, waxy-white petal, she hurried back to Brynna. Happy to be of some use, she packed a cloth bag full of medicants and other necessary items.

Whilst their hands were busied with these tasks, Llys gave Brynna a brief account of her capture, what she'd learned during her imprisonment, and her escape—but not of the intimate scene that followed her rescue.

During that same length of time, Adam set about seeking volunteers to join his small armed contingent in answering their lord's call. Wulf was beloved of his people and so many were anxious to sally forth in his defense that the matter of selecting only a few without offending those to be left behind required all of Adam's considerable diplomacy. The task was made the more difficult by the absence of the village's leader—the smithy, Maelvyn, was already in Lord Wulf's company.

Although Adam was further disturbed by the necessity to take Brynna and Wulf's still nursing infant with them on the dangerous journey, in an amazingly brief time the force was away on its quest, leaving Anya in Maida's care and Pip to guard them.

Chapter
13

"Two sorcerers!" Bishop Wilfrid's jowls turned red with irritation as he fair stomped from one side of his chamber to the other, casting darkly accusing glares at the two women just inside a closed door. "You claimed the ability to foil a single sorceress's escape only to return and report such wretched news?"

While Gytha's mirthless grin openly displayed her enjoyment of Wilfrid's frustration and distress, Elesa stood at her aunt's side near as upset by this unexpected fact as the bishop.

"I knew for a mistake the choice made by you and Saexbo, my immature leader. 'Twas an error to ally ourselves with Druids!" Hordath's words held a strange combination of smugness and disgust. "They have thus far been and can in future be of no worthy use to us. Have quit of them now before they further muddle our path."

"Muddle *your* path?" Gytha was incensed and the steam of her ire seemed to heat the dark coals of her eyes. "Hordath, it was *you* who failed to do away with Llys when you had her in your hold; *you* who chose not to place a guard at the door of her cell, as I recommended. Thus *you* are responsible for her escape."

Gytha took only one step forward but with it seemed to grow infinitely more fearsome as she went on with a scathing denunciation. "Moreover, 'tis you who must bear the blame for permitting Llys to carry away facts that, if revealed, might put an end to your precious scheme. And what sorry end do you seek? Why a crown whose power the pair of fools you are think to wield on behalf of Saexbo, an immature creature off in the forest playing childish games of hide-and-seek—and a greater danger to your dreams than any foe."

Again, as too oft in recent days, Wilfrid was forced to step between two allies near at daggers drawn. "'Struth, plans revealed to our prey afore time would jeopardize our intent." Irritated both by the need to intervene and by Hordath's weak-witted leader's deeds, through clenched teeth he gritted out an unpleasant fact.

"But since Saexbo's woman already has fled into Throckenholt Keep, doubtless with extensive knowledge of our plans, 'tis not what little information Llys learned before fleeing our hold that offers the worst peril."

Taller than the bishop by more than a handsbreadth, Hordath met Gytha's stony gaze directly. "Still, I question these Druids' usefulness to our cause."

The elder sorceress instantly turned the accusation back on its speaker. "Have you found a better method than the one I propose for holding Talacharn quiet while you seize ever greater stretches of land and amass armies of sufficient size to lead Prince Saexbo's challenge for his father's throne?"

"Force of arms!" Hordath snarled.

"Not even the ancient armies of Rome managed to subdue the warriors of Wales. But you deem yourself more able?" Gytha's laugh was chilling. "I think you'd succeed only in wasting precious time and too many men in a hopeless cause that would of a certainty cost you victory in the goal of taking all Northumbria."

"Your plan shows no more promise of success." Indignation rising apace, Hordath, too, returned the assault like against like. "You've said you will defeat Glyndor, reveal his powers to be less potent than those you possess. This, you claim, will so discredit the aging man in the eyes of Talacharn's people that they'll lose faith in him and yield to your command. A command you assure us will prevent them from coming to the aid of the sorcerer's grandson-in-law. And further an order for them to nowise interfere in Saexbo's seizure of the Northumbrian crown. Fine promises all." Hordath's hands clenched. "But what have you accomplished toward these goals? Nothing! And now there are two!"

Having lost control of the scene, if ever he'd had it, Wilfrid joined the fray. He turned to face Gytha with an accusing stare equally as scathing as Hordath's verbal condemnation.

Gytha's burning glare met and easily defeated those turned upon her. "Aye." She drew her impressive figure up to its full height. "Already have I sworn to deal with Glyndor. And when the destined time arrives, I will. The other"—she waved her hands dismissively. "Evain is young and cannot wield sufficient power to threaten *our* common goal."

Elesa, having met the young sorcerer and sensed his command of potent forces she'd once deemed her own province, was far less convinced. Still, she knew better than to challenge Gytha's claim and, in silence, followed her fuming aunt from abbey gloom into bright daylight.

Adam rode to the small party's fore with the two women coming immediately after him while, to guard their back, Cedric took the last position, behind even the four village men. Leading the way through forest shadows, Adam peered into the thick foliage on either side of the trail, alert to the possibility of concealed foes watching their progress. Indeed, he felt the gazes of unseen men as surely as if they stood square in his path. He wondered only why they wasted time in distant observation when successfully assaulting a force of limited size and strength would likely be no difficult chore. Had they a grander scheme planned? Did a trap lie ahead?

Three low blasts of a hunting horn echoed through the forest's pungent air. This signal had been intermittently repeated, and Adam began to question the wisdom of accepting such blatant reassurance that they were traveling in the proper direction as that and nothing more. Mayhap 'twas so. And yet might it not also be that the deep notes so oft repeated lured them into a waiting snare?

Adam lifted one hand in silent command to halt while reining his black stallion to a standstill with the other. There were faint grumbles from men unfamiliar with their leader, and yet the whole party obeyed when next he signaled them to follow him as he turned aside from the trail laid by years of heavy use. Adam was relieved that Wulf's men, strangers to him, had suppressed their misdoubts insofar as to submit to his wishes. Though they had almost certainly heard tales lauding his valor and might, Adam was fully aware that Lady Brynna's unhesitating compliance and Llys's uncomplaining courage had lent additional strength to his command.

'Twas difficult to believe that only a short time past he had thought Llys timid and weak. Now he knew that though she had the reticence of a creature in the wild, beneath a gentle surface she had its brave heart as well.

Adam was so deeply aware that haste might mean the difference between Wulf's life or death that time seemed to slacken to the pace of a particularly slow snail while his mount safely picked its way ever deeper into the forest's vast reaches. Breaking a new trail across ground spongy with lush undergrowth and the previous autumn's fallen leaves, the searchers moved through the dense greenery filling narrow spaces between close grown trees. Spreading branches intertwined above their heads to cast the path in gloomy shadows.

Now, as it had the last time she'd ridden behind the golden warrior, Llys's attention was inexorably drawn and held by the man who just as firmly possessed her love. 'Twas a gift plainly of no value to him, yet still it belonged to him. Her love was his to toss aside, for—despite a lingering suspicion that the emotion placed a strain upon, if not a block to, her link with the powers of nature—she'd come to know herself unable to stem its flow.

Clouded with pain, blue eyes rested forlornly at the point on Adam's broad back where the tip ends of bright hair brushed their stark contrast across the black of his cloak. Helplessly watching, Llys saw him shrug strong shoulders as if to rid them of an unwelcome weight. Thick lashes descended in the hope of hiding a measure of the shame flooding her with the distressing certainty that Adam had sensed her scrutiny and by this shrugging motion meant to show how unwelcome it was.

But it wasn't as Llys feared. Adam's shrug had been a vain attempt to shake off a vague feeling of foreboding. As an experienced hunter he strained to hear any suspicious sound. Instead, he became aware of the unnatural silence descending about them—as if by their stillness the woodland creatures warned him of lurking dangers.

Adam glanced back toward the women riding behind him. Their reactions appeared a clear sign that they, too, sensed something amiss. A faint grimness, he noticed, had replaced the gentle worry on Lady Brynna's face while Llys's apprehension seemed far more obvious. Her hands formed the familiar triangle while berry-sweet lips moved without sound. He assumed they were forming the eerie words of a Druid's prayer. Already he had come near to believing these enchantresses did in truth possess the gift of an affinity with nature.

Intending to make it more difficult for anyone waiting in ambush to pick off stragglers, Adam motioned his followers to move into as tight a group as possible amid a wildwood thick with trees and flourishing vegetation.

Z-z-zwing! Thwack! At the unmistakable sound of an arrow whistling through the quiet, followed by its solid smack into flesh, the swords of the men at either end of the band sang in their unsheathing. Stray shafts of sunlight pierced the gloom to glitter over sharp edges. Other men's weapons—daggers, spears, and clubs—also were menacingly raised, while a close, protective circle formed around the two women.

"Who is down?" Adam's question, though soft, was a growl so low it demanded an instant response.

After the briefest of pauses to take stock of their small force, Cedric responded, "No one of ours."

This surprising news turned amber eyes upon the speaker. "Then who?"

"'Twas me—Orm, youngest son of Ulford—who shot the vermin tracking you."

The party from Throckenholt turned as one toward the slight figure of a towheaded adolescent of mayhap sixteen summers stepping from between two towering trees with lowered bow in hand.

"Had to do it," a diffident Orm added. "How else could I safely beckon you into following me so as to secure treatment for Lord Wulf who lies mortally injured."

Adam glanced toward Lady Brynna. Though she was mute, in eyes deepened to gloomiest gray he saw the pain of worst fears confirmed. Even Cub, who—once fed—had slept quietly throughout their journey, seemed to sense his mother's distress. He woke and began a soft wail of protest.

The sight of Llys leaning close to lend her foster mother comfort brushed Adam, too, with a heartening moment of warmth against a bleak outlook. Under the spell of the beauty's compassion, he smiled faintly while watching Lady Brynna quiet her son even as she directly met his gaze with a wordless plea to hasten onward. Adam was also anxious to see aid reach Wulf, but the first step must be to make certain they would be led straight rather than astray.

"Who was it that first sounded the hunting horn?" Adam calmly asked. "And who is it now that so oft blows the summons?"

"'Twere Maelvyn who blew it first." Orm earnestly nodded a head of near white hair to indicate his understanding of the purpose behind these questions. "But I doubt you then heard its call, as 'tweren't much of a noise and made in the darkest hours." He grimaced in disgust.

Orm realized he'd strayed from his purpose, sheepishly shrugged, and continued. "'Twere my father, brothers, and I what hastened to answer that night call, and 'twere us what carried Lord Wulf to safety. Then 'twere my brother Ewell blew the horn early this morn—and got hisself coshed for doin' it. When he woke, the horn were gone. Proof 'tis as my father says: our enemies are cowards sneaking about in the night, avoiding an honest fight."

Suspicions near allayed, still Adam sought one more answer. "Do you know who sounds the horn now, thinking to trick us into harm's way?"

"Aye, Lord Adam." Orm proudly showed his knowledge of the famed warrior's identity while again nodding, although with considerably less fervor. "I know 'tis the same intruders what gave Father the gold coin to keep his tongue quiet."

"Thank you for your willingness to ease my suspicions." Adam gave Orm a grim smile. "And you proved your loyalty to Lord Wulf by taking quick action to free us of the foe tracking our path."

The youth swelled beneath the praise, and a bright grin bloomed despite the lingering of an honest concern for his lord.

"Now, as you've come to take us to your lord's aid,

Master Orm, let us be off with no moment's further delay."

In an instant Orm turned and set off at a trot easily matched by mounted followers. He guided them to a broad but shallow creek, absently calling back that these waters had originated from the spring behind Throckenholt Keep.

With his initial glimpse of the brook, Adam recognized the youth's intent and was impressed. Here was proof that Orm possessed the sharp wits and fine instincts to make him a wise tactician. It was clear that the course Orm had plotted would employ the best method for hiding their trail from trackers certain to come looking.

Splashing down the center of the stream's rippling waters while the mounted party rode in single file behind him, Orm continued onward. At length was seen a humble cottage with smoke rising lazily from an opening in the center of its roof to join a scattering of afternoon clouds beginning to gather across the once pristine blue of the sky.

"There lies my home," Orm proudly stated, motioning toward the little house seeming to rest peacefully in the center of a patch of land doubtless cleared with much toil.

All in all, the view of Orm's home indicated a simple yet comfortable existence—an impression confirmed by the appearance in the doorway of a beaming woman near as wide as she was tall. Though in her middle years, she could be no more than half her husband's age.

"Welcome to our house, Lady Brynna, Lord Adam." It seemed a well-rehearsed speech that had required every drop of courage the woman possessed, for she could only gulp and nod at Llys before stepping back and waving them inside.

Adam was not surprised to discover that once they'd all crowded inside, the abode's limited space was full to overflowing. Nonetheless, he took pains to politely thank Orm's awed mother and to greet Ulford as an old friend.

"'Twould've been too dangerous for Lord Wulf to linger here, you ken?" Ulford glanced nervously from Lord Adam to Lady Brynna and back, unsure if he ought to address his lady or the visiting lord. They both blessed him with reassuring smiles, and he went on with less hesitation.

"Secreted our lord away, we have. Took him off to a hidden refuge knowed to none save my family—and him. Maelvyn's been guardin' him since the wretched deed was done. And even he were blindfolded on the journey." Seeing their surprise that such was done to a man so important in the village, Ulford rushed to explain. "'Twere done 'cause were what Lord Wulf wanted. Said he would make certain sure our foes couldn't never force Maelvyn to tell its secret."

"Then blindfold us, if need be, but deliver me and our foster daughter with all haste to my husband's side." Holding a wide-awake and bright-eyed Cub in one arm, Brynna reached out to wrap the other around Llys's waist. "Pray let us waste no precious moment in seeing every possible deed done to restore your lord's health."

Ulford flushed with guilt for having failed to see that duty immediately performed.

"Too slow I am, milady. 'Twere why I sent Orm to fetch you. 'Tis why I send him now to lead you to Lord Wulf." Ulford nervously glanced sidelong at the golden man towering above the two ladies and cleared his throat. "Lord Adam, my lord says as what you should come, too. Albeit . . ." The word trailed into a tremor. "The others must remain here."

"Wulf is awake and able to speak?" This was the most heartening bit of news Brynna had yet been given.

"Aye. Sometimes." Ulford wrung his gnarled hands. "Be it other times he sleeps like the dea—" The last word was strangled by a horrified gasp echoed by a roomful of listeners.

Despite her own distress, the empathy that was so completely a part of Brynna's nature led her to gently pat Ulford's tightly gripped, age-spotted hands and give him a reassuring smile.

While Orm's mother hastened to provide her remaining guests with ale to quench their thirst, Brynna, Llys, and Adam were led from the cottage. Their guide carried in one hand a covered bucket of fresh water and under the other arm a bundle of resin-dipped rushes. Traveling now afoot, they moved directly into the dense forest behind the small dwelling. Orm explained as they went that several of his older brothers would take all the horses into a valley nearby where they could safely abide until needed again.

Moving over country more rugged than any Brynna had thought existed on her husband's otherwise gently rolling lands, they came to an unexpected rock outcropping. It was not high but broad at a base that looked like a solid wall of rough stone . . . until Orm showed the way through one of many long shadows and into a hidden cave.

Learning that Wulf's sickbed lay within natural surroundings lent the two of Druid heritage a measure of confidence reflected in the smile they exchanged. Indeed, this was the kind of familiar haven in which they had long dwelt. Here they were free to call upon the source of their powers, able to seek aid in restoring Brynna's beloved husband to health.

The deep gloom at the cave's entrance seemed to intensify as Orm boldly urged them to move forward through the darkness on a straight course over a downward path. Steep at the outset, it soon gentled, and a dim, flickering glow could be seen at the far end of an amazingly long passage. As they drew closer to that light's source they could see the pattern of shadows it sent to move across the rough surface of a stone wall at path's end. Following Orm in a sharp turn to the right, the seekers found their goal.

In one corner of the naturally formed chamber a crudely wrought three-legged iron stand supported a flaming resin-soaked torch. Llys blinked rapidly against the bright assault on dark-adjusted eyes. Squinting, she focused on a small ring of stones and the cook fire within, then looked beyond to the braced feet of a defender standing before a pallet laid directly on the floor.

At last Llys's attention moved over the patient, resting on the pallet, pale and either sleeping or unconscious. She instinctively offered a brief triad to restore Wulf, and another to lend her foster mother fortitude and comfort in her attempt to find the right combination of spells and potions for working that magic.

At the sound of their coming, the kneeling Maelvyn had leapt to his feet to courageously meet possibly threatening intruders with drawn sword at the ready. But when he caught sight of the new arrivals, his heartfelt relief found immediate expression.

"I thank God you are here, Lady Brynna!" The doubts Maelvyn had once harbored for the potency of her healing powers meant nothing against the problem at hand. "I've prayed to every saint whose name I could think of and begged God to speed you here!"

Adam remembered having made a similar plea for divine aid to help him find Llys . . . and he recalled too well his conviction the next morning that he'd been tricked by sorcery. As if it mattered, when the goal was won. And he much doubted anyone concerned would care in the least whether 'twas the gift of the Christians' God or the Druids' powers of nature so long as Wulf's life was saved.

Brynna resolutely moved past Maelvyn to the man apparently sleeping beneath a crude homespun blanket. And watching her, Adam for the first time questioned his earlier refusal to accept Wulf's reasoning that the God he believed had formed the world was also the source of the Druids' powers. He turned his thoughts from imponderable queries best set aside while questions of infinitely more immediate urgency must be answered now.

"How did it happen?" Adam quietly asked the clearly exhausted blacksmith.

As if marshaling his memories of the deed that had played over and over in his thoughts, Maelvyn wearily slid his sword back into its sheath and moved to crouch against the back wall before speaking.

"We spent hours combing the forest for sign of the missing maid. Night had well and truly fallen when we agreed to return home in hopes that you had succeeded where we failed—as I am thankful to see that you had." He glanced briefly at Llys, but his attention soon returned to unflinchingly meet Adam's gaze. "Of a sudden three men appeared, galloping straight toward us with blades bared. We gave a good account of ourselves—better than we got! Two were down and the third had turned tail to flee when some black-souled coward swooped down from the tree behind Lord Wulfayne and . . ." Maelvyn's pantomime of a blade slicing across his throat was far more chilling than could any words have been.

Brynna had been watching. She instantly turned and handed Cub to Llys before sinking down to kneel at her husband's side.

While her foster mother lifted the blanket away to carefully examine Wulf's wounds, Llys spread Cub's blanket in the corner opposite the torch. After settling the contented babe there, Llys began to unpack the satchel she'd carried into the cave. It was filled with vials and jars of elixirs and creams, a large number of clean cloth strips for bandages, as well as items to meet the mother and child's basic needs.

As she worked, Llys pondered all that Brynna had told her during the packing—the warning given by Evain and echoed by Glyndor of the ominous whirl-wind of dark powers rising from the earth to brew a storm the more menacing for its appearance at so precarious a time during nature's cycle of flowing energy. This was much as she had feared after her experience with Gytha and the black pendant. She had left the emblem of perverse powers carefully behind in the keep to await the moment she could pass it into Glyndor's hands. A deed Llys wished she'd done upon hearing him speak of a final battle. The conflict between him and Adam had so muddled her usually clear wits that she'd failed. Silently she offered a triad pleading for forgiveness and another begging help in seeing the pendant delivered to the one who could turn its dark powers to good purposes.

Brynna's careful scrutiny of Wulf's body revealed

naught but a few deep bruises and cuts. The latter must sting, yet they were likely as nothing compared to the slash at his throat that she'd put off viewing till last.

Llys had already set a small iron pot holding a portion of fresh water atop the fire's grate to boil when Brynna softly called. Together they began removing the heavily stained bandage crudely formed of strips torn from Maelvyn's cloak and affixed to Wulf's neck and throat.

Sensing Maelvyn's fear that he'd somehow failed to do a thing that would save his lord, Brynna glanced up to reassure him. "You did right to bind the wound firmly though not so tight as to constrict Wulf's breathing."

"Will he live?" Maelvyn's blunt question was the one of most importance to them all.

Before soaking the final piece of cloth in preparation for lifting it free where blood had clotted, Brynna responded. "That answer I can better provide if first you answer me this: when first he fell from his steed and the blood began to flow, did it spurt with the beat of his heart or slowly seep?"

"The latter . . . I think."

The warm smile Brynna set Maelvyn was answer enough to his query, and she bent her attention to freeing the wound of its less than clean wrapping. The injury was a livid slash from one side of Wulf's neck to the other. At the point on one end where it was deepest, red liquid began oozing anew.

Glancing over her shoulder to Adam, Brynna grimly announced, "My fears are proven true. 'Twould in truth have been deadly were Wulf hauled off to Throckenholt as he lies now. The journey would be certain to jostle and constantly reopen torn flesh."

Sorrowful gray eyes returned to caress the unconscious man. "Before any such undertaking is attempted, his wound must be given sufficient time to
mend."

Brynna directed Llys in how to help in the necessary tasks, during each of which together they would
sing powerful chants. While starting the lilting melody
with a soft, sweet triad of veneration, Brynna began
cleansing the gash with water Llys had set to heat and
into which had been mixed the tiniest drop of thyme
oil. The web of their enchanted words was spun faster
with strong notes of praise for this herb of mystical
powers able to forestall dangerous fevers. Then higher
rose elusive notes as Llys handed Brynna a jar containing an astringent salve, which she applied to a
white pad of folded cloth. Of a sudden the song
dropped into hushed words whose meaning was unknown to the men. Yet plainly they were an aching
plea made as the pad was softly laid across the livid
mark to be gently but firmly bound in place by
additional cloth strips.

When Brynna moved on to treat Wulf's lesser
injuries, a solemn Llys turned aside to lift Cub. The
baby, doubtless hungry, had begun to fuss. Although
Llys could do nothing to appease his hunger, she
tenderly rocked him while singing an old, old song of
comfort.

All three waking men had waited in what Adam
admitted could only be termed reverence while the
women sang mystical chants of incredible loveliness
and worked their healing charms. He couldn't—and
probably wouldn't even were it possible—prevent
himself from watching the young enchantress. Despite the immovable walls he still believed stood
betwixt them, erected by their diverse heritages, he

told himself it did no harm to watch from a safe distance. 'Twas true, his disbelief in a Druid's incantations had near evaporated. How could he dispute their power when he'd seen it proven? Indeed, in Llys's rescue, he'd been its agent. Yet distrust lingered.

Wulf claimed that their powers flowed from God, but was the reverse of divine power not also a likely source? And while Llys's chants seemed pure and of bright intent, what of the abbey sorceress? Were the two women not truly one and the same? And even if they were two separate beings, did their powers not flow from the same spring? Adam's early memories of a woman had taught him what he deemed a bleak fact—that all women were unworthy either of trust or of the love certain to expose his vulnerabilities to pain. So how had this enchantress so thoroughly invaded his defenses and twined herself into his heart?

Golden brows met in a fierce frown. This mental debate over the source and purpose of Druidic powers accomplished naught but the further endangerment of the already weakened platform of doctrines he'd been taught to hold dear. At risk was the faith he'd shared with the two beloved Aelfrics of his family. Guilt over the prospect of being a disappointment to them raised an invisible but infinitely more durable wall between him and the beauty amber eyes now stared at without seeing.

Wulf slowly roused under a familiar loving touch and gazed up into the lovely face of the mysterious sorceress who years past had captured his heart when for the first time he opened his eyes to find her treating his injuries. When Brynna found emerald eyes open and watching her, she was so overwhelmed with a relief that quiet tears welled up and spilled down soft cheeks. She had feared him hovering in the kind of half-life where Anya had so recently dwelt.

"Love you . . ." Wulf's voice was harsh and unable to speak above a whisper.

Brynna quickly laid her fingers across his lips and told him not to talk, but he moved his head very slightly from side to side and kissed the fingers blocking his mouth.

"Must . . ." It was plain that, though the words were difficult, he felt he must speak despite her disapproval. "Adam . . ."

Gracefully surrendering to his likely important wishes, Brynna turned and repeated the call too quiet to be heard by the frowning man.

Adam immediately approached the sorely wounded man and, seeing Brynna's discomfort with the situation, nodded his silent acknowledgment of the need for preserving the man's strength.

"I'm relieved that we've reached you in time for your Brynna to work the magic able to see you fully restored."

Wulf gave a strained smile in response.

"I go to make a strong tisane." As Brynna reluctantly rose she cast a stern look first upon her husband and then upon Adam. "But when 'tis ready, Wulf, you must drink it *all*. It will do many good things, not least of which will be the easing of you into a healing slumber."

"So be it." Adam gave the woman a wry smile. "The challenge of limited time we accept." He immediately turned his attention to Wulf. "Let me first tell you all that we have learned." Adam wasted no moment to assure him of having found Llys and then passed on the tale of her abductors—the bishop, two sorceresses, and Hordath, the man their king had assigned to keep a tight rein on his rebellious son, Saexbo. And, too, he stated his belief that this confirmed all their worst suspicions.

"Pray . . ." Wulf's single word was an effort yet he struggled with more. "Protect . . . mine."

"I give you an oath on my father's crucifix that I will do as you have asked." Adam quietly swore, and in a firm gesture of honor clasped his forearm to the one Wulf had painstakingly lifted. As Wulf could do nothing to remedy the wrong of either a slain messenger or the warning undelivered to their king, Adam had chosen not to burden the wounded man with news of these complications added to an already simmering stew of difficulties.

Although Brynna stood behind the man kneeling at her husband's side, Wulf had one more thing to say.

"Maelvyn . . . needed."

"Aye." Adam nodded even as he glanced toward the man who'd stood guard over his lord. "A good smith may be necessary to see this battle won. But I'll send Cedric to take his place as your protector."

Wulf merely smiled, too tired to speak again, near too tired to drink the first of the many potions Brynna meant to insist he consume.

Adam rose, and Maelvyn, having heard the exchange, also scrambled to his feet. The two of them turned toward Orm, patiently waiting in the shadows.

"We ought be off." Orm made no attempt to shield his relief that they appeared ready to depart. He'd been given responsibility for them and 'twas time and past to be gone but nowise could he have commanded a lord to do his bidding. "The sun falls fast toward day's end. You and all of yours must get safe from the forest afore nightfall, when dastardly cowards skulk in darkness to strike from behind."

Adam's answering smile was grim. He could but acknowledge what recent events had proven. Danger did linger in the night forest, long the province of thieves and cowards too weak to stand against their foes in the truth-revealing light of day. With brisk words he summoned the young enchantress to join them in preparation for an immediate departure. No matter his ambivalent feelings for Llys, it was she that he most wanted to see freed of the dense woodland's peril.

Llys handed Cub to Brynna and gave them both a quick hug before joining the men. She followed directly behind Orm while Adam and Maelvyn came after. In single file they slipped into the deep gloom of a passage through stone and climbed up to the daylight at its end.

Chapter
14

"Pip, you don't understand." Maida's soft brown eyes gleamed with tears perilously near to falling. The pair of them stood in the herb corner's shadows while the hearth's firelight bathed the pallet where an apparently oblivious Anya quietly played with a small group of figures formed of twigs and tied together with rags.

"Do you disdain me because your lover is of higher birth? Am I not fine enough for you?" Pip's bruised pride rebelled against her rejection. And no matter her flimsy defense, a rejection it plainly was, the certainty of which dimmed his spirits as thoroughly as twilight's descending haze blurred the horizon. "Only did I offer you a gift many another would welcome."

"The honor you would do me is a glimmering fantasy I would pay any price to attain . . . but never can it be."

The quiet desperation of her words failed to penetrate Pip's swelling indignation. He drew himself up to his full, impressive size while a sneer poorly shielded the pain behind the words he spoke. "Mayhap you prize the beatings of a nobleman more than the heart of a simple man who can claim no station in life greater than to say he is free and strong and held in honorable esteem by his lord."

"But there lies the problem all in all." Maida's tears flowed in earnest. "'Tis I who am not free." Voice muffled by the hands into which she lowered a flushed face in the hope of concealing her shame, she added, "Worse still, I am escaped from my master, the son of King Ecgferth."

As the explanation formed of melded hopelessness and shame fell from the weeping girl's lips, to Pip it sounded the death knell of his dreams. "Saexbo owns you."

Although it was not a question but rather a statement, Maida answered. "Nay. 'Tis the king who owns me, but he gave me into his youngest son's service."

"And 'twas Saexbo who fathered your babe?"

Maida's shame deepened, yet she nodded. "But he would deny it, were his royal sire to ask. And were Saexbo to discover I'd said as much to you or to anyone else, he would beat me until I no longer drew breath . . . as he has near done afore and more than once."

"Then I will barter with the king for your freedom." It was a desperate scheme that Pip well knew was unlikely to succeed. In the back of his thoughts stirred a faint relief that he'd sent the house thralls to their homes when the day was half gone, unknowingly lending privacy to this difficult scene, one able only to deepen tension in those awaiting the return of a band of rescuers and the news they'd bring—at best merely unhappy.

Maida gave Pip a forlorn smile of intended comfort. "You cannot afford the price Saexbo would demand his father seek in payment, if only to ensure that I never escape his cruel hold or reveal the brief existence of the tiny son who survived scarce three days." Mention of the babe who had died without a proper chance to live brought on a fresh bout of tears.

Into his strong arms Pip pulled the girl, whose resistance to him had long since faded into nothing. For the first time he felt inadequate to meet a challenge. While Maida silently sobbed against him, he discovered that the prize he most wanted from life could not be won by the physical might he took for granted. That realization opened an empty cavern in his soul, an endless need that could only be filled by this woman who literally belonged, body and soul, to another man—nay, to a vicious overgrown child.

"He can demand the price only if first you are recaptured." With this sudden and surely inspired scheme a bubble of relief welled up inside Pip. "Together we'll flee so deep into the trackless forest they will never find us."

"I would feel like the lowest of loathsome snakes were I responsible for your breaking of faith with Lord Adam. You claim he holds you in honorable esteem but the theft of a thrall would assuredly destroy his respect for you." Small hands curled into fists lightly pushing against a broad chest as Maida gazed earnestly up into Pip's frown. "Only think what such an action would do to your good name.

"And what of the family you view with such affection? Consider the shadow of shame that would be cast upon them if you were proclaimed a wolf's-head, ever hiding in the forest like a common thief, which in truth you would be if you stole a prince's property."

Pip listened to this unexpected wisdom from the woman so quickly become essential to him, wishing her arguments were not so dishearteningly logical. That Maida was unselfishly concerned for the ill it would do him rather than grasping for a hold to draw herself up from the mire of slavery only left Pip to love her the more.

"Besides," Maida calmly added, anxious to dissuade Pip from a course that could bring him naught but misfortune, "all such plans matter little, since I am as certain we'd soon be found as I am that Saexbo already knows precisely where I've spent these past days."

"How could he possibly know?" Disgust for the callow prince tinged Pip's words as, without a moment's pondering on the matter, he dismissed the possibility.

"Have you forgotten the woman who came here pretending to be Llys?" The quick grimace creasing Pip's broad face lightened Maida's tension enough to go on. "Doubtless she will have reported my whereabouts, leastways to those who, although Saexbo's subjects, are in truth his masters." Her scorn for an erstwhile owner and his cohorts went unshielded.

"Then why, pray tell, has Saexbo failed to demand your return, as is every freeman's lawful right?" Pip tried to infuse the question with skepticism, not wanting to believe that the treacherous prince was so well informed.

Maida steadily met the gaze of the only man who had ever viewed her as a person rather than an object of limited use. "Doubtless he finds the cost in time and toil of recapturing a worthless slave an unnecessary expenditure, what with events moving forward so smoothly."

Pip frowned and Maida rushed to clarify her reasoning.

"'Tis of small concern to him whether I am retaken today, tomorrow, or the day following when he is convinced that his assault upon Throckenholt will effect the same end soon enough."

"Are you so certain of his plans?" Pip asked.

"They're not Saexbo's plans." Maida sharply shook recently washed and shining brown hair. "But 'tis all the same, for in his name they are—by what I've heard here—being carried inexorably toward the end long intended."

Once again to the doorway, open to summer warmth lingering even at dusk, came unnoticed arrivals. Feeling Adam go rigid at the words overheard, Llys quickly took stock of the scene and all its players. A quietly watchful Anya sat on the hearthside pallet motionless and listening. The house thralls were nowhere to be seen, and the table was bare—a sorry sight with which to greet people returning from an even sorrier duty.

"What plans are these? What end do our enemies seek?" Adam's questions, directed at Maida, were harsher than would have been allowed had he not come so unexpectedly upon a conversation hinting at significant facts withheld and yet not as harsh as the bitter disgust in his next question. "And how is it that you know Saexbo so well?"

For all her honest desire to protect Pip from blame for her wrongs, these abrupt queries sounded like an obvious threat to her safety, and Maida's tenuous courage scattered. She instinctively turned to Pip and buried her face in the firm support of his broad chest.

Cradling the frail woman near, Pip immediately defended her from his lord's startling inquisition, answering the final question. "'Twas Saexbo who left Maida so thoroughly abused. He treated her, his thrall, with the same disesteem a man might show a dog." Pip's face hardened. "Nay, a hunting dog most men would treat with far more respect."

Llys's tender heart went out to Maida. The theory behind one member of humankind enslaving another was something she could not understand and far less accept. Compassion sent her two steps toward the trembling girl, distressed by the vision of timid Maida being subjected to any man's demeaning, vicious control.

Even as the cold questions fell from his lips, Adam regretted asking them. He inwardly berated himself for allowing strain spawned by a tangle of wild events to knock him so far off his normal stride he'd spoken so sharply to this girl that she cowered from him in fear. Clearly she needed gentle handling, a task Pip was apparently willing—nay, anxious—to shoulder.

"Striking a female, free or slave, is a weak man's attempt to appear strong." Filled with remorse for the wrong of words she'd likely felt as blows, Adam softened his low voice to a penitent tone, one lent power by his unhidden shame for the ill-said words. "Never have I been so lacking in confidence that I would lower myself to such despicable acts. And I crave pardon from you both for the unwarranted harshness of my questions."

Pip, relieved to see his lord's temper returned to its normal tight control, accepted the apology with a brilliant smile.

Maida's confidence was not so easily won, but she peeked from the protection of Pip's embrace and met the direct and steady gaze of amber eyes. In their unflickering depths Maida believed she glimpsed the soul of an honest man and a lord worthy of Pip's loyalty.

Despite regret for the barrage of callous questions, Adam dared not leave the matter unresolved. However, he trod onward with considerable care.

"With Llys's naming of those responsible for her abduction, the note left with the dead messenger, and my knowledge of the members of King Ecgferth's court and their relative positions, I've a fair notion of what is planned and the purpose behind it." Adam's words were calm, and he gave Maida a smile, albeit somewhat grim. At the same time he stepped full into the hall, quietly shutting the door. The action closed the small group inside a room grown dim with naught but the hearth's fire and the failing illumination of dusk to provide light.

"However," Adam said while advancing to halt at Llys's side, "your confirmation of my theories along with any details of what is soon to befall us may well mean the difference between an adequate defense and utter defeat. Maida, toward the goal of safety for yourself, for Pip, and for all of Throckenholt's own, will you share your knowledge with me?"

Llys sensed the tension turning the golden warrior's hands into clenched fists. Sharing his concern for the conflict undeniably looming ever nearer, she instinctively leaned closer into his aura of strength while at the same time offering him wordless support and compassion.

Maida's dark eyes flashed toward the encouragement on Pip's face before she took the risk of giving Lord Adam her trust.

"I will." The words were faint, and the instant after the brief compliance was given, Maida again buried her face against Pip.

Llys glanced up at the powerful man beside her who had all too often proved his ability to summon her attention without words. Adam felt the whisper-soft caress of blue eyes and could not resist answering their appeal. His reward was the tender smile blooming on rose-petal lips whose nectar he remembered so well that they were a temptation near able, even here before curious spectators and amid dire challenges, to draw him down to taste them once again.

Gazing into the amber eyes that had so quickly answered Llys's silent call—surely proof that whether he willed it so or not, Adam was as sensitive to her as she to him—the ache of his day-long rejection of her was soothed in some small measure.

But still, in the look they exchanged, she delivered a wordless plea for his patience with Maida. After having won a faint answering smile from the mouth that had been harsh moments earlier, she turned and crossed the room. Once standing beside the pair oddly mismatched in height, she lightly patted Maida's back and praised her for her brave willingness to aid her Throckenholt friends.

Adam acknowledged the fact that timid Maida, overwhelmed by a confrontation he'd been fool enough to precipitate, was unable to immediately continue. At the same time he saw with what trust Maida leaned against his young guardsman and the tender emotion with which her action was met. The sight awoke a longing in the dark depths of Adam's heart. Though mocking himself for the feeling, he wished that Llys could as guilelessly turn to him and that he could provide the same measure of untainted love. Cynicism curled one side of his mouth down. A sorceress without guile? And, from him, a love unstained by bleak experience? Impossible.

The last thought forced from Adam's throat an

unintended growl of disgust. In response the other three adults were startled into glancing toward him. They, as well as a young and watchful Anya, saw the tide of red creeping over strong cheeks.

Adam was mortified by the blush—a reaction he had not encountered since leaving childhood behind. Still he restrained the urge to either turn away or snarl his displeasure that it was so. He instead calmly spoke of an important matter cast into shadow initially by the unexpected possibility of firsthand information and then by intense emotion.

"Lord Wulf has been so seriously injured that moving him even the smallest distance would be unwise. Indeed, 'twould likely have killed him to endure the long, rough journey home."

Realizing that this news had only deepened the confusion of the couple who'd remained at Throckenholt, Adam felt compelled to explain the precise nature of Wulf's injury. Though emotionlessly stated, the harsh description both made plain the dilemma they'd faced and wordlessly justified the choice to leave Wulf behind in secret safety. Adam did not reveal the ealdorman's whereabouts.

Although Pip had known their host only a few weeks and Maida but a brief number of days, both were distressed by this news of so grave an injury. Yet their response was as nothing compared to the pain in Anya's quiet gasp—a reminder of her nearness that struck the adults with guilt for having forgotten the girl's presence.

Again as so oft of recent times, Adam was struck with guilt—an emotion he had rarely felt or deserved before this adventure had begun at Winbury Abbey. The tears glistening in the child's wide green eyes were the gentlest blame. He had been impressed by this young girl's decidedly unchildish ability to sit in motionless tranquillity listening attentively to all that was said—until this unhappy revelation of her father's fearsome wound. A wound he had described in a graphic detail that with wise reflection he would never have spoken before a child, far less the daughter of its victim.

"Fret not." Llys quickly moved to take Anya in a comforting embrace while reassuring her that all would be well. "Your mother and I have chanted our entreaties to nature's most beneficent powers and performed the deeds able, in the passing of time, to see your sire restored."

Despite proof lent by the revived good health of Wulf's white-faced daughter, Adam was nowise convinced of the sorceresses' ability to heal Wulf's wound. Lowering an impassive mask over handsome features, he shielded his doubts from the others. They faced troubles enough without knowing about the likelihood of the Lord of Throckenholt's demise, a loss that would surely sap the will of the local people to stand firm against aggressors. But if these two could be convinced of a Druid's powers to heal, then villagers already in awe of Brynna's curative talents would surely find it easy to accept that reassurance. Moreover, the prospect of such a remedy was as certain to spread as the news of Wulf's injury.

To shift the others' attention from an unpleasant reality they could do nothing to change, he returned to the abandoned subject. But this time he approached it judiciously and with words spoken in a voice carefully lowered into the dark velvet depths of a gentle invitation.

"Maida, mayhap later"—firelight gilded his thick mane as Adam moved toward the shadowed corner where she stood with Pip—"once we've supped, you'll tell me what you know of approaching dangers. Or if not tonight, then after we've slept. I fear no one here has been blessed with overmuch rest in many days, and if what you seem to suggest be true, we all may need revived strength and refreshed wits to meet what comes." Adam's white smile flashed a strong man's confidence.

Willing to comply and yet thankful for the temporary reprieve, Maida shifted her attention from the intimidating golden lord who filled even this sizable hall with his presence. Pulling away from Pip's embrace to tentatively approach the woman still cradling a child, she began a long delayed litany of thanks to the one whose return brought with it a renewed sense of tender comfort and warmth.

"I wanted to tell you of my gratitude for your welcome of a ragged stranger arrived unbidden to the keep's door, but there was no time before you left in search of Lord Wulf. And though I failed to do that deed prior to your capture by Saexbo's cohorts, I prayed for your safety each day you were held prisoner. I prayed, too, that the other, the impostor, would be gone." Her smile brightened. "God answered my prayers and for that I shall praise him always."

Anya had returned to calm, and Llys lowered her to the floor before giving a quick hug to the abused girl likely too familiar with the distress of unwelcome restraints. But a perplexed frown furrowed Llys's brow as Maida's words repeated in her mind. The other? A myriad of events had risen to tangle her thoughts as well as to demand both toil and attention since Adam had brought her back to Throckenholt. Was it only this morning? So much had occurred it seemed an aeon had passed.

In that lay her excuse for having purposefully kept her mind from pondering the strange accusations Adam had made after they'd awakened—pastel shades of dawn bathing bodies as closely bonded as the stones of the mystical cromlech behind them. Llys's frown tightened under pain increased by memory of the hurtful loss caused by Adam's incomprehensible repudiation of her. Leastwise incomprehensible till now when Maida, who knew nothing of that one-sided dispute, lent a measure of clarity by also speaking of another woman. Moreover, she spoke of the other, apparently Llys's double, as simple fact.

"Gave me a bad turn it did," Maida continued, "when you opened the keep's door that first night. But the moment you smiled and gently drew me inside, I knew you weren't the other one."

"What other one?" Three voices simultaneously demanded.

A startled Maida stammered her answer. "E-E-Elesa, of course." Her audience looked more expectant than informed and she stumbled on, striving to explain. "The younger sorceress. . . ." Still no sign of enlightenment. "The younger of the two drawn into the scheme by the bishop."

Doubting her ability to make the matter clearer, Maida glanced up toward Pip, who'd moved to stand at her shoulder. His encouraging smile lent her the spirit to firmly continue despite a lord's golden frown and Llys's obvious concern.

"Saexbo thought 'twas a fine jest, what with the

supposed piety of Bishop Wilfrid proposing the inclusion of Druids in their scheme." As she recalled the scene, Maida's lips lifted in a shy grin. "'Twas Hordath who stormed about—until he caught sight of Elesa. She cast her lures and pulled the man in like a big old bottom-feeding fish, and never did I hear him question the alliance again."

The white flash of Adam's smile rewarded Maida's increasing bravery. He had been sincere in his offer to allow Maida time to accustom herself to the notion of sharing what she knew of that strange alliance. However, once she'd begun of her own accord he deemed it wisest to continue onward before her apprehensions could again grow to daunting proportions.

"These two sorceresses, then, are the woman called Gytha, whom Llys met in the abbey while prisoner and this Elesa, who you say is the image of Llys?"

Maida nodded without hesitation but curiously questioned the lord's wording. "Do you not think Elesa looks as near to Llys as the reflection of the sky on a still pond?"

Adam forced a pleasant smile although a possibility once questioned that now seemed confirmed rasped a raw wound. If there were in truth two separate women with the same face, it meant he must squarely meet and admit his previous night's sin in taking an innocent woman's virtue. Guilt dug the deeper for his having wrongly used his disdain of Llys's heritage to block an indisputable fact from his mind, one proven in the midst of their passion. She had been untouched before he seduced her into matching his desire. And seduce her he had. Her willingness to surrender to a man of his experience did not excuse his misdeed any more than did the useless love he felt for her. A further growl of self-disgust died unheard in his throat.

Llys saw golden flames in amber eyes and sensed the disgust behind Adam's mask. She'd no doubt that Maida's words had been a potent reminder to him of his rejection of her, at the same time stripping away his excuse for repudiating her. Further, Llys felt certain that both this moment's emotion and the morning's denial were in reality born of regret for the sweet delight of their joining. Proof that he, like a skilled hunter who loses his taste for the prey once the thrill of the chase is past, wanted only to distance himself from their passionate encounter. Although she ought to have felt relieved at the removal of his threat to her link with nature, a pain she feared never ending confirmed it was not so.

Facing the other couple, Pip and Maida stood waiting with growing curiosity. Adam was first to sunder the silence allowed to linger far too long. To address the looming peril he temporarily pushed aside a deserved guilt for his wrongful deed.

"But why? What did the conspirators think to win by sending the impostor here?"

This was a query whose answer Maida had heard explained by the deed's perpetrators. "Hordath asked the same question, and the bishop assured him a sorceress in the midst of their enemy's camp would be able to create diversions and forestall strategies what might elsewise bring defeat upon them."

"But surely they knew she would be found out?" Adam thought their scheme a risky venture and questioned the wits of those involved in its planning.

Maida lifted her hands in an aimless wave. "They deemed it likely that nearing dangers would so distract the attention of those dwelling here that they'd fail to note small differences in manner."

Dark gold brows furrowed with disgust at the memory of how nearly that ploy had succeeded.

With hands now clasped tightly together, Maida solemnly continued. "Believed they that only the eyes of innocence would soon see through her guise."

An amber gaze met one of deep blue in wordless recognition of the reasoning behind the deadly trick played and the spell cast upon Anya.

"One question more I would ask of you." Adam turned a face carefully stripped of emotion toward the source of half-suspected explanations. "Did you hear these conspirators speak of me or my brother Aelfric?"

"Aye." Maida promptly nodded. "Your brother discovered that something beyond the work of God was being performed at the abbey. The bishop and Hordath had heated words on the dangers presented by his threat to write you with the revelation. What was to be done I did not hear, but . . ."

Adam's face was no longer merely expressionless. It had gone to cold stone. Although he had supposed as much, here was confirmation that Aelfric had been slain to silence him. It could only have been a fearful shock for Wilfrid when Adam appeared and spoke of the letter he'd received—news that had prompted the attempt to kill him.

"The bishop, a prince and his keeper, and two Druid sorceresses." Adam spoke in tightly controlled disgust, amazed by the odd collection of confederates that greed had spliced together.

Despite the golden lord's dark expression, Maida promptly responded. "But all together they represent only the springs providing water intended to flow together and then join others to become a mighty ocean of invincible power."

"What additional rivers are expected to merge in forming this ocean?" The chill of Adam's question was at odds with the flame in amber eyes.

"The seized shire of Throckenholt, added to the lands of Winbury Abbey, is meant to provide a strong base of power." Maida bolstered a wavering courage with the bright possibility of playing a role in seeing Saexbo and his cohorts fail. "Bishop Wilfrid told the others if that task is successfully done, he has the king of Mercia's sworn oath to lend his support in an attempt to wrest the crown from King Ecgferth."

Cold and expressionless, Adam's face revealed nothing of the surprise he felt. He had expected an attempt to seize the crown by the petulant youngest prince elsewise unlikely to reign but the possibility that the king of another of the five Saxon kingdoms would join the fray was infinitely more ominous. This revelation made it all the more imperative that the conflict be crushed before it grew into an all-encompassing war between kingdoms. He knew, as the bishop and Hordath ought, that should widespread conflict occur, Northumbria would be carved into insignificant pieces.

"They'll never take Throckenholt." Llys's statement contained calm certainty. "Talacharn's prince is Wulf's loyal ally and keeps a close watch. If he received reports of any threat to the neighbor sharing a common border, Prince Cai will descend from the mountains leading a force whose participants are in numbers I doubt the bishop and his conspirators expect." Slight shoulders shrugged beneath their cloak of black curls. "Between the Cymry force and Wulf's fyrd, the goal cherished by Saexbo and the bishop will be forestalled."

Despite all the dangers lurking near, of this single fact Llys was confident. Whether the Cymry force would be of as much use as she'd implied with the hope of lending encouragement was another matter since circumstances would have to be dire indeed for Prince Cai to appear. Llys bit hard at her lip. If Maida's tale was true—and Llys didn't doubt that it was—the situation *was* dire. Indeed, 'twas as Glyndor had foretold—a gathering of menacing powers during a dangerous time of restive natural powers.

Llys glanced toward Adam to see if her attempt to lend encouragement had been of use. The surprise and suspicion joined to furrow golden brows could only mean that Wulf had chosen not to tell Adam of Cai's promised assistance during their rides through the forest or long talks of lurking foes. But then, she ought have expected as much, considering Wulf's decision never to rely upon what he deemed a dubious defense built on the less than firm mooring of a secondhand loyalty, a promise not to Wulf but to Glyndor.

"Glyndor and Evain have yearly led Cai, prince of Talacharn, in publicly reaffirming his oath to come to Wulf's aid in time of need." Llys believed Prince Cai's solemnly given word would be upheld, but still she wished Wulf had spoken of the arrangement to Adam, as she doubted that Adam would accept it as a fact by her claim alone.

"The Welsh take their oaths most seriously. Should Cai renege on a promise given, his position would be forfeit, for in that country a prince holds his position not by birthright alone but by the will of a free people. So you see, Maida"—Llys smiled warmly at the girl whose knit brows revealed her bewilderment at the concept—"the lands you say must be joined in order to lure the Mercian king into their battle never will be united."

Llys spoke with the authority of one well acquainted with Prince Cai and aware of the utter trust he had placed in Glyndor since the bloodless defeat and humiliation of his predecessor, Vortimer, by virtue of a magical event known as "the great death of birds" in which she and Evain had aided Brynna.

As Llys finished her confident claim, Maida reluctantly explained the bishop's wretched scheme to foil Welsh assistance for Throckenholt. "That arrangement is well known in this area of Northumbria and is the reason why the bishop enlisted the aid of two sorceresses." Maida's face was bleak under a mixture of regret and alarm. "Gytha swore she would weaken Prince Cai's call to arms by destroying the faith of his people in Glyndor's powers."

"Gytha can't do that." Llys serenely smiled, yet behind her confidence lay sorrow. This was clearly the battle Glyndor had foreseen—the one that Brynna said the aging sorcerer welcomed as the end to his mortal existence.

Adam was not comforted by Llys's belief in her mentor or by her trust in a foreign prince's promised aid. No matter the mystical rites these Druids might perform, he firmly believed the looming conflict would be won or lost by human strength and cunning.

Noting that Adam was unable to trust in aid from Talacharn, and aware of her inability to convince him elsewise, Llys turned her attention to Anya. The youngster had returned to sit on the hearthside pallet, listening to talk of war with small chin bravely lifted despite the apprehension widening pale green eyes.

"Help me in a quest?"

Anya looked up questioningly. "For what?"

"For food sufficient to placate two huge warriors likely elsewise to become ravening beasts." With mock terror, Llys glanced sidelong at Adam. He obliged by growling again, although this time his snarl was velvet thunder that dissolved into a teasing grin even as he swept down upon Anya like a predator scooping up tender quarry.

Anya broke into giggles, and the merry sound lightened the spirits of all. The foolery continued as the child stood atop a chair at her father's table and, like a master commanding his servants, directed the adults in a search through baskets stored on the long shelves of the windowless wall and inside barrels beneath.

The hour was late for dining when at last the odd assortment of child, lord, sorceress, guardsman, and thrall gathered without thought to their disparate positions at a table whose planks were bare of white covering deemed unnecessary. By the flickering light of massed candles intensified by their placement atop a silver platter, they shared a quick repast of cold salt meat, slabs of deep yellow cheese, and hunks of bread baked the previous day. It was a simple meal and yet one warmed by the camaraderie born of their unspoken awareness of a common foe to be met.

They used damp cloth squares to wipe from hands the sweet residue of the special treat concluding their meal—freshly harvested peaches. Once done, Llys lifted Anya, small for her six years and light as thistledown, carried the child into her tiny chamber, and put her to bed.

The departure of Llys with Anya was the unspoken signal for the gathering's end, and those remaining at table rose. Adam moved to drop into a hearthside chair and stare into the fire, seeking certainty for troubling concepts he'd once thought firm but now questioned. However, the constantly shifting pattern of flames seemed merely a visual demonstration of his own unsteady doubts. Assaulted with self-contempt for his inability to prevent the sweet sorceress from interfering with his cool and rational thought processes, he picked up a thin, sturdy branch stripped of twigs. Wielding the tool with far more fervor than was justified, he prodded new life into a fire that should instead have been banked with ashes to see coals burn throughout the night.

On returning to the hall, Llys found that Pip and Maida had slipped back into the relative privacy of the herb corner's shadows, plainly intent on a few final moments together. Adam was sitting—definitely not resting—in one of the hearthside chairs while stabbing at half-burned logs and giving complete attention to the fire storm of sparks his action roused.

Llys decided 'twould be best to unobtrusively slip into her bedchamber without bothering the man who throughout the long day had demonstrated his wish to be apart from her—a disheartening fact Llys wished were untrue. She stepped through her small chamber's doorway, shoulders slumped under the weight of forlorn realities and memories of sweet delights gone sour for having been so soon disdained by her partner in their creation.

"I've come to plead forgiveness for my wrong."

At the soft thunder of words spoken so near, Llys abruptly turned to find the golden man filling the doorway. Her thoughts had been consumed by him, by intimate memories she'd treasure always no matter their pain, and now the physical impact of his unexpected proximity was wildly unsettling. With the pulse of her blood pounding in her ears, she comprehended no part of his request.

Adam gazed down into eyes of a sudden darkening to ebony. Did this woman so recently a virgin have any notion of what a temptation she was? Despite the heated hours of the previous night he thought not and warned himself to step back. Wulf had left this maid in his care and appointed him her guardian. It was a duty he meant to perform even though she needed to be protected from him—a man guilty at the outset but determined not to fall again.

After dark hours spent in his arms, Llys recognized the intensity of desire on Adam's face, and as he started to withdraw she closed the distance betwixt them. Although aware somewhere in the haze of her unthinking mind that he had not come seeking another night of fire and sweetness, she sensed this might well be her last opportunity to steal a few precious moments in the embrace of the man she loved. 'Twas a goal made more urgent by the fact that already he had demonstrated the ease with which he was able to turn from her, a sorceress whose inexplicable powers he mistrusted. That bleak memory added desperation to her determination to keep him from so soon abandoning her.

Fearing there'd be no future opportunity as promising as this, Llys wrapped her arms about powerful shoulders and laid her cheek lightly against his broad chest. She could hear the exciting sound of his heartbeat, pounding as fast and hard as her own. Rubbing her cheek against that strong wall of wool-covered flesh, she smiled as muscles flexed in revealing answer to her embrace. This involuntary response summoned wildly exciting memories—the feel of firm bronze skin and abrasive hair, memories that aroused pleasant sensations.

Under the control required to tamp down flames of desire fanned by the feel of tempting curves pressed against him, Adam tightened his jaw. Lying to himself that privacy for seeking forgiveness would see the deed more easily fulfilled, Adam wrapped his arms about Llys and urged her back a step into the small chamber. Once inside, he made what he knew for a moonling's error the moment it was done. He nudged the door shut behind him, closing them into dangerously tight confines intimately lit by the weak light of a single candle.

Berating himself for a fool and meaning to put her aside, Adam slid strong hands beneath a thick black cloud of silky hair to cup slender shoulders. He merely succeeded in forcing her to lean back, and when she glanced up, he found in a gaze gone soft with desire's dense mists a hunger as deep as his own. But his greatest mistake was made when his attention glided lower to drink in the delicious vision of alluring curves, soft and so temptingly near.

Filled with nameless wanting, Llys stopped breathing while molten honey eyes moved over her like a heated caress, lingering on bounty that all too clearly responded. When his gaze finally lifted she tumbled into the golden fires found in their depths even as his warm maleness beckoned her nearer still. She melted against him like wax to candle flame.

With the beauty melded to the hardening length of his form, Adam felt her tremble, heard the tiny catch in her breath, and his blood caught fire to race through his veins like windswept flame. As he realized that, unlike past experiences, the taking of Llys once had not lessened but rather had deepened his hunger for her, a low groan broke from Adam.

Llys heard the rough sound through a haze of passion while at the same time feeling him tense to reject her once more. To forestall the unwelcome action, she twined small fingers into strands of cool gold and unknowingly offered a most potent provocation.

Adam's honorable intent faltered when the pointed tip of her tongue darted out to touch a softly bowed upper lip. Beckoned by his own desire, Adam bent his golden head and surrendered to a desperate need to taste the ambrosia of her beguiling mouth once again. Crushing the enchantress full into his embrace, he gave her further proof of what dangers she provoked in teasing an experienced predator, building their kiss to a fever of passion so hungry a tiny moan welled up from her depths.

Reveling in the feel of Adam's hard mouth on hers, Llys lifted her body into the hard curve of his. 'Twas an action that tested the limits of Adam's control and proved them perilously near—so much for his famed restraint when so little of this sorceress's enticement threatened to break it.

Abruptly breaking the kiss, Adam gazed down at the woman in his arms. She was trembling wildly, her creamy cheeks passion-rosed and her soft lips moist, slightly swollen from his kiss and so tempting he still wondered if her allure was in truth born of a magic spell.

He acknowledged his mistake in giving in to the wish for time alone in her company, a threat to the right course for them both. But even an admonition this self-righteous was unable to cool the simmering heat of his blood. Indeed, even the honorable intention behind his determination never to claim her again only seemed to increase his desperate need for a last taste of the forbidden sorceress. Their diverse heritages ensured she could never belong to him, a fact that placed another, and to him far heavier, layer of gloom over an already dark tangle of dangerous challenges.

Although he desperately wanted far more of the yielding woman in his arms, he pulled away, knowing that if there be any hope of control, this embrace must stop *now*. He'd come to apologize for the theft of her chastity—an honorable intention threatening to end in the compounding of that wrong!

Still lost amid the cinders of a hungry fire, as Adam gently released her, Llys slumped against the wall's cool strength. She watched Adam quietly depart, wryly consoling herself with a fact revealed by the betraying rigidity of his clenched jaw. Plainly the end to their embrace had been as difficult for him as for her.

Once she was alone in the chamber's faint and flickering light, thick lashes dropped to her cheeks as if bearing the weight of doomed dreams. Fighting for cool logic to wield against the unhappiness of an expected yet unwelcome reality, she firmly reminded herself that his departure was doubtless a blessing to be welcomed. She should be grateful for this return to a serenity unshaken by any man's appeal—especially that of a Saxon who'd naught but disdain for her kind.

Hah! Llys's natural honesty scoffed at this useless attempt at self-delusion. Never would she be free of the scent, the taste, and the feel of the magnificent man she'd wrongfully permitted to become the center of her thoughts and dreams. As she had earlier admitted, no matter the fervor of her efforts, never could she force the constraints of reality over her unruly, ill-fated love for him. It had become a permanent part of her.

Crystal tears welled from the ache of an emptiness in her soul.

Chapter
15

Llys's eyes opened to the near darkness of her windowless chamber blessed only with the faint glow of a single coal such as each night was put into a small iron pot partially covered. From its heat each morning a taper could be ignited to lend light during preparations to meet a new day.

What with the muddled tensions of the previous day, last evening Llys had failed to carry a glowing coal with her when she retired from the hall. And yet by a coal's faint gleam, she could see the dim outline of the container waiting in its usual place within reach. 'Twas proof that the thralls had resumed their labors. Apparently, upon seeing her coal pot still in its position on the shelf, one of them had thoughtfully filled it and crept into her chamber to leave it for her use.

That had been a kind deed, and yet her dreary mood lingered. She lit a candle from the bright coal, relieving a measure of the surrounding dimness but no part of her inner dearth of cheer. Even after she had put aside the pain of a hopeless love, her anxiety for Wulf's survival lingered as did her alarm at threatening foes certain soon to launch an assault. And yet an infinitely more perilous threat must not be forgotten—the dark Druidic powers of which Glyndor and Evain had warned, powers she could now put names to but had no notion how to defeat.

Suddenly and as clearly as if the white crystal had spoken, Llys heard a silent rebuke for forgetting the black pendant. The past day's myriad troubles and dangers were no excuse for her feeble-wit's act of forgetting its hazardous presence for a single moment. She ought have given it over to Glyndor the moment Adam led her to the keep's door. Instead, already disconcerted by Adam's morning rejection of their night's passion, she had permitted her attention to be caught in the conflict quickly arising between the Saxon and the aging sorcerer. A wrong compounded by the silent departure of both her twin and Glyndor afore she'd a chance to turn over to Glyndor the pendant. And after that, when exchanging the tight red dress for one of her simple gowns, she had happily found her own bag and crystal. 'Twas a discovery which had granted her a much appreciated ability to leave Elesa's bag and the black pendant behind in the keep—though with care taken to ensure the pyramid's point was directed upward.

Llys sat upright, determination sparkling in sapphire eyes. She must get the black pendant to Glyndor with all possible haste. He would know how to wield it in ending the dark threat of perverted Druidic powers. If only she knew where to find him. . . .

Though in a tiny room blocked from any sight of what lay beyond windowless walls, Llys was certain dawn had come. Indeed she suspected it was far past daybreak as she'd found unusual difficulty in her night's quest for sleep and likely hadn't won her goal afore the sun began brightening the eastern horizon.

Rising, Llys looked over the limited number of gowns hanging from pegs driven into the wall at one side of the door. From their number she selected her favorite blue dress, the one taken from her and replaced by a monk's robes while Elesa wore the blue to enter Throckenholt in Llys's guise.

A good wash would have to wait until fresh water could be fetched from the spring, but, certain she was late in rising, Llys quickly donned the garb chosen. As she thrust her hands through sleeves wide at top but tight at bottom, she wondered what Elesa had been wearing the day she had left Throckenholt. Glancing over her meager collection of garments, she was relieved to find the one missing to be a dress she thought too tight and seldom wore.

After hurriedly brushing tangles from thick black curls, Llys stepped from the bedchamber to quietly enter a hall where Pip busied himself stirring life into the hearth's banked coals. She went still at the sound of a welcome voice stating a fact which the past night she'd attempted to wield as encouragement, seemingly with little success.

"'Struth." Glyndor nodded, and over his dark-robed shoulders fell white hair, thick despite his advanced age. "At our behest Prince Cai has positioned sentinels in his forest to watch and report any ominous movements or armed strangers approaching the borders of Throckenholt."

Adam answered with a cynical smile. Llys's assurances had failed to convince him of the Welsh prince's worth as confederate or use as an additional line of defense. And if the powers of the gentle enchantress had failed in that task, the aging sorcerer's corroboration had no hope of accomplishing more.

"Hrumph." Glyndor quietly growled his disgust for the Saxon's poorly shielded disdain of offered aid. Although he'd oft suspected Wulf suffered a measure of the same distrust, his granddaughter's mate had the excuse of having once been the target of a Welsh prince, Vortimer, who'd joined an uprising against Wulf's Northumbrian king. This Saxon, however, had no such excuse.

Adam steadily met the penetrating gaze beneath bushy white brows. He recognized Glyndor's irritation but refused to snap at the wordless baiting of a querulous sorcerer plainly waiting to test his mettle.

Seeing another storm brewing betwixt Glyndor and Adam, meaning to intervene, Llys hastened toward where they sat at the lord's table. Evain, too, sat there with Anya in his lap attentively listening.

"We've learned dangerous news that you must hear."

At the sound of Llys's musical voice, Adam's attention immediately shifted to follow the dainty figure's graceful approach.

"I've told them of Wulf's injury and Brynna's treatment of it." Adam thought to save Llys the repetition of a thing already done.

"'Tis not that." Llys slightly shook a cascade of black curls and turned her gaze to the aging sorcerer. "I speak of all that Maida imparted to us in the hall last evening."

Llys glanced over her shoulder toward the shadowed corner from whence Maida watched despite her inability to comprehend the Cymry words. Llys's gaze quickly returned to Glyndor. "To the bishop the odious sorceress Gytha has sworn herself able to weaken Prince Cai's call to arms by destroying his people's faith in your powers."

Though the mercurial sorcerer at first seemed unmoved, his solemnity soon erupted into an unsettling cackle of glee. Then his voice dropped into a rumble so deep it threatened to shake firm walls. "'Tis the battle I foretold."

The cryptic comment was all too well understood by its speaker's apprentices—but not by Adam. His impatience grew at this further talk of a wizard's imagined conflict when a very real danger loomed so near. Still, he calmed his irritation, telling himself he could bide his time a brief while longer.

Llys's fears had been confirmed by Glyndor's response. One way or another Gytha's challenge would end in the death of her mentor. Glyndor had made known his longing for this conclusion, in truth the opening of a door to a far better existence, but it would leave those behind heartsore at the loss and suffering from a grief and emptiness so deep it could be lessened only by his victory over the dark challenger.

Llys hastened to offer what aid she could, hoping it would be of some small use. "I've an item that may be of value as a weapon in that fearsome clash. I took it from a trap laid for me by the sorceress, Gytha."

While Glyndor stroked his long white beard and faintly frowned his skepticism, Llys hastily returned to her bedchamber. When she reappeared it was with Elesa's cloth bag held tight in one hand. She dropped to her knees at the elder sorcerer's side and from the pouch withdrew the ugly black pendant, all the while taking care to hold the triangle point upward.

Glyndor's scowl deepened as he cast a black-ice glare upon the emblem extended toward him. "'Tis a vile charm of vicious power—able to kill and easily tracked."

Although the sorcerer's stare was not turned upon her, Llys blinked against the fierceness of her mentor's reaction while Adam straightened up, balking at the thought of any peril, physical or mystical, turned upon the sweet enchantress.

"I deemed it a wonder that of your own you sundered their spell of binding." The sorcerer's dark eyes lifted to study the woman hesitantly nibbling her lip and apparently unaware of the great feat she had wrought. "The fact that you've been able to carry this safely here is . . ." Glyndor let the words trail into silence, yet with a slight shrug gave her a smile of admiration most rare to his lips.

Llys's pleasure in her mentor's praise was enhanced by relief for this proof that her link with nature's powers had remained unbroken despite her love for a Saxon unbeliever. Still, as conscious of Evain's bright grin of pride in his twin's accomplishment as Llys was, she restrained her own.

"Will it be of use?" Llys asked.

"Oh, aye." Glyndor nodded. His rival meant to instigate their conflict at the moment when nature's forces were in wild disarray and when his own powers were most vulnerable. With this odd black pendant he could control the timing of their meeting, a prospect that gave him great satisfaction.

Glyndor fell into silence and the twins, seeing he'd no intention of revealing any further knowledge of an imminent battle, which voiceless powers had imparted to him, knew better than to disturb their mentor.

In grudging respect for the beliefs of these Druids who surrounded him—an odd place for one who was the son and brother of Christian monks—Adam had held his peace. However, now that their talk alluding to an unworldly battle betwixt mystical powers had ended, he would wait no longer to discuss literal dangers too near.

"I assume that after you left us this past day you traveled through the woodlands surrounding Throckenholt's palisade, 'struth?"

No answer was forthcoming, and the strong firelight restored by Pip's good work glided over Adam's shoulder-length hair as he shook his head with disgust at the Druids' silence. Then, suspecting the sorcerers were offended by an apparent slight on the thought and toil they'd put into ensuring protection beyond Throckenholt village's walls, Adam rephrased his question.

"I realize that you've arranged with Prince Cai for a sentinel to watch in future, and I meant only to ask whether on your way to meet with the prince you saw any sign of forces in movement, particularly at night?"

Glyndor remained mute, but Evain's curiosity was pricked.

"Night? What alarms you about the shades of night?" Evain's sapphire eyes sparkled with amusement for this dread of darkness from the lauded Saxon warrior.

"Nothing alarms me." Accepting that the younger sorcerer was likely as prone to odd mood shifts as the elder, in response to his banter Adam smiled, though his lips tilted sardonically down on one corner. "Days past a ceorl reported an ill deed done in darkness and claimed that our foes have chosen the night as their province. 'Tis a fact seemingly proven by their cowardly assault upon Wulf."

Hair as black as a raven's wing gleamed as Evain tilted his head and answered. "We saw nothing." The brief statement was accompanied by an impish grin. "But then 'tis unlikely that cowardly men would reveal themselves to black-robed wizards traveling through the shadows of night by the light of a staff's claw-held crystal."

Amber eyes narrowed. Adam could well believe the fear such an eerie sight would put into the hearts of the callow Saexbo and his followers.

"And because of that ability to stymie men of such ilk," Evain said, "I propose to take the fallen messenger's place."

Adam frowned. Oh, he knew what the young sorcerer meant, but was not convinced of the wisdom in such an attempt, not least of all because he was a Druid sorcerer proposing to travel through Saxon lands to a Saxon ruler's court.

Evain saw Adam's discomfort with the proposal and purposefully misinterpreted it while at the same time making it difficult for the man to reject his explanation. "I will go to King Ecgferth, whose life and kingdom already have I once had a part in preserving. I'll tell him what wicked deeds have been here perpetrated—from the treachery of a 'pious' Christian bishop to his traitorous son Saexbo's assault upon his loyal ealdorman, Wulfayne."

"But what of Gytha?" Rising to her feet, Llys gasped at the vision of her twin brother in the same peril she'd experienced at the woman's hands. Her reaction was echoed by the small child in Evain's arms.

"Fret not." Evain fondly shook his head, eyes softening as first they met others of like hue and then shifted to comfort the distress in a pale green gaze. "The spell of binding can be wielded, and more efficiently, by another."

"One of greater power will keep the foolish woman occupied." Glyndor roused himself to make the mocking pronouncement involving his own mastery. "Thus, Evain will be able to slip through the net our misguided foes cast and wrongly think impenetrable. In truth 'tis a net able to hold only those who lack the skills and knowledge of a sorcerer."

Though Llys was unable to completely relax at the prospect of Evain in harm's way, she did have faith in her twin's power to control mighty natural powers and in Glyndor's ability to do as he said. She calmed her apprehensions with awareness that they were merely the product of love for a brother.

The three Druids turned their attention to the golden lord as if asking his approval.

As a famed tactician himself, Adam was both amused and annoyed by such talents being deftly wielded by this young man to trap him into agreeing to the proposed action. Ignoring Glyndor's satisfaction, Adam surrendered in a battle he wasn't certain he wanted to win in any event. Lifting his hands a short distance above the table, Adam let them drop to signal his agreement.

"For the sake of lending your journey what small aid and protection I can"—to the mockery of these self-deprecating words Adam added a wry grimace— "I'll write a message in support of your words and to it affix an item that will prove to my king from whom it comes."

Evain's bright smile flashed, acknowledging an accord reached betwixt them.

"Pip," Adam called to his guardsman. "Pray fetch my bags from my bedchamber."

Although as Pip's lord it was Adam's right to command the deed, he posed it as a plea to a friend. Such tasks were normally the duty of thralls, not freemen. And under usual circumstances Adam would not so slight a respected supporter's position but he thought with this task to accomplish two needs: first, the retrieving of the bags; second, the opportunity to see Pip walk more than the short distance between herb corner and hearth. Adam suspected that were Pip aware of his lord's purpose, the earnest young man might try to conceal his limp, if a limp remained.

Pip was startled by the appeal in English after so long a litany of unfamiliar words, but he was not offended by the request. He firmly crossed to Adam's chamber and then reappeared to carry the requested bags to his golden lord seated at the hall's far end.

"I thank you." Adam's grateful smile was bright. Searching through one of the two bags joined at the top, he pulled out a tightly stoppered vial of ink, a neatly folded packet of parchment sheets, a goose quill, and a small, intricately embroidered draw-bag. Using the first three, he quickly wrote a concise missive containing a list of ill deeds, their doers, and an outline of the scheme to steal the crown. After refolding the parchment sheet, he took a burning candle from the bronze platter and tilted it until wax dripped down to form a puddle where the edges of the missive overlapped. Then from the embroidered bag Adam quickly withdrew an object, which he pressed into the melted wax.

Once Adam had removed the curious instrument from the wax, Llys saw that the imprint it left was not unlike the one Ulford had drawn, the one that had revealed to the Saxon lords that its possessor was Prince Saexbo.

Glancing up into the slight frown of the woman standing at Glyndor's side, Adam sent her a potent smile. "'Tis the letter 'A,' the first in my name. My king gifted me with the ring for an appreciated service once rendered." Adam saw no reason to tell how once in the midst of heated battle he had saved his sovereign's life and been rewarded with this ring, much like those worn by the king's own three sons, although his was not of twined metals but all of silver.

Llys had no basis upon which to understand the token's significance, but the chilling ache of his past rejection of her was in some measure warmed by Adam's willingness to provide her with the explanation. Before anything more could be said, a loud knocking interrupted them.

Adam called an invitation to enter. Maelvyn hesitantly opened the door but remained hovering on the threshold in the doorway's long rectangle of light.

"As you directed on our return, Lord Adam, I've summoned the menfolk of the village so that you can give them an account of how matters stand. I've talked with others and assure you we all welcome your advice and leadership in meeting what comes. In truth we hope to learn from you how best to see them thoroughly routed."

The white flash of Adam's smile answered

Maelvyn's heartening faith in his leadership and his assurance of the villagers' support. Yet, knowing substantially more now—by virtue of Maida's disclosures—than he'd known even a few hours earlier when their small party rode through the palisade gates as dusk fell, Adam knew the task would be more difficult than he had then envisioned.

Amber eyes glanced toward the gentle enchantress, and the quiet trust he saw in blue eyes gone soft further strengthened his determination to repel approaching treachery. As Adam rose, he gave Evain the sealed letter that had been written to King Ecgferth. Then, as Pip's knee had plainly healed, Adam summoned him to come along as with a grim smile he departed to do what he'd pledged.

With the two Saxon men gone, Glyndor's dark glare narrowed in assessment of Llys. In the look he had seen exchanged between her and Lord Adam, he recognized the fall of yet another sorceress to a Saxon's lures. It annoyed him no end! Once in the past he had attempted at the outset of a like relationship to divert its flow . . . and failed. Disgust glittered in his penetrating stare.

Llys suspected the powerful sorcerer could see her love for Adam. But rather than seeking Glyndor's forgiveness for something which already she knew had become an integral part of her, Llys straightened and met his disapproval unflinching.

Recognizing a lost cause and unwilling to risk repeating the failure forced upon him in striving to keep Brynna and Wulf apart, Glyndor grudgingly shrugged. He comforted himself that leastways in teaching Evain he'd fulfilled the all-important purpose of a sorcerer's existence. He'd ensured the continuation of the generational links in the chain of knowledge unwritten and unknown to men untaught. And now only one further duty would he be required to perform before being granted the reward of a longed-for rest.

"Join us." The wide sleeve of Glyndor's black robe fluttered as he motioned Llys—more powerful than he'd suspected, despite her wrongful bond with an unbeliever—to take the seat between him and Evain which Adam's departure had left open. "It is imperative we speak of matters no Saxon must be allowed to hear."

"Anya," Evain said to the child he gently lifted and set on her feet, "poor Maida can't understand anything that's been said and has been left without even Pip to keep her company. She must be lonely. Won't you go and talk with her?"

Anya's green eyes narrowed in suspicion of her hero's excuse to be rid of her, but she grudgingly did as requested—although with a grimace of disgust to ensure Evain would know her not so foolish that she didn't see what he was about.

Having summoned Llys, Glyndor leaned his white-topped head against the dark wood of the chair back. Thus he consigned the responsibility for the next step to her twin, a young man who very soon would be left to assume all the duties of his departed master.

"As Glyndor's full strength and attention must be devoted to his conflict with Gytha," Evain said, "of necessity you must lend him aid by preventing your Saxon from obstructing his path."

Llys's first thought was to wish that Adam was indeed "her Saxon." However, she nodded compliance despite her certainty that 'twould be unnecessary as surely nothing could stop a powerful sorcerer from taking any path he chose.

Evain continued, saying, "While he and I are gone —and we will be—another challenge will arise, one that you will have to face and defeat alone."

Llys shrank back from her brother's prediction, feeling all her fears of a weakening bond with nature instantly increase fourfold.

Taking Llys's hands into his own strong clasp and leaning forward so that two sapphire gazes met and held, Evain refuted her unspoken anxiety.

"Many times over the years Brynna has told you that your link to the source of our powers is far greater than hers. Now, by the magic you wrought to sunder Gytha's spell, carry her foul charm free, and deliver it into the hands of her nemesis, you've proven that— even without the advanced training provided me— your powers are the match for mine."

Llys shook her cloud of ebony curls. She was unable to accept this claim, one she felt certain her twin had exaggerated so as to bolster her confidence and enable her to meet an ominous challenger. But who? Not Gytha. Glyndor would deal with the menacing sorceress and, mayhap by use of the black charm, put an end to her disturbance of natural currents, her bending of their flow into an ominous whirlwind. Therefore Evain must speak of a clash betwixt Llys and her mirror image. An unpleasant thought narrowed her eyes: Elesa must also be the one Adam had decried as the experienced strumpet in his bed.

"Remember . . ." Evain's voice summoned Llys from distractions. "Time has grown short. Soon the most treacherous crossing of nature's flow will be upon us." He knew the alarm his words would raise in

Llys, but knew also the importance of ensuring she was forewarned and thus able to stand prepared. "If the currents reach their weakest point at the same moment when these unfamiliar sorceresses wield malicious forces to brew their storm, 'tis too likely they'll spread throughout nature a poison able to forever still the voices to whom we call."

Llys frowned. If Evain intended to build her confidence with this prospect of the fearsome price failure would exact, he failed miserably. She felt the weight of an incredible duty fall upon her shoulders like the mantle of doom. How could she possibly meet and defeat anyone able to wield such vicious powers?

Glyndor peeked suspiciously at the young woman asked to fulfill a serious duty. Not convinced that Llys remained untainted after consorting with the Saxon, he growled another danger. This one would, he believed, reinforce any weakness Lord Adam might have caused.

"Lest you think the image of the voices of stone, stream, and river going silent unworthy of the conflict's cost, recall that should Elesa succeed, your Saxon might be in greater danger."

Llys had been struck by a double blow. Her eyes widened, and she gasped. The vision of Adam in jeopardy had the force of a slap, but her mentor's suggestion that she would ignore so vicious a threat to everything he'd taught her felt like a breath-stealing shock to her middle. And even when in the next instant she realized it was likely Glyndor's way to punish her for the displeasure she'd given him by falling in love with Adam, still it hurt.

"Hrumph," Glyndor groused, though a guilt very rare indeed warmed the face under a thick white beard. He wouldn't admit having been wrong in any choice he made—not even his suggestion that Llys could be so base. And he was furious with himself for so much as the momentary notion that he ought. Nonetheless, he offered a gruff comfort.

"Don't fret. I will have ended the greatest threat, and the one you'll meet possesses no powers to match those that you have demonstrated."

Llys gave the aging man a grateful smile although her confidence was no more increased by his claim of her power than it had been by her brother's. Again she asked herself how she could possibly defeat someone able to inflict such devastating harm.

Attuned to the workings of his twin's mind, Evain spoke. "A source of abundant power will soon appear . . . and you know that is so. Await its coming. Then trust in the power of the morning star."

Llys slowly nodded. There was no help for it. She must strive to see the feat done.

"And, too, remember that the other sorceresses' energies arise from the dark bowels of the earth and live in the night tempest while you, by entreating the brilliance of the morning star, will surely gain all you may need."

Thick black lashes fluttered down to rest on soft cheeks and shield Llys's lingering doubts from her brother. In the power of the morning star she believed. And she trusted her ability to successfully entreat its aid in small matters . . . but she mistrusted her ability to control its overwhelming power as either Glyndor or Evain might. Even the prospect of such an attempt was fearsome.

"Come, poppet," Evain called out, realizing there was nothing more that he could say on the matter.

Only could he, during his own dangerous journey, continuously offer chants seeking assistance for Llys's success in the task.

At the sound of Evain's voice, Anya's bright head instantly lifted from the game of draughts she'd been teaching Maida to play.

As Evain rose, he looked down into Glyndor's eyes, and all humor drained from his face. Both sorcerers were aware that this likely was the last time in life that their eyes would meet.

"Farewell, master sorcerer," Glyndor's voice was a soft rumble that spoke volumes more in praise and affection than was said in words. "And, in truth, you have mastered all that I could teach. Thus, when you return, my staff will be yours."

Llys struggled in the attempt but failed to restrain a faint sob. That Glyndor meant to gift his protégé with his precious crystal-topped staff was solemn proof his life's end was very near, and no matter their recent discord that fact lent a desolate ache.

Sorcerers do not weep, Evain curtly cautioned himself against the prickling presence of unwelcome tears. Despite the moisture glittering in Llys's eyes, he summoned a bright smile as he turned toward the child still hesitating in the herb corner's shadows. "Anya, give me a hug and a wish for good fortune."

Having heard the talk of Evain's intended departure and as fearful for his safety as Llys, Anya flew across the hall, pale golden locks flowing behind her as she launched herself into his waiting arms. "So soon?"

"The sooner to return with an army to guarantee your protection." He kissed her forehead and then, despite clinging arms, lowered her to the thick plank floor.

No matter what he had planned, when Evain departed the hall, both Llys and Anya accompanied him. They were determined to walk with him as far as the hidden rear gate. Once their small party stood before that portal, Evain turned to hug Anya once more and kiss Llys's cheek. As he did so, he whispered in her ear, "Remember the power of the morning star. Concentrate not on the weaknesses you perceive in yourself but on the star's powers, and all will be well."

Chapter
16

In the pale light of predawn a young lad arrived to summon Adam to the wall surrounding the small village. Knowing that if she asked, Adam would deny her the right to accompany him, Llys followed a discreet distance behind the powerful man as he strode along a hard-packed lane toward the gate. The first rays of sunlight glowed over Adam's golden hair as he rapidly ascended a sturdy ladder to the narrow walkway along the top of the wall. There he joined archers with bows drawn and arrows pointed threateningly down toward unwelcome visitors.

Refusing to be hampered by her skirts, Llys held them as close as safety allowed while she climbed the nearly vertical rungs.

Hearing the sound of a light step, Adam turned . . . and scowled, first at a woman where she ought not be and then at the wide-eyed men doubtless catching delectable glimpses of the shapely silken legs he well remembered. His glare sent oglers back about their important tasks even as he swooped down and with one mighty arm swept the beauty up to stand with him at one side of the gate.

Llys was unrepentant beneath the silent condemnation of the man she loved. Though he did not return her devotion, she refused to let him face danger alone, despite her certainty that he had done so many and many a time before. She purposefully shifted her attention toward the view that had brought them both to this site—a harsh vista upon which the soft pastels of dawn's light incongruously fell. The fact that it was expected did nothing to lessen the anxiety brought by the bleak sight of the armed force below.

"Did I think your intents peaceable, Prince Saexbo," Adam calmly said to the gangly youth, all skinny limbs and big joints but still filled with unjustified arrogance, "I would welcome you to Throckenholt in its lord's stead."

The adolescent prince's sneered response was offensive and revealed a mouthful of overlarge crooked teeth. "Aye, but Throckenholt's lord is *not* here." The words stank of vicious glee. "Although my supporters failed to be rid of you, I was more successful in having done with Lord Wulfayne. I personally saw to that."

"With the coward's act of striking an unprepared warrior from behind?" Dark gold brows rose in contempt. "In a wretched deed so dishonorable you take pride?"

Saexbo's temper, ever near the surface, was rasped by his cynical opponent's disdain. "We stand face to face! What will the lord of Oaklea do in defense of a shire not his own?" The prince opened thin arms wide in mock surrender. "Will you fire upon a group come in peace?" He paused, and his sneer deepened. "Even were you to do so and claim victory by foiling a scheme to claim the throne of Northumbria, your king would punish the ealdorman responsible for the treacherous slaying of his youngest son."

The options offered by this childish Saxon prince distressed Llys, yet by neither word nor gesture did Adam respond. However, Saexbo paid that lack no mind as he spitefully asserted, "I have you trapped."

A sardonic half-smile turned one corner of Adam's mouth down while he regretfully shook his blond mane. "Your father is a wise man, and though he has been far too indulgent with you, he is not blind to your failings."

Adam was aware that the larger problem lay not with this insolent boy but rather with Hordath—an ambitious man his king foolishly chose and gave the task of controlling a wild princeling. Hordath was the danger, and for some reason he was not here. A curious, telling fact.

"We offer you no harm, Prince Saexbo, but neither will we open Throckenholt's gates to you." The mocking smile accompanying this laconic statement was boldly intended as a further irritant.

The trail of deeds Saexbo had wreaked upon the night forest Adam believed was now explained. Not only was Saexbo the spoiled youngest spawn of an important man but his small band of companions, too, was composed of the landless whelps of highborn lords. Doubtless this irresponsible pack had viewed careening about the dark woodland, terrorizing any who came to hand as naught but a lark.

"Then we will wait till you come out." Saexbo was thoroughly annoyed with the man who seemed unimpressed by his trap. He tossed back a mop of straggly brown hair, amazingly thin for one of his youth. "And you must. Eventually you must come out." His last words sounded like the peevish grumbling of an increasingly ill-tempered toddler.

With fresh water springing up behind a keep filled with the abundant foodstuffs he'd ordered be brought in from outlying farms the previous day, Adam was more amused than threatened.

Under his opponent's unwavering smile, Saexbo's ire descended so far into a childish tantrum that he actually stamped his foot.

Llys abruptly became aware of the youthfulness of the entire company. For a moment she thought her initial distress at the prospect of armed foes at the gate unwarranted. But in the next instant she remembered that these adolescents were responsible for the assault upon Wulf and likely the murder of the messenger he had dispatched to King Ecgferth as well.

"Don't even think of attempting to sneak out the back gate." Saexbo's words were a snarl. "'Tis not so well hidden we were unable to discover its position. Even as we speak it stands guarded against such a foolish action."

Amber eyes narrowed against the insult. "I recommend that you don't make the error of imputing your own weaknesses to me. Never have I been so dishonorable as to flee from battle."

Llys had been aware of Adam's scornful amusement at the absurdities of these ineffectual besiegers, but now she sensed a bolt of tension abruptly stiffening his powerful body. Positioned on his left, she stifled an urge to take his arm in support, knowing how unwise it would be to distract a man in such a situation— particularly one who had not wanted her there in the first instance.

"And I accept as an intentional slight," Adam coldly continued, "your suggestion that I might be as craven as you've proven to be, with your skulking through night woods to launch attacks upon the backs of the unsuspecting."

Adam's sword sang as he pulled it from its sheath. "If by the insult 'tis battle you seek, then let us meet face to face. Together, while your men and mine stand aside to watch and later swear to the truth of the deed, let the two of us, armed with swords alone, settle this matter now."

Saexbo quailed at the prospect of matching his questionable strength against that of a famous warrior. Every hint of color drained from the self-important youth's face as he blustered a few unintelligible words and then determinedly shifted the focus of the confrontation by leering at the lovely creature at Lord Adam Brachtward's side.

Incredibly uncomfortable at suddenly finding herself the object of so much male attention, Llys had to summon all of her fortitude to keep from shrinking back. At the same time, Adam resheathed his sword, wrapped a strong arm about his tender enchantress, and held her as far behind the protection of his back as the narrow walkway permitted.

"So, Lord Adam, though already you've stolen my thrall to serve your needs," Saexbo's smirk was woefully unsteady, "you also keep near to your side a whore who is the very image of the one my guardian, Hordath, finds so . . . so intimately entertaining."

Fierce temper flared, and even from the distance enforced by Adam's position high atop the wall, the golden flames in amber eyes threatened to sear the aggressor. Saexbo stumbled back, knowing that with the action he revealed himself to be a coward but unable to prevent it being so.

A frustrated Saexbo issued a useless threat. "Never

doubt you'll be watched while we wait for your surrender." With this he turned aside to order his pitifully few youthful supporters to establish camp where they stood.

Adam lingered to observe with wry amusement the actions of these callow adolescents playing at war but obviously possessing little notion of the tactics involved in actual conflict. Their inexperience was glaringly revealed by how close against the wall they were pitching their camp. If Adam had intended to destroy this pitiful lesser flower of the Northumbrian aristocracy, his task would have been simple, requiring very little effort from him or from those at his command. A barrage of arrows and spears loosed straight down or a few upended caldrons of hot liquid would have sufficed to send their number fleeing like scalded cats.

Of a sudden a white smile flashed across Adam's face. He could near have thanked these misguided whelps for gifting him with so fine an opportunity to meet looming dangers. 'Twas an uncomplicated tactic but certain to win him success in this conflict's initial skirmish—one lending him strength and easing the way toward victory in the final battle.

Adam's amusement faded, and his arm unthinkingly tightened about the tiny waist of the woman still in his hold. All too soon other men would descend to bolster this foolish prince who would be king. It would be unwise, and he was not that, to think the newcomers would be else than battle-hardened warriors. He daren't waste a moment more but had best be about making appropriate arrangements.

Llys had sensed the source of Adam's amusement, seen the flash of inspiration in his smile, and when his expression firmed with determination, she knew he had made his decision as to how he would handle this clumsy siege.

Adam chose to descend the ladder first so that, as Llys closely followed, the view of any man foolhardy enough to watch would be blocked. Of course, it also meant that as they descended she was very nearly in his arms. Her wildflower fragrance teased his senses, and her soft form brushed against him often enough to distract him with heated memories and useless wishes for what he dared not permit. While Adam felt her nearness with every fiber, Llys's awareness of the handsome man was equally impossible to repress.

Once on firm ground Adam surprised Llys by proffering his forearm in a gallant gesture. She hesitated, glancing up only to fall into fathomless amber depths. Sensitive to the attention of many turned their way, she pulled her gaze away, a task harder than near any other she'd been called to perform. Then, to further waylay surreptitious interest, she formally laid her fingertips atop his strong arm.

In a silence aching with thoughts of what could never be, Adam led Llys back down the narrow lane bordered on either side by cottages and shops. He was aware of the invisible shroud of unhappiness he had wrapped about her the morning after their lovemaking. And he no longer tried to deny to himself that it was love . . . but he knew it was hopeless for two of such diametrically opposed beliefs.

Llys sensed Adam's renewed rejection even as he escorted her up wooden steps leading to the keep's door. His aloofness deepened her pain, but still she smiled gentle encouragement for difficult tasks ahead, and blue eyes warmed with promised comfort. Although they hadn't spoken of the matter, she was aware that the unimpressive group outside the palisade constituted a minor annoyance compared to the host that would descend all too soon.

Adam left Llys at the door. The responsibilities demanding his attention thwarted his desire to linger in her company. And a fine thing that, he admonished himself, since such an action could only widen the chinks in the emotional armor he must instead fortify against the bewitching maid's invasion.

Stepping slowly into the hall, feeling as if lead weights had been attached to her feet, Llys found Glyndor napping in a hearthside chair. As was his wont, he was carefully composed with hands folded atop a long beard while his white head rested against the seat's tall back. Llys's melancholy mood deepened under the realization that, with the vitality of snapping eyes hidden by closed eyelids, her mentor looked alarmingly older.

Forcing her attention away from Glyndor, she glanced toward the others who had remained here and waited with increasing dread. Wanting to lessen Maida's fears, Llys told her only what she would certainly hear elsewhere—that Saexbo had arrived to camp outside both the palisade's front and back gates. And, too, she repeated how he had taunted Adam with the punishment he would face if he slayed the king's son. But tell Maida of the princeling's words concerning her, Llys would not. Instead, she assured both the girl who had escaped from the brutal prince and the apprehensively listening Anya that Adam had a plan to end Saexbo's threat.

Llys's audience pressed her for details that she couldn't and wouldn't have given even if she knew them. She had heard Adam command Maelvyn to find as many lengths of sturdy rope as possible, but she had no notion what task he planned for their use.

Smiling serenely, she shifted the subject to mundane matters by begging their aid in preparing ingredients for a stew, as the house thralls seemed too overcome with apprehension to be of service.

Again it was Anya who directed them to the baskets and barrels where foods were stored. Once strips of salt venison, diced onions, crumbled parsley, and other such ingredients were placed in an iron caldron, they struggled to arrange sturdy hearth rods on which to hang the heavy container safely above low-burning coals. Even while the two women and one young child performed these sometimes noisy tasks, Glyndor remained in motionless slumber.

The call to face Saexbo had come before Adam had eaten a morning meal, and important duties prevented him from returning at the midday hour. Thus, when he returned at midafternoon, he felt near as ravenous as only the night past Llys had teasingly warned Anya he might become.

When the door was thrust open, blue eyes flew to the man who, though tense and weary, entered the hall with a firm stride and determinedly reassuring smile. Llys's expression softened into something far deeper than mere admiration for the man's physical perfection.

"Pray assure me that you have something for me to feast upon. Elsewise . . ." With a ferocious growl he swooped down upon a fair-haired child who broke into giggles as he scooped her up into his arms.

"We've put a stew to simmering for the evening repast." Llys motioned toward the hearth. "But if you can be sated with such simple viands as bread, cheese, and the lone peach that remains from last evening, then you need not ravage the child."

With mock regret, amber eyes narrowed to scrutiize his prey. "Ah, well, methinks these bones lack ufficient meat to satisfy me."

As the golden giant so like her father set her on the loor, Anya gazed up in trust and solemnly asked, 'Are you going to save Throckenholt for my papa?"

Adam dropped to one knee before the child and ook tiny hands into the strength of his much larger ones. "I will do everything in my power to see it so."

"As will I." The gruff statement came from the sorcerer unexpectedly come to tower above them. 'And for that reason I must now depart."

"Depart?" Adam immediately straightened and, meeting the sorcerer face to face for the first time, discovered the two of them were of an equal height, their unyielding gazes on a level. "No one can depart Throckenholt until the siege—a foolish one but a siege nonetheless—is quelled."

"Nay, *you* can't, but *I* can and I *will!*" Glyndor's response snapped through the air like a whip.

Llys saw Adam's strong chin lift against the sorcerer's lash, and golden fire flare dangerously in amber depths. She went to him and, as had become a habit, slipped a restraining hand into the crook of an arm whose strength was not hidden by its layer of fine tawny-hued wool.

"If you stand in my way, Saxon"—Glyndor's lips twisted with disgust—"Wulfayne may die, and your petty warfare will come to naught."

"Grandsire"—Anya used the same name for the aging sorcerer that her mother did, although in truth he was her great-grandfather—"please save my papa."

The distress straining the child's voice smothered unspoken in Adam's throat his harsh response to the sorcerer.

"Anya." The golden lord's voice softened into a deep burr as he attempted to explain their unpleasant predicament without deepening the little girl's apprehension. "Anyone who steps outside Throckenholt's gates enters mortal danger. But don't fret, your mother will see your father's health restored."

"Danger for you, Saxon." Though Glyndor reached out to stroke the child's pale blond curls with amazing gentleness, it was to Adam's assertion he responded. "But I shall be protected by the power of my staff. The foolish prince and his playmates can do me no harm."

"'Tis true, Adam," Llys earnestly affirmed the sorcerer's claim. "You must accept that it is so."

While the two strong-willed men argued, Llys had remembered the oath she had given Evain, wherein she promised to exert her best efforts to ensure Glyndor not be barred by "her Saxon." She was relieved to discover that for this small duty only must she effect the momentary distraction of others' attention—Adam's in particular. Normally neither the presence of an unbeliever nor the restraints of man-made walls would be permitted during the casting of so potent a spell as Glyndor plainly intended. . . . But, a somber Llys wordlessly acknowledged, what needs must, must be.

A golden head turned toward the quiet plea's sweet source. Then, even as a skeptical amber gaze melted into the mysterious depths of blue eyes, there began a strange event. Words roaring like the winds of a storm filled the hall, echoing against the four walls, which seemed inadequate to contain their power.

Adam's attention immediately shifted to the black-robed wizard whose joined hands held aloft a staff whose glowing crystal emitted beams of eerie light. With the motion of a whirlwind, white hair whipped and flowing black robes swirled about the sorcerer's feet as his thunderous words shook the walls. In the shock of a single instant, silence fell, and Adam blinked in disbelief.

One moment Glyndor was there. The next he was gone leaving only the harsh thud of a closing door behind.

After Glyndor mysteriously vanished, Adam ate a quick meal and returned to men laboring to fashion ladders of rope. He didn't reenter the hall until the dark of a moonless night had fully conquered the sky. The evening's long delayed repast, thick slabs of two-day-old bread soaked under an abundance of savory stew, was consumed by a party smaller than that of the previous evening by virtue of Pip's absence.

The house thralls had not returned after being allowed to retreat to their hovel early that morning. After the meal, Anya and Maida were again intent on a game of draughts. Glancing their way, Llys wondered who was entertaining whom. Adam left the table and sat in a hearthside chair, in his clasp a crockery mug filled with a fine measure of bitter ale. He sat but did not relax. Every muscle was tense while he alternately stared blindly into the hearth's circle of soot-darkened stones and glanced toward the door as if impatient for someone's arrival.

If not already done, then soon his plan would be put into motion. Adam heartily wished it were he who led the way. However, he took his responsibilities seriously, and such a deed would pose too great a risk to the continuing safety of Throckenholt as a whole. Thus he was left with the most difficult task of all—waiting.

Llys felt Adam's tension and wished there were

some deed within her power to perform that would lessen his strain. After a moment's quiet pondering, she concluded that a distraction from worries plaguing him would achieve the desired goal—even if that distraction came in the form of an unwelcome interruption, and from an equally unwelcome source.

"I know from Brynna that your father and brother, both Aelfric by name, were monks." Llys moved to stand within arm's reach of the brooding man and gazed down on the strong planes of his face, more cleanly etched by the fire's shifting pattern of shadow and light. She was well aware that the subject raised was a tender one, yet thought that tempting his anger would likely be the best path to her goal and deliberately continued. "But when I asked after your mother during your first days in the keep, you went silent. Will you tell me about her now?"

Adam was thunderstruck by this sudden assault launched directly at his most vulnerable point from an utterly unexpected quarter. His eyes widened, and the next instant the same amber gaze that so oft flashed with golden fires proved it could freeze as well as burn.

Llys felt as if the sharp blade of an icy knife had pierced her heart when Adam turned upon her the chill of his outraged attention.

"My mother?" The word was a cold sneer. "She was the epitome of your sex—greedy, self-centered, and solid ice to the core."

No verbal reply came from Llys but, startled, she delicately lifted her brows. To Adam that instinctive reaction spoke volumes about his own nature, about the betrayal of it in his telling response to her question. He was shocked to realize for the first time that he was as guilty as the mother he'd condemned for near a lifetime.

Llys saw that she had succeeded in thoroughly diverting the golden man from the quagmire of troubles ahead but took no pleasure in the feat, not when in so doing she'd driven him back into the even more unpleasantly tangled paths of his past.

"I regret my prying. I sought to turn your attention from concerns causing you such distress. Instead it seems I've only compounded them." Llys instinctively lifted her hands toward Adam. Then, realizing the man who had already rejected her on more than a single occasion would likely disdain her touch, she clasped them tightly together at her waist.

"I beg you will forgive me." Although still wanting nothing so much as to soothe his aching heart, she feared to stumble and more deeply bruise his wounds.

"Nay, 'tis I who am sorry." Adam helplessly shook bright hair. The gentle compassion in cloudy blue eyes convinced him that the gentle maid was undeserving of his cynical disdain, and one of his large hands reached out to clasp her dainty fingers. The sincerity of Llys's apology increased his remorse and left him fervently wishing for the ability to unsay hasty words.

"Long have I prided myself on being strong enough to stand firm beneath the demands of any coming battle, but here I've shown myself as much a boastful fool as Saexbo and his friends. I've proven it true by permitting the pressures of looming hazards to so strain my control that I erred in lumping you into a barrel full of unworthy companions."

He lightly tugged her down to sit in the matching chair he pulled close to his own. "I will not burden you with my unhappy tale." When she made to argue the point, he lifted hands, palms out, to forestall the words and softened the refusal with one of the slow, devastating smiles so rare to his lips. "I am as committed to holding my painful memories in tight privacy as you are to keeping secret your Druid spells."

Peeking sidelong through dense lashes at this man beloved, Llys wondered why he could not see how little the two matters had in common. Where his tale was apparently a personal tragedy, there was a far deeper and infinitely more far-reaching purpose behind the secrecy surrounding Druidic knowledge. Without pausing to consider the wisdom of such an action, she sought to help him understand.

"That choice is not mine to make. 'Tis a matter of generations upon generations accepting the limitation in exchange for the privilege of receiving a measure of the knowledge unwritten."

Adam had heard the last phrase oft enough in the past fortnight and more that he didn't blink, but his curiosity did force him to pose a single question. "Then *any* person who is willing to accept this limitation may seek the 'knowledge unwritten'?"

"Nay." A dark head firmly shook while a wild rose blush flooded delicate cheeks first with embarrassment for the unclear wording but more for her poor judgment in speaking of secret matters at all. "Only a chosen few of those born to the heritage are permitted the gift of an ability to speak with the soundless voices of nature, the right to call upon them in due respect and great awe."

"The gift." Adam quietly repeated the term.

This caused Llys to wonder if he meant to belittle her earnest explanation, one she should not have spoken. But, no, his amber gaze revealed no sign of insincerity. Reassured, though she knew she should say no more, Llys took the risk involved in clarifying what she had already said.

"We of the chosen few do not ask for the gift but rather are blessed with the honor to varying degrees. 'Tis our heritage and our destiny—one we must fulfill or accept the fearsome responsibility for allowing the powerful voices all around us to go silent for lack of those able to converse with them."

Dark gold brows furrowed. "You sound little like the pagans among my fellow Saxons."

"I am *not* a pagan." The suggestion was an insult against which Llys straightened, blue sparks flashing from her eyes. "I am a Druid."

"'Struth, an enchantress." It was not a question but a quiet statement, as he had long since given up the foolish attempt to pretend she was anything else. Amber eyes, warmed to honey, visually caressed the sweet beauty so near.

The gentleness of his response robbed Llys of the fierceness in her defense. Off kilter, she solemnly nodded even as her suddenly shy gaze skittered away from the potency of his allure. Staring at the hand still wrapped in his mighty clasp, Llys tilted her head to one side, causing a soft mass of ebony hair to fall forward. Orange gleams of firelight caught and glowed in each dark curl.

The sight summoned to the fore of Adam's mind memories ever too near daylight thoughts and the constant subject of his night dreams, memories of the shattering intimacy of their time at the base of an ancient mystical monument and remembered images of the moments yielding an elusive delight after he'd awakened. Too well he recalled his intimate study of the glorious beauty he'd claimed, a luminescent vision pillowed against her cloud of silky black hair. A delicacy that was his for so fleeting a time.

Llys glanced up into the unshielded emotion in a velvety gaze. Physical surroundings faded under the more potent reality of his nearness. Llys unthinkingly leaned closer even while Adam tumbled into mysterious blue depths and bent toward her sigh-parted lips. . . .

"'Tis done, Lord Adam!"

Pip's victorious call was punctuated by the thud of something harshly dropped on the floor just inside the door, an action immediately followed by Maida's gasp of alarm.

Adam instantly rose and turned toward the odd sight of his youthful guardsman standing above the firmly bound Saexbo, grinning with pure delight. Somehow, while long anticipated, these arrivals had made an unexpected appearance. Striding closer, Adam saw that the prince could only view him through one eye. The other was swollen shut, and bruises were already darkening elsewhere on his sulking face. Adam's attention shifted back to Pip's unrepentant grin.

"Your command was that I not kill this stripling prince," Pip said, "and I did not. Only did I think it my duty to aid my king in teaching his immature son leastways one lesson about becoming a man."

Dark gold brows rose in mocking demand for an explanation of such inventive reasoning.

"I learned when young that experience was the best teacher." Pip's eyes narrowed with contempt as he gazed down at the furious prince. "So I deemed it my duty to give this unwilling student a lesson on how it feels to be subjected to the blows of a much larger and much stronger abuser."

As Pip finished speaking, he turned his attention toward the slight figure of Maida lingering in shadow. In her eyes he saw no fear, only recognition of the feat done for her. Silver tears welled in brown velvet eyes—this time not in sorrow but in unspoken love.

Chapter
17

"Saexbo and the rest of you besieged the village of Throckenholt?" The bishop's question contained such a wealth of disgust it seemed to echo against the stone walls of his abbey chamber. "What sorry impulse drove him to that poorly timed—nay, witless—deed?"

Before the trembling youth, subjected to this verbal lashing, could answer, a glowering Hordath waved his cohort's questions aside to demand an answer to his own.

"Tell *me* how it was that from an armed camp the foe besieged could so blithely capture your prince and erstwhile leader?"

The boy, Merl, had no worthy answer to give, save an increased trembling that set his teeth to chattering.

"Begone!" Hordath snarled. The youth lost no moment in fleeing.

"They deserve to be whipped!" Filled with fury, Wilfrid made no pretense of pious compassion. The folly of Saexbo and his friends endangered a scheme long and carefully plotted. For this sin, in his view, they deserved no mercy.

"Should their aid come to naught," Hordath's cold voice intoned, "'tis doubtless a deed their fathers will wreak upon the ambitious whelps."

Hordath had no compunction in using the youngsters' greed for power to his own benefit. Yet he despised these younger sons of noblemen for their willingness to turn against fathers as well as king for the sake of winning positions within a new monarch's court.

"First, even before our smooth plan was well under way, your unmanageable charge thoroughly mucked it up with his childish woodland games. Now the addle-pated brat has rushed to do a deed much better left to sane heads and firm hands." Wilfrid glared at Hordath as if he were responsible for the siege.

"Before you blame me for Saexbo's ill-advised deed," Hordath instantly responded, "remember that it was I who discreetly persuaded the prince that his position was so poor he ought to fight for rights that otherwise would never be his. And without a prince we can manage, our goals would be lost."

Wilfrid reluctantly nodded, but his querulous frown did not fade.

"Moreover, while you criticize Saexbo, what of the worthless pair of sorceresses you insisted would be of such great aid? Seems they've entirely disappeared and just when arrives a moment they might be of some use."

"Gytha *is* gone." Wilfrid nodded while folding his hands in an attitude of forced complacency over the ample shelf of his belly. "She said the appointed time had come to perform the feat which we've demanded be done."

Wilfrid would not admit to Hordath his own discomfort with the memory of how surprised and annoyed Gytha had seemed to be with the arrival of the confrontation supposedly planned by her.

"Don't expect me to mourn her absence." Hordath crossed his arms over a beefy chest.

"Hah," Wilfrid sneered. "You seemed happy enough to have the younger woman ever hanging upon your arm . . . and more."

"Aye, but such are matters one *assumes* a pious priest cannot understand." Hordath would be pleased when the need for this alliance was past. He'd been forced to endure far more than enough from this worldly bishop, and he welcomed the prospect of its end.

"Why waste precious moments on unimportant matters when we've a very real challenge of our own to face. Come, let us lay out such tactics as will secure success in this vital battle, wrongfully hastened though it has been."

Brynna whirled to face the source of a familiar thumping—the rhythmic sound of a crystal-topped staff repeatedly tapping against the entrance tunnel's stone floor and steadily drawing nearer.

"Grandsire, how did you find us?"

The aged sorcerer stepped from the tunnel's darkness, ignoring the stocky Saxon guard and the silent threat of his broadsword's bared edge glittering in the light of a single resin-soaked torch.

"After lo these many years and all that I've taught you"—Glyndor wasted no attention on this small chamber at the end of a long approach nor on its sparse furnishings but shook his white mane in disgust—"you dare to question my ability to work so simple a charm?"

"Never would I question your power to work any spell." Brynna moved forward to greet the unexpected arrival with a forlorn smile. "'Tis only that your deed proves how inadequate are my own abilities." She gave a slight grimace. "I chanted a spell of shielding— one which you penetrated with ease."

"Hrumph." Glyndor's quiet growl made evident his annoyance at being so poorly welcomed with this news that she'd sought to prevent his appearance here.

Brynna hastened to soothe his affronted dignity by clarifying the purpose behind her attempt to confuse the path of any come seeking, although she was certain that intent was already known to him.

"I sought to protect our small band against the dark sorceress who I fear means to seek us out for the sake of finishing the deadly task at which another failed."

"She comes." Glyndor serenely nodded. "I summoned her, and she comes."

Shocked that the grandfather she loved and respected had purposely called the fury of perverted Druidic powers down upon them, Brynna blankly stared at him. Though long used to his mercurial mood shifts and possessing a lifetime's familiarity with decisions oft incomprehensible to her, she was unprepared for this abrupt deed of mysterious intent.

"Hrumph." This second growl contained a seldom heard gentleness. "I know what I'm about. Or would you question my interpretation of unspoken words as well?"

"Nay!" She instantly responded, though concern curled her lips downward. "'Tis my inability to hear the same words that leads me into misguided, unfounded fears."

Glyndor's answering smile was crooked. He repented the urge to snap at the woman assuredly weighted by too many woes over a span of too many weeks. Reaching out in a rare demonstration of affection, he brushed back from her delicate face the wild tangle of curls gone unbrushed while toiling to see her beloved Saxon restored.

"How fares Wulfayne?"

The gentleness in his voice was as startling to Brynna as his use of her husband's given name.

"He's failing," a somber Brynna replied. "In the first hours he revived, and I was confident that he would quickly recover. Then during the night he fell into a deep sleep from which nothing either wielded or chanted could rouse him."

"Like Anya?" The question was quiet but filled with a meaning Glyndor was certain had already occurred to his granddaughter.

"Aye, like Anya." Brynna's voice ached with sorrow. "His flesh mends well, but his spirit is absent."

"Clearly once Gytha learned of his wound, she cast the same spell over this leader of her foes." Black eyes glowed with distaste. "But just as Evain sundered her hold upon Anya, I will break the vise about Wulf. 'Tis why I've chosen this place as the site of my final battle."

Brynna's first thought was shame for having even momentarily doubted her grandfather's motives in seeking out this hidden haven. In the next moment she was near overcome by an inner conflict of emotions threatening to pull her in twain. The happy relief lent by confidence in her grandsire's ability to see Wulf freed from Gytha's vicious grasp stood in direct contrast to the prospect of certain grief looming in the inevitable end to his long anticipated battle.

Sensing her chaotic state, Glyndor stated a firm reminder, along with an amazingly gentle reproof. "The energies I must wield in commanding the forces whose aid will be necessary to win our goal on Wulf's behalf cannot be controlled in else than complete serenity."

In these words Brynna recognized an oblique plea for the departure of a less than tranquil her. Moreover, she heard the unspoken demand that she take with her the Saxon guard whose disbelief likely would be a dangerous disruption of the smooth flow of natural powers required for success in this grave task.

It would not have been safe for Brynna to leave the cave, even accompanied by the stouthearted Cedric, drawn blade at the ready. But by moving down the long entrance tunnel to its far end, they could place sufficient distance between themselves and the sorcerer. Despite persistent tension over the deed at hand and the battle to come, Brynna found amusement in Cedric's reaction when she asked him to come with her into the tunnel, leaving Glyndor in privacy with an unconscious Wulf. The guardsman's relief was evident in the alacrity with which he snatched up and lit a fresh torch. Doubtless talk of such inexplicable matters as spells and charms made him so uncomfortable that he welcomed even a temporary escape.

As they moved ever deeper into a darkness against which the torch seemed inadequate, behind them an eerie light began to glow. Though she could not see Glyndor's extended staff, Brynna knew 'twas the increasing brightness of its claw-held crystal that flooded the tunnel's blackest reaches. And all the while her grandfather repeated strange words over and over again, his voice gaining in power and depth until even the cave's solid stone walls seemed to shake.

When the tunnel returned to a gloom lessened only by the torch's wavering light, anticipation filled Brynna. She rushed Cedric in returning to the chamber at its end.

Though Wulf continued to lie flat, his smile flashed toward the woman he loved. Between his potent smile and the gleam in his green eyes, Brynna knew the danger was past and that, although his flesh was still not fully mended, he would recover. He held out his arms, and she hastened forward to sink carefully down into their welcome embrace.

After a few impatient moments of stroking a long white beard and watching the tender reunion, Glyndor interrupted. "The time is very near, and I go now to meet my final destiny."

Brynna gently pulled away from Wulf's strong hold and rose to reluctantly face her grandfather, as if to forestall his departure and thereby delay the inevitable conclusion.

"The world is calm, but soon a tempest will rise," Glyndor flatly stated. "Do not venture into harm's way. Remain in this safe shelter and wait until stillness reigns again. Then come to me. I will linger long enough to bid you farewell."

Wanting to hug the man never comfortable with such displays of emotion and filled with gratitude for Wulf's restored health, Brynna thought to take a step forward, but the sorcerer foiled her wish by slipping into the shadows with more nimble haste than might have been expected for one of his age. Deep melancholy washed over Brynna, weighting her down with a sense of great loss.

Wulf reached up to clasp his forlorn wife's hand in

warm comfort. While a single tear slipped down her ivory cheek, she again sank to her knees beside the anchor in her life, further reason to be grateful for such a grandsire as Glyndor. He had been responsible for so many gifts—everything, from his acceptance of Brynna as an orphaned girl-child, to his winning from secret powers the right to train her in knowledge unwritten. And now, despite Glyndor's long-standing resentment of the man, he had saved her beloved Saxon. But doubtless most important of all, the gift without which none of the others would matter, he had ventured forth to destroy the overwhelming threat not only to Wulf's king but to all of Brynna's heritage.

In the forest beyond the hidden cave, Glyndor stood amid night shadows, eyes closed and patiently waiting. Sensitive to the quiet solitude of his surroundings, he heard the first hint of a rising storm in the faint rustling of leaves. It brought a smile of peaceful satisfaction to his lips. Too long he had been forced to wait for this culmination of his destiny, as welcome was the chill breeze lifting white hair like a flag to signal his presence.

With unnatural haste the wind swelled into a primitive howl. Raindrops splashed against his uplifted face while through narrowed eyes he sought a first glimpse of the one foretold.

A crash of thunder rolled overhead as Gytha strode boldly from the deep gloom between towering trees. Thick tendrils of unbound hair whirled in rhythm with the storm. She believed the white streaks in her black mane were a symbol of her bond with dark thunderclouds and bright bolts of lightning—in truth, to the unleashed fury of all primal energies, the source of her powers.

"You would challenge me?" Glyndor calmly asked, motionless although his black robes whipped around him. Seemed even the usual black ice so common in his eyes had melted into calm pools.

"Have I not proven it by the tempest risen at my command?" Gytha's eyes flashed with dangerous lights. As she waved one arm, the wide sleeve of her dark gown swirled on the gust of wind her action summoned.

"Aye," Glyndor serenely agreed and with a slight smile added, "but what you can raise, I can tame." Slowly he lifted one hand, palm out. And though the storm raged on, a stillness settled about Glyndor, allowing his thick white hair and black robes to gently fall and rest against him, unmoving.

"'Struth?" Gytha refused to be shaken by this small spell cast by an aging wizard who was surely losing strength with passing years. Her laughter was as wild as the storm, and she welcomed the flare of her temper as the gift of further power that to her it was. She sought to drive that vitality even higher by taunting her opponent into losing his own temper. "'Tis well known," she taunted him, "that for the lack of such an ability you lost your only son in the battle of Winwaed Field."

Hers was a malicious blow but one that Glyndor had long since learned to absorb unshaken. In pride of a mage's power he had once allowed himself to be goaded into rousing nature's fury—a wrong for which he'd paid with the life of his son—and the lesson taught by that sorry deed he had so thoroughly learned that now his confidence remained as steady as his unwavering gaze.

"'Struth, indeed." A quiet smile curled his mouth.

"'Tis why I made attaining that skill my life's goal . . . and why I have so thoroughly succeeded."

Gytha's heavy brows met in a frown as fierce as the rolling clash of thunder, and she hissed, "In your claim I hear the hollow echo of a baseless boast."

When Glyndor's smile merely widened, Gytha loosed the full force of her anger. In demand for like rage from nature she thrust her arms upward to a night sky whose darkness was intensified by the thick layer of clouds she'd summoned and from which she called down vicious bolts of lightning.

Safe in the eye of the tempest, Glyndor stood in a circle of calm and began a soft chant. Slowly he rotated while his low voice steadily increased in volume and power, spinning a web of peace out from his core.

Gytha fell back to avoid meeting defeat at the hand of this one who was unexpectedly able to subdue the very source of her strength. Worse still, defeat at the hand of the famous sorcerer, as well known for his erratic temperament as for the marvels he wrought. Overcome with rage, she made a last desperate attempt to sunder the wizard's power-sapping tranquillity and thereby to prevent the crushing defeat it meant for her.

Shrill voice rising ever higher, Gytha invoked the most dangerous of spells by calling to the powers in the earth's blackest depths. The tempest enfolded her in its dark embrace, and lightning struck at the ground about her feet until with a fiercely urgent wave she sent the bright bolts toward Glyndor.

Glyndor's smile widened with honest joy. For this moment he had waited. While slowly spinning, he'd pulled from the bag at his waist her pendant—the black emblem of perverted Druidic power. When she directed the deadly streaks of light to strike him, he lifted the charm and with both hands held it, sharpest point up, in front of him.

Gytha's lightning struck the pendant and, increased a thousandfold, was deflected back at the vile sorceress. Her form disappeared even as her shriek echoed through the forest and then descended to be absorbed and forever imprisoned in a bleak, mute void.

Exhausted by his feat but warmed with justified satisfaction, Glyndor slid down against the stone wall beside the cave's entrance and settled at its base. He could feel the call of a pleasant peace, longed for and now awaiting his coming, but he fought the summons to linger a short while longer.

As soon as the inhuman cry died away and with it the storm, Brynna started toward the cave entrance. Stepping outside, she was instantly aware of a unique occurrence. All of nature seemed to be rejoicing in Gytha's defeat. Although stars again glittered in a cloudless sky, even in the midst of night a chorus of birdsong cheered the air and the voices of many animals joined the jubilant melody.

Smiling wistfully, Brynna found her grandfather resting near the cave's opening. She dropped to her knees at his side and took one aged hand in hers.

"Brynna, I beg you will not mourn me." He squeezed her hand while giving her a stern black glare. "Rather, celebrate the victory won. And 'tis done for good and all. Gytha is no more."

Brynna nodded but could not prevent the ache in her heart for the loss of his support and, though he might deny it, his love of her.

"I want you to know, Brynna, that I have seen how

well you've fulfilled your destiny, the one early revealed by your affinity for all ailing creatures in need of your curative powers."

That her grandfather had lingered long enough to speak of his pride in her and to reassure her of the rightness of a once questioned path made her silent tears flow more freely.

Then Glyndor ruefully confessed a wrong, a most rare event. "In my pain over your father's death by my own folly, I was wrong to demand so much of you. And I am fortunate to have been forgiven my error insofar as to have been sent another."

His smile warmed, but his voice weakened as if its message was in truth a part of his release into the welcome next sphere. "Evain will do well in my stead." After each phrase he drew a deep breath, gathering air to go on. "My staff I've promised the young sorcerer. . . . He's earned it and will wield its powers wisely. . . . Against the possibility that I might fail . . . I left it in the tunnel's shadows. . . . Beg you will see it safe into Evain's hands."

Brynna sensed him slipping further and further away. Tears now flooded her cheeks unashamed.

"One more thing I've learned . . . must be told before I'm freed." His voice was no more than a whisper, and Brynna bent forward to place her ear near his lips. "Ought to have guessed." He gave an infinitesimal shake of white head. "Hidden by haze of dark peril. . . . Only now . . ."

Brynna realized that he was striving to tell her that while he awaited her arrival the powers of sorcery had parted their mists to speak more news to him. She gently frowned. What more could there be now that Gytha was defeated? Wanting to believe that with the elder sorceress gone the younger could be no danger, she refused to think of Elesa—a choice that was taken from her.

"The likeness between Llys and Elesa . . . Evain, too. Not shapeshifter. . . . Three babies."

Startled, Brynna pulled back a short distance. Her grandfather was right. Given their bond with secret voices, they all should've guessed. The Druid father of Evain and Llys had been blessed, though he must have thought it a curse, with not two but three babes.

Brynna would've asked more, but Glyndor's eyelids seemed to have grown too heavy to lift, and she would waste no more of his precious final breaths.

"Grandsire . . ." All other thoughts were scattered by grief at his passing as Brynna earnestly whispered her own farewell. "We will always honor your memory in our hearts and with our deeds."

A pleased smile lifted Glyndor's lips as he drifted into the peace he had awaited for so long.

The deepest hours of night had come, and yet Adam, filled with tension for the coming day's conflict, lay awake in the dark of his chamber. Saexbo, still bound, had been deposited in the small windowless room on the hall's far end while Anya shared her parents' bedchamber with Maida. The brawny Pip presented a not inconsequential barrier to their prisoner's escape as he dozed on the floor across the makeshift cell's door. Armed villagers stood guard beyond the hall's portal.

Through the welter of concerns filling Adam's thoughts stole an awareness of quiet sobbing on the far side of the wall against which his pallet lay. He knew all too well that Llys slept there. The fact of her nearness had lent him many a sleepless hour abed.

The lonely pain in her voice was not something Adam could simply ignore. He feared himself the source of her hurt—either in his taking of her or in the next morning's rejection. After their quiet time and talk only hours past, he felt himself even more the fool to have doubted that she was as gentle and quietly courageous as he was now certain she was. His love for her was not something that his armored heart could deflect. Its tender coils had won the battle by never fighting it at all.

And no matter who or what the reason for her distress, he knew he must comfort his beloved enchantress. However, fearing her good name would be tainted were he seen entering her bedchamber, he took care in stepping softly from his room, quietly entering hers, and shutting the door behind him to close them in the intimacy of a room lit only by the faint glow of the single coal in a tiny iron pot.

Lost in quiet sorrow, Llys neither heard Adam's approach nor realized the source of a comfort slowly stroking dark curls until Adam carefully lifted her into his strong arms. Then she buried tear-damp cheeks in the curve between his throat and broad shoulder while he cradled her curves close to his chest and leaned back against the wall separating their rooms.

As slowly Llys calmed, she became all too aware of the identity of a welcome pillow for her sorrow. Ashamed of her loss of the control so important to a Druid, she buried her face the tighter against him as shield for her precarious emotions still teetering on the edge of grief.

Adam sensed the change in her tension and gently wrapped his fingers in the curls at the back of her head to tug until she lifted her face toward his. The lingering shimmer of unfallen tears pained Adam. Driven to know if he was responsible for her pain, he softly asked, "Why are you weeping?"

"Glyndor is gone." The last word broke on a tiny sob.

Confusion put a slight frown between bronze brows. "Aye, you were there when earlier today he left." The aging sorcerer was her mentor, but the man's earlier absence hadn't brought tears.

Llys shook a tangled mass of dusky curls. "His mortal days are ended." She took a deep, unsteady breath. "He has passed through the door to a better existence."

"How did you hear this?" Even as he asked, Adam suspected he knew the answer.

"I feel it"—through tearstains a smile appeared, and though forlorn, it was welcome to Adam—"here."

He watched as Llys laid a curled hand against her heart, just as Brynna had in explaining how she knew Wulf was injured. But this time, not for an instant did he doubt the accuracy of knowledge thus gained.

"You believe me?" Llys asked, hoping it was so but fearing it wasn't.

The faint light of a single coal glowed on golden hair as he nodded. "No matter my training, I've seen too much to longer disbelieve." Gently he pulled her into a comforting embrace.

Llys was uncertain whether his words were praise or insult but Adam soon calmed her anxiety.

"I was raised to believe that Christians are the carriers of right and champions of good while Pagans are inevitably soaked in the black slime of every conceivable sin. Never was there any suggestion of something in between," he softly spoke into the dark curls atop her head. "Yet in the few weeks since I came to Throckenholt and learned of your Druid ways, I've found it no longer so simple a matter to divide wrong from right and good from evil."

This was so strong a reminder of the conflict Evain had warned her she must wage that Llys trembled.

Having no knowledge of the duty Evain had given Llys, Adam mistook the source of her distress and feared that she was remembering his denunciation of his mother and his rejection of her following their night of passionate fires and sweet delight.

"I was wrong not to answer when you asked about my mother."

Soft lips parted as Llys started to assure him that he need not force himself to speak of painful memories he had rather remain private, but his fingertips blocked her words.

"I had barely completed my first decade when my brother Aelfric was born." His fond smile had a bitter curl. "Even before he was weaned, our mother deserted us."

Llys gasped, leaning back horrified at the mention of such a wicked deed, and for a moment Adam's smile warmed. Then he continued, and his expression went to impervious stone.

"The pagans of my race do not regard the marriage bond with the same sanctity as do Christians. To a pagan 'tis merely a pact that can be easily sundered by either spouse." While Adam paused, his hands unconsciously curled into fists. "My father wed my mother as a Christian, but she departed with a pagan, and we've neither seen nor heard of her since."

Llys recognized the bitter disgust in his voice as the

source for all the barbed shards that he had flung toward her. "And now I understand why you claimed all women are greedy and self-centered."

A sardonic smile accompanied Adam's continued tale. "It was a fine start, and in the many years before my arrival at Throckenholt I saw little to alter my opinion."

Llys's heart leapt with the small spark of hope lit by his oblique hint of a change taking place here. Then he mentioned the abbey, which had so oft been twined with his inexplicable distaste for her, and she listened intently.

"When I arrived at Winbury Abbey to seek my brother, I was introduced to a Druid sorceress named Llys. She was as wicked as I believed every woman to be. Even did she laugh with cruel glee when the bishop told me of Aelfric's 'suicide.'" Adam's eyes burned with the fires of stinging memories. "When assaulted, I was brought to Throckenholt and awoke to find that same Llys tending me with what I could only believe was a feigned gentleness."

"But it wasn't me," Llys whispered, grateful on one side for the simple explanation but aching for him on the other. In an instinctive gesture of comfort for his years of painful distrust, she caressed his cheek.

Adam caught her hand and buried a kiss in its vulnerable palm. "Nay, it wasn't you." He discovered this compassionate woman was as able to heal a wounded spirit as a physical injury. "And I regret the time it's taken me to plead forgiveness for my inability to see clearly through the distorting haze of my bitter past and accept the blessing you are."

Thrilled by words she'd never thought to hear his deep velvet voice speak to her, Llys slipped silken arms about his strong neck and tangled her fingers in thick blond hair to urge his mouth down. Adam needed no further inducement to reclaim the berry-sweetness of her lips. Their kiss went so immediately deep and hot that she moaned beneath its sensuous demand.

Afraid that in the depth of a need too fierce he'd been rough, Adam pulled his mouth away, seeking restraint to handle the tender enchantress as gently as she ought be. But while his head was thrust back and amber eyes clenched shut against the enticing vision she presented, her lips brushed welcome torment over his throat and down to the laces of his tunic. And when small fingers released their hold on his hair to tug at the ties, he carefully set her aside, freeing himself to ruthlessly rip the cloth barrier away.

Fascination darkened blue eyes as with his action powerful muscles flexed beneath their mat of bronze curls. Even before he aimlessly tossed his garment into the shadows, she reached out to stoke the hard, wide expanse of the massive chest rising and falling so heavily she could feel his hunger spreading its ever more desperate need to her.

Shuddering beneath the caress, Adam pulled her back into his arms. His mouth opened over hers, devouring her eager lips until she melted against him, seeking more, ever striving to get closer.

Then with a satisfied smile Adam shifted his lips to kiss smooth cheeks and nuzzle a throat that arched under the burning touch even as he struggled to free her of a simple homespun gown. It proved remarkably uncooperative with fingers afflicted with haste-induced clumsiness, a difficulty the experienced man had never in past encountered.

"I want to feel all of you against me again as I have in nightly dreams and daylight fantasies." The low growl sent shivers of desire through Llys, and when with the last word Adam at long last rid her of the recalcitrant gown she was as pleased by its absence as he.

His hands returned to cup the bounty of her breasts. Llys quietly gasped, lifting into their hold, and when warm, sword-callused hands contracted on throbbing flesh, a moan of anguished pleasure rose from her depths.

At her ardent response, passion blazed through Adam's veins and his mouth laid a trail of fire across passion-flushed cheeks to reclaim hers in a devastating kiss. She pressed aching curves against his strong torso, and he was pleased by her uncontrollable need, a hunger near as deep as his own. He settled on his back and with hands on her shoulders urged her upward and held her immobile above him. Desire glittered in the amber gaze moving over sweet flesh, and then he lowered her enough that he was able to alternately stroke tantalizing fire over deep rose tips with his tongue or tempt with the more exciting pleasure of drawing them full into the heat of his mouth.

Shaking under such unbelievable delights, Llys lowered her heavy lashes as she twisted her head to one side, sending a curtain of ebony curls down to brush the side of his face with its silky caress. Lost in desire's urgent demands, Adam lowered her to the pallet and rose above her to let golden flames burn over the reality behind so many tantalizing dreams and delicious memories as he removed the rest of his own unwanted clothes.

Despite closed eyes, Llys felt the heat of his gaze as if it were a physical caress and was far too caught up in desire to recognize or wish to hide the helpless response assuredly visible to him.

As Adam stretched out at Llys's side, she flowed toward him as naturally as water downhill. In silent praise, her hands again explored the erotic combination of hard muscle and abrasive hair before sliding up to measure the width of his shoulders with awe. Reveling in the feel of his powerful body, with her small pointed tongue she ventured to taste his flesh as he had tasted hers. The surface of his magnificent chest rose and fell heavily as she moved her mouth across it. Sensing the potent desire growing in him, she grew bolder.

Enjoying Llys's curious exploration, Adam curbed a need to crush her temptingly pliant form to his aching body despite the intensified provocation—until her lips found a flat masculine nipple. Then his labored breathing caught on a harsh cry of hunger. He pulled her against the whole long length of his powerful form and swept his hands down the satin curve of her back, mindlessly bringing her hips into contact with his.

The intimacy dragged a shattering moan from her throat. Lost in blazing sensations, Llys shifted recklessly. She dug her nails into the firm flesh of his neck in a silent plea for relief. But Adam reined in his own wildly insistent cravings long enough to caress her every curve and tease every sense with stinging pleasures until she groaned with a frustrated desire as deep as his own. Only then did he gently urge her to lie back and shift as he settled himself full atop her slender length—hard chest against soft breasts, hip to hip, thigh to thigh.

Llys clasped Adam's hips closer still in an attempt to provoke him into providing the delight of a fulfillment that was his to give. He responded with a powerful thrust that merged her wanting flesh with his own, and the enchantress yielded to a song surely the most powerful spell of all for the love at its core. Adam held her tightly bound to him, as their twined bodies surged in the hot, wild rhythm of passion. The pleasures were overwhelming, yet Llys clung to the beloved source of such sweet music and desperately strove to match his power until at last the near unbearable tension of an ever increasing tempo burst in a shower of glittering sparks.

Wrapped together in soft clouds of contentment, they drifted into gentle dreams, oblivious to the challenges and dangers looming near.

Chapter
18

"Aye." Pip steadily met his lord's gaze while nodding with earnest fervor. "I have news of vast importance, else never would I have called out for you."

Only the faintest hint of day's first light had begun to brighten the eastern horizon, and Pip had far rather not have been forced to awaken his leader, even less with the unpleasant tidings he bore.

"Then get it said and have done." Although Pip's call had been quiet, it had been a rude awakening and an unwelcome end come too soon to warm contentment, leaving Adam in no mood for a laggard's pace in the telling. Thankfully Llys had tarried in dreams even while he, by the dim glow of a single coal, had searched out garments hastily discarded with no concern for where they landed. He'd thrust his legs into his chausses' loose leggings before slipping from Llys's chamber as quietly as possible but had carried the tunic, which he now tugged over his head—a too revealing fact.

Pip rushed to do as his lord bade him. "During

night's darkest hours reinforcements arrived to take up positions beyond the palisade wall."

Despite Pip's attempt to look unconcerned, curiosity glittered in the gaze he couldn't prevent from sliding sidelong to the closed chamber door from which Adam had emerged. 'Struth, to accommodate a captive prince, sleeping arrangements had been changed for the night but not, he was fairly certain, those involving Lord Adam and the young sorceress.

Amber eyes narrowed against this announcement of an event expected but come with surprising speed. Adam nodded and said, "Have the two villagers at the outer door guard Saexbo while you go to the gate and assure those standing watch there that I'll soon join them."

Though Adam was anxious to get on with the dangerous duties at hand, everything from cross-garters to the jerkin studded with large interlaced metal rings waited in his own chamber. Harmless as Pip's curiosity most oft was, Adam would not rouse it more by being seen to step from one room but return to another—a fact which if, even inadvertently, passed along the gossip vines might bring Llys unearned shame. Suspicion the loyal young guardsman had aplenty, but only that, and Adam chose not to tempt him with more.

After Pip's departure, Adam hastily prepared himself for the unpleasant task ahead and set off down the village lane to the gate at its end. As he had done before greeting Saexbo only the past day, Adam climbed the sturdy wooden ladder to confront unwelcome visitors. But this time it was no longer a matter of two small groups of inexperienced youths uselessly blocking gates. Those whose encampment had filled abbey lands now completely surrounded Throcken-holt's palisade with battle-honed might.

Two leaders stood below, radically different in their callings—one an erstwhile man of peace, the other with expertise in war—but bound together by greed for the power and wealth to be wielded behind a weak king. They remained quiet, giving the shire's tempo-rary lord time to observe and, with right wits, surely recognize the hopelessness of his position.

"Do you surrender?" Hordath hadn't a bishop's training to patience and was unwilling to waste over-much time in unproductive silence.

Adam's smile was the vision of cold cynicism. "For what worthless reason would I do that?"

"To save your own hide!" Hordath snapped back.

"Though I appreciate your fears on my behalf," Adam mocked, "I am confident of my ability to preserve my own health. Thus 'tis not with my life you ought be concerned."

Hordath lifted his chin against the other's disdain and drew his husky form up to present its most fearsome guise. "Idle boasts will not protect you from *my* sword!"

"Indeed not. Nor would I wish it so. With pleasure I will meet your challenge to do battle one to one." Adam's cynical smile deepened for this challenge near a duplicate of the one he'd offered Saexbo, the first to lay Throckenholt siege.

"But given the threat you mean to Lord Wulf and all that is his"—Adam ruefully grimaced—"honorable duty insists I put personal pride aside and warn you that my life or that of any person within these walls can be called forfeit only at the price of your princeling's."

"We can set fire to this wall and to the village inside!" Wilfrid harshly broke into the conflict. He refused to acknowledge the effectiveness of the vise Adam had placed about a long planned and anticipated scheme of vengeance to bring down the king who sought to take away the worldly power and wealth that were most important to him. "In the panic certain to follow, while you fight through smoke, Saexbo will be rescued."

"Are you so certain he still lives?" Adam's mocked. Here was a prospect the men come to Saexbo's aid had not considered. It shook their confidence.

"How will you explain Saexbo's death to his father, *our* king?" All humor gone from the piercing golden gaze pinned to an impious bishop, Adam followed his well-struck blow with another. "And if the pawn you meant to put on the throne is gone, how can you hope to win the power you seek?"

"How will *you* explain Saexbo's death?" Wilfrid slyly asked, certain a powerful defense lay in this turning of the question back on the resented foe who lived now only because of the ineptitude the bishop's foolish minions. "If in truth Saexbo died after you took him captive, you will have even more offenses to explain."

"Nay." As Adam calmly shook his head, golden hair glowed even in the limited light of predawn. "'Twould be a most simple task for I would needs speak but the truth of your wrongful deeds, of the wicked acts perpetrated by a bishop—including even the murder of an innocent monk."

The ealdorman of Oaklea's eyes blazed with the dangerous fires Wilfrid well remembered from their confrontation in his abbey chamber. Although the bishop would not shrink back, an expression grown grim revealed his awareness of how willing King Ecgferth would be to believe ill of him.

Adam was amused by Hordath's glance of contempt toward his ally. Deliberately he added, "Also I would speak of how Hordath—a man to whom the king had entrusted his son—not only led that too impressionable boy into treason but loosed him to wreak havoc on the good people of Throckenholt in a vicious rampage that included a coward's assault upon Wulfayne, one of Ecgferth's most trusted ealdormen. And Wulf *lives* to show the scar and to bear witness to Saexbo's attack."

"Not so!" A reed-slender soldier stepped from a crowd of many to stand between the two leaders at the foot of Throckenholt's gate. "Wulfayne is dead, or soon will be, no matter the healing arts worked upon his flesh." With this confident claim the soldier removed a helm, releasing a sorceress's wealth of black curls. "By the powers Gytha wielded, he was destroyed."

Of a sudden Adam realized that Llys once more stood at his side to face a besieging force, this one far deadlier than the first.

"You are wrong, Elesa." Llys quietly spoke. Having awakened to find Adam gone and having then learned about the arrival of this greater danger, Llys had realized that the moment Evain warned her to expect had come. Here waited the conflict she must meet, and in calm certainty Llys faced her mirror image.

"'Tis Gytha who is no more." Llys's voice held a strange pity for Elesa, who was now left, as was she herself, without a mentor. "My foster father lives and will soon return to his home and to the people of Throckenholt, none of whom either you or this army can endanger."

Welcoming an instantly ignited wave of white-hot rage, Elesa wasted no effort on a denial. Rather, in response, she began a peculiar song that initially embarrassed her cohorts. But as the sound dropped lower and strange gusts of wind began to blow, they grew frightened.

Elesa's voice expanded into a roar that whipped the dirt and long grasses at her cohorts' feet into strange patterns. The unnatural turbulence twisted the soldiers' garments in directions at odds with one another. Then the promise of dawn's bright shades were blocked by the sudden appearance of dark clouds which, in answer to arms wildly waved, raced across the sky to collide in thunderous crashes. Observers fell mute at the display of such fearsome powers.

Llys, too, faltered. But only for a moment. The memory of Evain's confidence in her bolstered her courage while she recalled his caution that if she wished to defeat and scatter darkness she must trust not herself but far greater powers. With a lilting thrice-repeated chant of supplication to the forces of a dawning sun Llys began.

When the tempest's clouds slowed and even began to recede, deepening fury strengthened Elesa's commands, preventing nature's upheaval from fading into calm.

Though separated by the distance from walkway to ground below, the two who were so much alike stared into each other's unwavering blue eyes. To Adam their relative positions seemed like a symbol of the difference between them—high and bright against earthly and dark. And although the only weapons the women wielded were their voices, Adam sensed in their clash a danger far more ominous than that of honed steel.

Llys's voice lifted into a soaring melody with words holding no meaning for the listening men. Yet their attention was commanded upward as her hands rose, palms up as if she were reaching for a distant gift. Then her hands came together over her head, fingertips joined above while thumbs met below to form a triangle pointing toward the opening between fleeing clouds and the light gilding their edges. In answer to her supplication, an amazing spectacle appeared.

Gaping witnesses watched in awed silence as a single bright orb streaked through a sky, from which the stars had faded. The brilliance of this magical morning star drove lingering clouds into abeyance and left the beauty of a long tail across a clear, colorless sky of early morning.

Llys's eerily beautiful chant, with its incomprehensible words, faded into peaceful silence as she slowly lowered her arms. An initial dazed hush broke into cries of praise from all of Throckenholt's own. But Llys's sympathy was roused when she looked down and saw Elesa lying in a crumpled heap upon uneven, heavily trodden ground.

Adam felt Llys's compassion for her foe and it more thoroughly convinced him of the blessing given by his tender emotion for the incredible enchantress he'd claimed and would do all, give all, to hold forever safe at his side. The differences in their heritages meant nothing compared to his love for her. In truth, having seen her wage a battle of light against the darkness the sorcerers had warned against, he no longer saw a difference at all. His Christian faith taught belief in the struggle between good and evil. His Llys was struggling for the same honorable goals as he. Sliding his hands beneath the shiny curtain of her curls, he wrapped his arms about her shoulders and gently pulled her back to rest against his strength. Llys welcomed his wordless support, grateful that, despite recent grief and the challenges yet to be met, her difficult feat had come to a right end and ensured Adam's safety from dark powers.

As the couple on the palisade walkway watched, it became clear that the besieging force would offer no further threat. The warriors had splintered into confused disarray, muttering between themselves of defection from an alliance proven wrongful by their sorceress's failure and, in truth, by the wickedness of a bishop who would seek such aid. Loyalty oaths given the source of foul ambitions were easily betrayed with none willing to claim sufficient knowledge to decry the misdeed of another. Before the throng stationed around Throckenholt's wall could break apart and scatter, however, they found themselves surrounded by another, larger ring of armed men led by King Ecgferth.

Wilfrid and Hordath, who had turned traitor to their king, were left undefended and were immediately taken captive by warriors wielding gleaming swords to good effect. Hordath snarled as his arms were roughly bound behind his back, but the bishop silently stared at his royal opponent from narrowed eyes full of spite and a silent vow of retribution.

Although startled by this most unexpected arrival, Adam grinned down at the rider who removed his helm to reveal silver hair that gleamed as bright as his own golden mane.

"Your majesty," Adam called. "Temporarily standing in Wulfayne's stead, I bid you welcome to Throckenholt."

King Ecgferth gave a warm smile to his ealdorman, though Adam was lord of lands other than these. "I thank you for holding Throckenholt safe for its lord and my kingdom for me." He started to ask after the beauty tenderly held by the woman-disdaining Adam, but the noise of the gate being opened intervened.

While Adam aided Llys in safely descending the ladder, the king's guardsmen continued their task of taking captive traitorous warriors, who rued their foolishness in not having abandoned their leaders' cause much sooner. The prisoners would be bound and transported to the king's hall, from whence punishments were rendered.

Throckenholt's gates were fully open by the time Adam and Llys reached the ground, where they immediately turned to greet a dismounting king.

"You are soon arrived, Sire." Adam's smile lacked the cynicism Ecgferth had thought a permanent part of it.

"We rode all night. I fear our steeds are much wearier than we." The king ruefully stroked his neatly trimmed beard.

Adam nodded but glanced knowingly at the young sorcerer a pace behind the king. In order for the king to have appeared so quickly, Evain must perforce have arrived at the court with unnatural speed.

Evain serenely smiled, but his eyes glittered with amusement for Adam's perception—unique and plainly born of his love for a sorceress.

Adam returned his attention to his king and saw that Ecgferth's curious gaze rested on a blushing Llys with more than passing interest. When that intense gaze shifted to him, Adam knew a formal introduction was expected, even though Evain had doubtless spoken to the king of his twin sister.

Golden hair caught the morning star's lingering light as Adam nodded and with pride complied with the wordless request. "This is my liege, Ecgferth, king of Northumbria,"

Llys smiled while Adam completed the formality with words that lent such pleasure the wild rose brightness of her soft cheeks increased.

"And this, Sire, is Llys, *my* enchantress who, get I my way, you'll meet many a time at Oaklea in coming years."

Llys glanced up and happily sank into the unshielded love in molten honey eyes.

"Llys and I have met before." Ecgferth was fondly amused at the miraculous sight of his too cynical supporter fallen to the gentle lure of not merely a woman but a sorceress! "Though she was but a child and may have forgotten, I never will."

Startled, Adam blinked, but then a bright smile flashed. Of course, Ecgferth's throne had been saved years past by the magical "great death of birds," a feat accomplished by the Druidic sorcery of Llys, Brynna, and Evain.

"So . . ." Ecgferth saw that Adam comprehended his meaning. "You see how familiar I am with her fine talents. Although it seems you've an infinitely deeper appreciation of her value, doubtless something you find most precious."

While Adam and his king retreated to the keep's hall to discuss the events of past days and to make plans for those ahead, Llys arranged for Elesa to be carried into her own chamber. She then turned attention to the massive task of marshaling preparations for a great feast of celebration to include the whole of Throckenholt, their king, and his army.

With the merry help of grateful villagers the deed was done. Trestle tables were hauled into the daylight and assembled to stretch down the village's single lane from gate to keep. Though simple, the food was abundant, hearty, and certain to be much enjoyed.

When the sun in its day's final glory rested on the western horizon, the long, long table was crowded on both sides with the people of Throckenholt. Their king sat at its head, Adam and Llys on his right and, to Ecgferth's surprise, Pip with Maida on his left.

At the meal's start, the king rose to his feet to offer a toast. "Once again, Adam, I owe you a debt of such proportions as can never be repaid. First, my life you saved. Now my kingdom . . . although that is a deed for which you must share credit with the lovely sorceress at your side. To Lord Adam and the lovely Llys!"

The king lifted a precious silver chalice high, and those in the crowd immediately responded by raising theirs as well. Adam wrapped his strong arm about Llys's shoulders to hold her soft form near while the toast was drunk.

When the meal commenced, a nervous Maida couldn't help but glance apprehensively toward the king—who owned her as a thrall.

Well aware of the woman's discomfort, Ecgferth frowned. Her nervousness was unwelcome at such a feast as this. What with a traitorous son, he had pains of his own but had left them behind to join the people of Throckenholt in celebrating the deliverance of their lands and his realm. Despite his determination not to permit Saexbo's traitorous deeds to muddy his evening's enjoyment, thoughts of the son he'd already dispatched to his dead mother's people in the far, far north—home of the barbaric Picts—intruded.

Adam saw Maida's discomfort and Ecgferth's resulting frown. A white smile flashed. Filled with more peace and happiness than he'd ever known existed, he wanted to see that the young guardsman who'd helped in Saexbo's capture would be given his heart's desire. Adam placed his gleaming silver goblet on the table and turned to his king.

"I would beg a boon of you, Sire."

Ecgferth's brows rose in surprise. This was a rare event, for although he owed much to the man, Adam —unlike others who vied for positions near the throne merely for the sake of seeking unearned rewards—had never asked anything of him.

"Whatever you ask, I must give in recompense for all you've done in my behalf."

Adam shook his head, uncomfortable with the thought of performing duties for gain beyond those mutually owed between a monarch and his subjects. "'Tis a small matter. One I seek not in payment for what I give in duty owed but rather asked as a gift from a friend."

With a fond smile, his admiration for Adam growing, Ecgferth nodded a head as bright a silver as the nearly empty goblet in his hand.

"The thrall, Maida, is your property although you gave her into Saexbo's hands." Adam steadily spoke. "The boon I ask is her freedom."

Ecgferth was startled. He looked between his friend and the sorceress so lovely she seemed to glow. Surely Adam could want no other woman.

Llys's gaze had gone soft for Adam's thoughtful request but saw the king's confusion and sought to lessen it. "In the days we've shared here, I've come to value the maid and would appreciate the gift of her companionship."

"She is yours—thrall or free as you choose."

Ecgferth's mouth curled in a curious smile, but he shrugged as he looked between Adam and Llys.

"Then Maida goes with us, a free woman, on our return to Oaklea . . . with my *men.*"

Pip gave a whoop and unabashedly hugged a wildly blushing Maida, whose smile could've flooded the night with sunlight.

As the meal continued and wine flowed in as steady a stream as the ale, Ecgferth revealed his plans for disposing of their erstwhile foes. He had already told Adam in private that he'd banished his foolish, ever troublesome son to the north. Now, with no care who might hear, Ecgferth stated his intent to send the treacherous Hordath into exile across the great North Sea. And, though Adam knew his king would have preferred to see Wilfrid imprisoned, instead the less than pious man would be put on a ship setting sail for Rome and the Holy Father to whom he claimed loyalty—although loyalty was not a quality either Ecgferth or Adam thought Wilfrid likely to feel and less to act upon.

At the end of a meal during which horns of ale had been freely emptied and flagons of wine passed in great abundance, musical instruments were brought out and trestle tables cleared to make room for dancing.

Llys soon discovered she was expected to dance with near every man in the village—and with a great many of the king's warriors as well. While whirling through the steps, she caught glimpses of Evain dancing with Anya in his arms, first laughing and later dozing gently against his shoulder, small arms curled about his neck. The hour grew late with no sign of a lessening in the celebration. Laughing but wearied by rounds of dancing, she was pleased when Adam appeared to claim her from the arms of her previous partner—a stout ceorl who'd stood guard over Saexbo.

Despite the milling guests, Adam pulled Llys with him into a dark private corner of Maelvyn's smithy where he took her into his arms for a passionate kiss too soon ended.

"Llys, pray, may I have a private moment with you?" Evain asked.

Feeling Adam stiffen against not merely the unwelcome interruption of their embrace but a perceived threat to their union, Llys instantly smoothed soft palms over the fine wool of the sleeve covering a strong arm. For the first time she realized that during all the events transpiring during precious few hours she hadn't paused to ponder Evain's possible response to her love for this Saxon.

"Brother . . ." She hesitantly began but Evain quickly intervened and, with a sorcerer's sensitivity to others' emotions, calmed her spreading anxiety.

"I feel your happiness and am pleased. No doubt your Adam will be as worthy a husband for you as Wulf is to Brynna." He offered his forearm to Adam who hesitated for no more than an instant before joining his to the one offered as a symbol of family bonds accepted.

"But, Llys, I've come seeking you to speak of Elesa . . . our sister."

Llys smiled faintly. Since the moment she and Elesa had faced each other in conflict she'd begun to suspect this relationship.

Evain went on. "Although I feel I must leave you and go to Brynna's aid until Wulf can be returned here, as soon he will, I chose first to talk with Elesa."

Llys nodded the rightness she recognized in this action.

"Gytha was our aunt, too," Evain stated. "Our father knew that people are fearful of any man whose wife bears more than one child in a single birthing. Two would be suspicious. But when born to a Druid sorcerer revering the magic of triads, three babies at one time would bring horror . . . and doubtless danger. When three of us were born in a single night, he recognized the need to act for the safety of us all. He carried one of his two daughters to his sister in another cantref, thinking he would bring her home again in time . . . but, as we know, he wasn't given that time."

"Was it the grandsire we never knew who taught Gytha the secret knowledge?" Llys asked.

"Nay, not apurpose." Evain ruefully shook his head. "Gytha was barred from Druidic training by her father, a sorcerer, but by lingering near and listening while he passed the knowledge to her brother, our father, she heard enough to acquire the knowledge on her own. Elesa says she was most proud of having won her powers without the aid of a master. 'Twas why she was so certain her skills would enable her to defeat Glyndor."

Two pairs of like blue eyes met in unspoken sorrow they both felt for their mentor.

"And she taught Elesa her ways." Llys's question was really a statement.

Evain grimly nodded. "But with *our* aunt Gytha's final defeat and your having defeated the powers she thought unconquerable, Elesa learned the limitations of her training. I offered to show her how to turn such powers to beneficent uses, but she fears them now and chose instead to break her crystal and forever sunder her bond with the voiceless spirits of nature. While I watched, that she did."

Llys gasped. To her such a deed would be the ultimate punishment, but mayhap to one trained in dark ways, their forfeiture would be a relief.

Evain continued. "Elesa spoke of her childhood home in the south, a place she said was happy before Gytha's spells earned the fear and hatred of foes who burned their haven." The images raised were a reminder of unpleasant events he and Llys had seen in their youth, and an expression of distress flashed across Evain's face. "It is Elesa's desire to return to the south. After helping her fill a satchel with food, I shielded her from sight by the light of my crystal and saw her safely free of the keep and into the forest."

Evain and Llys gazed into each other's eyes in wordless confirmation of a wrong having been made right. "Now," Evain said, "I am off to lend what aid I may to Brynna and Wulf. Are you like to be here when we all return?"

Adam immediately nodded, blond hair falling forward. "We will remain here until Wulfayne returns safe and whole. Then, as you are the only sorcerer I am ever like to know, I will ask that you perform whatever Druid rite is necessary to bind Llys to me as my wife."

Evain solemnly nodded in answer to the favor honorably asked before he slipped into shadows as abruptly as he had appeared.

Once Evain had gone, leaving them again alone, although in a privacy proven less than certain, Llys nestled closer against the powerful man who was hers to claim.

"In all the years and despite the many women I

knew before we met, I have never loved another. Now that I've found the source of such a sweet delight and endless peace that you are, I'll never let you go." The soft velvet of his eyes stroked the tender beauty guilelessly yielding against him. "By both Druid and Christian rites we shall be bound to each other forever."

"And I shall love you until the end of time and beyond." Llys had heard an echo of the bitterness his mother's abandonment had begun. Silently she promised to spend the rest of her days filling the void and proving he need never fear being deserted again.

Llys gazed up, and her blue eyes darkened to the shade of the midnight sky above as Adam bent to claim a soul-binding kiss, which she returned full well.

POCKET BOOKS
PROUDLY ANNOUNCES

CHANTING THE STORM

MARYLYLE ROGERS

Coming in Paperback
from Pocket Books
Summer 1994

The following is a preview of
Chanting the Storm . . .

Spring
A.D. 688

Spirits of meadows and woodland bowers, of eternal stone and fleeting flowers, of gentle dew and mighty sea, thrice of you I plea. Dainty form clad in soft yellow perched on a stool drawn close to one of a pair of small windows whose shutters were thrown wide, Anya exercised her habit of solemn patience while continuing an unspoken chant. *Once to grant serenity, twice to warm Evain's memories, and thrice to hasten him home to me.*

Anya had been waiting in near this same position since dawn, gazing at the path leading to the door of Throckenholt Keep. Now, as she earnestly repeated her soundless litany, the deepening pastels of a setting sun lent a bright aura to her slender body and glowed on the cloud of pale blond hair cloaking her shoulders. Even while chanting she prayed that what power silence robbed of her words might be compensated for by their fervor.

The daughter of a Saxon Christian and Druid sorceress, Anya saw no reason to hesitate in combining a

Christian prayer with a Druid chant. She worried only that her triads failed to possess the ethereal beauty and effortless rhythm of either her mother's or Llys's chants. 'Twas the best she could do without the formal training denied her by a loving father's insistence that his children be raised as Christians and by a mother's honest belief that her half-Saxon children were by their mixed blood blocked from attaining mastery of Druidic forces.

Aware of a sudden that her unusual restlessness had drawn the notice of both her mother and Llys, Anya realized she'd allowed her mind to wander. From so early a time she could not name the day she'd listened closely, quiet as a mouse, and long since learned enough to know that serenity and unwavering attention were the first steps in wielding Druidic power. Were her chants to be of any value, she must focus on them alone.

Spirits of meadows and woodland bowers, of eternal stone and fleeting flowers, of gentle dew and mighty sea, thrice of you I plea. . . . Leaf-green eyes closed tight, Anya concentrated on her goal—Evain's coming.

Even the fact that Evain was not journeying here to see her but rather in answer to his sister's desperate plea failed to lessen Anya's delight. Blocking all thought of the keep's hall, of thralls laboring at the central hearth over a belated evening meal, of her mother and Llys, she fervently repeated silent triads.

Brynna sat in her shadowed herb corner at a long table burdened with an array of vials, measuring bowls, and pottery jars. The methodical pounding of a small pestle to grind tiny seeds in a stone bowl was a task so oft repeated over many years that it permitted her to work without thought to the sleeping tisane in which they'd be steeped.

Instead a gray gaze darkened with anxiety lingered upon the daughter filled with palpable anticipation. Despite the lovely vision presented by her golden child bathed in daylight's final glory, to Brynna's mind Anya had as well have been shrouded in bleak mists and leaning out over an unseen precipice. Brynna near wished that Evain would not answer the call too likely to tempt Anya into a headlong fall.

Over the years Brynna and Wulf had watched in amusement while as toddler and then awkward child Anya idolized teenaged Evain—a harmless youthful fancy. But now Anya was a maiden full-grown and her unwavering admiration had become a worrisome thing intensified by the fact that the boy to whom Brynna had stood as foster mother, of sorts, had matured into a devastatingly handsome young man. The potency of Evain's natural attraction had been increased by experience gained in having been pursued by a great many females during the past decade and made the more dangerous for mystical powers joined to his physical strength. A danger particularly to Anya.

Evain was a Druid sorcerer whose heritage and destiny demanded the fulfillment of an all-important duty owed both to the past and to the future—one in which a half-Saxon mate could have no part. Thus, nothing could come from the deepening of Anya's feelings for him. Nothing but pain for Anya. And of that Brynna wished to spare her daughter. Regretfully, there existed no mystical chant able to alter human emotion.

The overworked pestle had ground seeds into an unnecessarily fine powder before it was stilled by another's gentle fingers settling atop Brynna's hands. A dark head highlighted by strands of silver lifted to meet the solace of Llys's sapphire gaze.

"Trust Evain." Llys spoke so softly only Brynna would hear. As the mother of a healthy pair of twin boys and a toddling girl, Llys could easily comprehend her foster mother's concern but also knew her brother too well to doubt his honor. "He cares too much to hurt her."

Brynna's smile failed to reach her eyes. "I fear 'tis as inevitable as the thunder that follows a strike of lightning." Seeing the other woman's distress over the truth in her statement, Brynna felt guilty. First, for thwarting

Llys's attempt to comfort. Second, for even momentarily regretting Evain's coming when it was so necessary to aid in Llys's desperate cause.

Unaware that the two older women were quietly discussing her, Anya maintained her concentration by summoning to mind the image of the darkly handsome sorcerer, her beloved Evain. The fervor of her chanting intensified until some inexplicable inner voice urged her to look through the window.

Green eyes flew open to glimpse the answer to her pleas striding through twilight's purple mists. Anya leaped to her feet so quickly her stool crashed to the side. Paying it no heed, she rushed to throw wide the iron-bound planks of an oak door, dash down the front path, and hurtle herself against the longed-for figure.

"You're here! Oh, Evain, I'm so glad you've come at last." The words were muffled against his broad chest, but she soon leaned back and tilted her chin upward to ask, "Why have you stayed away so long?"

One strong arm wrapped tightly around the dainty figure while the other held a stave topped with a crystal clasped in a bronze eagle's claws. Evain gazed down into a piquant face radiating an unshielded emotion he dare not return. 'Twas the answer to her question, yet one he would not state aloud for fear of opening a subject best buried in silence. In truth, he wouldn't have ventured coming to Throckenholt at all but for his sister's urgent request that he meet her here. Aye, only affection for his sister and awareness of the desperate purpose behind her summons had forced him to risk reentering a tempting web woven by sweet innocence and forbidden love.

And yet nothing could prevent him from drinking in the reality behind too many daydreams and night fantasies. Large silver-green eyes dominated an elfin face with high cheekbones and pointed chin while her petal-pink lips, top bowed and bottom full, were far too enticing. And the more inviting now when they were so brief a distance below his own.

"Come in, Evain." Calling from the cottage's open doorway, Brynna's voice was sharp and sundered the dangerous enthrallment she saw too clearly. But her tone softened to add, "There's stew and fresh bread waiting to be eaten."

Evain glanced over the top of Anya's blond head, smiling an apology for the momentary lapse in his guard and gratitude for the interruption. Asides, he was both hungry and thirsty.

"I pray you can spare me a mug of ale as well." The beauty continued clinging to his side, but it was with a restrained brotherly affection that he wrapped his arm about her and led the way into an abode where burned a fire whose warmth was welcome against the spring evening's chill.

Three women and one man took seats at the high table of a lord gone to join his king in defending a threatened kingdom. By the fact that Evain had chosen to sit between his sister and foster mother, Anya recognized his justness in turning attention toward the serious need for which he'd been called. And, as was her habit, Anya retreated into a shell of patience, silent but intent upon hearing all that was said. Once each had been served with trenchers of bread drenched in savory stew and Evain had his big earthen mug of ale, he quietly listened while his sister spoke of the matter which had drawn him here.

"As you know, Wulf joined our king in meeting with the foes of Northumbria. And you know, too, that after he saw one of their leaders wearing Adam's helm and armor, we thought him dead." Despite now possessing worthy reason to question that assumption, Llys's voice still ached from months of what she hoped was needless mourning.

"Less than a fortnight past, to Oaklea came a traveler. After wending a path through the kingdoms of Wessex and Mercia he found his way to our door. For the price of a meal and a night's abode, he delivered this missive."

Llys carefully laid a square of folded parchment on the table and nudged it toward her brother.

Evain went still before returning a full spoon to the trencher which he then moved aside. Gingerly he slid the clearly precious parchment nearer. The ragged paper crackled in its cautious opening and, curiously, several pieces of candle tallow fell to the table's bare planks. They were initially ignored while he gave his attention to the message in his hands. It was with unconscious gratitude for the wisdom of their foster father, Wulfayne —who had insisted that, in addition to Glyndor's Druidic training, he and his sister learn the rudiments of writing and reading—that he read the scribbled message: "Healthy but in stone."

The letters were roughly formed and smudged, leaving little doubt but that they'd been written with a bit of crudely sharpened coal salvaged from a fire gone cold. Yet, though cryptic and unsigned, its meaning was as clear as the identity of its author.

"Realign the tallow pieces," Llys urged, heart in her throat. Although she'd been certain of the letter's source the moment it touched her outstretched hand, she was anxious for the reassurance to be granted by a brother as convinced as she that this was not merely a cruel hoax.

After Evain nudged the three largest chunks of broken tallow together, the identity of the message's source was confirmed. Pressed into their center was a stylized letter: *A*. One such as those so oft used in illuminating the manuscripts copied by scribes in monasteries.

None at the table could doubt but that the mark had been produced by the ring whose metal strands were twined into the first letter of Adam's name. The ring was a distinctive one given Adam by King Ecgferth in thanks for having saved his liege's life. Ever secreted upon his person, Adam had long used it to mark formal approval of documents and to sign personal correspondence.

"When Wulf returned from the unsuccessful negotiation between our king and his opponents, he told me of

the foe who proudly wore Adam's helm and armor—"
Brynna broke a long silence. "And he spoke of looking
for but failing to see the ring upon him."

"Adam was wise not to sign his name." Evain nodded
both acceptance of Brynna's statement and his certainty
that the letter had truly been sent by a captive Adam. "I
fear that had it been recovered by his captors, his life
would've been . . ."

Llys shivered while through her mind ran visions of
Adam being tossed into the sea or a bottomless peat
bog—both furtive but known practices for assuring the
permanent disappearance of a foe.

Sensing the distress caused by the implication, Evain
regretted not having better guarded his tongue. To direct
his sister's thoughts away from bleak possibilities, he
asked, "Whence did this message originate?"

"The one who delivered it claimed 'twas given him in
Wessex by a man who had traveled south." Llys's answer
was immediate. "Said the first man was unable to recall
precisely where or who had given it to him."

That the source of Adam's letter could not be firmly
stated was no surprise to the listeners. Unless a lord sent
his own trusted messenger, most written communication
passed through many hands before reaching its destination.

When the meal was done, thralls removed the trenchers and retired to the small hut provided by their master.
The hut was a gift of uncommon consideration for slaves
but one also able to provide Wulf and his family with an
even rarer treasure—hours of privacy. Alone and free to
openly discuss secret matters unknown and never to be
revealed to those unworthy of being taught, Evain and
the two sorceresses reached an agreement. They would
take the scrap of parchment out into nature's haven.
Once within arms whose embrace was ever open to those
able to commune with its silent voices, they would chant
the rising moon.

Anya quietly rose when, to intently discuss needful

details, the tones of her mother and the two siblings instinctively sank into whispers. Slipping from the abode unnoticed, Anya hastened down two wooden steps, around the keep, and into a circle of oaks. In his bride's honor, near two decades past, her father and planted these trees, joining them to the mighty one long growing at this site.

Anya approached that venerable oak, gently singing the triads of respect and gentle pleas for permission to use its shield which she'd learned from a mother unaware of how attentively her child listened. Then, in a darkness preceding the moon's appearance, she hiked her pale skirts up to billow over a low-riding belt of plaited reeds, leaving the hem to brush her thighs. Once done, Anya began to steadily climb. The bark was rough on her soft hands, and she feared that, even carefully folded over a belt, her linen skirts would have tears difficult to explain. Still, she had no regret for the deed. Anya had just settled herself into a crook between sturdy limb and trunk when the other three entered the oak grove below.

Evain placed the missive from Adam in its midst. Next, atop the scrap of parchment, he, Llys, and Brynna laid their crystals. The three then moved together, not into a circle but a triangle. Eyes shut and arms extended with the closed fingers of one's hand touching at tips against another's while thumbs met below to also form triangles at each joining, they began chanting an eerily beautiful tune. The wild song's deep tones sank and gained strength as the trio slowly revolved around soon glowing white stones. When the notes soared higher, the three Druids moved ever faster, and the crystals burned so brilliantly 'twas as if the rising moon itself had come to rest in the grove's heart.

In branches above, Anya was awed by the charm of what, by a tale told far and wide, she recogized as the eternal triad of balanced power. Aye, though these haunting verses had a different purpose, this must surely be the same powerful rite that the three had once performed to send a massive army fleeing.

As the otherworldly entreaty's final notes dipped, swirled, and soared through the treetops like rising sparks, each chanter bent to lift their own crystal and reverently cradle it in cupped hands. Gazing into bright centers, one by one they spoke of visions revealed within luminous depths.

"I see men dressed in the armor of ancient invaders." Brynna recognized the garb by virtue of the costume passed through her family from generation to generation until Glyndor had seen Wulf so attired to aid in a rescue of her.

Fascination filled Llys's voice as she said, "I see the southern forest and crashing sea beyond."

Both the eerie glow and waiting silence lingered until at last Evain shared his vision. "I see a sprawling stone palace . . . surrounded by dense forests and shrouded in storm clouds." His words summoned his companions' attention and their crystals went dark, but he gave them a grim smile. "Leastways we have learned enough that I know my destination and may go forth warned, prepared for the difficult quest."

"You go?" Llys's brief question held both fear and hope.

Evain nodded and while the brightness of his crystal faded, the light of a fully risen moon rippled over the thick black mane a watcher above intently studied. "Both you and Brynna have children to raise and shires for which to care," he sensibly answered his sister, strong chin lifting in demonstration of his determination. "Asides, alone I am better able to thread my way through the forest of foes and pass unscathed through the storm."

Brynna remained silent. She saw too well the verity of Evain's claim. Loving him as a son, she feared for him but could not honestly dispute his words. Asides, he'd been both well trained to military skills by a great warrior, her husband, and taught all manner of mystical powers by her grandfather, the famed Druid sorcerer Glyndor. With these comforting facts she soothed her apprehensions for his safety.

From the branches overhead, Anya listened to frightening words. It was not totally unexpected, but she'd refused to earlier consider the likelihood of Evain's clearly stated intent. She laid her soft cheek against the trunk's rough bark, an unthinking echo of the need to face harsh realities. 'Twas true that neither her mother nor Llys could desert those dependent upon them—both children and entire shires. Not when the only males remaining in Throckenholt and Oaklea were either very young or old and infirm. Anya forced an unwilling spirit to accept the unalterable fact that Evain must take up the challenge of finding and freeing Adam.

While Brynna and Llys retreated to the keep, an idea slowly took shape in Anya's thoughts like a new fire gathering strength. The older women had duties to bind them near their homes, but not she. Focusing on that glowing inspiration, Anya straightened—an action that nearly sent her plummeting to the ground. She tightly clutched both a limb overhead and the one below to steady her balance. Yet even this immediate proof of her vulnerability did nothing to lessen her belief in the merits of a fine plan able to provide aid for Evain . . . and also permit a measure of the time in his company she craved.

Anya assured herself that the ease with which she'd recovered her secure position foreshadowed an ability to safely pursue her goal. Surely nothing existed to prevent her from assisting the success of Evain's mission. A cold flash of reality shivered through Anya. Nothing, that was, except Evain himself. Still, Anya reassured herself, she was sharp-witted enough to find a way around that impediment as well.

Maintaining a tight hold on thick branches, for an unmarked length of time Anya sat motionless to ponder the matter. She devised and discarded a plethora of convoluted ploys until in the end she settled on the simplest. Filled with a sense of success in overcoming the first obstacle, she glanced down only to discover additional difficulties. Not only had a deal more time passed than she'd realized but below rested another problem unforeseen.

Evain, as had his mentor, Glyndor, disliked allowing the barriers of man-made walls between himself and the spirits of nature, the source of his powers. Thus, when visiting Throckenholt, never did he sleep within its walls. Anya had never known where he made his bed until now, when it was clear his habit was to sleep in this grove. Stretched out on his back and wrapped in a long black cape, head pillowed on satchel, Evain lay sleeping directly beneath her towering perch.

This was a problem indeed. Doubtless the ladies inside the keep had thought her safely abed before they set out to perform the rite she'd witnessed. And were she not in her small chamber when dawn came, there'd be questions she couldn't answer without jeopardizing her plans. There was no help for it. She must find her way down from this tree and into the keep unseen. Moreover, to wait longer here would be to tempt the night chill to rob her fingers of necessary dexterity and make matters worse.

With senses honed by training as a warrior and sharpened by the skills of a sorcerer, Evain had become aware of being watched. That the attention focused upon him lacked any threat of danger prevented him from immediate action. It was not until he heard soft sounds above that his eyes opened to a too enticing sight.

Moonlight picked out the light-hued skirts tucked up beneath a belt riding slender hips and glowed on the elegance of shapely legs. Only a bit above his standing height, small, bare feet descended the rough bark of the oak's trunk with care. In the instant during which he was torn between rebuke and unabashed admiration, the dainty maid's toes slipped.

Despite desperately grasping fingertips, Anya fell with a soft shriek. Her heart-stopping fall had an even more exciting ending as she was caught in Evain's arms and crushed tightly against his broad chest. Not wishing to lose the joys of this unexpected gift of fate, she instantly buried her face in the crook between his throat and shoulder, thinking that if he meant to hold her until her heart resumed its normal pace she would be in his embrace forever. But it seemed her future afforded no such good fortune—leastwise not without her help. A fact made plain when he lowered her feet to the ground and started to put her aside.

To defeat what Evain likely viewed as an honorable choice, Anya twisted about to wrap her arms around his neck and wantonly press herself full against him. She loved the feel of his warm strength, the powerful muscles tensing where her breasts flattened against him. Her heart ran wild as she rose on tiptoes to lift her lips toward his.

Evain was thoroughly aware of the many reasons this must not happen, but for far too many months—nay, years—he had dreamed of sharing just such a burning embrace with the elfin beauty. Those heated memories were responsible for leaving him utterly unprepared to withstand the trembling maiden's innocent onslaught.

Evain's firm mouth brushed achingly across hers, gently bit at her lips, probing and tenderly coaxing until he had heated the kiss she initiated as an inexperienced child into a devastating merger of souls. Wild sensations swept over Anya, stealing her breath and turning her bones to water. She melted against him with a hungry moan, tangling shaking fingers into the cool black strands of his shoulder-length mane.

The sound of Anya's hunger sent Evain over some vague precipice of blind pleasure, and he lifted her delicate curves intimately tighter into his hard form. But even as she yielded without sane restraint, Evain became aware of his wrong. Having sampled the berry nectar of her mouth—indescribably sweet and the more precious for its scarcity—his guilt intensified under the realization that it could never, must never, be tasted again.

As Evain abruptly pulled his mouth from hers, Anya cried out against the loss and lifted heavy lashes to gaze with palpable longing into the mesmerizing lights glittering in the sapphire depths of his eyes.

Irritated with himself for his foolish actions of questionable honor and with her for so easily knocking him off kilter, Evain struggled to mentally restore an even footing.

"Go to bed, little poppet." Evain employed the teasing name he'd long used for the dainty elfling child she'd been and still was—almost.

"I've grown up." Aching with a never before experienced frustration, Anya instantly took exception to his implication of inexperienced youth, never mind that 'twas true.

"Have you?" The cynically smiling sorcerer's tone left no question but that he doubted the fact and for the first time Anya caught a glimpse of what danger this man could be to her. However, 'twas a danger more thrilling than perilous and one she refused to fear, just as she refused to rise to the bait inciting an argument.

Seeing Anya's delicate features settle into the lines of patience which were their wont, Evain cupped slender shoulders in strong hands and turned her toward the keep's path with another caution: "This adventure is *over*"

Although Anya walked away without verbal response, she concentrated on her carefully designed plan and wordlessly disputed his claim. *'Tis not over! It has only just begun.*

Look for

Chanting the Storm

Wherever Paperback Books Are Sold
Summer 1994